... has always been a city girl at heart. ... tory at Oxford University she entered the allegedly glamorous world of television, beginning her career as tea and coffee co-ordinator for Nickelodeon UK.

Progressing to researcher and then to assistant producer, her contracts took her to MTV and finally to the BBC, where she worked for several years.

Since 2000 Jane has enjoyed a double life as a part-time PA which has given her more time to write and feel guilty about not going to the gym. Jane's novels include *Lost and Found*, *Technical Hitch*, *Like Mother, Like Daughter* and *Confessions of an Agony Auny*. Find out more at www.janesigaloff.com

The Romancipation of Maggie Hunter

JANE SIGALOFF

MIRA

MIRA is a registered trademark of Harlequin Enterprises Limited, used under licence.

MIRA Books, Eton House, 18-24 Paradise Road, Richmond, Surrey, TW9 1SR

© Jane Sigaloff 2007

ISBN 978 0 7783 0165 3

59-0907

Printed in Great Britain by Clays Ltd, St Ives plc

Mr D, this one's for you.

ACKNOWLEDGEMENTS

Huge thanks as ever to all my family and friends.
Your general cheerleading and omnipresent support
are appreciated on a daily basis, even when
I don't call for a few weeks.

Thanks especially to my best girls for being there every
step of the way: the good, the bad and the even better.
Also much gratitude to my agent Carole Blake,
to Sarah Ritherdon and the team at MIRA in the UK
and to Margaret O'Neill Marbury, Rebecca Soukis
and all at Red Dress Ink in North America.

Definitions

Romancipation: *the freedom for women to love whom they choose whilst retaining their own space and identity. Arguably the final stage in women's liberation.*

Commitment: *1. Imprisonment. 2. Action of committing an offence. 3. Involvement of a moral, political, artistic, financial or social nature restricting freedom of action. 4. A pledge. An undertaking. Often leading to a shortness of breath and irrational panic. Typically begins with the exchange of front-door keys, moves on to merging of DVD collections and on occasion leads to marriage and children—no longer necessarily in that order.*

History

A bird's-eye view of the last fifty years or so.

1960s   Women's liberation movement demand equality and less flammable, better-fitting brassieres the year after Lycra is invented. The contraceptive pill becomes available—just as miniskirts come into fashion. Divorce Reform Act means men can now be penalised for behaving unreasonably. Weight Watchers founded. Fortunately aspartame founded soon after. Life has never been sweeter.

1970s   Women born now are taught that there's nothing men can do that they can't do better and take their emancipated status for granted. Microwave ovens and cheap domestic appliances mean women have more time for their own interests. Decline in UK birth rate.

1980s   Madonna. Martina Navratilova. Margaret Thatcher. Women take centre stage in all fields and stay there. Told that they can have a successful career, a successful marriage and a family without making a day any longer than twenty-four hours, the pressure mounts.

1990s   *The Sex and the City* years—proof that women really wear the trousers (and the best shoes). Women work hard, play hard, look great, love living on their own and when it comes to men, won't settle for second best. Okay, so it's a TV show not a documentary but why let a tiny little thing like that get in the way?

Noughties   Organic revolution. Our bodies are temples. Women still having it all, but some starting to admit (if somewhat guiltily) that it's bloody tiring trying to do three things at once and they'd quite like to stay at home with the children and cook more.

Prologue

Maggie stared at the coffin being lowered in front of her and wished she could get Queen's 'Another One Bites The Dust' to stop playing on her mental jukebox. She needed to get serious, but the thought of anyone actually being inside the box was so inconceivable to her in this age of David Blaine, David Copperfield and other high-concept illusionists that she almost wanted to call a halt to proceedings and ask someone to open it up just to make sure Adam hadn't in fact made a quick getaway and was restarting his life on a beach in Australia without her.

It wouldn't be the first time he'd deceived her. She'd trusted him completely and he'd completely let her down. Then he'd bloody well gone and died before she'd even had a chance to shout at him properly.

Almost numb from the head down, Maggie felt Eloise gripping her arm as the vicar started another round of prayers and thanked the powers that be for providing her with a significant other she could count on. The last five days had passed in a blur as help had arrived from all sides, some of it invited, some unsolicited. She hadn't been allowed to do anything for herself, even think.

As the sun beat down on her pashmina-covered shoulders, everything about the afternoon felt like a hoax. Twenty-nine-year-olds did weddings not funerals. Plus, every interment she'd seen on television or at the cinema was accompanied by grey skies, the wind whipping through almost leafless trees and men in overcoats. Yet here they were, gathered today, on one of the hottest days of the year so far. The black wasn't helping anyone keep their cool as the assembled crowd committed Adam's body to the earth and him to their memories.

Staring into the grave, idly she wondered how long it would be before IKEA would start producing cheap assemble-your-own or, at least, get-a-close-friend-to-assemble-one-for-you caskets. So much for partying like it was 1999. Her prince had come. And then gone and left her for someone else before leaving the planet altogether. From now on, July fourth would be known as Newfound Independence Day for one Maggie Hunter.

It couldn't have just been a fling or a drunken misdemeanour. Oh no. Adam, it turned out, was a man who liked to do things properly. A full-blown affair for one of the two years they had been together, which meant that she'd effectively been wasting her life with him fifty percent of the time. Now it was his funeral, literally. But finally she was free. Or at least she would be when this mourning sickness was over.

Five days ago it had been an ordinary summer Sunday and, like hundreds of other women all over London, she'd woken

up determined to try to inject some life into a less than sat-
isfactory relationship rather than calling it a day and starting
from scratch. She'd read the magazine articles; she knew
what she had to do.

It had been a smile of a morning. No clouds cluttering
the warm blue sky over London. No portents, no comets,
no rivers of blood, no italics in her diary advising her it was
Judgement Day (UK).

With the benefit of hindsight there had been a black man
dressed in his Sunday best and a battered straw hat using a
loud hailer to urge all sinners to repent as she'd descended
the escalator into the fetid bowels of the London Under-
ground on her way to surprise Adam at the airport for the
first time in months. She remembered thinking that if God
was going to send anyone a message in this age of technology
and instant communication, he wouldn't be leaving it to any
man to deliver it. After all, he'd managed a burning bush
more than two thousand years ago, so it wouldn't be unreasonable to think he'd be moving with the times. There'd have
been SMS messages, a viral advertising campaign, a world
stadium tour, a podcast or even a Godcast.

As she'd stood in the arrivals hall at Heathrow, Maggie
must have watched every passenger on the flight from JFK
come through the sliding doors from customs, her excitement at her spontaneity and the romance of airport reunions
gradually fading. She soon tired of her self-constructed game
of matching the arrivees to their families, yet despite the fact
the screen was adamant that his baggage was 'in hall', there
was no sign of Adam.

When she'd finally admitted defeat and called his mobile,

he had chirpily informed her that he was already at home. Disappointed, she berated herself for trying to live her life as a feel-good movie. Just because Meg Ryan and Tom Hanks had managed to run into each other at the top of the Empire State Building after the viewing deck had closed, just because Richard Gere had arrived in his white limo before Julia Roberts had set off for the bus station at the end of *Pretty Woman* didn't mean that she and Adam were destined to sprint across the swirling carpet at Heathrow arrivals into each other's arms, even if she had picked out her favourite floaty summer skirt that morning.

She wondered if a couple of years down the line her favourite movie heroines' lives would become as mundane as hers seemed to. Was Annie Reed stroppy in Seattle and nagging Jonah to keep his room tidy and the toilet seat down? Was Vivian Ward a slightly less Pretty Woman pairing cashmere socks and catching up on the ironing whilst Edward worked late on a deal? It was no wonder so many romantic comedies ended at the point the couple got together.

Her mood had improved when she'd returned home to flowers and mid-afternoon sex but when, whilst dropping a post-coital tea bag into the kitchen bin, she'd noticed that the discarded boarding pass lying face-up had Friday's date, Adam hadn't known where to look or where to start. It didn't matter. It merely confirmed what her female intuition had been hinting at for months.

Guilty confession over, he'd left to buy cigarettes to restart smoking. She'd muttered something acerbic about how they wouldn't kill him fast enough and then, it was true, she had wished him dead—but only to herself and only for about five minutes. And it's not like she had a history of wishes coming true.

The coffin was shorter than she'd been expecting and Maggie wondered if Adam had enough room. He'd always liked to sleep on his side and often with one arm stretched out in front of him, a bit like Superman at take-off. As the first shovel of dark, moist earth rained down on to the anaemic wood, a muffled sob pawed at the heavy silence and Maggie closed her eyes firmly, trying to blank out his mother's pain. No parent should have to witness the funeral of their own child. It wasn't part of the job description.

At this precise moment, and although she would probably never be able to admit it for fear of appearing less nice than she actually was, Maggie personally felt something closer to academic curiosity than to heart-rending sadness. It wasn't that she was a particularly tough person. She'd bawled when the family cat had to be put down, she always sobbed through *E.T.* and she had even started welling up at the happiest moments in films recently, as they'd only high-lighted the shortcomings in her own relationship. But if there was a silver lining to be found amongst Adam's dirty laundry it was that arguably she'd had a lucky escape. Her life wasn't over.

Not that anyone other than Eloise and her mother would have suspected that anything was wrong in Maggie and Adam's world. She should have been nominated for an award for her role as Best Supporting Girlfriend, especially when his job had taken him to New York for most of the past six months and, as she now knew, into the arms of Eve. Adam and Eve. Would you believe it? A twist of fate's quirky sense of humour.

As the prayers continued, she stole a glance at the not-so-mystery blonde opposite, a discreet three rows back. Her highlighted hair had been ironed straight, a style that now only accentuated the fact that her face was twisted with grief, her flushed cheeks glistening with tears in stark contrast with the pale calm of Maggie's own. Eve Redland had no idea that Maggie knew who she was. But when your boyfriend plays away and then leaves you at home with a broadband connection, a suspicious mind, access to his inbox and his company intranet, he leaves himself wide open.

Eve looked like a lawyer at a big city firm which, Maggie mused, was hardly surprising. She was well dressed, well worked out and, well, more attractive than the picture on the company website suggested. Not a red talon in sight, only evidence of a French manicure and a round brilliant cut diamond set in platinum dangling from a simple necklace. To think that she had even let herself get excited when she'd seen the spine of a Tiffany catalogue in Adam's briefcase three months ago. Maggie sighed with disappointment and at once a chair was produced for her from somewhere. She waved it away. She was going to have to relearn to stand on her own two feet.

She'd really fallen for Adam, their initial email banter almost as frenetic as their sex life. For the first time she'd really been in love. And it seemed to be mutual. They'd declared their feelings repeatedly, and not just after sex. The future seemed rosy. But once they'd settled down, played house and merged CD collections, it just broke. No hysterics, no apology, no real understanding of why things had to change.

She hadn't gained weight or developed a penchant for

growing underarm hair. He'd been away working on a deal and in the process had found himself a dealbreaker. Maybe if she'd left him the first time he'd let her down instead of giving him a second chance, he'd have been rolling around with Eve on a king-sized bed in a Manhattan apartment instead of fumbling distractedly for his lighter as he stepped off the pavement at the wrong moment. She'd never really shouted at him before that afternoon, previously preferring to save her anger for a rainy day. But people always said it was better not to bottle things up, and it had made her feel better to get everything out of her system, if not for long.

As all heads bowed reverentially, Maggie peered over her sunglasses, grateful for the lenses' ability to repel UVA, UVB and HOWRU? rays. As everyone scrunched their eyes closed in prayer, the vicar's words providing comfort and a focus for their disparate emotions, Maggie had her first real opportunity to scan the assembled crowd. There must have been nearly two hundred people gathered there. Men and women from every living generation had come to pay tribute to St Adam, representatives from each of his life stages on his journey from prep school to the firm. Every one of his peers was silently vowing to kick their jaywalking to Starbucks whilst on their mobile phone habit and every parent secretly thanking their God that it wasn't their child being buried this afternoon.

She glanced at her parents, heads bowed, hand in hand. They were an exceptional couple, apparently ordinary from the outside, pure gold underneath their Marks & Spencer clothing and their tendency to bicker about the unimportant things in life. Maggie wondered how many marriages lasted thirty years these days. Nothing was expected to last for life any more. Not even a set of saucepans.

At the rear of the crowd, a few feet back from the others, a man in a dark blue suit wearing a white shirt without a tie stood alone. As he looked across towards the grave and so to her, Maggie bowed her head, ostensibly returning her focus to the ground although, shielded by the fashionably large lenses in her sunglasses, she covertly stole another glance before giving Eloise's hand a squeeze. His hairline might have receded a few centimetres but she'd have recognised that profile anywhere.

From the distance, her university crush was still head-turning and she wondered how she was looking before reprimanding herself for being so shallow graveside.

She'd first spotted Max French during Freshers' week in the autumn of '89 as he'd ambled through campus. His jeans had been faded in all the right places, his Converse All Stars once black, then grey, clearly lived in and loved in. His T-shirts were always tight enough to titillate. As female admirers assessed what lay beneath, their hormones were further stimulated by the faint scent of male aerosol deodorant always left in his wake; a vapour trail that reduced many female undergraduates to strike a 'Bisto Kid' pose as they sniffed out their chosen one.

Tentatively she looked up again, but the moment had passed and as she thought she felt Eve look over, Maggie studied her shoes, ostensibly deep in prayer, her mind wandering back ten years to the early nineties.

Max had been the guy boys wanted to buy a beer for and who women wanted to gift-wrap their virginity for. Confident without being cocky, attractive without being vain, his desirability had only been augmented by the fact he'd gone through university almost permanently unavailable. As he passed apparently seamlessly from one tall, slim, sporty girl with perfect teeth to another, Maggie, conversely, had meandered through her student years in outsize sweatshirts overindulging in cheap lager and even cheaper chocolate digestives wondering why she didn't have a constant stream of men in her life and her mailbox. A mailbox, quaintly, for real envelopes. She'd written every word of her final exams with a pen on paper, made all her undergraduate phone calls standing still, whilst putting actual money in a slot. In many ways it had been a much more ordered time.

On the few occasions she'd ensured her and Max's paths had crossed, they'd exchanged several sentences of witty repartee as she'd flicked her hair from side to side. They'd even danced together—or rather next to each other—a couple of times, but they'd never reached an attending-a-funeral level of friendship. Maybe, despite her increasing doubts, there was a God after all, or perhaps the herbal stress-alleviating capsule Eloise had made her take earlier had had hallucinatory side effects.

Maggie felt a slight upturn in her mood. She might have been a bit down on the trusting-men thing, but she was definitely in the market for a bit of meaningless, aerobic, getting-over-it sex. Apart from the almost-widow thing, she was looking so much better these days. Plus Max was unrequited and unfinished business. Maggie covered her mouth with her hand. She had a horrible feeling she had just been smiling.

Chapter One

Three years later. December 22. Christmas. Present.

What do you buy for the man who has everything? How much do you spend on your first Christmas together when you don't want to look mean but you don't want to look desperate either? Should it be a predetermined percentage of your monthly income or the same each? And a mere seven months in, who's going to ask the million-dollar or, potentially, several-hundred-pound question. Maggie grimaced. Finances were an area in which she was never going to be able to keep up with Max and, while the old-fashioned girl in her loved being taken out for dinner and dreamt of semi-precious gifts, the single-sex educated side of her demanded she see herself as an equal in every respect, even when her current account dictated otherwise.

It was too late to add anything to the bag of freshly wrapped presents now. She had left the flat feeling laden with gifts although the packages appeared to be shrinking ever smaller as she approached the restaurant. Rationally she ran through the items for at least the seventh time since leaving home.

- *Charcoal-grey John Smedley merino wool pullover. (Main gift.)*
- *DVD box set of* The A-Team—*first complete season. (Fun present to demonstrate she has been paying attention to their conversations over the last seven months and doesn't take herself or her TV viewing too seriously.)*
- *Gordon Ramsay cookbook. (Never a selfless purchase when dating a man who can cook—plus item includes colour photos of Mr Ramsay.)*
- *Clarins For Men facial exfoliator and moisturiser. (Now concerned items are too nurturing/metrosexual/maternal.)*
- *Signed autobiography of latest English cricketing legend who has apparently already been to hell and back despite having not yet reached his thirtieth birthday. (100% no risk. Heavy hint dropped by recipient-to-be.)*
- *Special Edition Signed Double DVD of Red Connelly's career-launching action movies:* No One Dies *and* No One Dies Again. *(Free gift from a satisfied A-list client and much better suited to a male DVD collection than to hers.)*

Now slight concern that overall gift contains too many DVDs— around fifteen hours of entertainment in total. Doesn't want Max to think she is encouraging him to become couch potato. Although a few more nights in would be good for her bank balance, waistline and the longevity of her liver.

★ ★ ★

As Maggie stepped up the pace, the stiff paper of her Christmas carriers pricked her conscience and her shins with every other step, daring her stockings to ladder as she walked fast as she could without running. Despite the fact she'd managed to arrange her appointments so she could pop home for a shower after work and it was only just above freezing outside, she could feel a film of sweat on the nape of her neck starting to curl her just blow-dried hair from the inside out.

Twenty-two minutes behind schedule, thanks to a spontaneous detour to buy a pair of shoes that had winked at her from a shop window on the Kings Road, she was now armed with incriminatingly fresh purchases. Who cared if the economy was struggling if it meant sales started before Christmas?

It was a women's prerogative to be late—although, she suspected, a very annoying one and best kept within fifteen minutes of the original rendezvous time. She hoped he had at least ordered himself a drink.

Max sat in the leather-backed booth at the restaurant and wondered why, if waiting was part of the male job description, he was so bad at it. He hadn't brought a newspaper and he'd already tidied up his emails. Suddenly aware that he was jiggling his leg under the table, he forced himself to be still and to breathe slowly. It wasn't that he was impatient, merely still operating at work pace. Plus these were exciting times.

Not wanting to waste a second of Friday night euphoria, he slipped his muted PDA out of the inside pocket of his brown corduroy jacket to check the screen. No messages. And then there she was. Radiant, rosy cheeked and on her way to his table.

Proudly, he got up to kiss her. 'Hello you.'

As Maggie handed her coat and scarf to the waiter, Max's gaze slipped to Maggie's cleavage before he dragged it back to her eye level. It was her fault for wearing a plunging neckline. It might as well have been an arrow. She was glowing, her décolletage shimmering.

Maggie smiled. 'So sorry I'm late.'

He spotted the bags. She was forgiven. 'For me?'

Suddenly sheepish, she nodded. Could it be that she should have been blasé enough to ignore the whole tradition of presents altogether?

He rubbed his hands together with comedic glee. 'You shouldn't have. Okay, you should have. I love Christmas.' He reached across the table. 'Can I open them now?'

Maggie put the bags on the floor on her side. 'Is it December twenty-fifth yet?'

As she sat down she momentarily lifted the back of her top, giving cooler air a chance to do its clever convection thing. She hoped her deodorant was going to live up to its marketing and wished she'd doused herself in a little more perfume before leaving home. Then again, she hadn't wanted to assault Max with a left hook of floral sensuality on arrival.

'But surely you want to be able to see my face when I open them?' He almost pouted. 'Unless of course you change your mind and spend Christmas morning with me. I promise to release you in time for lunch.'

'Ten out of ten for persistence…'

'I prefer persuasive or even tenacious. So?'

'I'm sure you'll survive Christmas morning without me.'

Max shrugged. 'I guess there's always next year.' Max

moved on. 'So, is work still hectic? Surely people aren't thinking about moving house this close to Christmas?'

'Terrible traffic.' She was sure she should have been saving white lies for moments when it mattered.

Max frowned. 'You didn't drive here, did you?' He patted the inside pocket of his jacket.

'Of course not.'

His shoulders relaxed. 'Good.'

'Why?' Maggie flicked her hair playfully while it was still straight enough. 'Planning on getting me drunk?'

'I've got to get you into the Christmas spirit somehow.'

'There's been far too much of that after work this week.' Maggie had promised herself she would stick to gin and slimline tonic before her waistline started to resemble Santa's.

'How about a glass of champagne to start?'

'Perfect.' In the absence of any Saturday appointments, this Friday night she had the willpower of a gnat and Maggie could feel herself starting to unwind already. Thank goodness for Max French. For the first December in a while, it did feel like the season to be jolly.

Max looked up from his rare steak, his next mouthful poised on his fork. 'So I've had an idea for your Christmas present…'

Maggie had noted the lack of parcels on his side of the table but, not wishing to come across as a spoilt eight-year-old, and her inner optimist having decided there was probably a sackful being stored for her in the cloakroom, had remained mute on the subject. Now, secretly she was disappointed. Everyone knows you can't unwrap an idea. Plus, in the seven months they'd been dating so far, neither of them had had a birthday, so this was an unofficial test. Max was shaping up for a C minus.

'…but I just wanted to check something with you first.'

The bottom line was Max was a heterosexual man and therefore an automatic member of the more disorganised sex. In his world it was only December 22 and there were two more whole shopping days until Christmas.

'Fire away.' She coated a chip in Béarnaise sauce and popped it in her mouth. A morsel of comfort.

'Are you a size eight, a size ten or a size twelve?'

Saturated fat on its way to her thighs, Maggie had never felt less romanced in her life, plus she was sure she hadn't been a size eight since she'd been eight years old. At least she hadn't been according to UK sizing. In the States she was still an eight or a ten, one of the best reasons that she could think of to apply for a green card and move west. That and HBO. And Max's lopsided grin was starting to annoy her.

'Just kidding. Now for a serious question. Sun or snow?'

She frowned. In the course of debating whether to be realistic or optimistic when answering the size question, she'd stopped listening. 'What?'

Damn. Forgetting who she was with, she'd gone for the terse teenage response complete with irritability and furrowed brow. At least she hadn't pronounced it *wot*.

Undeterred, Max's eyes shone with mischief. 'Sun or snow? For our first holiday?'

Maggie sat back in her chair, her hands in her lap. Following a gullible phase in her early twenties, she didn't take kindly to being wound up. 'Very funny.'

'Really.' Max put his hand on his heart. 'It wasn't a joke.'

'Our first holiday?' Maggie leant forward. She couldn't control an expanding smile. Adam had bought her a fountain pen for their first Christmas. And she didn't even really have a desk job.

'Well, it is the holiday season, is it not?' Max was enjoying the moment. One of the best things he'd found about being financially secure was the facility to sweep your nearest and dearest off their feet and away somewhere unexpected.

Maggie laughed. 'To think I thought the "holiday season" was just Gap's way of ensuring they could sell woolly hats, scarves and fleeces to every religious denomination. I can't believe I've been getting it wrong all these years.'

Max grinned. 'Well, what do you get the woman who is impossible to second-guess? I thought that rather than try and choose something you probably won't like, wear or need, I'd whisk you off somewhere for a week instead.'

'A week?' Just checking she'd heard him correctly, Maggie chose a word from the preceding sentence at random and squeaked it out.

'I could probably manage ten days.'

Maggie blushed at his miscomprehension. 'A week would be perfect.' A holiday for free? She felt like she'd won the star prize on a game show. 'Wow. Thank you.' Her bag of gifts was suddenly feeling microscopic.

'I just thought I'd better get your permission before booking anything. I know you don't like surprises.'

'I don't?'

Max shook his head. 'Not unless you've dropped a large hint first.'

Maggie wondered if that was true. She'd always thought she was very laid-back.

'I think it's a control thing.'

They both laughed. When it came to taking the lead, they could both be as bossy as each other.

'Well—' Maggie raised her glass '—consider yourself in charge.' To think she'd doubted him.

'Really?' Max raised an eyebrow.

'Only for holiday planning purposes.'

'Of course.'

'One carte blanche at your disposal.'

Max nodded. 'I think this might be more exciting than getting a platinum AmEx.'

'The Hunter Carte Blanche is *much* more exclusive.'

'And I know you're probably fuming because you think I haven't gone to any advance trouble and I'm just going to throw money at the gift problem when, no doubt, you've been agonisingly thoughtful but…'

God, he was good.

'The thing is I can't think of anything I'd like more than to have some time away with you.'

'Not even the complete first season of *The A-Team?*'

Max feigned indecision. 'Actually that's a tough call.'

Beaming, Maggie pulled up her sleeve as far as her elbow. 'A holiday would be amazing. I'm grey with winter.'

'I thought grey was the new black.'

It was a hypothesis he would be able to confirm when he unwrapped his main present.

Maggie absently ran her hand over her now clenched stomach muscles and wondered how soon she could be ready for a bikini moment. It was one thing to be naked for a sympathetically lit—make that almost dark—boudoir moment when your hormones were out of control, your legs were waxed and your alcohol levels were high, but three-hundred-and-sixty-degree exposure to sunlight in swimwear and without make-up could be very unforgiving, especially in the midst of a British winter and in male company. Male company that you wanted to love what he saw.

'So, sailing or skiing?'

Cellulite forgotten, Maggie paused. She didn't want to be picky, but where was the lying on a white sandy beach, listening to music, reading with no activity option that she and Eloise had perfected over the years? Or at least that she had perfected over the years, whilst Eloise eventually tired of being a human sundial and sauntered off to explore the area beyond the pool and the restaurant.

'I was thinking we could charter a yacht…'

She guessed you didn't get to be a successful entrepreneur by lying down for a week at a time.

Not an experienced sailor, Maggie delved into her archive of idealised seafaring images which apparently included the Duran Duran 'Rio' video, *Some Like it Hot* and Goldie Hawn before she went Overboard. She imagined herself reclining on a gleaming white boat, sunlight bouncing off her fresh pedicure, a cocktail in hand, sarong flapping in the breeze and wondered if there'd be a pool on deck or whether that was only on cruise ships.

'…or well, you can't beat a week in the mountains.'

An image of Bridget Jones planted face down in the alpine snow flashed across her mind. It was time to come clean.

'I'm afraid I don't ski.'

Max looked surprised. 'But you have all the kit.'

Maggie blushed. 'The ski jacket and moon boots are fashion items. Neither have ever travelled to altitude, unless you count the London Eye.'

'And you love frosty mornings.'

'From the inside of the car, with the heating on.'

'Oh I see.'

'Disappointed?'

'Just surprised. I mean, you're pretty sporty.'

Seven months in and Max didn't know the whole truth. He must have been misled by the charity bike ride she'd done in China three years earlier in a fit of grief and the fact that Eloise's old tennis racket resided in her umbrella stand. The reality was, she'd joined a gym mainly for the steam room, the sauna and the resident beautician. She'd hated games at school. If any of the sports teachers had paid closer attention instead of using her to keep the equipment cupboard tidy, they'd have realised that she'd allegedly had the most prolonged menstrual cramps and possibly the most chronic verruca outbreak on record in the Western World. Not something she'd be bringing to the attention of the *Guinness World Records* or indeed her latest suitor.

'I blame my parents. They preferred a tan to thermal underwear. Plus we couldn't afford two holidays a year on two teachers' salaries. And you can't read while you're skiing.'

'I'm sure you'd pick up the basics in a couple of days. You'd be carving your way down the slopes in no time.'

Maggie shook her head slowly. 'I have to warn you that when Eloise tried to teach me to ice skate I developed a terrible case of Tourette's syndrome…'

Max laughed.

'Besides, I've always regarded a holiday as an opportunity for me to take most of my clothes off rather than to put more on.'

If this relationship was going to work he was going to have to put up with the Real Her rather than the Ideal Her. In her world Ski was a yoghurt not a sport.

'Well, a man can't argue with that.' Max clinked her glass. 'Sailing it is.'

That was it? No further justification required? No emotional blackmail, no protests? Surely life couldn't be this simple.

'So, how does the Caribbean sound, say early February?'

Maggie almost clapped her hands with excitement. 'Perfect. I'm owed a few days off.'

'Although in the future you might have to let me go skiing with the boys occasionally.'

'What is it with boys wanting to feel henpecked?' Safely on the offensive, Maggie allowed her self-protective core to get a little bit excited. In the future.

Max smiled and wisely moved on. 'You're going to love sailing. You'll never have seen so much blue sky. As for the stars at night…'

'Aye-aye, Captain.' Excitement simmering, it just slipped out. Maggie couldn't believe it. Especially as she had a few genuine nautical terms in her lexicon; port, starboard, sail and rigging—although she had a feeling the latter was only found on old pirate ships.

To Maggie's relief, Max didn't appear to have been listening, which on this particular occasion was a good thing. It looked like he'd already left for their holiday.

'Have you ever snorkelled with a sea turtle?'

'I'd rather snorkel with you.' She hadn't had a holiday for nearly a year. But could she trust her junior, the cocky but inexperienced and misleadingly named, Simon Senior, not to screw things up in her absence? She was going to have to. As long as she was back for city bonus time. The effect on the housing market was almost instant.

Maggie would have pinched herself if she hadn't been sitting in the middle of a restaurant. Finally at the ripe old age of thirty-two she was on the perfect date. Despite everything Adam had put her through, she had made it to a committed but non-claustrophobic relationship with a fully domesticated, aesthetically pleasing Homo sapiens who washed and shaved regularly, still had a full(ish) head of hair, wasn't in debt, didn't mind watching reality television, knew she had once owned a Shakin' Stevens poster, had once had a perm, that she lost her virginity to Genesis (album playing, not a gang bang), that she'd never read Shakespeare or Dickens and had slept soundly on her only trip to the opera. She wasn't sure she could believe in *the* one anymore but Max French was certainly A1. She only hoped he didn't turn out to be mad Max.

It may have been only seven months in, but he still called when he said he would, he got on well with his parents (still together), his sister and his brother-in-law. He'd successfully charmed her parents. Eloise had awarded him eleven out of ten and now he was going to book them a holiday. On a bloody yacht. True, she had been known to feel nauseous on a ferry crossing, but that had been years ago and her horizons needed expanding. Rod Stewart started sailing through her mental jukebox as Maggie racked her brains for a less embarrassing theme tune for her newest hobby. 'Club Tropicana' danced into the mix before David Gray came sailing away just in time.

Anthem selected, a vision of a sun-kissed, slimmer version of herself diving perfectly into clear blue seas from a great height came to the fore before she substituted it with a cellulite-dimpled, less athletic, paler image. It was definitely time to buy a new bikini. Her favourite black one was desperately lacking in elasticity after its recent use in a health club Jacuzzi.

'Well, I'm delighted that's sorted. Let's block out some time in the diary as soon as we can.' He returned to his meal with gusto.

Maggie wasn't sure she'd ever known anyone able to chew and smile at the same time. She loaded her fork and then reloaded it with a more demure mouthful. They say you know the reason you're going to leave a man as soon as you meet him, but as yet she hadn't encountered any dealbreakers. Granted, he left toast crumbs in the butter, balled his dirty socks before leaving them next to the laundry basket, checked his emails at every opportunity and purchased peach-coloured toilet paper, but these were all things she was sure she could learn to accept or retrain, in the case of the latter simply by editing the default shopping list in his e-Trolley—a device so clever it not only packed his groceries but delivered them to his front door.

'Margaret Joanna Elizabeth Abigail Hunter.'

Smarting at the use of her very full name—the use of which only ever signalled trouble—Maggie returned her attention to the table.

Maximilian French was waiting patiently and when, as if on cue, a waiter appeared with two fresh glasses of champagne, her most recent mouthful of dinner hesitated on its way to her stomach.

Max was flushed but his wine was virtually untouched. Plus, Maggie now noted, while she'd been savouring every calorie, he'd clearly been herding the majority of his food around his plate.

Suddenly short of breath, she forced herself to breathe in. And out. Was this what hyperventilating felt like? And how come everyone on the television or in films always seemed to have a small brown paper bag to hand when they needed one? She only had her shopping bags with her. Big enough to put over her head but that was about it.

He leant in. 'I've been thinking…'

When would men learn to leave thinking to the girls? Plus she was sure she'd told him before, generally speaking and after a number of cocktails, that she regarded proposals in restaurants to be as classy as glacé cherries in a fruit salad. Besides, it was far too soon. Maggie drained her water glass, but her mouth remained dry.

Max wiped his suddenly sweaty palms on his napkin.

As Maggie watched his hands disappear below table level, her pulse rate performed a hop, skip and a jump. She hadn't had a manicure for months. Her cuticles had cuticles.

He leant forward in his seat, as close to her as the width of their table allowed. And then there it was, on the table in front of her, a ring box.

Maggie's first instinct was to look around her. Thanks to

the position of their booth, the other diners were either oblivious or being incredibly discreet.

'Max…'

Even in the one syllable she could hear the slight tremble in her voice.

'Maggie.'

She didn't dare open it. Being fussy may have been intrinsic to a woman's charm but when it came to being picky she could have been a world champion and, as he'd mentioned only minutes earlier, was surprise averse. In which case…what was he playing at?

Her hands remained on her lap, her fingers repeatedly knitting themselves together. 'You shouldn't. You didn't…'

As he opened the box for her, Maggie wondered if anyone had ever suffocated sitting upright. She'd never been convinced she was the marrying kind.

His body language conveyed total calm. 'You're right, I didn't.'

And then there it was. No diamonds, no ball and chain, but a key. The one she knew opened his front door. She exhaled noisily.

He grinned at her reaction. 'I was just thinking that things would be easier if we lived together.' He leant back and raked his fingers through his hair.

Easier? So much for can't-live-without-you passion. Plus, now, despite the fact she knew she had told Max several times that she wasn't sure she believed in marriage, she was disappointed. How could she hope to find a man who understood her when she didn't even understand herself?

'I'd just really like it if you didn't have to go home, well, ever basically. And before you try and talk me out of it, we spend almost every night together already.'

Every night except the crucial ones she kept to herself for depilation, beautification and ten hours' sleep.

'I know you think I am a serial monogamist.'

Think? All the evidence was there. 'Which is better than being a serial killer...' She did her best to smile. She'd dreamt of this moment in the late 1980s. An era when she'd also believed that jeans looked better when they had holes in the knees.

'It's true I have had a few serious relationships over the years—'

Maggie couldn't help but interrupt. 'You've virtually been going steady since you were sixteen. In most cases there was a personnel overlap.'

For the first time, Max appeared to be blushing. 'I'm afraid I can't change the past although maybe I could commission a hagiography?'

She reined herself in slightly. 'You're just a typical male.'

'I'd argue that I'm atypical—in all the best possible ways. I mean for a start, I'm not afraid of commitment.'

'Come on. You just don't like being on your own. When there hasn't been a girlfriend in your life or your house, you've almost always moved a friend in to stay.' Subconsciously Maggie had folded her arms across her chest. Commitment-phobia wasn't solely a male preserve.

'Hey, relax.'

If Maggie wasn't good at surprises she was even worse at being told to *relax*.

'Look, I know we're supposed to be taking things slowly,

but it's not how I feel. You're different. We're different, don't you think?'

'I'm having a good time, if that's what you mean.'

'That's an important part of it and don't forget, I've built a career on spotting unique opportunities. I don't want to sit back and miss this one.'

'I bet you say that to all the girls.' Despite her trepidation, her smile was on full beam.

'Hand on heart, this is a first for me. Historically it has always been the women who bring up the subject of cohabitation, in one way or another.'

Women. Plural. Maggie tried not to imagine a crowd scene of clamouring exes.

'First they fill my bathroom with rows of bottles, then their flatshare/lease/car parking permit comes to an end and, well, you know the results. You, on the other hand, won't leave so much as a hairbrush at my place.'

Max leant over the table.

'So what do you say? Just think, no more underwear stuffed in glove compartments and briefcases, no toothbrush in your handbag, no need to wear the same outfit two days running, less risk of finding the milk in your fridge has turned into unofficial yoghurt.'

A formal, considered, non-heat of the moment, not post-coital or even close to coital moment. Maggie was stumped. She and Adam had moved in together in the days when they could barely afford to live apart.

She knew she was supposed to kiss him now, to say yes, to even shed a tear of overwhelmed excitement. Instead she stalled for time. How could she possibly say 'Let me think about it' without ruining everything?

Aside from the fact that she had vowed she was going to grow old on her bespoke sofa, alone, it didn't help that the key was to a house which, if she was being picky, he did happen to have shared with several previous girlfriends. However it was at least three times the size of her current abode, had steps up to the front door, which she had always wanted, and had decent shops and Notting Hill within strolling distance, whereas her locality was only good for placing a bet, having a kebab or dry-cleaning (and usually in that order).

'You want me to move in to your place?'

'I just want to take us to the next level. I know how much you adore your flat, and it's a great flat, I'm just not sure that realistically there's enough space for us both….'

Maggie's train of thought took a detour. Where on earth was she was going to find tenants who weren't going to trash her place? She'd sanded every skirting board herself. Hey, she'd had the time.

From where he was sitting, Maggie was unresponsive. Concerned, Max changed tack. 'I know you're probably thinking that you're just the next in line for a door key.' He paused. 'Truth is, I don't know how I can get across that I'm serious, without making you run a mile. Or even a marathon.' He smiled warmly.

He was good at this. Her gut instinct was to say yes. Then again it's not as if her instinct had an unblemished record. Maggie had learned very few real lessons en route to her thirty-third year. In fact the only ones she could remember were:

- Never buy a white bikini—not a mistake you make twice.
- Never expect anything to occur to a man without heavy prompting.
- You won't lose weight unless you eat less.

and

- You can't trust a cohabiting partner.

Apparently deep in thought but actually deeper in panic, Maggie stared at the tablecloth, zooming in and focusing on the weave of the white linen. She knew that eventually she was going to have to look up. The ring box was open on the table between them.

Max waited for her to give him full eye contact. The longer she took with her answer, the surer he was that he knew what he wanted.

'I know it's soon, but I love you, Maggie. Take your time. This is one offer without small print or a closing date.'

As he watched a half-smile freeze on her face, he gripped the stem of his champagne glass harder. 'And I do have plenty of room.' Bugger. That sounded wrong.

'Size isn't everything, Mr French.' Maggie's riposte was flirtatious as she forced herself to enter the spirit of the moment before she ruined it altogether.

I love you too. It might have been the clichéd response, but it was definitely what he wanted to hear. Yet she still found it hard to say 'I love you' sober, face to face, in broad daylight even though she was ninety-five percent sure that on this occasion, if she even knew what love was, it was the case. She'd been playing a game with herself for the past couple of months. The rules were: if she didn't tell him she loved him, she couldn't get hurt. Trouble was, she knew she was cheating herself.

'I suppose we could live at yours…' Max was tentative. He was starting to sweat with the effort of trying to crack the Da Maggie Code. 'Or I guess we could buy somewhere new together. I just didn't want it to, you know, be too big a deal after, well, last time. We can take it as slowly as you like. As long as we're together, that's the most important thing.'

He wasn't used to misreading situations. He was even less good at not getting what he wanted out of a meeting and yet Maggie's unpredictability was one of the things he found most magnetic about her.

Over on the other side of the table in 'No live-in Man's land' Maggie was trying to keep things in perspective, but in an increasingly risk-averse, marrying-later, commitment-phobic society she couldn't help thinking this was tantamount to a proposal. 'And you're quite sure you want me to live with you every day?'

Max nodded. 'Day and night.' He raised his glass—he needed his drink now. 'To us—if I may.'

Maggie wondered if he'd used that exact line in the past, before berating her cynical side.

'You do realise I hate doing the washing-up and I tend to leave my shoes under the coffee table?'

Max nodded. 'I also know that you like to go to sleep listening to music, that you can't construct a sentence until after your first cup of tea, that you sleep on your back or your left side and always floss your teeth before bed however much you've had to drink and have been known to wipe your eye make-up on the hand towel.'

Maggie was lost for words. Not a condition she was familiar with. She envied Max's easy display of his feelings as she blushed.

'Well.' A procession of tears arrived uninvited. More, Maggie suspected, out of shock and fear than anything more romantic. Was she really ready to put all her eggs in one basket and all her shoes in his wardrobe? Her twenty-one-year-old self would have already been on her way home to pack and practice her new signature having decided that Maggie French sounded great. Then again, the twenty-one-year-old Maggie Hunter would probably have been dumped a few weeks later. When it came to relationships, she had always been an all-or-nothing girl. Now, it seemed, she was more 'all for one'—herself.

Max placed his hand over hers, delighted that at last there had been an emotional reaction and pretty sure it was an encouraging one. 'We're great together. Everyone thinks so.'

Her Adam's apple apparently suddenly the size and texture of a large jam doughnut, Maggie did her best to swallow and nodded.

'It is quite soon…and don't worry, I realise you've got baggage. We all have.'

Maggie wondered if it was a coincidence that Max was stroking her ring finger.

'I know you were determined to grow old on your own.' Max took her hand. 'But you don't have to. From now on, you have nothing to worry about.'

Smile tight, Maggie was happy for Max to believe she was

speechless. 'Under Pressure.' David Bowie popped into her head and stayed there. She clearly had to say something. Preferably something nice.

'And what about my sofa?' Maggie stopped herself five words too late. It was sofaux-pas. Even if post-Adam and pre-Max it had been the most important item in her life, she could and should have kept it to herself. There were plenty more sofas in the world but, despite the rumours to the contrary, not that many fish in the sea.

Max laughed. 'And that, Maggie Hunter, is why I love you.'

Maybe she should have been begging him to marry her before she was carted off to a lunatic asylum where, no doubt, she could have all the time she wanted on the couch and on her own.

'Look, why don't you sleep on it? The idea I mean, not the sofa.' Max kissed her hand. 'I'll still be here tomorrow. And the next day.'

'Cool.' Maggie smiled.

Max slid out of his side of the booth and joined her on the other side. As he kissed her, all Maggie's doubts temporarily disappeared. She knew she was a great person to live with: easy-going, even tempered—provided she got her own way—fairly tidy without being obsessive about it and a semi-decent cook. She'd loved living with her. But she had no idea what Max was really like behind closed doors. That said, she was never one to turn down a challenge. Martha Stewart and Nigella Lawson had better watch their home-making backs. Maggie Hunter was thinking about picking up that front door key and entering the building.

Chapter Two

Maggie was awake. So awake it seemed impossible she had ever been asleep.

The champagne had done its job, there'd been kissing in the cab, the foreplay had been amazing and then— The flashback ended abruptly and Maggie realised that the Agent Provocateur thong she'd playfully selected after her pre-dinner shower was still on. She must have passed out before they'd got very far. Damn. Romance wasn't dead, just drunk.

Now sober enough for her lacy underwear to be feeling uncomfortable, she wriggled out of it, hooking her toe over the black lace as it dallied round her ankle, anxious to liberate herself completely. As waves of movement radiated from her side of the mattress, she peered over at Max. Could he really be sleeping through her lingerie gymnastics? Maybe he was sulking? Perhaps she should wake him with a kiss to apologise for earlier? Or a blow job? She leant over him and paused. On the verge of a headache, she didn't really want to have sex now.

Rolling away, she let her arm hang off the edge of the bed and rummaged in her handbag until, to her relief, her hand closed around the velveteen ring box. He clearly hadn't demanded his door key back yet.

Tonight would definitely have been easier if she hadn't buried her last cohabiting partner not long after he had stopped taking her out for dinner and started taking her for granted. Propping herself up on her pillow, Maggie watched Max with affection. He was completely at peace, yet if her side of the duvet was anything to go by, she had recently been fighting for her life.

The room was quiet except for Max's regular breathing and the occasional siren spiralling up to the top floor from the street below as her life flashed forward forty years. Maybe if she added a Catherine Cookson novel and a pair of shop-bought magnifying reading glasses to her bedside table, this was the shape of things to come. And what shape was that anyway?

Max was blissfully oblivious to her mental pacing. Hopefully by the time he regained consciousness, she'd have rebooted her optimism at their new status-to-be. From the outside looking in, and indeed from the inside looking out, they appeared happy. Max French and Maggie Hunter. One life, one letter box, from this day forward.

Maggie was sure she'd feel better once she'd told Eloise. Over the years she'd stood at many of life's crossroads and Eloise had never failed to jump-start her excitement. Just as well; tonight she'd truly stalled.

As her emotional pendulum swung slowly from contentment to crisis and back again, Maggie tried to hone her main concerns:

—Her furtive addiction to music television and derisible soap operas.

—Her love of spending lazy work-free Sunday mornings in outsize sweatshirts and unflattering pyjama bottoms, often not showering or applying make-up until just before going out, which frequently wasn't until the evening.

—Her love of pottering on her own for hours, busy doing nothing.

—His clutter-free bathroom.

—His clutter-free life.

—Returning to a world of golf clubs under the bed, damp sweaty black socks in the laundry basket and a Corby trouser press gathering dust in the corner of the bedroom.

—Having to be considerate when cooking/using the last tea bag/selecting TV to watch/having friends over/wanting to pick your nose.

—Having to ask Max whether he'd be home for dinner or, better still not asking, but then wondering how long to wait before cooking and eating her own supper.

—Having to eat proper meals instead of serving herself cereal or broccoli with grated cheese for dinner in front of the television.

And of course, the top news story this hour:

—Was he *the* one or just the next one?

Maggie stared at Max's eyelids, and silently started counting down from ten. The contestant was oblivious but this was a test. If he woke up before she'd reached zero, he was on her wavelength. But if he opened his eyes, was she going to say yes before enticing him to finish what they'd started earlier or was she going to close her eyes so fast that he'd think she was still asleep? Apparently the rules of engagement, or just living together, were yet to be finalised.

Ready to start, Maggie took a deep breath.

Ten

There really was no need to panic. Max was an exceptional man. Perhaps not quite as exceptional as she was, but definitely premier league. If he had asked her out for a mere drink fifteen years ago he would have made her year. And now look what had happened.

Nine

There are no guarantees in life. Not even when you pay extra. She could spend her life worrying about what might be or just enjoy the moment while she was young enough to bounce back if necessary and her skin still had some elasticity.

Eight

So what if Max was a minimalist and had what could only be described as a show bathroom? How could he not understand that shelves were there to be filled and that offers in the chemist were impossible, indeed foolish, to resist. Buy two, get one free made perfect sense. Even if you then had to buy four to get two free to ensure you had the right ratio of shampoo to conditioner for the long run. Maybe this was the perfect moment for her to learn to streamline a little.

Then again her (untidy) mother always said that immaculate homes were usually owned by dull people. Was Max boring?

Seven

Woe betide him if he used all her Jo Malone shower gel. Some things were not okay to share.

Six

Or got pubic hairs in her massage sponge.

Five

If she moved in he would know that she bleached the hair on her arms in winter, only ever used super or super plus Tampax and occasionally got cystitis.

Four

He probably wasn't that observant. And he was kind. She'd never heard him shout except on the phone, once. Or did his lack of volatility mean that he wasn't truly passionate?

Three

Maybe she could suggest they get a lock for the bathroom door. She never wanted him brushing his teeth, sprinkling talcum powder on his balls or clipping his toenails into the bath while she was having a pee.

Two

Just because you lived together didn't mean you really had to share everything, just the good stuff. They were definitely going to be using her towels and linens.

One

She was thinking about *towels?*

Zero

Move in. Move on. Move in. Move on. Move in. Move on. Despite her best focused staring, Max was still asleep. Guerilla tactics required. Coughing, she tugged at the duvet. He murmured and turned over, presenting his back to her and an irrational sob sprang to her throat.

Boarding school had a lot for answer for. Thousands of pounds spent a year training Britain's finest to sleep through dawn, alarm clocks, fire drills, lesson bells and, probably, babies crying. Maggie swallowed hard. They hadn't even discussed children.

Maggie wondered why men didn't appear to analyse everything so much. Maybe there was limited space for every eventuality on their hard drives after all the sporting statistics, James Bond trivia and memorable quotes from *The Office, Blackadder* and *Star Wars* that they seemed to be able to reproduce at a moment's notice? And yet she appeared to have the capacity to question everything. A channel in her brain that she didn't subscribe to and hardly ever indulged in, but it was always there in the background, posing a constant stream of questions but never providing the answers. The quiz show from hell. And she couldn't find the mute button.

She wished she could sleep. Being overtired definitely wasn't going to enhance her state of mind. And she had been hoping to wake up in a better mood altogether. Maggie snuggled up against Max and scrunched her eyes closed before breathing deeply in an attempt to relax. She was sure everything would seem much more manageable in daylight. She synchronised her breathing with his, hoping to be lulled to sleep. She was all in favour of progress, except perhaps in the case of nuclear weapons and biological warfare, but why did things have to change?

If she moved in to his place, she was never going to be able to break wind sub-duvet with the wild abandon of a singleton, never be able to sleep in the star position with her head wedged between two sets of pillows, never be able to dance around the flat and punch the air euphorically after he'd gone home the morning after the night before….

A few minutes later, sleep was no closer. Sliding herself to the edge of the mattress, she checked her watch— 3:07 a.m. Officially the middle of the night, as opposed to midnight which, these days, was really just late evening. Gingerly leaving the bed, she slipped on her bathrobe and, after walking into the kitchen, stood at her sink and stared out of the window into space.

Eloise opened her eyes. Something had woken her. She propped herself up on her elbow. Or at least that had been the intention, but either her left arm wasn't there or some joker had replaced it with a lead one. Either way, the command from her brain to her arm bounced back.

<internal error>
<pathway obstructed>

Suddenly panicking as she recalled a documentary she had recently half watched, she wondered if she could have had a stroke. Urgently, using her right hand to move her inconceivably heavy limb, she shook it back to life via an attack of almost unbearable pins and needles. Once restored to full working order, she used both hands as a neck brace and, supporting herself, slowly sat up from what seemed an unfeasible sleeping position on her armchair. She only remembered closing her eyes for a moment. The remains of her almost finished Indian takeaway were still on the coffee table and the television was on.

Memories of her evening started to return to her. Another job rejection followed by another engagement party. Marriage was the latest epidemic sweeping London and Eloise had never felt so acutely in need of immunity. Declarations of everlasting love shouldn't have been allowed so close to Christmas—a season that was already nauseatingly coupley. And on the employment front, she hadn't really wanted to be a receptionist at a film company; she just fancied the idea of being Orlando Bloom's wife.

She was sure the evening would have been much more fun if Jake had been able to join her. She'd always suspected that his biggest clients' Christmas drinks would overrun and he had sent her a text around eleven excusing himself, but she was tiring of being a team of one, of living alone, of having sole rights to the remote, of rarely being woken with a kiss and a cup of tea even though she allegedly had a boyfriend.

She and Jake had been seeing each other for as long as Maggie and Max had, technically a little longer, and while their once, sometimes twice and very occasionally thrice weekly get-togethers were always entertaining and often sex-filled, it didn't really feel as if it was going anywhere fast, or even slowly. Maggie and Max had undertaken them, having found themselves in one of those easy partnerships that Eloise aspired to. A merger rather than a takeover. She feared it was time to call Jake for a board, or should that have been bored, meeting.

Out of habit, Eloise checked her phone as she regained full consciousness. There had been a time when she and Maggie would have exchanged texts at the end of every evening they hadn't spent together and several on a Friday night, but her wing woman had flown. When it wasn't the morose middle of the night, she was delighted for her, even if Eloise had always maintained that life would be better curled up in the arms of a lover, with a hand to hold and a life to share and Maggie conversely had always reminded her about the snoring, the early-morning halitosis and feeling obliged to make conversation first thing when all you want to do is listen to the radio. Then again Maggie had been an only child. With three older brothers, Eloise liked having her thoughts and sentences interrupted and her days hijacked.

Seeing Rob at the party had definitely thrown her. It had been so many years now since they'd argued over anything, that at first she'd been delighted he was there. But while she knew he'd been with Helena for a while, she didn't know they'd got engaged until she'd almost been blinded by the size of her engagement ring. Talk about dangling a carat.

The way things stood at the moment, Maggie would be the next to head off into the ark, hand in hand, out of the storm. Meanwhile out on the plains, in the worsening drought, Jake would barely commit to going to the cinema the week after next.

She knew she needed to be busier. She still hadn't found her purpose in life. Thirty-two years on the planet and her CV was more of a See Me. She'd thrived much better at school, when her days had been structured and someone had been there to make sure she was advancing in the right direction.

Eloise yawned as she picked at a cold piece of naan and used her fingernail to check between her teeth for stray leaves of sag before pawing at her face, tacky with the remnants of her make-up. Time to hit the bathroom, then again if she was going to have a hangover she might as well look the part, too. It was much harder to feel sorry for yourself when your breath was minty and your skin was cleansed, toned and moisturised.

Stiffly she got to her feet and carried her tray of congealing leftovers to the kitchen. Jake or no Jake, there hadn't been one quality single man at the party. As she tipped the foil cartons into the kitchen bin, she watched the remains of the orange Tikka Masala sauce slip through the gaps between the rubbish. She didn't want to be the cliché thirty-something woman that men were warned about, but if she and Jake weren't going anywhere together, she really needed to be brave and branch out on her own before her eggs and her enthusiasm passed their sell-by date.

Ten years ago she'd probably have felt as if she'd bagged the man of her dreams. But in her early twenties she still hadn't realised that men don't change. They might get a bit tidier and learn to cook more than one dish but they don't switch from lager to bitter, from Coke to Pepsi, from non-callers to callers, from tending to be apathetic to being inspirational.

It was all about timing. Max was as affable now as he had been at university, despite his success. Over the years Maggie had metamorphosed into a better-looking, well-dressed, more confident version of herself. Eloise couldn't believe they'd remet at a wedding of all places. Everyone knows you're more likely to win the Nobel Prize than fancy the single man they sit you next to at a wedding reception.

Chapter Three

Seven months earlier

'Why is it that when people invite me to their weddings I feel duty-bound to say yes?'

Maggie's nose was almost touching the full-length mirror next to her chest of drawers as she applied her mascara, wondering why at the age of thirty-two she still needed to have her mouth open whilst applying eye make-up.

'And why can't couples just get married in London instead of making their guests commit to a whole weekend of celebrations in a place they've decided means something to them but frankly is just a hassle to everyone else?'

Pausing to rest her jaw, she turned to face Eloise, who was sprawled on her bed, half reading, half flicking through a magazine, apparently simultaneously performing a series of leg stretches. Maggie desperately wanted to swap days with her or at least join forces for a girlie Saturday. She'd rather have been going to work.

Suddenly aware of a silence, Eloise looked up as her female standard-issue dual concentration replayed the last sentence of Maggie's rant for her. 'I thought Jeremy owned a weekend cottage in Chipping Campden?'

'Fair point. Maybe I'll have to let him off on that count of nuptial narcissism. But this will be two funerals and a wedding in the same family in less than three years.'

'And still no sign of Hugh Grant.' Eloise knew her jocularity was due largely to the fact that she didn't feature on today's guest list and that the next twelve hours were her own to waste as she pleased. That said, with her preferred partner in crime unavailable and nothing in the diary, the day probably wasn't going to live up to its potential.

'I do have other things to do.' Maggie's tone was laced with irritation at her own incompetence as she aggressively separated a few eyelashes with her fingernail.

'You have to go. Prove you're okay to Adam's family. Do your duty and all that jazz.' Eloise sang the last three words. She'd seen *Chicago* in the West End several times. Sadly she suspected she was fifteen years too late to start training as a dancer. And yet she was sure it was hormonally impossible to feel depressed while you were dancing or singing. Unless of course you were singing 'Nothing Compares 2 U.'

'Duty is so two centuries ago. And what about Adam's duty to me to be faithful?' Maggie sighed. 'Bloody dead ex-boyfriends with fathers remarrying.'

Eloise nodded. In her current role as a sounding board, she wasn't required to actually say very much at all. Her eyes darted back to the magazine for retail inspiration. She was wondering whether to go shopping later and was still debating if her legs were now too old for a miniskirt. She shook her head as she flicked through the photo shoot. 'How many more times in our life is the fashion world going to try and persuade us we should be wearing striped T-shirts and wide belts?'

Maggie winced. 'Ah, the 1980s. Not my best-looking decade.'

'Not anyone's best-looking decade. Shoulder pads. Puff-balls. Blue eye shadow. Why is there no fashion tsar pressuring designers to come up with new ideas or, at the very least, legislating they just stick to the good ones?'

Maggie's focus had slipped back to her day. 'The trouble is, Jeremy still thinks that Adam was perfect.'

Eloise interrupted her best friend. 'Mags, we've been through this a billion times.'

'UK billion or American billion?' Maggie flashed Eloise an apologetic smile. 'Sorry, lovely. I don't think I'd thought through the practicalities of actually having to be there until I woke up this morning.'

'No bad thing. You'd only have got yourself in to a state earlier and at least this way you'll be able to tick loads of people off your to-visit-or-call list in one fell swoop.'

Maggie grunted her grudging acceptance that Eloise may have had a valid, if small, point. 'I'm just not sure I can cope with hours of wide eyes and sympathy.'

Eloise loved Maggie like the sister she'd always longed for in a family of brothers and therefore was allowed to get ir-ritated when Maggie overlooked the fact that the world did not revolve around her. 'Look, It's just one afternoon and evening. And you're more sorted than most people I know.'

Maggie cackled maniacally. 'Ha ha, my master plan has worked. That's what you're supposed to think.'

'Seriously, I wish I was half as happy as you purport to be.'

'Oh come on, El, you've got a fab life. A mortgage-free three-bedroom flat just off the Fulham Road, every episode of *Friends* ever made on DVD, the perfect body shape for Seven jeans, money in the bank, me…'

'That isn't everything.' Eloise hadn't meant to snap, but a plan-free Saturday when you were feeling a little bit too single and your best friend was busy all day and evening was as good for the soul as watching *Crimewatch* last thing at night when you lived alone.

'Just remember that men can pick up desperation from several postcodes away.'

'I get frustrated.' Eloise paused. 'Today is mine for the taking and yet I wish I had a man to do nothing with, to give the sports section of the paper to, even someone to cook for. There's little attraction in trying out new recipes for one. And despite the fact I make myself incredibly busy, I'm lonely. There I've said it now.'

Maggie stopped talking about herself.

'I know you claim to love being on your own…but we're not the same. I'm dying to meet someone who I want to date for more than a couple of weeks and who wants to date me back. And I do want children.'

'Steady, you're making me nervous.'

'I know we're looking younger, feeling younger, but we're well into our thirties.'

'We're in our barely-thirties.'

'We're thirty-three next birthday.'

Maggie couldn't help thinking that in the dating world good things always happened to you when you least expected it, not when you had devoted yourself to finding the path of true love and then setting up camp in the middle of it. These days Eloise thought of every man she spoke to, let alone dated, in terms of marriage. If she could only divert the energy she spent on worrying about finding a man to finding alternative energy sources, Maggie was certain Eloise would have saved the world from global warming by Christmas.

'And even if I met someone tomorrow and things went really well, I probably wouldn't have a child for, say, two years.'

'I didn't realise you had the gestation period of an elephant.'

Eloise hadn't heard her. 'Of course, that is assuming we can still have children by the time we get round to trying.'

'Breathe, El, you're scaring me and I'm not even a practical contender. If you really don't meet the right guy, or if it all gets too late, you can always adopt. There are children all over the world who need loving homes. Or if you'd rather keep it simple, buy some sperm.'

'Simple? What do you suggest I tell that child when he or she wants to know who its daddy is?

'Mummy couldn't find a boyfriend but really wanted to have you?' Maggie laughed. She knew she was being facetious, but she really needed Eloise to lighten up before she bought herself a husband over the Internet.

'Don't worry, I'm not asking you for child support or your ovaries.'

'Thank goodness for that.'

Eloise grinned at Maggie.

'Now what?' Maggie wasn't sure if she was concerned or relieved by the change in mood.

'Don't shoot but they say in here—' Eloise flicked back a few pages before proffering her open magazine as Exhibit A '—that in one way or another you've met the man you're going to marry by the time you're thirty.'

'From now on you're only reading *The Economist*.' Maggie glanced at the garish headline. 'What total crap.'

'Why do you always have to be so dismissive?'

'I prefer realistic and it's not like we were inundated with suitors in our not-much-sex-in-this-city flatshare.'

'Just because you haven't kept in touch with your exes.'

'Ex. As ever, the clue is in the title. And the hypothesis is flawed. If he wasn't good enough the first time around, why on earth would you bother tr—'

Eloise interrupted. 'It doesn't say you've necessarily dated before, just that your paths have crossed.' She paused. 'I suppose you may not even remember meeting them.'

'Doesn't sound like he was going to be the earth-shattering one then. Who are the "people" that come up with this stuff? The same misguided individuals who say that if you don't eat carbohydrates you're going to lose three stone?'

To Maggie's concern, she could see Eloise had come over all wistful.

'I was thinking I might look up some old flames. You know, just in case. What's the harm?' Eloise shrugged. 'At least it'll keep me busy. I thought I might start with Joe….'

Disbelieving, Maggie stared at Eloise via the mirror. 'The stalker?'

'So he rang a few times.'

'Every evening. For several months. You even started turning the lights off at the front of the flat so he thought you were out.'

One of the downsides to having lived with your best friend is that your poetic licence is revoked.

'That was only once and he still remembers my birthday.'

Maggie raised a warning brow. 'No, El. Promise me you'll call Ghostbusters before you try and track him down.'

Eloise avoided eye contact with Maggie. 'Okay then, how about Dan?'

'I thought someone told you he was married.'

'Damn, I think you're right. Then again, there's always his mate Toby, the litigator.'

Maggie frowned. 'I don't remember him.'

'He was yummy.'

'He can't have been as good-looking as Dan.'

'Different. Striking rather than traditionally handsome.'

Maggie stopped to think. 'Nope. No recollection what-soever.'

'You were probably going through one of your super-dismissive periods.'

'And just say, hypothetically, you do track him down—what are you going to say?'

Eloise shrugged.

Maggie shook her head. 'Look, you know how much I love you.'

'Why do I sense a "but" coming on?'

'Please please get a full-time job and immerse yourself in a less inward looking project. What about the survey they rehash every year that says most people meet their partners at work?'

'I've had more careers than I can count.'

Eloise had been everything from a Starbucks barista to a landscape gardener. Jackie of all trades and master of some. Just yet to be really inspired.

'You need something full-time or at least more-time, something that'll challenge you mentally.'

'I know.'

'You'd really benefit from…' Maggie stopped. 'You know?'

Eloise nodded. 'I'm really trying to make the right move this time. I'm actually thinking about going on a counsel-ling course.'

'I wouldn't say things were that bad.'

'To train as a counsellor.'

Maggie smiled at her misunderstanding. 'Sorry. It's just your list of qualifications must be in double figures by now. Why don't you teach something you've already qualified in? Adults, children, you'd be amazing. And just imagine how rewarding it would be and how appreciated it would make you feel.'

'I already do the library trolley at the hospital and my radio show.'

'Ah yes. *Ward FM, Bedpans Today*—whatever it's called. That's, what, five hours a week or something?'

Eloise was silent. These days her radio show was the high-light of her week. And this week it had been cancelled. No wonder she was having a bit of a downer.

'I'm not trying to be nasty.'

Eloise folded her arms across her chest. 'Sometimes you don't need to try.'

'Sorry. Look, I just think you need to help yourself before you help all these other people. And stop kidding yourself that everything would be okay if only you had a lovely boyfriend.'

Eloise stood her ground. 'Only if you stop pretending that everything is perfect without one.'

'Everyone's different. I'd rather have my independence.'

'I'm not planning on giving all of mine up. I just want to share myself with someone else.'

'I'm not sure there's enough of me to go around.'

'Don't you want someone to rock your world?'

'Been there done that. He rocked my world and then my boat before capsizing it altogether.'

'So that's it now, for ever?'

'Who knows, but I like being in charge.'

Eloise gave Maggie what she hoped was an empathetic rather than a patronising smile. 'It's normal to be nervous about commitment.'

'You haven't been on a counselling course yet.'

'Bridget Jones might have been itching for her happy ending, but don't think she signed a joint lease without several bottles of Chardonnay and a lot of soul-searching. I'd be nervous, too.' Eloise corrected herself. 'I will be nervous, too.'

Maggie looked at her watch. 'How on earth did we get on to this? We're both single. And now I'm going to be late.'

'I know underneath that designer dress, there's a closet romantic waiting to be rediscovered.'

'If you don't shut up, I'm going to lock you in the closet and then your patients won't even get their lunchtime request show.'

'It's been cancelled this week.' Eloise sighed. 'They're up-grading the studio.'

'I'm sure they'll be quite happy listening to City FM instead.'

Eloise shook her head. 'With me they get to listen to the songs they want to hear, plus they get an all important visitor—imagine how long a day is, just lying on your back waiting for your next crappy meal to arrive and, besides, I love doing it. And it is a way of giving something back to the community.'

'So aim higher. Go for a job with a big station.' Maggie softened. 'I think what you do is amazing but, just think, you could cheer up thousands of people, millions maybe, instead of a handful—and get paid for it.' Maggie applied her lip gloss. 'Anyway, I help the community.'

Eloise frowned. 'You help the treasury.'

'I help people find their perfect home.'

'For a fee.'

'People are happy to pay for a good service.'

'They don't have a choice.'

'I save them time, stress…' Maggie took a deep breath. This conversation was going nowhere but a huff. 'Well, if you're not brave enough to really go for it as a radio presenter, I still think you'd be a fantastic teacher.' Maggie hoped she hadn't overdone it. She just wanted to galvanise Eloise into action, and in order to do that she had to penetrate her shell of pseudo-ambivalence.

Eloise returned her focus to her magazine. 'You know what they say about people who become teachers.'

'You're patient, interested, interesting, and you get on with everyone you want to. I genuinely think this could be your calling.' Thanks to her father's success, Eloise had no need for a regular pay packet. Not necessarily a good thing.

Eloise was so taken aback at the force of Maggie's compliment that she considered it. 'I guess I could teach languages.'

'You could teach anything you put your mind to.' Maggie slipped her shoes on and rechecked her appearance in the mirror.

Eloise nodded enthusiastically then stopped, apparently in thought. 'Only one problem.'

'Shoot. I'll solve it.'

'It's an industry full of women.'

Maggie could have screamed. Instead she sighed. 'It's as if you're waiting for a man to come along before you even start trying to live your life.'

'Retracing my romantic steps would be a project. Maybe I could even write a book about it. I've always fancied having a go at that.'

'You're not alone there. I can see it now—*EXpect the worst.*' Maggie repeated the Ex bit in case Eloise had missed it in its verbal state, which she had.

'Hey, that's kind of catchy.'

'I was joking. Or I guess you could start a business.'

'Because being an entrepreneur is such an easy option.'

'What about all your dreams?'

'Not sure I really had that many. Not of my own. What would my company do?'

'Make chocolate underpants. Build gardens in hospitals. Start up a radio station for pets left at home on their own all day. You just need to come up with something the Western World shouldn't be able to live without. And then you won't have time to worry about all the other stuff. You might not even have time for lunch every day.'

'Look, I know your career comes first.'

'That's got nothing to do with it. Imagine the sense of achievement in seeing people doing things your way.'

'I'm not giving up on the man thing.'

'Who said anything about giving up. It's just important to do other stuff at the same time because if you do meet a great guy—'

'When.'

Maggie was always nervous when Eloise used that tone of voice.

'When you do meet him, what are you going to say you do for a living? Search for Mr Right?'

Eloise shrugged silently. Not a good sign. Maggie wished she'd been a little gentler. Especially as she was about to go out for the rest of the day.

Sulkily, Eloise responded. 'Okay, so maybe going backwards isn't a good idea, but I still think I have to be proactive. Take Jeremy. Sixty-three years old and back in the saddle again barely a year after his wife of thirty-eight years died.'

'So much for true love.'

'He only promised to be faithful to Anna until death did them part which, sadly, it did.' Eloise shrugged. 'Plus, you can't blame him. He's one of the last men standing from the "can't boil an egg" generation of husbands.'

'He could afford to get a housekeeper.'

'He lost a son and a wife within two years of each other. And at the point some people would want to curl up and die in front of daytime television, he's getting married again.'

Maggie sighed. 'How about you just have some meaningless sex—with contraception, of course?'

'Check. Done that. Which is more than can be said for you recently.'

'I gave it up for Lent.' Last year. But who was counting.

'Lent finished a month ago.'

Maggie shrugged. 'I've been busy. Hey, maybe there'll be a band there tonight.'

'What's that got to do with anything?'

Maggie shrugged. 'I've never slept with a musician, plus I only made it to the gym once last week so I could do with the workout.'

Eloise shook her head. 'I'm not sure that you should be flirting in front of Adam's entire family.'

Maggie opened her make-up bag to check she had everything and decided to add a few finishing touches. At this rate she wasn't going to have time to do anything on arrival.

Eloise watched her wave her Lancôme wand. 'Mags, if you put any more mascara on that eye, you're going to look like the *Clockwork Orange* poster.'

Maggie returned her cosmetic sword to its cylindrical scabbard and, for the first time in as long as she could remember, she sneezed. It was unstoppable. A mascara massacre. Fucking typical.

Eloise caught a glimpse of the clock on Maggie's bedside table. 'Blimey, shouldn't you be heading off? There's nothing like following the bride up the aisle for making an entrance.'

Eloise walked over to the mirror to inspect Maggie close up as Maggie licked her finger and tried to erase the spidery mascara shadow now drying just under her eyebrow and just below her eye, without smudging any of her earlier handiwork.

Lecture apparently forgotten, Eloise handed her a tissue

and hovered at her elbow. A human hummingbird. 'Has global warming been particularly acute in Knightsbridge?'

'Pardon?'

'I swear you've developed a tan.' Eloise looked from her arm to Maggie's and back again.

Maggie blushed under her foundation. 'I may have invested in eight minutes of self-confidence. Twice.'

Eloise shook her head. 'You're not allowed to die before me.'

'Everything in London is carcinogenic.' Maggie found her car keys and grabbed her handbag. 'Right. I'm off.'

'Good.' Eloise's unofficial role was to get Maggie to the church on time—or at least to the motorway in time. The rest was up to her driving skills and her satellite navigation. 'Invite? Sense of humour?'

Maggie peered into her bag. 'Check.'

'Overnight bag?'

Maggie shook her head. 'I'm driving home later.'

'Why on earth aren't you staying down there?'

'And have to make small talk with everyone over a fried breakfast I don't want? I'd much rather be back in my own bed tonight, plus I've got loads of paperwork to catch up on at the office tomorrow.'

'If I need to get a job, you definitely need to get a life.'

'At least I now know what I want. Most people have to wait until after their first divorce to find themselves. I suppose you could say I had a lucky break.' Maggie took a deep breath.

Eloise forced a hug on Maggie. 'I know today is tough and awkward and, go on, admit it, sad even, but you're Maggie Hunter, a legendary coper in these parts. Just think

Jackie O rather than Jackie Stallone. You need to glide not stomp through this afternoon and evening.'

Maggie hugged Eloise back. 'I wish you were coming with me.'

'Tragically I wasn't invited.' Eloise couldn't have been more delighted.

Maggie exhaled as she prepared to face the past.

'Hey, one second, I just remembered I brought something over for you that'll cheer you up.' Eloise produced a torn-out dog-eared page of a magazine from her bag. It had been folded so small it resembled a colourful receipt. 'Remember Max French?'

'Is Harry Potter a wizard? I still can't believe he sloped off after the funeral without saying hello.'

'If he was even there in the first place.'

'I promise I wasn't making it up.'

'I didn't see him and I actually knew him at university. He was always a bit of a fantasy figure as far as you were concerned.'

'Hardly.'

Maggie regretted her denial immediately. Eloise had been an eye witness. 'At least my university crush was on a man.'

Blushing, Eloise presented her find. 'Turns out you were way ahead of your time. Max was voted the thirty-fifth most eligible bachelor in *Miss Magazine* New Year's Hottest List.'

Maggie shrugged. 'So?' She was much more difficult to impress these days.

'You're single and so is he.'

'The only two single people left on the planet, well, apart from you, of course, we met before we were thirty, it must be fate and…hang on, New Year's list? It's May.'

'So the magazine was a few months old. I found it in the doctor's waiting room.'

Maggie's tone became accusatory before it switched to concern. 'Are you okay?'

'Fine I hope. Just time for my three-yearly cervical smear.'

'Nice.' Maggie could empathise only too well. One of the many routine things about being female, along with spending thousands of pounds over the years on sanitary ware, that you had to take in your stride.

'Especially when it makes you realise you can count the number of times you've had sex since the last one on one hand. What are we like?'

Maggie shrugged. 'Like all the other single women in their thirties.'

'Ah, but you see, we don't need to be. I have a plan.'

Maggie rolled her eyes. 'If only you put this much energy into something constructive.' She feigned casual interest. 'So, what *is* Mr French up to these days?'

'He was one of the guys behind *Feeling Fruity*.'

'What is that, Viagra with vitamin C?''

'Where have you been? It's a smoothie company and it's just been bought for millions of pounds.'

Maggie did an aural double take. She could have sworn Eloise said millions.

She nodded confirmation. 'He's the entrepreneur the city is watching. Richard Branson's natural successor, apparently.'

'Without the beard, I hope.' Curious, Maggie reached for

the article again. 'I'd definitely have put money on him being married by now.'

'I read an interview with him a year or two ago which said he was too busy for romance.'

Maggie was always secretly impressed by Eloise's ability to keep up to date. She knew who the prime minister was, but when it came to popular culture Maggie couldn't help feeling she was starting to lose her grip. Then again, one of the reasons she was good at her job was because she treated all her clients exactly the same—usually because she had no clue where they fitted in to the big social and celebrity hierarchy, unless they had distinctive names like Madonna or Oprah or Red.

Maggie studied the page. Eloise had circled a blurry photo the size of a postage stamp, but even with skin the colour of a satsuma, Max French was still a wow. Or maybe her standards had slipped since college, when she'd turned up assuming she'd be spending the next three years in the brat pack rather than with a gaggle of Adrian Moles.

Eloise, watching her, leant in conspiratorially. 'So? Want to join me on my history tour?'

'I'm late, remember. And don't forget your and Max's paths crossed way before you reached thirty. He could be it. Live life to the Max, why don't you?' Maggie stole one last glance at the picture. A fond reminder of an era that was infinitely less complicated than she'd realised at the time. 'Just remember to thank me in the speeches. He's still gorgeous. How could you not have fancied him?'

'It must be a chemistry thing.'

'Or an eyesight thing. The man looks like Rob Lowe.'

'More like Ricky Gervais these days.'

Maggie gave Eloise the page back. 'I'll bet his PR just paid for him to be included.'

Eloise raised her eyebrows in surprise. 'Do you really think so?'

Maggie nodded. 'He must be married to one of his supermodel girlfriends by now. Remember Kirsty? Legs up to her eyebrows.'

'Maybe he's divorced?'

'Nah, far too young.'

'Says the woman who buried her last boyfriend.'

'If you could possibly rephrase that.' Maggie's thoughts flitted between the present and the past. 'And who can forget Olivia Double-Barrelled? Tall, slim, fashion conscious and blemish-free—quite an achievement for an undergraduate.'

Eloise laughed. 'Only because we were living on toast, pasta and pesto.'

Maggie giggled. 'Go on, come with me this afternoon. I'm sure they'd be delighted to see you. If not, it'll be a nice drive and you can go shopping or something.'

'And buy what? A cream tea? An antique? A National Trust tea towel? Come on, I'm throwing you out of your flat. But first, the real reason I came round…'

'Shit. Well remembered.' Sprinting back to her bedroom, Maggie rummaged on her dressing table. One of the few disadvantages to living alone and attending weddings without a plus one is that you have no one in-house to help you with the fiddly clasp on your favourite bracelet.

Chapter Four

Maggie scoured the reception looking for table numbers hidden amongst the peach and white petals as she wove her way between the cream-satin-covered chairs. She could see tables six, seven and eight but not nine.

Nine. Nine. Nine. It was rapidly becoming an emergency. A smile fixed on her face, she ignored the trail of sympathetic head tilts and whispers that had been following in her wake all afternoon and sashayed confidently to the table in the corner on the far side of the dance floor. To her relief, her name card was at the centre of the first place setting she came to and her seat was facing the wall rather than the rest of the room. She couldn't wait to sit down.

Mayday Mayday. Max sat low in the driver's seat of his gleaming silver vintage Porsche 356 Speedster wishing he had a less noticeable car as he watched the last of the guests arriving at the hotel for the reception and wondered if he should just restart the engine, drive home and send a note of apology.

He'd never attended a wedding on his own and, thanks to the fact that the he'd left the directions on his kitchen table and Chipping Campden wasn't a one-horse town, he still hadn't. However, the reception was now looking unavoidable despite the fact that if he'd read the invitation properly he would have known he should have been wearing an ordinary suit instead of tails.

He hated being overdressed. Now everyone would assume he was either a lottery winner or gauchely posh and find it acceptable to discuss shooting pheasants. Max sighed. If only he'd had a top hat, cane and patent leather shoes, he could have bluffed his way as the cabaret. He had a baseball cap, jeans and trainers lurking on the back seat, but that was it.

Opening the car door, he put his new Italian loafer straight into the only muddy puddle in an otherwise bone-dry car park. One of those days. Smoothing down his tailcoat and ignoring the slightly damp sock on his right foot, he locked the car. He'd attended plenty of weddings of his peers but this was his first among sexagenarians.

Despite his best intentions, he hadn't seen Jamie since Adam's funeral and he'd been strangely flattered by today's invitation. Now Jamie was best man to his father. Adam's death had definitely left a void in the drinking buddy department, a gap Max was only too happy to fill. Hopefully starting as soon as possible.

'Hi.' Maggie flashed her best high-energy approachable grin at the expectant group as she sat down. Despite the fact that she knew at least thirty people at the wedding, she didn't recognise one face at this table. One by one the others stopped mid small-talk to welcome her to the fold.

'Maggie Hunter. Friend of groom. Or at least used to date his youngest son, Adam.'

Silence spread round the table.

'Yup, the one who died.'

Forget pins dropping, you could have heard an electron spinning in the silence that ensued as the fellow inhabitants of social Siberia exchanged glances, unsure what to say next.

Maggie shook out her napkin and reached for a glass of pre-poured no-longer-quite-cold-enough white wine as the conversations stuttered back to life around her. Luckily the hotel had found her a spare single/box room/walk-in wardrobe above the kitchen. She didn't care as long as it had a bed and a lock on the door. Eloise had been right on this occasion. More than two units of alcohol were imperative if she was to survive the rest of the day on what was definitely the singles table.

Maggie was used to being seated with life's leftovers at weddings. Apparently it was all about even numbers. Maggie couldn't help thinking it was a spectator sport for couples. Sipping greedily, she forced herself to concentrate on concocting an appropriate interjection on the table's current hot topic of wireless computer networks and Internet service providers.

A man to her right, possibly in his forties, with hair as pale as his complexion, bravely pulled his chair a little closer as Maggie observed that the place on her left was still empty. She was on her own.

'Hi, I'm Blake.'

His voice was quietly intense as he proffered a clammy hand for shaking, his wrist so limp that Maggie was concerned she might end up with his hand in hers, literally.

'Pleased to meet you,' she lied as she returned her half-empty glass of wine to the tablecloth and wiped all traces of Blake on to her napkin. 'Maggie.'

'As you just said.'

Nodding, she rubbed her forehead with her non-contaminated hand, foreshadowing a potentially ruinous headache. Thankfully she'd already had a long chat with Jeremy, so an early departure was definitely feasible. An effusive thank-you letter and he'd be none the wiser. Maybe she could even bribe the banqueting manager to let her know what the first dance had been to.

Blake smiled, revealing a set of stained teeth. 'So, what do you do?'

Maggie did her best to disguise her sigh with a smile. What did it matter? She could unequivocally state she was never going to see Blake again after today. That said, they had to talk about something. She resigned herself to a dreadful interview cum conversation. 'I work in property.'

'Well.' A self-assured smile played on his lips. 'I guess we could all say we work *in* property, except those of us who work outdoors.'

He said 'us' as though he was a man of the people—which he definitely was not.

Maggie rubbed her temples firmly with her fingertips, hoping a genie might appear. Instead someone started talking behind her.

'So I see they've put the youngsters as far away from the top table as possible. I'm almost flattered that they still think I might throw a profiterole.'

Mr Pale & Not at All Interesting shot Mr Already Much More Interesting a look over her shoulder as Maggie wondered whether she should turn around and face her saviour. His voice was deeply promising. She felt sure its owner would, sadly, be fat and bald.

Max sat down in the empty chair to Maggie's left. He had been hoping he'd be sitting with Jamie. He had a life full of friends he rarely saw and really wasn't in the mood to meet seven more. 'Sorry to interrupt.'

'No apology required.' Turning, Maggie prepared to introduce herself to the latest addition to this circle of hell.

Swivelling to look over his shoulder at the top table, Max surveyed the rest of the reception from his seat. 'It does feel like we're in exile…'

Maggie's jaw was slack. It was definitely him and, in what was nothing short of a miracle, she had reapplied her lip gloss less than fifteen minutes ago. She couldn't believe she hadn't checked the seating plan after Jeremy had given her the table number.

'…or maybe it's just that we're the only guests still young enough to be able to hear the speeches from here.'

'Max French?' She hoped it had sounded like she'd just plucked his name from her long-term memory and was testing it out. Thanks to Eloise and *Miss Magazine*, Maggie felt a little too up to date.

'Yes.' Max lingered over the syllable as he rushed through his mental Rolodex. She did look vaguely familiar. He decided to gamble. 'Were we at college together?' With two years at a mixed sixth-form college, a three-year degree and an MBA under his belt, the probability was high.

As Maggie beamed, he tried and failed to remember anything specific about her, starting with her name. He glanced at her place setting, but the name card had fallen on its face. He couldn't help thinking he was about to follow suit.

Suddenly acutely embarrassed, she blushed at his hesitation and proffered a hand for shaking. 'Maggie Hunter.'

He nodded enthusiastically and charmingly. 'Of course.'

'I wouldn't be surprised if you didn't remember me.'

'Of course I remem—' Max raised his hands in surrender. 'Okay, you've got me. I'm afraid I don't recall exactly where you fit in to the big picture. I'm guessing it was a while back. Then again, apparently drinking lots of Diet Coke affects your memory.'

'Really? No good being slim if you can't remember who you are.'

Max smiled appreciatively. 'The research suggested it had to be litres a day rather than a couple of cans, but how depressing to have reached the age where I can't quite match a face and a name. Next I'll be repeating myself.'

'I can hardly wait.' Maggie berated herself for not being more memorable. That said, Max had been the one-who'd-got-away or, more accurately, the-one-who'd-always-been-going-out-with-someone-else. She, on the other hand, was the one who'd been half a stone overweight and in need of a hairstyle. In a way it was quite positive that he hadn't recognised her. Ego bruised, she decided to go on the offensive. 'Great outfit.'

Maggie sat back in her chair and watched as Max squirmed, momentarily self-conscious. It was an easy point for her to score, but her Diane von Furstenberg wrap-around self-confidence always made her feel invincible and flirtatious. A dangerous combination.

'Okay, so it's fair to say that I didn't get to where I am today by reading invitations properly.'

'Don't tell me, your PA forgot to flag the dress code.'

Max laughed. 'Put it this way, by the time I realized, my only alternative was jeans.'

'Not denim. Not at a wedding.' Maggie's theatrical overreaction was well received. 'Cloth of the devil. The scruffy devil no less. Or it is if you're over sixty, not a rock star, and it's a special occasion.'

Maggie hesitated, stopping their easy banter in its tracks. 'I didn't see you at the ceremony.'

Max leant in conspiratorially. 'I forgot the map, too. Stupidly, I didn't think there'd be more than one church here. I'm afraid I'm a true Londoner. I always assume that everywhere in the country is village sized—one post office, one church, one newsagent and about fourteen pubs. Did it all go well?'

'Well, two people committed to each other for the long haul, if that's what you mean.'

'I suspect it's much easier to do that in your sixties than it is in your thirties.'

Maggie smiled. 'Absolutely, although if you believe what you read…'

'I try not to.'

'Well, apparently we're all going to live a long time.'

He wasn't listening. Maggie could tell. The rest of the day

was shaping up perfectly. Keen drip versus self-absorbed dish. Back to the migraine plan.

Max shifted in his seat. 'This is going to sound a tad cheeky, but do you think you could vouch for me being at the church? Say I was sitting with you, that sort of thing. I mean if anyone, like, well, Jamie basically, was to ask…'

'You want me to lie?'

'Yup.'

Maggie wouldn't normally have hesitated but, aside from the fact she was enjoying her moment of being useful, fibbing about being in church? Plus, as Max had been seated next to her, there more than likely was a God after all and Maggie didn't want to risk pissing him or her off just yet.

'I just need an alibi—that is if your boyfriend doesn't mind?' Max scanned the table.

Maggie sighed wearily. 'This is the singles table.'

Max took another look and his eyes widened. 'So this is what it's like on the other side, in the world of solo artists.'

'Please don't tell me this is your first time.'

'I sit beside you like a virgin.'

'Finally you've made it through the wilderness.'

Max looked at her blankly. He was clearly not a Madonna fan. Maggie decided to move on swiftly. 'So.' She was starting to feel quite drunk. Wittily as opposed to staggeringly so, but merrily, not-to-be-trusted-anywhere-near-a-car, and therefore definitely staying. 'So, how do you know Jeremy?'

Flushed, she sat back and fanned herself with a handily placed wedding breakfast menu, unleashing a cloud of hidden pastel hearts and horseshoes. A tissue paper church bell adhered itself to her Juicy Tube glossed lip and she wiped it away assertively on her napkin, taking a tiny bit of her lip surface with it.

'Jamie and I were at school together. And I've always got on well with his old man. We had a few holidays together. You know the sort—four boys whittle themselves a wigwam and nearly come a cropper in a homemade go-cart in Dorset.'

Maggie laughed, 'My holidays involved reading the Famous Five rather than being them.'

'The difference between girls and boys manifests itself early.'

'Along with the peeing-standing-up thing.'

'Exactly.' Max was relieved. While all his mates had almost enviously assured him it was incredibly easy to pull a single girl at a wedding, they had also warned of the potential moose lurking. Fortunately there were no wildebeest on his horizon at the moment.

He refilled both their glasses with the wine on the table. 'How about you, how do you know the groom?'

Maggie was thoughtful. 'I didn't realise you were at school with Jamie.'

Max shrugged. 'I was at school with lots of people.'

'It's just you'd think our paths might have crossed again in the two years Adam and I were together.'

Max paled. 'You were the Maggie dating Adam?' Instantly awkward, he fiddled with his cutlery, aligning it carefully whilst stealing a couple of sidelong glances. She didn't look like the Maggie at the cemetery. Then again maybe she did. Different hair. Longer? Darker? Less black clothing.

'That's me.'

'I didn't realise…I didn't think…' Flustered, Max forced himself to finish a sentence. 'I'm sorry. I've spent most of the last few years at the office. When I resurfaced I barely recognised my life let alone the people in it, including my then girlfriend.' While he'd been in meetings, Catherine had completely redecorated and styled herself as Mrs French without checking with him first. She'd had to go.

'Had she been spending your bonuses on plastic surgery?'

'Pardon?' Still in something of a tailspin over Maggie's identity, Max looked confused.

'It was a joke. Not my finest. Rest assured I won't be using it again.'

Max revisited the last few exchanges and finally grinned. 'I get it now.'

Maggie could feel her cheeks had become rosier. 'Anyway, at least that makes sense.'

Max frowned. 'Sorry, lost me again.'

'Well, I thought I saw you at the funeral and then I thought I must have got you confused with someone else.'

'I was there only briefly.'

But he'd been there. Maggie clenched her fist in a victory punch under the table.

'Are you okay?'

Maggie nodded and relaxed her arm. Oh Eloise Forrest of little faith. Just wait until she had a mobile-phone-friendly moment.

'I would have stayed longer. It's just…' Max paused. 'Well, funerals aren't really my thing.'

'Nor mine.' Maggie's expression gave nothing away.

Max smacked his palm on his forehead. 'Please forgive my astounding lack of tact. I will impale myself on my cake fork if you so desire.' Chivalrously he prepared for death by prong.

Maggie shook her head. 'No need.'

'So.' Max polished his dessert fork on his napkin and returned it to its place in his setting. 'How are you doing?'

'I'm fine. Good actually. Life after death couldn't be better.'

Maggie laughed and, taking his cue from her, Max half joined in, struggling to be appropriate but feeling his way.

'Well, you're looking great.'

'Thank you.'

Suddenly she loved weddings.

'I mean all things considered.' And then it happened. Max French, university crush, thirty-fifth most eligible bachelor and totally unexpected wedding bonus, put his hand on her arm. Maggie took his tactile side in her stride.

Despite Maggie's rapid champagne and wine consumption, her safety catch was still on. If there was such a thing as a right time and/or place to set the record straight on Adam, this definitely wasn't it. 'It's been a while. Life goes on, and it was a good turnout.'

Max hesitated, not quite understanding what she meant.

'At the funeral, I mean. Loads more people came along than I'd expected.'

'Adam was a popular guy.'

'He certainly was.' Maggie suddenly wondered exactly how many of the women dressed in black he'd slept with.

Max leant in closer. 'I have to confess to standing at the edge of the crowd sentimentally wondering who on earth would turn up to my funeral. And then I dashed off to catch a plane.'

'I wish I'd been able to jet off somewhere. Forget honeymoons, the time you really need a holiday is after a funeral.'

'I'm afraid I don't really know what to say. I could wheel

out the old cliché that time is an excellent healer—which fortunately happens to be true.' Max dipped his head and lowered his volume slightly as a mark of respect. 'It must have been a terrible time for you.'

Maggie had often wondered why making your co-con-versationalist strain to hear was supposed to demonstrate compassion. She decided to change the subject.

'So I guess your ego must be dining out now that you've been named and shamed as one of Britain's most eligible bachelors.'

Max's hairline receded a few centimetres as his eyes widened in surprise. 'I didn't think anyone sensible read that magazine? In fact I was assured by my sister that no one would see the article.'

'My best friend is addicted to trashy mags and is very much in the market for a man. She's always looking for the next big thing, be it handbags, careers or a shopping list of suitors.'

'Maybe you should introduce her to me?' Blake had pulled his chair round, apparently determined to force his re-entry into the conversation. Maggie wondered why male self-confidence clearly had no correlation to looks. While millions of women were worrying about their bottoms looking a little on the large side in a pair of jeans, the worst-looking men in the world rarely stopped to think if perhaps they were being boring.

Maggie decided to ignore him and addressed Max. 'So, the university smoothie decided to make it his living.'

Max laughed. 'Something like that.'

'You make smoothies?' Blake wasn't going anywhere.

Judging by his pallor, Maggie was amazed he even knew what fruit was.

'Well, I did. We recently sold the company.'

'It was a huge deal.' Maggie was showing off on Max's behalf. He ignored her interjection.

Blake nodded. 'Interesting.' He enunciated the word so carefully that it sounded like an entire sentence.

Maggie could see from Blake's expression that he was dreaming up a battery of detailed questions for Max. Instinctively Maggie wanted to protect him and, if she was honest, herself, from the crossfire. Max got there first.

'Not that interesting. And not all my projects have been as successful. I lost a lot of money last year on some IT software that was supposed to be in every home by now.'

Blake's features lit up. 'Was that the XVMRC190?'

'I honestly couldn't tell you. I was just one of the mugs who invested. It was supposed to mean you could use your mouse as a remote control or something like that. The prototype looked good at any rate. Hey, it could have gone either way.'

'So…' Max's rerouting of the conversation made it quite clear he felt the same way she did about Blake. 'How's widowed life been treating you?'

'I'm not a widow. We weren't married.' Maggie immediately regretted her defensive tone. 'Sorry.'

Max waved her apology away.

She wondered how close Max and Jamie were. 'To be frank, things hadn't been perfect between us for a while.'

'I bet well-meaning but tactless idiots like me aren't helping.'

His self-deprecating concern was touching if slightly

mistimed. She really didn't want to be thinking about Adam now. Somehow she'd managed to block almost half of 1999 out of her memory. All she could recall was an emotionally airbrushed version.

She fiddled with a lock of her hair as she tried to get the balance right.

'You know, in some ways, it's not that different to being dumped, except there's nowhere to send a Christmas card when the dust has settled and you are trying to be civil. It took time, but now I am fine. Really fine.'

'I suppose at least you don't have to deal with him going out with someone else.'

If only he knew. Maggie forced a smile through tight lips as Max swept the room with his gaze. He lowered his voice. 'I'd say it's very good of you to come today. Quite a tall order, I'd have thought.'

Maggie appreciated his empathy. 'In actual fact, it feels a bit like I've popped into a bygone era, a previous life almost. Three years is a long time. Longer than we'd been together and…' Maggie stopped herself in case her wine started doing the talking. If only they'd developed some sort of kit to help you detect men who cheat, just a simple test where they had to pee on a stick or something.

Max nodded. 'If it's not the wrong thing to say, you seem in remarkably good shape.'

'Thank you.' Silently she praised herself for finding fifteen minutes between clients to have her eyebrows threaded on Thursday.

As the starters arrived Maggie wondered who in the seventies had decided that melon and Parma ham looked good together or whether they had just been the last two items languishing in some chef's fridge along with iceberg lettuce, peeled prawns and Thousand Island dressing.

'So.' Max parcelled his melon expertly in ham. 'Who did we both know at college?'

'Do you remember Eloise Forrest?'

Max stared into his white wine glass as if hoping a vision of Eloise would appear, crystal-ball style.

Maggie decided to help him out before Blake noticed the lull in conversation and decided to gatecrash.

'Five feet five inches. Light brown hair, actually quite blonde hair in those days. Dark blue eyes. Sporty, skied a lot—I think she might even have been ski captain—hilarious if you think it didn't snow once in the UK while we were students. She had a very pink fluorescent ski jacket—then again, it was the very late eighties. And big tits. Well, relatively. She's not Jordan or anything.'

Tits? Was she a teenage boy in disguise? And there were ways to describe women without resorting to bust size. Maggie thought about going to the loo and staying there.

Max snapped his fingers. 'Eloise, of course. I remember the jacket.'

Maggie applauded his tact.

'Wasn't she, isn't her dad the guy behind Forrest Fires?'

Maggie nodded. 'She's also the one who reads *Miss Magazine*.'

'Dan Forrest is one of my business heroes. Such a simple idea to have an indoor barbecue and they've remained in front despite the flood of imitations on the market. Max shook his head, clearly frustrated he hadn't thought of it first.

'Eloise and I were definitely out on the piste a couple of times together as it were. Probably with you.'

Maggie smiled benevolently. There were skiing types and then there was the rest of the world.

'So what's she up to? Married? Kids?'

'Nope. Not yet.' And he was asking, because…? Because they had to find enough small talk to see them through to the speeches.

'Did she go into the family business?'

'No.'

'It must have been tempting.'

'She was determined to be her own person.'

'Good for her.'

'That said, she still hasn't quite found her true vocation.'

Maggie immediately regretted her lack of loyalty. Over fourteen years of friendship and she was criticising her best friend in front of an almost stranger just because she'd fancied him for years. She was pathetic.

'She'll get there. I still don't know what all my goals are. This weekend, it's to have fun and get Jamie really pissed after his speech.'

He looked around the table and then leant in conspiratorially. 'My married friends tell me that the strike rate at singles tables is very high. You know, girls going all misty eyed at their desire for a wedding of their own.'

Maggie folded her arms. 'Sorry to disappoint, but we're not all itching to be Mrs Anyone.'

'Of course.' Max tilted his head cheekily.

'Seriously.' Maggie was adamant. 'Commitment isn't what every girl dreams of.'

Max was bemused by her defiance. 'I think deep down all my girlfriends have been hoping for marriage and children.'

'The ego has landed.'

'And I'm not saying that's a bad thing, just a woman thing.'

'Maybe that's what happens when you date blondes.' Maggie smiled in a concerted effort to lighten the tone. She couldn't bear men being smug about being the answer to every woman's prayers. Even Max French. Especially Max French.

Max started to nod, then stopped himself. 'You're kidding, right?'

Maggie smiled ambivalently. 'You should venture to the dark side sometime. You might be pleasantly surprised.'

'I think the misunderstandings usually started when we were living together, but it was always easier to have them on site.'

'Love at on site. Wow.'

'Hang on, I'm not talking about the wooing stage.'

'Ah yes, of course, lull the girl into a false sense of expectation and only once she's settled in to your place do you let her down.'

Max raised his arm from the elbow. 'Permission to defend myself?'

'You can try. I speak as a previous cohabiting partner who was misled.'

'Clearly he was the wrong man.'

Maggie smiled. 'Without a doubt. But you can't say that here.'

Max reddened. 'Adam?'

Maggie nodded.

'Shit.' Max was muttering, almost to himself. 'He was

probably too handsome to need to understand how to treat a woman well.'

Maggie wondered when Max had last looked in the mirror. 'Easy to say now.'

'He was always very confident.'

'It's okay. You can say cocky. Same quality, different attitude.'

'But Jamie's always been much more of a gent.'

'I think that would be too weird, don't you?' Maggie found herself laughing at the thought.

'I didn't mean you and him.' Max couldn't understand how he'd tied himself into such a huge knot. Communication was allegedly one of his skills. He made a mental note to make the next topic of conversation something non-contentious like recent films or favourite holidays.

'I have a question.'

'Thank goodness.' All his own fault, Max was dying to move away from the present subject.

'Speaking of handsome, confident men, what's Max French doing on a singles table? Hang on, let me guess, you've been single for what…thirty-six hours?'

'Actually it must be six months now. Well, since anything serious.'

'And before that?'

'I was living with a girlfriend.'

'And before that?'

Max studied his napkin, helpless to defend himself. 'A different girl. Look, Kat appeared while Louisa and I were on our last legs. It wasn't intentional, it was just bad timing. Well, for Louisa.'

Maggie hadn't thought about the fact that there'd probably

always been a queue. Being on the right side of the man drought must have been fun sometimes.

'But with a couple of exceptions over the years, I haven't been that serious about any of them.'

Maggie shook her head slowly. 'And to think women actually look for men to make them happy.'

'I mean not in the long term. I liked them at the time.'

'Sounds like true love.'

Max was sheepish. 'True lust mainly. I've only really been in love once.'

'And in the case of the others, it never occurred to you to move on before they moved in?'

Max smiled. 'It wasn't like that. It was never about taking a big step.'

'Not for you maybe.'

'Well, now that I'm on my own I have to say I'm quite enjoying myself.'

'Welcome to my world. Living alone is the new living together.'

Max frowned. 'I do run out of loo roll at least once a month, and my fridge has more different types of beer than vegetables in it. Plus, I never used to have to defend myself quite so much at weddings when I was on the couples tables. It's much easier over there. You'd probably say boring.' Max smiled.

Maggie softened. 'I might. But personally I'd rather live alone with a couple of pot plants than get to fifty with the perfect garden and an unhappy marriage.'

Max proceeded with caution. 'Don't you ever find weekends on your own can be a bit difficult?'

'I love nothing more than having a day or two with no plans, no agenda. And I often have to work at weekends.'

'It's funny, Chris and I—'

'I thought you said you were single?'

'Christopher. Temporarily homeless pending finalisation of divorce, so staying for a few—'

'So you're not living alone at all.'

'I'm not living *with* him and he's not there all the time.' Max paused. His tone was apologetic. 'I haven't really lived alone since I was at boarding school.'

'You're joking.'

'Well, with the exception of a few weeks here and there and a month or two in hotels when I've been away working on deals. And I like having company.'

'You see, I think that's a problem.'

'Because I don't intend to die alone?'

Maggie smiled. 'That's not what I meant. It's just now there's a generation of women whose main aspiration in their twenties is to get themselves a bachelorette pad. They'd rather pay a cleaner than pick up a duster. They don't really cook or iron, and they'd rather sue than sew. Sure they want relationships or, failing that, flings, but it's all on their own terms.'

'Believe me, there are plenty who can't wait to start nesting. Plus if God had meant for man to live alone, why did he give the Sony PlayStation two controllers? And it says so in the Bible.'

Maggie frowned. 'I don't remember any reference to video game consoles in the version we had at school.'

'Seriously, it says in Genesis.' Max paused as he tried to

recall the exact quote. '"It is not good for the man to be alone." Or something like that.'

'It's definitely not good for man or a relationship to be alone with a computer game.' Or indeed to quote the Bible as a source in casual conversation. Why did there always have to be a catch?

He sensed her unease.

'Hey, it's the only quote I know. Along with "on the seventh day he rested." Some other advice I'm very happy to take.'

Relieved that Max had probably not been born again, after all, Maggie decided to return to her original point. 'The trouble is if you've never spent any real time on your own, how can you possibly know who you really are?'

'It says so on my driving licence. So, my little feminist, how long have you lived alone?'

'Nearly three years now.'

'Any cats?'

'Fuck off. No cats, no soft toys. Hand on heart, I've never been happier.'

'But, well, if…' Max stared at his water glass searching for tact and diplomacy. 'If Adam, well, put it this way, if he hadn't, you know…'

Had an affair? 'Been killed.' Maggie decided to provide Max with the end to his sentence he'd been expecting.

'…well, you two could have been married with kids by now.'

'Or divorced.' She leant in towards Max. 'I know it doesn't fit the love-lost mould but I don't think we would have worked long term. It was definitely love at first, but we only really moved in together because it was easier—and cheaper—than living in two separate places. It's not a mistake I'll be making again.'

'And you're never lonely?'

Maggie laughed. 'Chance would be a fine thing. I have friends and family I don't see enough as it is and I deal with people all day and often work evenings, so I cherish my nights at home alone. Especially after a long week of driving all over the country.'

'To put men in their places at weddings?' Max's smile was mischievous.

'To help my clients.' Maggie was trying to be discreet, but she had a strange feeling she was sounding a tad shady. 'I'm a property finder.'

'Any time, any place, anywhere?'

'Any home, anywhere in the UK but mainly London and the south.'

'Sounds interesting.'

'I love it.'

'Ha. Of course you do. I knew it.'

'Pardon?'

'You're one of those women who live to work, who fill their lives with their career.'

'Something you'd know all about, I imagine.'

Max stopped crowing. 'So who do you find places for?'

'Anyone who needs me. I head up a team at Home.'

'That must require so much self-discipline. I rent a serviced office to stop me pottering all morning when I'm supposed to be working.'

'*Home* is the name of the company. We're a small firm based in Knightsbridge.'

'Very posh.'

'Fine for work. I actually wouldn't want to live there.' Maggie stopped herself. 'You don't by any chance live in…'

Max shook his head emphatically. 'Weirdest property you've ever seen? Famous clients?'

Maggie raised an eyebrow.

'I get it. You could tell me, but then you'd have to kill me.'

'And that would be a terrible waste.' Maggie listened to herself. If she hadn't known herself better, she'd have said she was flirting. But her clients were treated with total discretion, whoever she was sitting next to. 'If you get where you live right, it's your refuge, your sanctuary, your cave, your castle.'

'Your mortgage,' Max quipped.

'That too. But properties, like us, all have a history. It's fascinating.'

Max was impressed by her passion. 'So, talking shop for a moment, do you think now is a good time for me to invest some capital in a second property?'

'If you pick the right area, it's always a good time in London.'

'And what's the best way for me to find out what my options are?'

Maggie flicked her hair, flirtatiously wondering if she could make herself an option, at least for a night or two. After all, Max was unfinished business.

'Probably easiest if you make an appointment to see me at the office, or I can come to you, whatever is easiest. Let me give you my card.'

Maggie rummaged in her clutch bag and almost produced anti-shine blotting paper, her emergency credit card, and car breakdown membership before finally finding a slightly handbag-soiled business card which she watched Max slip into his tailcoat pocket and hoped he'd remember where he'd filed it before he attended another wedding in several years' time.

Chapter Five

Eloise took a sip of her coffee and wondered why it tasted so much better in a paper cup at TLC, a few hundred metres from a mug in her kitchen. In an increasingly hectic society it was a practical indulgence. No time to stop and chat to your neighbours but always time for an overpriced coffee even if you didn't actually stop to drink it. A generation of children now knew the difference between a skinny macchiato and a decaf cappuccino long before they could spell either.

Tea, Literature & Coffee was Starbucks without the bucks but with books and attracted the more literate, more liberal residents of Fulham Village—a village in which a fiver for a cup of coffee and a cookie was a steal. Early on a Saturday morning there were almost as many Bugaboos as blokes, as fathers were despatched to spend some quality time with their offspring and as a result their organic babyccino was a top seller. Yup, due to some clever marketing, toddlers now demanded an egg-cup-sized cup of warm milky froth adorned with a dusting of chocolate powder.

Importantly for the single girl, coffee provided the perfect motivation to shower and dress, plus it enabled Eloise to be sociable without actually having to say a word—except *large skinny latte*—to anyone.

This afternoon she had braved the pavement to contemplate the meaning of life and panini alfresco. Saturday supplements were scattered across the battered pine table and anchored with an arbitrary collection of ashtrays, books and elbows. She rummaged in her bag for her iPod nano and plugged herself in. A blast of gangster rap nearly shattered the calm of her afternoon. Switching from her gym playlist to music to muse to, she prepared to face the world on her own terms with her personal soundtrack.

Couples spilled out of restaurants and filtered into the constant pedestrian traffic as an apparently endless stream of families strolled and rolled past, and Eloise longed to be one of them.

There were almost as many buggies as cars in London these days and the largest of them definitely warranted some sort of congestion charge. It was no wonder child obesity was at an all-time high, their chariots so comfortable that none of them would ever want to walk anywhere. Eloise could still remember the rough nylon of her red-and-white-striped pushchair cutting the circulation to her lower legs off at the knee and the rudimentary frame poking in to her back, the bone-shaking plastic wheels juddering on the bumps of the pavement. She hadn't been able to get on to her feet fast enough.

A man not dressed for exercise hurtled through the scene,

halting abruptly a few metres away. He was breathing hard. Either he'd just mugged someone or he was on some sort of sponsored shuttle run—in jeans and the sort of trainers not designed for sprinting.

Catching his breath, he scanned the surrounding area frantically. Slowly Eloise took another sip of her coffee, enjoying the view.

'Frankie. Frankie.' His panted delivery was urgent.

Lots of heads turned. Everyone's but Frankie's, it would appear. Surreptitiously Eloise paused her music. With the headphones still in place, at least she didn't look as nosy as she really was.

'FRANKIE.' His tone changed from concern to anger. He shook his head vigorously and muttered furiously. 'God, you can be a naughty bitch.'

Silently pedestrians clutched their handbags a little more firmly, increased their pace and avoided eye contact. A few crossed the road as Eloise tried and failed not to stare.

He didn't look like a nutter. He wasn't waving an empty whisky bottle or foaming at the mouth, and he didn't look like he was going to smell of vintage body odour or urine. His jeans slouched over a pair of battered classic white Nike trainers. His navy T-shirt might have been faded and a little frayed, but it had definitely been washed recently.

The laid-back nature of his outfit, however, was betrayed by his wide-eyed panic. As he scanned and rescanned the area, without thinking, Eloise gave him what she hoped was a reassuring smile. Immediately he jogged the three steps to her table, surveying the road at all times. She removed a headphone.

'You haven't seen a small chocolate Labrador go past, have you?'

Eloise smiled. 'Oops, sorry it was delicious.'

He didn't smile. 'Chocolate as in brown.'

Now he was irritated and Eloise remembered she knew nothing about him. She responded with a little more gravitas. 'Frankie?'

The guy nodded and then sighed.

'Sorry, no.'

'Shit.' Almost shouting, he punched his thigh hard, the self-inflicted aggression startling Eloise. 'My sister is going to kill me. She thinks I'm irresponsible enough as it is.'

'I'm sure…' Eloise wasn't aware what she was sure of. Fortunately she wasn't about to come under scrutiny. He was muttering to himself quite manically. Suddenly he looked as if he might cry. Eloise decided to help. It's not like she had anything more pressing to do.

He rubbed his forehead. 'I should have given her a proper walk this morning. I was just sending a text message, I looked up and DAMN it. I'm toast. I am such an idiot.'

'How old is Frankie?'

'Old enough to know better.' Nothing could remove the stabbing nausea at the back of his throat as he kept an eye on the pavement. 'She's around four, I think. Actually if the twins are nearly four, she must be five.'

'Maybe he smelt a cat or a squirrel or a kebab or something.' In her days as a volunteer at Battersea Dogs Home, Eloise had never ceased to be amazed by what dogs ate. 'Do you think he might have headed for the park?'

His shoulders were starting to slump. 'I guess.'

'Do you always take the same route?'

'Pretty much.' He rubbed his stomach distractedly, and Eloise noted that underneath his shapeless T-shirt he was in very good shape indeed.

'My sister *will* kill me if anything happens to that dog.' He shook his head at the sky.

'We just need to try and think Labra—'

'Susan definitely loves that dog more than me. Frankie was her first child. They thought they couldn't and then along came…sorry.' Try as he might, he couldn't calm himself down. 'Bet you're wishing you hadn't looked up now.'

Eloise wasn't sure. 'Why don't you check the park, meanwhile if he comes back here, I'll—' She had completely forgotten this wasn't her problem.

'She.'

'She.' She, she, she. Eloise was the same with friends' babies. Dressing your children in pink and blue might be politically incorrect, but it certainly helped embarrassing blunders for the first few months when, Eloise found, clothed, they really all looked pretty similar and, if she was honest, usually not that beautiful.

'Thanks, you're a legend.'

Eloise beamed at the compliment although she had a sneaking suspicion that in order to be a legend, you had to be dead.

'Everyone else is looking at me like I'm some sort of a weirdo.'

'Maybe if you stopped pawing at yourself so much?' She raised an eyebrow. 'It looks like you're coming off heroin or something.' Eloise wondered what she was doing. For all she knew, he was high as a kite and the dog was a figment of his drug-addled imagination.

Car brakes screeched a hundred metres down the road. All traffic, motor and pedestrian, slid to a temporary halt.

'NO.' His voice soared from high to low and Eloise held her breath as she watched him sprint to the scene as fast as he could. She hadn't noticed any needle marks.

Grabbing her bag and abandoning the last few bites of her late lunch/early supper, she couldn't help but be drawn towards the commotion. A reluctant addict to reality television programmes, Eloise had finally succumbed to the lowbrow revolution.

To her relief there was no sign of an animal lying on the road or the pavement and, within seconds, the traffic had resumed its staccato progress towards South Kensington. The man, however, was now on his hands and knees, peering through wrought-iron railings down into a basement stairwell. Despite the fact he was shaking slightly, he looked far from feral.

Eloise approached tentatively. 'Okay, just so you know, now you really look like a weirdo.'

'Thanks.'

She followed his gaze to the foot of several steep stone steps, where a brown dog in search of a safe house trembled on all fours. Her eyes were edged with white.

'Frankie?' Eloise's voice was gentle.

At the sound of her name, Frankie turned her attention to her fellow female and then growled nervously.

The man sat up, running the hand that had moments earlier been on the pavement over his forehead, over his head, to the back of his neck. 'She never growls.'

'Was she hit?'

'No. I don't think so. No.'

'Do you think maybe she should have been on a lead?'

'Do you think I'm not feeling shitty enough?' His tone was sharp.

Point made, Eloise smiled at Frankie, hoping to get a warmer reception and, opening the gate, slipped into the stairwell, sitting herself down three steps from the top. Rummaging in her bag, she found a half-eaten muesli bar from yesterday and, after placing some of it on the step below her, pretended to munch on the rest. Frankie watched her and barked. As Eloise ignored her, studiously continuing to nibble her portion, Frankie raised her nose and sniffed hard. Slowly, tremulously, she started to climb the stairs towards her and two seconds later Eloise had her hand on Frankie's collar.

'So what are you, a dog whisperer?' His tone was a combination of gratitude and irritation.

Eloise gave him a smile as she scratched Frankie's ears.

Sweating, he smiled weakly. 'From now on, I'm not leaving the house without a bag full of goodies.'

'How do you think they do it at Crufts?'

'Well, one dog and his man are very grateful. Can we buy you a coffee to say thank you?'

Despite the fact that Eloise was almost trembling with caffeine, she couldn't possibly say no.

'Sure. You look like you need a cup of hot sweet tea.'

The man looked at his watch. 'Shit. Sorry. I hadn't realised it was so late.'

Eloise wondered in which time zone 4.25 p.m. on a Saturday was late.

'How about tomorrow?'

A likely story. She knew she should have washed her hair that morning. 'Great.'

He proffered a hand. 'I'm Jake Chambers.'

'Pleased to meet you.' She shook it firmly. Had she forgotten to introduce herself or was she playing hard to get? She hadn't decided yet.

'And you are?'

'Eloise.'

'Seriously, let me buy you a coffee, or lunch. How about we meet back at that coffee place, say tomorrow at one?'

Eloise wondered whether to pretend she was busy, then again she didn't want to increase the risk of him not turning up.

'Cool.' Eloise wondered if he'd be there.

'You understandably have no idea, but you just saved my life.'

Supersinglewoman raised a hand to wave them off as they jogged away together. As she strolled back towards her front door she realised she was walking tall, almost swaggering in fact. Jake seemed like a nice guy. But that of course would depend on whether or not he kept his word.

Chapter Six

Maggie concentrated on not looking as drunk as she felt, as she watched Jeremy twirling Ivy across the dance floor to Van Morrison's 'Brown Eyed Girl.' There was something exciting about witnessing two people in synch. Or at least there was if you were a woman. She suspected the *Dirty Dancing* effect was lost on most straight men of her generation who viewed any dancing, especially in public at a wedding, as a painful obligation and an endurance sport.

Ivy was radiant. She had clearly won the race to Jeremy's side. The number of widows and divorcees present testament to the fact that

a) women live longer than men

b) the dating scene gets worse the older you get

c) Viagra works

d) toy boys are so last season

Max had unfortunately disappeared to prop up the bar

with Jamie on the other side of the room and, as the song drew to a close, Maggie felt Blake sidle over. From Jeremy's enthusiastic hand signals, they were now all welcome on to the dance floor. Either that or he was going to spend his retirement guiding planes around airfields.

As Blake stooped to find her ear, a blast of acidic white wine on his breath curled into her nostrils. 'Would you like to dance?'

Maggie would rather have donated a kidney. She kept her bottom on her seat and hooked her feet around the chair legs for extra security. 'No thanks.'

'Go on. It might be fun.'

'I know it won't be.' Maggie smiled generously and reached for her glass.

Blake moved on to the next girl along who, moments later, was being held nice and close. Maggie relished her narrow escape. Even under the influence of rather a lot of alcohol she had kept her dignity. Or at least she would, provided no one insisted she stand on one leg or walk along a straight white line.

Finally alone, Maggie released her wine glass and poured herself a large tumbler of water. She rolled her neck to release the day's tension and stretched her legs under the table. It wasn't quite nine o'clock and yet it felt as if it should have been approaching midnight. Just one dance—to at least appear to be having a good time—and then she was going to slip upstairs to bed. With a bit of luck she might even catch the Saturday night movie although, if she was honest, the chances of her staying awake in anything resembling a horizontal position were very slim indeed.

'May I?'

Max towered over her, his already significant height advantage compounded by the fact she was sitting. His tie and tailcoat had been discarded and the top button of his shirt was undone. The pint glass in his hand was almost empty and Maggie wondered if the space that in women was occupied by a womb and all its accessories was, in the simpler sex, all bladder, so enabling the consumption of pints of liquid after a three-course meal. Fortunately for her, wraparound dresses were by virtue of their design, expandable.

Behind him the dance floor was packed with over-fifties trying to make their old dance moves fit music that was merely meant to encourage you to shake your booty. As the uh-oh intro of Beyoncé's 'Crazy in Love' started playing, she felt her head start to nod. Maggie generally didn't do dancing at weddings. Then again Max French wasn't usually the man asking.

Just over four minutes later she was hot, sweaty and grinning from ear to ear, no longer caring whether her dancing had been good, bad or ugly. Flopping into a chair, she dispatched Max to the bar while she got her breath and her perspective back. He was clearly a bit of an expert when it came to the ladies, and while he might have saved her day, she was loving her status quo—a status quo which, just for the record, had nothing to do with ageing rockers dressed in denim with receding hairlines and defiant, if limp, ponytails.

Deciding to end the night on an endorphin high, she clocked Max queuing for drinks before slinking away to bed. In her current state she didn't trust herself not to sleep with him and, as she had reminded herself several times in the silent campaign to retain her dignity she'd been waging with herself all evening, he hadn't even remembered her from university. And now, if he still remembered her name in the morning, or better still, a few days later, at least he knew where to find her.

As she closed the door to the smallest bedroom ever, Maggie nearly knocked herself out on the television suspended from the Artex ceiling on a bracket she hoped was strong enough. Carpet swirling nauseatingly beneath her feet, she gave herself a static shock as she flopped onto the bed and peeled back the stained velour bedspread to reveal a set of pink polyester sheets. She wished she had pyjamas. As it was, she was going to have to wear her dress again in the morning. After wrapping a small scratchy towel around her waist, Maggie passed out whilst trying to work out how many hours it would be before she was safe to drive, long before she'd even turned the TV on.

Max completed a third circuit of the venue, still holding Maggie's white wine spritzer, before returning to the bar, and to Jamie. It looked like it was going to be a boys' night after all.

'Maxy, my man.' Jamie put his arm around Max. 'Next you'll be drinking Malibu and orange.' Jamie took a drag of the cigar the groom had given him. To think he'd thought his father didn't know he smoked.

'On my own, apparently. I don't suppose you want a spritzer? Or can I get you another bitter?'

'Most definitely. I am the Best Man and tonight you are my Best Friend.'

'The one who turns up every three years or so.' Max was contrite.

'You movers and shakers are all the same. So how's Maggie?'

Max paused, unsure of protocol. 'What do you mean?'

'I mean, how's Maggie? We've all lost touch with her really. Aside from Christmas cards.'

'And weddings.'

'And funerals, sadly.' Jamie paused. 'Dad's always been incredibly fond of her.'

'You can understand why.'

'It was his idea to sit her next to you. A carefully selected chaperone, if you like.'

'We had a good evening.'

'He almost thought she was too good for Adam at first….'

Max noticed Jamie battling with his emotions.

Jamie shook his head. 'I still can't believe he's not coming back.' He drained his glass. 'But good to see the old man so happy tonight.'

'Definitely.'

'He deserves it.'

Max nodded. 'He certainly does.'

'And having Ivy around really takes the pressure off me. I am no longer his only family member and the sole focus for his concern.'

'Well, none of you need to worry about Maggie, she's on great form. Quite a feisty one.'

'She needed to be. I'm glad she's doing okay.'

'Of course, I had no idea she was *that* Maggie at first.'

'Damn, I think I was supposed to brief you.'

'No harm done. We managed. Apparently we were also at university together.'

'You're kidding? Small world, isn't it.'

'Sometimes.' Max paused. 'Anyway, I think she's done a runner.'

'Uh-oh, don't tell me the legendary French charm has failed you.'

'I wasn't.'

'Oh yes you were. I've been watching you.'

Max shifted his weight awkwardly.

'You don't need to be embarrassed.'

Max drank the spritzer in one. Anything was going to be easier than this conversation. 'I'll get the beers in.'

'Excellent. In the meantime, I'm going to rescue my friend Philippa from the idiotic Blake.'

'Yeah, who *is* he?'

'Ivy's nephew.'

'So you're related to him now?' Max couldn't resist mischievously raising an eyebrow.

'Yeah yeah. See you back here in a few.'

Max stood at the bar, drunk and alone. He was sure one dance was supposed to lead to another.

Chapter Seven

'Team meeting. Ten minutes.'

After spending most of Sunday in bed, the wedding was starting to resemble an elaborate dream, and part of Maggie was relieved to be back in the real world this Monday morning. Expertly she wove her way between the archipelago of desks in the open-plan office and reached her corner room without dropping anything. However in the process of dumping her soft brown leather briefcase on her desk, she dislodged a leaning tower of post.

The perfect start to her day immediately marred, she sighed as she gathered up the envelopes and shrink-wrapped brochures, most of which were instantly junkable. She had a spam filter on her inbox, she didn't see why she couldn't have one on her in-tray, or at least have one of the secretaries throw away the circulars and brochures for garden furniture. She only had room in her life, and on her balcony, for two pots of geraniums.

Her concentration momentarily hijacked by a towel and bed linen catalogue, she heard a polite cough at her open door and guiltily filed it in the bin. If she was thinking about purchasing sheets that needed ironing and towels that cost more than shoes, she should probably have been setting up a standing order with Oxfam.

'Come in.'

She looked up. And then she looked up further.

If there was an award for tallest employee of the year or even the decade, Maggie felt sure Lucan would have won it hands down. Hands up, he would have swept the board—and the ceiling.

She smiled encouragingly. 'Everything okay?'

'Just wanted to check if you, like, wanted a coffee from across the road.' His normally pallid cheeks were feverishly rosy.

Lucan successfully headed up the rentals department at Home thus giving Simon, the self-appointed team joker, the opportunity to refer to him as Rent Boy. Lucan had just taken it all in his forty-inch stride, and either he was better at drafting a rental agreement than he was at sentence construction or the huge demand for property to rent in central London meant he had the most straightforward job in the world. He also, Eloise reckoned, had a monumental crush on Maggie.

'Please don't go especially for me.' Although the prospect of a real coffee as opposed to one that involved pouring boiling water over freeze-dried granules in the cupboard that doubled as a kitchen was very alluring.

'I've got a few orders.'

'Then I'd love a latte with an extra shot.' Caffeine as good as on its way, Maggie felt herself sit up a little straighter.

He beamed. 'Brownie?'

'Girl Guide, actually.'

Lucan laughed. A sound that most resembled someone who had swallowed a mouthful of seawater struggling to re-capture their breath.

Despite the fact she knew she hadn't been that funny, she was happy to have improved his morning. 'Better not though. You have one for me.'

She wasn't overweight per se. She was just at the top end of her weight scale, which either meant the scale was wrong; that she was largely muscle—unlikely unless it was manufacturing itself; heavy boned—a case she'd been arguing since her teens; or ate more than she needed to. Worse still, since the company had provided her with a dark grey BMW convertible she drove almost everywhere. But thanks to a flat on the top floor of a mansion block that didn't have a lift, Lycra and the fact that this year curves were finally in, she looked fine from the distance and not that bad from close up. It would all be fine provided her metabolism didn't think about slowing down, ever.

As Lucan observed her rummage for the right change in her purse, Maggie wondered what the difference was between watching and staring. Thanks to Eloise and her hare-brained articles, she had started to look at men she'd first encountered in her twenties with an air of assessment.

Searching for conversation, he nodded for no apparent reason. 'Anyway, I'm glad you're feeling better.'

As far as the office was concerned she'd had a nasty twenty-four-hour bug.

'I think I may have an allergy to weddings.'

He laughed again. 'Well, good to have you back.'

She'd only missed an afternoon and at least her hangover hadn't involved any leg-over. The morning after the night before was much easier to deal with when bodily fluids hadn't been exchanged with phone numbers.

'The team definitely functions better with you here.'

Maggie nodded. 'Thank you.' She had a team—a far cry from school when she was always in the last three to be picked for anything. Her competitive gene had only really kicked in when she'd got to the workplace and the rewards had been tangible.

The phone flashed an incoming call and Maggie dismissed Lucan with a five-pound note and a wave of her hand. He cleared her office in two strides.

She scrabbled on her desk for her headset and hit the speaker button as she put it on. 'Maggie Hunter.'

'Maggie love. It's Mum.'

'It's Monday morning. I'm rushing to a meeting and I was just about to retrieve my messages.'

Carol Hunter scoffed. 'Well, it's not as if you have to *go* anywhere to get them, is it?'

'No.' Maggie reminded herself to be patient. 'But I do need to be up to date.'

'Well, I won't keep you. I was just calling for a catch up.'

Two contradictory statements back to back. Maggie had started to suspect that retirement, rather like childbirth, erased your ability to remember what life was like before. Her mum still hadn't quite grasped that just because Maggie answered her phone didn't mean she had unlimited time to chat.

'I did in fact leave you a message on Saturday evening.'

'I was at Jeremy's wedding.'

'I know. I hope you gave him our card.'

Maggie knew it was still on the windowsill by her front door. 'Of course.' She could post it tomorrow.

'Good. I was just calling to see how it went. Obviously better than expected, because you were still there.'

'It was drinks and dinner.'

'I actually thought you might have phoned us.' Carol sounded suitably put-out. 'Or even popped in—you must have almost driven past.'

'I totally forgot to check my messages. I spent the day in bed. Some sort of bug.'

'Oh darling.'

Maggie immediately felt guilty for making her mother worry. She logged on and, as she waited for her emails to come up, clicked on the breast cancer site to donate a free mammogram. A good deed under her belt before nine-thirty and it hadn't cost her a thing.

'Should you be at work, do you think? That's how epidemics start, you know.'

Maggie smiled at her mother's inbuilt sense of responsibility. Once a deputy head, always a deputy head. 'I'm fine today. Just no time to talk.'

'You're always in such a hurry. It can't be good for you. And it's no wonder you never meet anyone.'

'I'm not trying to—'

'I know the spiel, but it's not like your generation are all happy either. You need to make time to give life a chance to happen. You all even speak faster than we did.'

'I'll-call-you-tonight?'

'I look forward to it. You do have our number, I take it?'

'Chat tonight. Love you.'

No sooner had she put the phone down than it rang again.

Rolling her eyes, Maggie flicked the button on her headset. 'No, I can't make it for supper. Nice try, but I have stuff to do at home.'

'That's handy because, one—you're not invited and, two—I'm not sure my girlfriend would like it, not that Petra really eats in the evenings.'

Maggie's stomach lurched as Red Connelly's famous tones accosted her in stereo. Along with the rest of the UK, she'd watched a rare TV interview with him on Friday night and now he was on the phone, on her direct line. Not a licence for her to be that direct. Damn.

'Many apologies. I thought you were someone else.' She shook her head, silently admonishing her lapse in professionalism.

'Clearly.' His tone was bemused. 'What can I say? Poor guy.'

'It was my—' Maggie interrupted herself. Red was a client. And a famous one at that. The banter only needed to be one-way. 'Good weekend?'

Maggie wondered whether box-office-busting action heroes dating central European underwear models had bad weekends.

'Not bad. Busy.'

'I loved your interview.' So what if she sounded like a sycophant. It happened to be true. Plus he collected properties like other people collected shoes. And that was good news for commission.

'It feels like one after another at the moment. You know how it is….'

She could only guess.

'But the new film is released next month and the test audience loved it, so I can't complain.'

'The skydiving scene in all the trailers looks phenomenal.'

'Own hair, own teeth, own stunts. At least for now. Adrenaline's about the only drug that's legal these days.'

He laughed at his own joke, one that Maggie remembered verbatim from Friday night's interview. She wondered if actors learned a script for every part of their lives.

'Anyway, just wondered if you've had any joy finding me somewhere in the middle of nowhere with a drawbridge and a moat infested with paparazzi-eating sharks.'

'Sharks rarely eat each other.'

'Hey, good one. And so early on a Monday. What did we do before coffee?'

'Think before we spoke? They were much safer times.'

He laughed. 'You're flying today. I'm nowhere near my best until much nearer midday.'

Maggie suspected that was because Red was nowhere near his duvet until the early hours of the morning.

'So, anything to whet my appetite?'

'I've got a great Grade II hamstone farmhouse in Somerset with a coach house that could be converted into a screening room that I think you'll love, but there are a couple more places I want to check out personally before we go and view. I daresay on your schedule you could do without a wild goose chase. Can I give you a call later on in the week?'

'Nothing for me to go down and see today?'

Maggie hesitated. 'No. Soon but not quite yet.'

Red was silent.

'Is that a problem?'

'When I spoke to Simon on Friday, he said you might have a couple of things to view today and it looks like I could carve out a few hours later on. It's the perfect day to go for a drive. And I was hoping to combine it with Jack Barclay lending me something expensive for a test drive.'

'Until I know I have something I think you'll love, I really wouldn't want to be wasting your time.'

'Understand. But between you and me, I just can't wait to get out of my place in London and spread my wings, or at least be able to get undressed without the shutters being closed and not risk some sodding telephoto lens pointing at my dick.'

Maggie found plenty of space for herself in London. But then she didn't have her face all over fly posters, in magazines and staring down from billboards at roadsides and on tube platforms.

She tried to think of anything but his private parts. 'I have no doubt we'll have something perfect for you. How about I call and update you first tomorrow morning?'

'My first thing is usually elevenish.'

'Great. We'll speak then. And my apologies about earlier.'

'No problem. I love women who say what they think. Then again some might say I just love women.'

If recent tabloid rumours were true, Red loved everyone. Maggie put the phone down and shuddered. He was too smooth for his own good. But way too rich and high profile to risk upsetting.

Checking that she had a dial tone and had definitely hung up, Maggie opened her office door and her lungs.

'SIMON.'

Every office had a Simon. A larger-than-life barrow boy made good who thought his cheeky chappie persona would enable him to charm everyone he came across with a level of confidence that overrode his average looks, overgelled hair and appalling taste in ties. This one was unfortunately the nephew of the MD and therefore unimpeachable. In a staff of twenty it was impossible to bury him in paperwork and while he was the most junior, he was also the most vocal and definitely a salesman. Maggie just wished he'd been selling fruit & veg rather than exclusive properties. His suit, fat tie and slip-on shoes reminded her of an England footballer in number ones.

He strolled in confidently.

'Morning, boss. Loving that suit on you. Have you been working out again? Oh and been meaning to talk to you about organising a team-bonding night. How about a casino? Or maybe beers and ten-pin bowling?'

Maggie closed her eyes for a second and took a deep breath.

'Did you tell Red Connelly we had a few properties lined up for him to see?'

'Yes, I had a good weekend, thanks. Shame Arsenal lost but you can't win 'em all. You just wait until next season.'

'Did you tell Red—'

Simon cracked his knuckles. 'Not in so many words.'

'Which words did you use exactly?'

Simon shrugged. 'He called on Friday afternoon. Sounded like he wanted to hear some positive news…I like to oblige if I can, if you know what I mean. Apparently he got fifteen million pounds for this last film. I mean that's obscene.'

'So you thought you'd help him and help us by inventing some good news?'

'To be honest, and it doesn't happen very often, I was a touch star-struck. I mean Red, on the phone, to me. Simon Senior. Plus I'd been out for a quick drink at lunchtime with the girls, so I was in an accommodating mood as they say…'

'The girls' were the secretaries but, the way he talked about them, his bitches. As it happened Michelle was twenty-five, her favourite colour was pale blue, she was married to her childhood sweetheart and rarely drank. Cherie, by contrast, was forty-something, a single mother who knew how to have a good time and not the sort of woman you wanted to cross. Maggie imagined she drank cider. Pints of. Or Scotch. Ditto.

'It was Cherie's birthday, you see. Anyway I might just have got a bit carried away, but he sounded pleased enough.'

'Not so pleased this morning though.' Maggie shook her head. 'And, aside from the farmhouse in Somerset I found last week, do we have anything for him to see?'

Simon studied his bitten fingernails. 'Maybe one or two places…'

'Anything definite that the owners might be considering selling and/or fulfil his criteria?'

Simon folded his arms across his chest in mock defence as he made eye contact. 'You're always so demanding.'

'Simon. This isn't a joke. It's people like you that are giving the profession a bad name. You're letting the side down.'

She paused for disciplinary effect. He was uncharacteristically silent. Maggie hadn't finished yet.

'Red doesn't need the hard sell. We're not trying to shift a couple of car stereos or a pound of overripe apples. We're dealing with the apex of the property market and you're behaving like a wide boy. You're a bloody cliché of a salesman.'

Simon stood up a little straighter. 'I'm a cliché. Coool.'

'No, not cool. Less cool in that I bet you can't even spell cliché.'

'C-L-E-E-S-H-A-Y.'

Maggie let her head drop into her hands.

Simon rallied. 'Hold your horses. I'll find something. There are houses everywhere.'

'I know I don't need to remind you that Red is a very important client.'

Simon shook his head, then nodded, then shook his head again. He'd forgotten the question.

'And he's only guaranteed to be in the UK for the next few weeks, so we need to move fast without rushing. If we all need to be flat out on this, just let me know. It's not a problem. Yet. But I don't want it to become one, either.'

'Relax. When Simon says it'll be fine, it'll be fine.'

'How's your day looking?'

'Not bad. I've got a meeting in a few minutes.'

Maggie could feel exasperation approaching. Simon specialised in looking busier than he was. He'd be great when he got to management level; however, now she needed him to actually do some hard work. Hard work that involved making phone calls from a comfortable chair, not digging holes. 'The meeting with me?'

'You got it. But the rest of today is pretty free-form.'

'Not any more. Skip the meeting. Reread the spec and

my notes in the database and I want a shortlist by the end of the day. Call the local agents in Gloucestershire, Somerset, Wiltshire, Hampshire and Oxfordshire. Call your contacts, think laterally and remember—'

'I know, the client is anonymous at this stage.'

'Anonymous meaning…?'

'They don't want to read about the fact they're moving from LA, New York and London to the English countryside in the papers?'

'You got it.'

Simon paused at the door. 'And how are you feeling about the idea of a team outing?'

'I'm thinking we'll talk about that later.'

'Right you are, boss.' As Simon swaggered off, Maggie sat back in her chair and delivered a silent prayer to the suspended ceiling. Maybe he could head up a team in Siberia.

Nearly ten minutes to go and there was no sign of anyone moving from their desks. She closed her door, turned her back on them all and, resting her feet on the printer table, replaced her headset and called Eloise.

Despite Simon, she was feeling fairly invincible. Red would probably be happy with the £3m property in Somerset, plus she'd managed a perfect ten hours' sleep, which combined with the five or six she'd managed on Saturday averaged out at between seven and eight a night. She felt so much better than she had twenty-four hours earlier.

'Hello?'

Eloise was on the end of the line before Maggie had even heard it ring.

'El? Were you sitting on the phone?'

'Spooky. I was just about to call you. We're just so psychic sometimes.'

'Are you okay?'

Eloise was speaking faster than normal, positively sprinting through her syllables.

'I'm great. JC has only just left the building.' For once she had news.

Maggie paused. 'You had the Messiah to stay?'

'No, the guy with the dog I met on Saturday. Jake. Jake Chambers. Didn't you get the message I left you yesterday morning?'

'Em, no. By the time I got back from the wedding all my energies were focused on not being sick. I think I must have had food poisoning. Yesterday was all a bit of a blur. I didn't make it as far as my answerphone.'

Eloise sighed as Maggie stole the spotlight. 'You were probably just hungover.'

'I really didn't drink that much. Just a few glasses of wine.'

'Oh really?'

'And a few sips of champagne. And one tiny glass of port. Actually, maybe two of those.'

'And yet you're okay today?'

'I feel great. Almost euphoric.'

'Welcome to the world of not being twenty-two any more.'

Maggie wasn't in a hurry to dwell on that. 'So, you met a guy on Saturday?'

'Jake Chambers.' Eloise enunciated his name as proudly as if she had made him herself. 'But apparently quite a few people call him JC.'

'That's dodgy.'

'Oh come on.'

Maggie bristled. 'It's a free country. I'm allowed to have an opinion.'

Eloise paused. 'But you don't even like Marmite.'

'I'm sorry?' Eloise had lost her in the apparently logical jump from the alleged son of God to yeast extract.

'So, I'm just saying that our tastes are not the same.' Eloise was being surprisingly feisty.

Finally Maggie understood. 'You slept with this guy, didn't you?'

'Come on. I hardly know him.'

'And yet, you said, he just left…'

'He came back after lunch yesterday.'

'And you only met him on Saturday?'

'He'd lost his dog, I found her, that's all you need to know.'

'Is he handsome?'

'Dark hair, dark eyes. Boyishly good-looking.'

'You mean scruffy?'

Eloise thought back to his jeans, trainers and hoodie. 'Maybe a little.'

'And last night?'

'He bought me lunch to say thank you. Then we hung out, listened to music, watched DVDs, got a takeaway.'

'With the dog?'

'Just the two of us, Frankie belongs to his sister. We had a fun evening, he crashed on the sofa. I went to bed, alone.'

'Sounds like you've been married for years.'

'Honestly, Maggie, I think he could be great. And he's in-credibly laid-back, which is probably good for me.'

'Or bad for him.'

Eloise laughed. 'And he's much more interesting than I thought he would be.'

'So he's definitely the one?' Maggie's tone was cheeky.

'With a bit of luck he'll be a one.'

Maggie sat back in her chair. 'Has it occurred to you that he might borrow a dog every Saturday to facilitate the striking up of conversation with attractive women?'

'Do you have a conspiracy theory for everything?'

'Pretty much.'

'It was the middle of the afternoon.'

'So he's unemployed.'

'On a Saturday. Honestly, you're worse than any parent. And he has a job. He designs websites.'

'Excellent. A computer geek. How pale was his skin?'

Eloise laughed. 'He was tanned.'

'Definitely between jobs then.'

'He's simply not a nine-to-five man. And website design is more creative than technical.'

'Since when were you an expert?'

'He's also a singer-songwriter. He used to be in a band.'

'Hang on, he's starting to sound like the product of your imagination. You haven't built a boyfriend, have you? You're not going all *Weird Science* on me?'

Eloise giggled. 'I can barely operate my email. The best thing is he's not like anyone I've dated before.'

'And at our age do you think that's a good thing?'

'Hey, it's always good to try something new.'

Maggie wasn't so sure. She'd spent thirty-two years honing her likes and dislikes.

'He even sang me a few lines of a couple of his songs last

night. He's good. And he had a hit, well one, when he was part of a band, it must be about ten years ago now. And well, "hit" may be a bit strong. "Feel my pain."'

'It sounds like you've brought it on yourself.'

Eloise was enjoying her newsworthy moment, 'No, that was the name of the song.'

From deep in Maggie's musical archive a chorus was struggling to get out. Gradually it came into earshot. 'Hey, I think I remem, was the band called Crash?'

'Yes!' Eloise was impressed and excited. 'How could you possibly know that?'

'Wasted youth. Make that wasted life. I think the song was on one of the compilations I had.'

'So he wasn't lying.'

'Surely you've checked him out on Google by now?'

'I haven't had a chance yet, he's only just left.'

'Sounds like you've bagged yourself a one-hit wonder. Or at least a quarter of one. Guys and Dogs. It sounds a bit like a West End musical. So does he wear black drainpipe jeans? And how long is his hair? Crash all had ridiculously big hair, if I remember correctly.'

'Shaved head.'

'Bald?'

'Fuzzy. Think Justin Timberlake.'

'Tattoo? Piercings?'

'None that I could see.'

'Alcoholic? Does he do drugs?'

'He did have a couple of beers with his lunch, but then again so did I. He's normal. Or at least as normal as we are. At least I think so.'

'So, in fact, not normal at all.'

Eloise smiled. 'You're the one who told me I'd meet a man when I least expected it.'

'There must be some hilarious fanzine sites. I can't remember the name of the bass player, but I think he was sort of cute.'

'I'll see what I can do.'

'I think I'd rather remember him fondly. By the way, I don't know if you've had an age conversation yet, but I think he must be a few years younger than us. Are they still touring?'

'They split when they left university. But he's still writing new stuff, solo stuff, you know hoping that maybe one day…'

'He'll meet someone in the street who he can sing to.'

'Shut up. I've got a good feeling about this one.'

'Name me one person you haven't had a good feeling about.' Eloise paused.

'So when are you seeing him again?'

'We haven't planned anything.' Despite the fact he'd kissed her goodbye on the lips, suddenly she wasn't feeling so sure at all. 'So you survived the wedding.'

'Apparently so.' Despite herself, Maggie was beaming.

'Good to see Jeremy?'

'Surprisingly so, you were right.'

'See. And you weren't answering your phone on Sunday morning because?'

'Prepare to be smugger still. I took your advice and stayed the night.'

'Hah. Hence the hangover. Good for you. You've got to let go sometimes. Anyway, I'd better let you get on. Just wanted to check you'd made it back in one piece. Fancy seeing a film on Wednesday evening?'

Maggie wasn't ready to change the subject just yet. 'Guess who sat next to me at dinner?'

From the silence, Eloise sounded as if she was genuinely thinking. Maggie gave her a couple of seconds before giving her a clue. 'Max.'

Okay, so it was the punchline, but she was tight on time. Eloise's delivery sped up. 'He was there?'

'It's quite incredible. He's decided I'm the one and has been following me around since Adam died.'

'He has?' Eloise sounded happily overwhelmed, almost tearful.

'El, the world is not a giant chick flick.'

'I can't help it if I'm a romantic.'

'You can be a worldly romantic.'

'I'm not sure that you can. Hoping for true love is a bit like believing in Father Christmas.'

'It turns out Max was at school with Jamie.'

'So he *was* at the funeral.'

'Believe me, I'm not one to forget a face, or at least not that face.'

'And?'

'Well, aside from the fact that initially he didn't have a clue who I was, we had a nice dinner and one sweaty dance.'

'So not married then?'

'Nope—although it sounds as though he's had a few near misses. Thanks to your freakily well timed briefing, at least I knew what he was up to.'

'That's got to be fate. It wasn't even this month's issue. So, should I be taking him off my list?' Eloise's tone was mischievous.

'Hardly. I slipped off to bed while he was at the bar.'

'I love it. So saucy.'

'My bed. Alone.'

'Hang on. Rewind.'

'Look, he didn't even remem—'

'You didn't even say goodbye?'

'Not exactly. No.' Maggie frowned. 'But I didn't, it wasn't that sort of—'

'Next you'll be pretending you don't care if you never see him again.'

'Well, *never* seems a bit extreme.'

'But you haven't exactly given him the green light, sounds like more of a No Entry sign to me.'

'I'm quite proud I took myself to my room before I did something I'd now be regretting.'

'You don't know that's how you'd feel.'

'You didn't see my room! Seriously though, I'd be sitting by the phone just in case he felt like calling, wondering if he was ignoring me. I'm too old for that.'

Eloise interrupted, 'Now you'll never know. Not that it matters. I mean you're never having another serious relationship again, ever, remember?'

'Exactly.'

'Although I would just like to mention that U-turns are very fashionable this year, along with leg warmers.'

'I'm happy to live without both.'

'Has he changed much?'

'It's not like I knew him very well. But he was pretty good company.'

Eloise knew Maggie well enough to know less was more.

'Max bloody French. Blimey. What is that, thirteen years of foreplay?'

'Hardly, we weren't in touch for ten years.'

'Details, details.'

'Plus, foreplay suggests there's going to be a main event.'

'Exactly.'

'Speaking of which, guess who else was there at the wedding?'

Mood buoyant, Eloise barely paused. 'Adam?'

'That's not funny.'

'Sorry.' Eloise halted her giggle just in time. 'I didn't mean to be flippant, it's just that Jake and I watched a programme last night on the paranormal channel.'

'There's a whole paranormal channel?' Maggie wondered if spirits could channel their energies through it. 'What next, the "think I might have a bit of a cold" channel? The Aries channel, the Libra channel, the—'

'That's not a bad idea, you know. I met a chap who ran a couple of channels when I did that screenwriting course. I might give him a call and see what he thinks—if you don't mind of course.'

'Be my guest.' Maggie loved the fact that Eloise's innate optimism was apparently indefatigable and unlimited. They complemented each other perfectly.

'So.' Eloise remembered she'd interrupted herself. 'Who else was there?'

'Alexander the Not So Great.'

Eloise laughed. Adam's cousin had got his nickname when he'd failed to find Eloise attractive.

'And how was he?'

'Married.'

'I thought we decided he was gay.'

'He has a wife.'

'That means nothing. Although I guess I'd better tick him off my list if he's married.'

'He was on your list of boyfriends reunited?'

'You can't be too picky.'

'Clearly. Although I suppose I should take comfort in the fact you're not prepared to wreck marriages in pursuit of the one who got away, or the one you can't even remember properly.'

'Of course not. I hope to be a wife myself one day.'

'Ah, if only your careers teacher could hear you now.'

'There's nothing wrong with wanting to be happy.'

'Surely your total happiness is too much pressure to put on a mere male mortal? Especially a total stranger you picked up in the street.'

'You met Adam at a petrol station. And you lent him money.'

'True.' Maggie sighed fondly at the memory of the flustered walletless man in a pinstripe suit pacing the forecourt by his recently refuelled mini. 'Totally out of character. I should have known it was all going to end in tears.'

'Are you going to give Max a call this week?'

'Fortunately it's not a dilemma I have to debate. I don't have his number.'

'If you can find an eight-bedroom house for a Hollywood director in Notting Hill in a week I'm sure it's well within your capabilities to track him down.'

It had been a career coup. And a lucky one. Her phone hadn't stopped ringing ever since. 'Hey, I'm not the one determined to trawl through my past loves, almost loves, could-have-been loves, best-friends-of-loves.'

'Go on. Mock me now, but just wait until—'

Maggie heard a knock at her door and checked her watch.

'COME IN. El, I'm going to have to go. I have a meeting.'

'Hey, you called me.'

'For a quick chat.'

'I haven't finished yet.'

'We'll have to adjourn.'

'Call him.'

'I gave him my card.'

'A crucial part of the story you omitted mentioning.'

'It was just business.'

'Of course it was, and clearly none of my business.'

Maggie swivelled around in her chair to find this morning's main topic of conversation standing at the entrance to her office. Max had swapped the penguin suit for jeans and a pale pink shirt and the just-dressed simplicity of his outfit made him appear very handsome indeed. Sensing gossip, her team were milling around the office behind him, never keener to start a meeting in their lives. Lucan squeezed past Max and handed over her coffee.

'I have to go.'

'Call him.'

'We'll see what we can do. Thanks. I'll be in touch soon.'

Leaving Eloise puzzling over the business-like end to her call, Maggie whipped off her headset, ran her hand through her hair, pulled her chair up to her desk and, slipping her feet back into her shoes, sat up efficiently.

With a nod of his head, Lucan indicated Max. 'Max

French. He said he had an appointment, but I can't find it in the calendar.'

Maggie looked over to Max, who flashed her a conspiratorial smile.

'I told him he could pop by sometime. He's an old friend of mine who's thinking of moving.' That last little titbit was crucial to get the nineteen other employees off her back.

Maggie gave Lucan her best I-know-it's-not-your-job-but-please-please-could-you-ask-him-if-he'd-like-a-coffee and gestured for Max to come in.

Lucan cocked his head in Max's direction. 'Wanna drink? Water? Juice? Coffee?'

'An espresso would be great.'

'Sure.'

'Oh, and Lucan?'

He beamed at Maggie.

'Let the team know the meeting's on hold for now.'

'Will do.'

'Thank you.' Maggie ushered Lucan out and Max in, closing the door behind him. As the door clicked shut, she could sense the disappointment from the other side of the dividing wall. Now not only were they going to have to do some real work but they couldn't eavesdrop either.

Max fiddled with his car keys. He'd been going to give her a call sometime and then he'd found himself in Knightsbridge and there'd been a meter free.

Maggie tidied a pile of papers on her desk. 'We didn't make an appointment, did we?'

Max shook his head. 'I was just passing.'

'First thing on a Monday morning?'

'I'm always up early. Anyway I just wanted to check you were okay.'

'Since Saturday?'

'You disappeared.'

Maggie shrugged.

'I thought Blake might have abducted you.'

Maggie laughed. 'You could have just called.'

'I was thinking about what you said.'

Maggie hoped she could remember everything. The last half a bottle of wine was a bit of a blur.

'Maybe I do need to find something new.'

Something? Maggie was all ears.

'I've been in that house a while. And now I can afford to invest more, I don't want to miss my chance. Who knows what the future holds.'

Relieved to be able to focus on the thing she did best, Maggie offered Max an armchair before sitting down at her desk and finding a pad and pen. In some ways she was an old-fashioned girl.

'Any idea where you'd like me to start? Penthouse? House? Apartment? Maisonette? Old? New build? Conversion? Do you want a garden? Central London? Somewhere further out? What sort of size? So many Des Res, so little time.'

Max tried not to look overwhelmed. 'You're the expert.'

'Let's start with the basics. Area, price range.'

'Central, north-west, west or south-west London. Up to a million, one and a half at a stretch, but only if it's worth it.'

Maggie wrote multimillionaire down followed by a series of exclamation and question marks before covering her tracks with a marker pen and writing £1–1.5m. Surely he should have been in *Miss Magazine*'s top five, not languishing in the thirties. Maybe Eloise had got it wrong and that was his age.

'And whereabouts are you living now?'

'Notting Hill if you're being generous. More like Ladbroke Grove, Westbourne Park area.'

'Flat?'

'House. Three-bedroom. Four if you count the study/nursery/box room.'

Maggie was impressed. 'Interested in selling?'

Max shrugged. 'I'm probably being oversentimental, but it was my first place. I'd rather not. I've done a lot to it.'

'And is not selling going to have a knock-on effect on the capital you have for your next asset?'

Max shook his head. 'I should be okay. I mean obviously I'd have to let one of them.'

'Right.'

'I'm not sure what to do really. I would really value your opinion if you have time. Maybe you should come and see the house sometime.'

'Absolutely.'

Maggie couldn't deny she was curious.

The door handle creaked open as, scowling, Lucan appeared with a coffee. It was service without a smile as he handed Max the tiny cup and left.

Max took a sip and forced himself to swallow. It was the consistency of molasses.

Maggie watched him. 'No good?' She didn't want to be the one to tell Max that they only had instant coffee in the office since the deluxe coffee machine had broken. Lucan had clearly improvised.

Max tried to find his voice. 'Quite strong. I don't suppose you've got time to pop over this morning, have you? I've got a few hours free, a professional coffee maker in my kitchen and I have beans in my fridge all the way from Costa Rica.'

'Well, let me tell you, I have beans from Heinz.'

Max smiled. 'Honestly, these are fantastic.'

Maggie wondered if he was always this modest. 'I do have meetings.'

'Of course.'

'Lots of meetings.' Maggie looked at her almost empty diary on screen. Monday was usually her day in the office for catching up on all the details and all her paperwork. Then there was Red.

'Maybe some other time? Late this week could work for me.'

Then again what was the point of being in charge of her diary if she couldn't mould it to fit her life occasionally? And, she reminded herself, whatever she might have hoped or imagined, this was actually business. She stared at her computer.

'Actually I could move some things around so I don't have to be back until one.'

'Perfect.' Max got to his feet.

'Address?'

'Don't worry, I'll drive you.'

'You might be hijacking my morning, but you don't get to kidnap me too.'

'I'm an excellent driver.'

'You could be Michael Schumacher. Company rules, I drive myself and I'm happy to give you a lift. I've got a lovely little BMW. If you're good, I'll even put the roof down.'

'I've got a Porsche.'

Maggie groaned inwardly. Of course he had. Wealthy men just couldn't help themselves when it came to purchasing cars.

'And it's on a meter. Plus I don't like to leave her for too long. Do you think you can find your way to 122 Newton Avenue?'

Maggie nodded. 'I have an excellent co-pilot who gives clear and calm directions, never swears at me, never holds his breath in when I squeeze through a narrow gap, turns the radio down or changes the CD.'

Max smiled. 'Sounds like the perfect man.'

Maggie sighed wistfully. 'Bit of a chip on his processor but hey, you can't win them all.'

'Excellent. I'll see you there then in, say, half an hour or so?'

As Max started to leave, Maggie sat down at her keyboard, the image of efficiency. She looked up. 'See you then.'

Typing her team a brief email moving their meeting until the end of the day, she logged off, checked her make-up and headed out to the car park. One of the things she loved most about her job was nosing around other people's properties. And it was fair to say she'd been hoping Max would invite her back to his place for years. His digs had been the most Desirable Residence on campus.

Chapter Eight

'Hot milk?'

'Why not?' Maggie was welcoming any excuse to prolong her visit. Monday morning in Max French's kitchen beat Monday morning in Maggie Hunter's office, by a mile.

This was no quick caffeine fix. Max's coffee machine had more pressure gauges, valves and levers than she had seen since the physics laboratory at school. By the time the coffee reached her cup, it had really been squeezed through its paces.

The kitchen was filled with the scent of fresh coffee. Rather like toast, it was one of those things the anticipation of which was even more delicious than the final product. Although with a piece of shortbread in one hand and a very tasty mug of coffee in the other, Maggie knew she had made the right choice. Breakfast was a meal that was designed to be lingered over, not condensed into a handbag-sized bar for women to nibble on their power walk to the tube.

'I know it was bit cheeky to turn up this morning unannounced, but I literally was driving past.'

'On your way to Harrods to buy the newspaper?'

If she'd known he'd had a vintage Porsche she might have had to waive her not-letting-clients-drive policy. The only vintage car she'd ever owned was the Ford Escort she'd learned to drive in and that had been more clapped out than collectable.

'I was due to have a breakfast meeting at The Wolseley with a TV producer, but it was cancelled at the last minute.'

'Should I be expecting you to be beamed into my sitting room every week night?'

Max shook his head. 'Definitely not. She just wanted to talk about me being on a panel.'

'Celebrity Big Brother? Celebrity Love Island?'

'Over my dead body. Anyway, I'm hardly a celebrity.'

'Exactly, you'd be perfect.'

Maggie wondered if she'd overstepped the mark.

Max didn't seem phased. 'I'm delighted to report I'm being courted for something more serious. Apparently I'm a media-friendly player in the business world. Only clearly not that friendly as I ended up having breakfast on my own. So thank you for restoring some purpose to this morning. I hate wasting my time.'

She watched as he prepared everything meticulously, cleaning up as he went along, loving the fact that when men did anything creative in the kitchen they reverted to their Blue Peter training and got all the ingredients ready first, in case they forgot anything, whereas women tended to make it up as they went along. A bit like life really.

Maggie sat at the breakfast bar, which was basically an extension of the dark grey granite work surface. The double doors leading on to the small garden had been flung open, allowing the few rays of May sun in to join them. Spring seemed to be getting later every year.

Maggie was experiencing a serious case of fridge envy despite the fact that it was almost the same square footage as her kitchen. American in stature and attitude, it was wider than most people's front doors.

She watched Max reach into a cupboard and select a Superman mug for himself.

He caught her staring and smiled apologetically. 'It was a present.'

Damn. Maggie thought she'd kept her expression neutral. 'I was hoping you hadn't bought it for yourself.'

'Along with my "I ♥ me" tea towel?'

'Exactly.' She grinned.

'Actually Polly gave it to me years ago. With the benefit of hindsight, I think now she'd be more likely to have chosen a Darth Vader one.'

'Nasty break-up?'

'Tricky. Apparently she'd already told her family that we were engaged.'

'Subtle.'

'I'm surprised the mug has lasted this long. Quite a few other things from her seemed to have vanished. I think Kat systematically destroyed the lot—always an accident, of course.'

'It's clearly a SuperMug.' Definitely her worst joke ever. Maggie willed herself to treat Max like any other client. She looked around as professionally as she could. 'Fabulous kitchen. Do you know who designed it?'

Max shrugged. 'I'm afraid I just paid the bill. Polly would know. Best bit about it as far as I'm concerned is the fridge.'

Maggie was losing track. She'd spotted a collage of photos in the downstairs loo featuring a number of blonde women in exotic locations and Max in various states of undress and muscle tone, but none of them had been labelled.

'She will have made someone an excellent wife by now.'

'Hopefully the guy in question will have asked her first.' Maggie noticed the flourishing herb garden on the window-sill behind the sink. A straight man who remembered to water plants was a rare commodity. Some might say caring. Others would say they were just herbs. Or that he had a cleaning lady.

Max smiled, gentlemanly refusing to be goaded into a bitching session. 'To be honest I don't think I've used the Aga since we split up. It's a bit *Country Life* for me. I prefer having a thermostat and a glass door. Hence we got both.'

'Coward.' Maggie's tone was challenging.

'I prefer scientist.'

'So what went wrong?'

'I just always forgot there was anything cooking until you could smell burning, by which time it was all over.'

Bemused, Maggie smiled. 'I meant, with the girl?'

'Polly or Kat?'

'I'm afraid I'm getting confused now.'

Max smiled. 'Hardly surprising. There have been a few.'

'In residence?'

'Fewer. And Pol was a while back now. In fact she and I split up the weekend after Adam's funeral. We were in Rome.'

'Long way to go to say goodbye.'

'It wasn't the plan. I'd just booked us a trip because I deserved a break and I'd read about a new boutique hotel. Of course she decided it was a moment.'

Maggie shook her head and smiled. 'Thanks for reminding me how much easier my life is now. No hidden agendas, just my own.'

'Polly was a walking hidden agenda.'

'How long were you together?'

'Three years, maybe four?'

'Well, there you go.'

'There I go, where?' Max must have missed a sentence.

'Four years hard labour, she was well within her rights to get excited. Especially if you whisked her away to Rome as a surprise. Poor love.'

'I just wanted us to have some quality time together, a bit of fun and the sort of sex you don't have on a Saturday night when you're sharing a takeaway and watching *Parkinson*….'

Maggie wondered if he'd forgotten he was talking to a woman and whether or not she should take that as a compliment.

'But from the minute I opened my eyes, rolled over and pulled her in for a hug that Sunday morning I could tell there was going to be a problem. And a talk. The sort of conversation that reduces me to monosyllables just at the point I should be at my most articulate. All I'd wanted was a lazy day, one of those really thin pizzas and a glass of red wine, maybe some buffalo mozzarella, a stroll through the Piazza Navona with an enormous ice cream…just some fun after the funeral.'

'Clearly not what she wanted.'

He stirred his coffee and shook his head. 'I was only thinking about me. The funeral really threw me.'

'Believe me, I can relate to that.'

Max winced.

'Seriously, I'm fine now, but there's nothing like a bit of death to make you reassess your life.'

'Poor Pol. She'd geared herself up for a totally different weekend. I probably should have seen the signs. She'd packed saucy underwear, she'd even had a Brazilian. It had been a perfect Saturday. Sadly Sunday didn't go the same way. We'd split up by eleven, leaving us eight more hours of minibreak to endure.'

'What did you do?'

'Pol spent a fortune at the spa. Then for some reason I apologised—I think mainly to make the flight home easier, and to stop her purchasing any more Dead Sea Mud treatments.'

'You live and you learn.'

'You'd have thought so, but it was almost exactly the same with Louisa. A great first year and then she spoilt it all by wanting to get married and have children. Surely all those magazines she insisted on reading must have advised against issuing an ultimatum to your cohabiting partner. Plus I don't think you can depend on someone else to make your day every day.'

Although she agreed with him, Maggie wondered whether she should have been taking the side of his ex-girl-friends; for the sisterhood, and for the sake of balance.

'Kat, on the other hand, wanted to chop my balls off even though she knew she'd be far better off finding someone who wanted what she did.'

'Let me guess. Marriage and children?'

'Plus someone to talk dirty.' Max almost blushed. 'I have no idea why I am telling you this.'

'You can't stop now.'

'To be fair though, Kat had every reason to hate me. In fact when we split up, I didn't have to move my lips or a muscle in the process.'

'How come?'

'I had made her position untenable.'

Maggie caught his eye out of the corner of her own. 'By seeing someone else?'

'No.'

'Good.'

Max paused. 'Does thinking about seeing someone else count?'

'You confessed?'

'I may have been spotted sipping a few cocktails with the lady in question a couple of times.'

Maggie shook her head. 'That's prize bastard behaviour.'

'Nothing happened.'

'Don't you see? It already had. So it's true, the era of nice guys is over.'

'No.' Max was indignant. 'And who really splits up with their other halves properly these days. They either start seeing someone else or let them drift. And it's not always the men. At least I was honest with her.'

Maggie was silent.

Max sensed this might be the perfect time to return to business. 'So, what's your verdict?'

'I would have expected more from you.'

Max looked around him. 'On this place?'

'Of course. Yup. Right.'

'Your professional opinion, if possible…'

Maggie was relieved to be back on familiar territory. 'Good-sized rooms, great bathrooms, sympathetic use of original features plus a few complementary new ones. All in all it's very marketable, a few idiosyncrasies of decor but nothing that can't be easily changed.'

The limited edition modern floral watercolours were definitely nothing to do with Max, nor, she suspected, was the choice of hot-pink bed linen in the spare bedroom. The Bose stereo and obscenely large flat-screen television in the den on the other hand were one hundred percent man. As was the table football in what had probably been intended to be a dining room. And he had been quick to mention that the framed signed photo of The Chelsea Squad was Chris's and only holidaying in the sitting room, safe from sabotage, until his divorce came through.

She looked around the kitchen again. 'How long have you lived here now?'

It was an innocent enough question, indeed necessary in her profession, and yet today it sounded as much of a pickup line as if she'd said *So, do you come here often?*

'Six years.'

'Well, I can guarantee you'll be delighted with the increase in value and the Aga will be a definite asset if you do sell. And, just so you know, the average Briton moves every seven years, so it's no wonder you're getting restless.'

'I didn't realise the seven-year itch applied to property, too?'

Maggie smiled. She'd never thought about it like that before.

'If there isn't a "one" when it comes to jobs or partners, then why should there be "one" when it comes to houses?'

Max sat back in his chair. 'My problem is, I moved three times a year when I was at boarding school. I've done enough packing and unpacking to last me a lifetime.'

'You're preaching to the converted. I am determined to grow old on my sofa exactly where it is now.'

'And I know this place seems big for one.'

'Don't forget about your lodger.'

'He'll be off again soon. And I like having this much space. I just need to buy a few more pictures and books. Jo took a few with her when she left….'

Jo. Once Polly had sorted the kitchen, Max had apparently gone through at least one woman a year. But Maggie had noticed the shelf of cookery books on the dresser was depleted. Jamie Oliver was propping up Nigel Slater who was supporting a very old Robert Carrier. Maggie had been given the very same edition by her mother when she'd gone to university. Mr Carrier had apparently been the Jamie Oliver of his day.

Mug in hand, Maggie meandered over and helped herself to the most dog-eared volume before holding it upside down to see where it opened. 'So, is fish pie your *pièce de résistance,* you-see-I-can-really-cook-if-I-try dish?'

Max laughed. 'Maybe.'

Maggie shook her head.

'Hey, at least I cook. Some men just order food in.'

'Not in the early days. No one's ever tried to seduce me over a deep-pan pizza.'

'Then you haven't lived.' Max grinned.

From her new location, Maggie was in full view of the kitchen clock and, to her alarm, the morning was nearly over. She took her mug to the sink. 'I've got to get back to the office.'

'Thanks for coming.'

'It's a lovely property.'

'It's my lovely home.'

There they were, two detached and desirable properties in what some would describe as a crowded marketplace.

'You'd have absolutely no trouble selling…'

Max proudly ran his hand along the surface of the kitchen table as if he'd planed it himself rather than bought it at auction at Lots Road.

'And if you do decide you want to buy somewhere a bit more man about town, our rental department could look after this place for you. Alternatively, you could just make the finishing touches here your own and buy somewhere else to let.'

'I'm not sure home improvements are my thing. I find it hard enough to pick out a tie let alone a colour scheme or a style.'

'You'd be surprised.'

Max didn't look convinced. 'I could get a cute interior designer.'

'Total waste of money you could spend on the actual contents.'

'But at least everything would go together. I don't suppose you'd want to give me a hand? Just until I get into the swing of things. I'd pay you for your time.'

Maggie shook her head. 'Just because I look at a lot of properties doesn't make me an expert. And there aren't enough hours in the week as it is.'

Piles of as-yet-unread Sunday supplements towered at one end of Max's antique pine kitchen table. This was the sort of kitchen that made you want to settle in for a few hours, your hand curled round a mug, setting the world to rights.

'And thanks for delicious coffee.'

'That tall guy from your office has a lot to learn.'

'And not just about espresso. Anyway, if I can help with anything—wallpaper aside—give me a call.'

Max nodded. 'I think I should probably buy an investment property while I can.'

Maggie could smell the commission and it was still Monday morning. 'You'll be amazed at what's out there. London really has it all.'

'Who knows what the future holds.'

'Who really wants to?'

'Do you mind if I ask you a personal question?'

Maggie hesitated. That would teach her to fling her personal views around. 'Fire away.'

'Where do you live?'

And now not quite the question she'd been hoping for. 'Little Venice. Two bedroom flat and if you think your garden is small, you should meet my balcony.'

Max found himself hoping that one day he would.

'The place was falling apart when I bought it, but I did it up room by room. Post–Adam I was determined to have everything my way.' Maggie had been living together with her flat for nearly three blissful years. 'Look, can I tell you something…' She knew that trying to force a bond with Max was childish, but then so was pretending she didn't want to be invited back to this kitchen again.

'Of course.'

'In confidence.'

Max rubbed his palms together. 'Better still.'

'Seriously, this mustn't get back to Jamie. Or to Jeremy for that matter.' She wondered if this was wise.

Max sensed he was on the verge of some excellent gossip. Whoever said men weren't interested in that sort of thing was lying.

'Message received. Zero distortion.'

Getting up, he walked over to where she was and rested his bottom on the work surface.

Maggie took a breath. 'Adam was having an affair…'

Max's expression remained the same.

She increased the flow of information '…for almost half the time we were together.'

His eyes widened with apparent disbelief. 'Seriously?'

'Oh yes.'

'Who was she?'

Maggie paused. So much for "poor you." Instead "was she hot?" Testosterone was a fascinating thing. 'Someone in the New York office.'

'A big cheese from the Big Apple?' Max noticed Maggie wasn't smiling. 'How did you find out?'

'The first time was just a hunch, about a year after we moved in together, then…'

'Hang on, the first time? Same woman?'

Maggie nodded. 'He promised me it was a one-off.'

'And you believed him?'

'I really wanted to and I only discovered they'd actually become an item the afternoon he died. We had an argument

and he stormed out. That was the last time I saw him alive.'
Maggie could feel tears in her eyes. She could hear the door
slam, smell his aftershave and then silence, until the phone
rang. And yet it seemed dulled. As if it was a scene from a
movie she was recalling.

Max put his arm around her and rubbed her shoulder. It was
less of a hug and more of a massage. But his proximity was definitely having a positive effect on her pulse rate. 'How awful.'

As Maggie smiled through her watery eyes, everything in
the room moved into the sort of pattern you see through a
kaleidoscope. The strong coffee wasn't helping. 'Apparently
Eve was married. Adam told me that as if it was going to
make me feel better.'

'Who knows?'

'It didn't help at all.'

'I meant who knows about his affair?'

'My mother, probably my father, although he's never said
a word, Eloise and now you. And Eve, of course.'

Max was speechless.

'The funny thing is I only really discovered who I was
when he left me. It's taken some time, but I've honestly never
been happier. Anyway, my point is…'

Max was enchanted by her determination to stand alone.

'…my advice is don't compromise. Although I guess you
didn't get to where you are today by playing it safe.'

He smiled. 'My instinct hasn't let me down yet.'

'Well.' Maggie picked up her bag. 'Good to see you again.'

'And you.' Max turned to face her. 'Would you consider
having dinner with me?'

Maggie glanced at the diet bookshelf. 'Fish pie?'

'Hey, it usually turns out okay. Or we could eat out.'

'Let's do that.'

'How about Thursday evening?'

Maggie admired his skills. A date night without the pressure of a Friday. 'I'll have to check my diaries.'

'You do that. And in the meantime—' Max looked around the room '—I've always fancied something with a river view.'

'Interestingly enough, I think Jack Carlisle is thinking of selling his penthouse in Battersea.'

'The actor?'

'There was a feature in one of the papers last week. Kids on the way, they need something bigger.'

'Can you get me an appointment?'

'Of course.'

'Fantastic.'

Just business. So now she had to find Max the perfect place and herself the perfect outfit before Thursday, just in case.

Chapter Nine

December 23, seven and a bit months later
The morning after the night before

Maggie stood in the queue at TLC and wondered how Eloise could possibly be late when she only lived a two-minute walk away. A Rat Pack version of 'God Rest Ye Merry, Gentlemen' was filtering through the tinsel-festooned speaker; the girl at the till was wearing a Santa hat and gingerbread latte was the coffee of the day. In normal circumstances, Maggie would have been revving up for a rant, but either she was a woman who had recently won a man over or they'd laced their air conditioning with good cheer. She was starting to learn that the only way to handle the festive season was indeed to be jolly, to emigrate or to hibernate. And she'd left it too late for the last two.

'A skinny—not at all festive—large cappuccino and…'

Maggie scanned the cake display area. 'Ooh…' She succumbed to her surroundings. 'I suppose I'd better have a Christmas muffin.'

Said item looked suspiciously like a regular raisin muffin with a bit of white icing and candied peel that she'd probably pick off the top, but unlike most people she knew, she loved Christmas cake, and wedding cake for that matter which, going on recent numbers of weddings at which she had been present, was fortunate. She'd always thought that if you substituted the bride and groom atop a wedding tier for a snowman, sleigh or sprig of holly you'd get a Christmas cake, cunningly guaranteeing year-round employment for fruitcake bakers.

Eloise cruised to the front of the queue just as Maggie was paying. Her hair was an interesting style. Somewhere between just washed, iced, and frizzing rapidly. She must have been freezing. Literally.

'The usual please, Jenny, and I don't suppose you could be a sweetie and bring them over?'

Eloise squeezed Maggie's non-plate-holding arm and pecked her on the cheek. 'Morning. Don't say a word.'

'It's not that ba—'

'It's a fucking disaster. I left my hairdryer at Jake's last week.'

'He doesn't have a hairdryer?'

Eloise shook her head. 'Three boys. Two almost bald. Jake can towel dry his in thirty seconds.'

'And you don't own more than one?'

'Rest assured I'm about to buy a lifetime's supply. So, what's brought you this far south on the last shopping Saturday before Christmas?'

'I just thought it'd be nice to catch up face to face before we descend into Christmas proper and you disappear into a mass of family for weeks on end.'

The Forrest family Christmas was always wall-to-wall relatives, endless lunches for twenty and more quality time together than most people managed in a lifetime, whereas Maggie's was achingly sedate: two parents, one daughter, a selection of good books, a CD of carols and the inevitable board game.

Eloise observed her best friend as she settled into an armchair, trying to ascertain what was different. 'Are you sure there isn't raw egg in the topping on that muffin?'

'Pardon?'

'You're pregnant, aren't you?'

'Have you lost your mind?'

Maggie didn't understand why everyone assumed that when you were dating someone in your thirties, you were secretly hoping for children, when most of the time she was half hoping for difficulty in conceiving. She was planning to be a fantastic Godmother to Eloise's inevitable brood, responsible for their first alcoholic drink, first 18-rated movie (at around 14), first totally impractical pair of shoes (girls), first pair of Calvin Klein boxer shorts (boys) and first trip to see *Avenue Q*. When it came to the idea of changing nappies, the thought of breastfeeding or indeed growing a child in an area she had finally got flattish, she couldn't get at all excited. She was clearly missing a hormone.

Determined there was a reason for Maggie's presence, Eloise squinted at her. 'Getting married?'

'Yuh, because, I mean I wouldn't phone you or anything.'

Maggie shook her head but the edge of a smile escaped, mainly out of relief that while he'd popped a question he hadn't popped *that* question.

'You're grinning.'

'Am not.'

'Are too.'

'So, it's Christmas time and I'm in a good mood.' Maggie was relieved that after her stormy night her overriding emotional state this morning was one of excitement with a few scattered concerns and a prevailing wind of change. Plus she had an idea.

'Exactly. Something is wrong with this picture. The question remains, what?' Eloise rubbed her chin thoughtfully.

Maggie paused. She didn't want to ram it down Miss Dying To Settle Down's throat, but she knew that withholding relationship information would

a) be impossible to achieve for more than a maximum of forty-eight hours going on their current call frequency

b) carry the death penalty in the State of Eloise Forrest.

'Unless of course in the process of dating Mr French you have become Captain Christmas.'

'Hey, I may be having more regular sex these days, but I'm still me.'

'Regular as opposed to irregular?' Eloise's expression was mischievous.

'Regular as opposed to never.'

Eloise sighed. 'I just hoped that Max might be corrupting you. Not sexually, just emotionally and seasonally.'

'Whose side are you on?'

'Mine. Always.'

Maggie grinned. 'Good. He's just a man. He'll screw up eventually.'

'I'd say Max is as good as it gets. I'd marry him tomorrow.'

'You would?' Maggie raised her eyebrows. Then again Eloise would probably marry anything that could say 'I do' these days.

'Well, if I was you, I mean.'

'He's not perfect.'

'And you are?'

'Well...' Between her and her, she thought she came pretty close.

'I dare you to make an unofficial tick list...I'm telling you, he's premier league.'

Maggie paused for a moment to collect her thoughts from far and wide. 'Um, kind?'

'Check.' Eloise drew a tick in the air with a flourish.

'Funny.'

'Check.'

'Successful.'

Faced with a win-win situation, Maggie was starting to enjoy the game.

'Aesthetically pleasing.'

'Check—for you. Although he is pretty stylish for a man in the business world—'

Maggie interrupted. 'Apart from that beige duffel coat he loves wearing at weekends.'

'I think it's cute actually.'

'Only because you don't have to be seen out with it. I don't recall Paddington Bear being emulated on any catwalks, ever.'

Eloise ignored her. 'Plus he's going places, owns his own property.'

'Properties.' Maggie smiled.

Eloise sighed. 'Jake doesn't even own a car.'

'You don't need a car in London.'

'Stop trying to make me feel better.'

Maggie buttoned her lip.

'And in all seriousness, Max is committed to you, and it's not like he hasn't had long-term relationships in the past…'

'Too many of those if anything.' Maggie had already forgotten her recent self-imposed vow of silence. No wonder she couldn't stick to a diet for longer than a series of *Big Brother*. Make that an episode.

Eloise clapped her hands. 'Now jealousy is a great sign.'

'I don't care about his past relationships.'

'Of course not.' Eloise winked at her.

'I just don't like the feeling that I am one in a continuous succession of girlfriends.'

'He makes you feel like that?'

Maggie shook her head. 'Much worse. It's all my own work. I just wish he'd spent a little more time in his own company instead of always having a live-in companion. It might make me feel a little more special. I mean I like to think I'm one in a million, several million even.'

'You know you are, he knows you are. Isn't that enough? Couldn't you just try and look on the bright side for, like, ten maybe fifteen minutes.'

'Hey, this is me in a good mood. And I know I'm a lucky girl.' Maggie brightened, encouraged by Eloise's enthusiasm and suddenly shy as she remembered what she was doing there in the first place. 'Actually, as it happens, I do have some news.' Maggie carried straight on, not wanting to give Eloise time to react. 'Last night Mr Perfect asked me to move in with him.'

Propelling herself with her feet, Eloise gave Maggie a rugby tackle of a hug almost knocking over Jenny, who'd just arrived with the coffees. 'I knew it. It would have been my next guess.'

Maggie hugged her best friend.

Eloise pulled away first. 'No champagne here, but we could crack open a Snapple if you like, or a smoothie?' Eloise was overcome with a hybrid of opposing emotions. 'Awesome news. Now that's a Christmas present.'

Maggie decided not to mention sailing.

'It won't be long until you're in the same boat.' Maggie hated herself for the platitude, but she knew it was what Eloise wanted to hear.

Eloise nodded bravely. 'Can you believe that this time last year we were still both single.'

'I had a great Christmas.'

'We were shamefully hungover on Christmas Eve and on Christmas morning.'

'Totally your fault for buying me a cocktail shaker and a box full of ingredients and then letting me open my present on the twenty-third.'

'Trying to work our way from A to Z was your mistake.'

'We only made it as far as Harvey Wallbangers.'

'I thought we made it to Martinis?'

'I only made it to Ibuprofen.' Maggie smirked as she recalled her mother's disapproval when she'd turned up for lunch in sunglasses.

'So what I can get you to celebrate. Bit of cake?'

'I'm all muffined up, thanks.'

'Another coffee? Or shall we decamp to a wine bar?'

'At eleven a.m.?' Maggie ran her finger round the rim of her mug.

Eloise waved at the counter. 'Hey Jen, how about a shot of caramel syrup in a latte for my cohabiting best friend.'

She hadn't even said "skinny."

'Do you know how many calories are in one of those things?'

'It's a treat.'

'It's a calorific time bomb.'

'Treats by definition have to involve guilt.'

'I'm going to be sharing a bathroom.'

'You're going to be sharing everything.' Eloise waggled her eyebrows in a suggestive fashion.

Maggie's stomach twisted involuntarily. She ignored its protest. It was all going to be fine. Better than fine. No panic required.

'You've always dreamed of steps up to your front door. Now you can pretend you're Carrie Bradshaw, only you've got the whole house.' Eloise sounded genuinely thrilled.

'It is exciting.' Maggie's eyes were bright. 'Even though you know I'm not great with change.'

Eloise had always believed what goes around comes around. She was due a jackpot any time soon. 'Did he get down on one knee?'

'Shut up. Just because you're the only person I know who doesn't forward through "Hopelessly Devoted toowowowo Yooo"—' Maggie aped Olivia Newton John '—when watching *Grease*.'

'It's touching.'

'It's boring. Anyway, he did put his door key in a ring box which, once my pulse had returned to safe levels, I have to say was a nice touch.'

Maggie watched Eloise convulse with excitement and wondered if there was something wrong with her. Then again Eloise had been planning her wedding since her eighth birthday and Maggie still couldn't visualise hers.

'That is so adorable and only one step away…'

'Don't say it.' Maggie wasn't ready to hear the rest.

Eloise was miles, and years away. 'Imagine if you'd known at university that in twelve years' time you'd be moving in with Max French.'

'I'd have panicked. Twelve years was a lifetime away. I'd probably have thought that we'd all have pet robots and cars that hovered just above the road by now.'

'Instead everything's just the same.'

'Except for tiny phones that work everywhere, that take photos and that you can listen to the radio on, oh and my waist measurement.'

'You know what I mean. We're still agonising over boys. And now you might even be getting married.'

Maggie froze. She was still coming to terms with proposal number one. 'I'm warning you. One step at a time.'

'Oh come on, we all thought we'd be sorted by the time we were thirty.'

'Since when does moving in with a man equate to being sorted?'

'When he's rich, successful and owns a whole house in west London it does.'

Maggie glared at Eloise, who shrugged. 'Sorry, my mistake, I forgot about your inner Germaine Greer.'

'Obviously I'm delighted he asked me, but I can't help thinking, what's the big rush? I'm happy as I am now.'

'Maggie Hunter…' Eloise's eyes narrowed as she concentrated on reading between the lines. 'You did say yes…?'

'I…if we're being one hundred percent pedantic…'

Eloise flung her head back in her armchair dramatically.

'I didn't say no, but I may just have passed out before…'

'Maggie.' Eloise's voice was uncharacteristically shrill.

'It all came as a bit of a shock. I was expecting a swish dinner, not a door key.'

'I think *surprise* would be a better choice of word.'

'Anyway, this morning I do have a spring in my step. And you've really helped so, thank you. I know you think I'm nutty about this kind of stuff.'

'Think? It's oh so easy to play the independent woman card from within a relationship, but it doesn't wash. Honestly Mags. Look around you.'

Maggie paused as she surveyed the motley crew of fellow caffeine addicts. Most were there alone.

'Enjoy this moment. There'll be plenty of time for you to be bitter in your forties and fifties when you're not having any sex.'

Maggie nodded sagely. 'I am happy. But I'm just a bit nervous. I mean I'm hardly the cake-baking type, am I?'

'Shut up. You make homes for a living.'

'I *find* homes for a living.'

'You even plumbed in your washing machine for goodness' sake.'

'That's hardly difficult.'

Eloise raised an eyebrow. 'You're talking to the woman who paid someone to come and change her kitchen light bulbs. Make sure you say yes properly. And nicely.'

'I'm sure Max will have assumed it is all systems go. He isn't used to people saying no—well, not women at least.'

Eloise let her head slip into her hands.

'Don't worry. You have my word. I'll cook him a steak or something. Exfoliate and wear sexy underwear for a week or two…'

Eloise nodded approvingly. 'Good. Sometimes I don't understand what you are so afraid of.'

Maggie shrugged. 'Just the usual, that in a matter of months I'll have to pick myself up and start all over again.'

'This one's been a long time coming. You picked him out years ago.'

'Along with the rest of my fantasy league—Harrison Ford, Richard Gere and Brad Pitt. Do I have any of their numbers in my mobile phone? Plus we really hardly know each other.'

'The older I get, the more I think you recognise someone who's right for you in an instant, rather like you recognise your suitcase on a luggage carousel amongst so many similar items.'

'Let's just see how it goes. It's relatively early days and it's not that serious.'

'Oh yes it is. I l-o-v-e it.'

'I really was very happy on my own.'

'It's not an either/or thing.'

'But a part of me feels, well, like it's limiting. You know one door shuts, but which new one is really opening?'

'His front door! And no one wants to grow old without someone to play Scrabble with, to scratch the bit of your back you can't reach, to help you down steep stairs and, of course, to show you a very good time between now and infirmity.'

'From here to infirmity. Jeez. I can hardly wait. And why can't you and I look after each other in our twilight years?'

To Eloise's relief, Maggie winked.

'Thanks to all the preservatives we ate as children, odds are we'll be ancient together.' Eloise paused. 'It's amazing though. It's all karma.'

Eloise had lost Maggie at preservatives. 'What is?'

'Well, if Adam hadn't died, then Anna might not have deteriorated so fast, Jeremy may not have met Ivy at a coffee morning and you wouldn't have remet Max at their wedding. Also if Adam hadn't been shagging around, you might never have moved on quite so well.'

'Beautifully put, if I may say so.'

'Plus, as soon as you decided you were taking yourself off the market for good, you were as good as married. Men can just sense indifference.'

'Now you're making me nervous again. Maybe I don't want to know exactly what the future looks like. I want to choose what I do. Me, me, me. Not we, we, we.'

'You can always be single inside.'

'I really had got to a point where I felt I was better on my own.'

'And yet you always cry in films like *When Harry Met Sally* and *Sleepless in Seattle*. You're an oxymoron.'

'Hey, watch who you're calling a moron. Just because I have baggage and Max doesn't seem to have any.'

'Just put yours in storage and for God's sake put him out of his misery.'

'Okay.' Maggie paused.

Eloise's eyes twinkled with mischief. 'Say it.'

Maggie addressed her mug. 'I guess I sort of do love him.'

'That didn't hurt, did it?'

'No.' To her surprise it didn't. Next time she'd look up. Maggie straightened. 'Hey, that reminds me, I don't suppose you could do me a small favour.'

'Always.'

'I had an idea at about three o'clock this morning.'

Eloise sat back in her armchair. 'Absolutely not.'

'Wait. I haven't told you what it is yet.'

'You dreamt it up in the middle of the night, that's all I need to know.'

'It's when some of the best eureka moments happen.'

'I thought that was in the bath.'

'Look, you know I've got loads of stuff....'

Eloise could almost feel her knees twinge as she remembered helping Maggie move in to her top-floor flat. She'd had backache for over a week. Who on earth kept every back issue of *The Week* anyway? She bet Maggie had never reread an article in her life.

'I'm really sorry, but I think I'm getting too old to spend an entire weekend carrying boxes up and down stairs.'

'Don't be silly, I'm not asking you to help. Well, not with fetching and carrying. Not this time. We'll get a removal company.'

Eloise didn't want to pull Maggie up on her easy use of

'we' in reference to her and Max, but to the not-so-casual observer, it was most promising.

'So what's this idea?'

'I just wondered, whether, maybe, I could keep a few things at your place.'

Eloise simply looked at her. 'Max has got a four-bedroom house.'

'And you've got a three-bedroom flat.'

'But as we're not sleeping together and you're not paying my mortgage, I don't have to put up with your clutter.'

'It'd just be a few clothes, maybe a handful of DVDs, a box of trashy novels, my foot spa, a few toiletries.'

'Toiletries?'

'Max is so anal about his bathroom. It's all sandstone and mirrors. There's only one slim cabinet. I just don't want to overwhelm him.'

'He's spent enough time at yours to know you come with products.'

'I'm just asking you to lend me a couple of drawers and then when I fancy getting away from it all, or need a girlie night, I could come round.'

'Slob out, watch embarrassing movies in your baggy university tracksuit bottoms whilst giving yourself a facial and a pedicure?' Eloise's voice was rising in disbelief. A tone change which Maggie mistook as excitement.

'Genius, eh?'

Eloise folded her arms across her chest. 'Absolutely no way.'

'Why not?'

'Because it's daft. You know you can come round any time you need to escape.'

'I think it's quite a modern approach actually.'

'Are you planning on telling him?'

'Of course not.'

'Then I'd say it's quite a dishonest approach.'

'Just look at it as a safety valve, an escape hatch if you like.'

'You're not going to prison. You shouldn't need parole.'

'Just for a few months until I'm settled. I promise I'll move it all in eventually.'

Eloise was silent. Disapproving but silent. A combination Maggie could cope with.

She frowned. 'I suppose I could give you a couple of months of transition, but then I'm taking it all to the charity shop.'

Maggie put her hand on Eloise's. 'Thank you.'

'But—' Eloise interrupted herself. 'If you're this nervous about it all going tits up, maybe you're right. Maybe you shouldn't move in now.'

Maggie was all ears if, strangely, a little disappointed. She'd never had a garden before.

'What if you were to hold out until he asks you to marry him? That way he doesn't get exactly what he wants without having to give you more commitment. Then maybe you'll feel he's taking it seriously enough to show him your depilation products and childhood teddy bear.'

'Surely it's better to have a trial run without committing to a life sentence?' Maggie wondered whether it was physiologically possible to actually feel her blood pressure rise. 'Anyway, way too much about me, how are things with Jake?'

'Not bad. Quite good sometimes.' Eloise fiddled with the handle of her mug. 'I just don't feel like we're really going anywhere. When we're together and it's good I wonder why I doubt him, but then we have a few days apart and I start to wonder whether this can be it.'

'Hey, it's early days.'

'It's seven whole months. I mean look at you and Max.'

'We had a history. Plus he's that sort of man.'

'Romantic, impetuous, decisive.'

Maggie had to hand it to Eloise. She was a professional stirrer.

'A serial monogamist who doesn't like to live alone.'

Eloise shrugged. 'I don't think Jake has had a serious relationship since the Dark Ages.'

'So give him time to reach his Enlightenment. He's probably still getting his head round having a proper girlfriend. Where is he for Christmas?'

'With his sister, which is probably just as well seeing as he thinks Christmas is a waste of time, that it's materialism gone mad. Suffice to say I'm not holding out for a huge present.'

Maggie was a mere yuletide amateur in Eloise's presence. 'I'm sorry.'

'It's undoubtedly for the best. I'm not sure he's ready to meet the brothers.'

'More like you're not ready. I can't believe you've managed to avoid it so far.'

'It's not hard when we only usually see each other a couple of nights a week. It's a bit like dating was in your teens.'

'Snogging to twelve-inch singles, sitting by the phone wondering if he's dumped you and you're the last to know…ah, those weren't the days.'

Eloise smiled wearily. 'We are going out to celebrate New Year's Eve together.'

'Definitely a positive sign.'

'Even if we're together but not?'

'I don't understand.'

Eloise sighed. 'New Year's Eve was traditionally one of his non-negotiable nights out with the boys. Although this year girls are allowed. Yippee-yi-yay.'

'Bound to be much more fun than an overpriced meal for two with a couple of glasses of wine in a fashionable restaurant as you reflect on what you haven't quite achieved in the preceding year before trying not to doze off on the sofa before Big Ben strikes twelve.'

Eloise smiled ruefully. 'I suppose, except we either need to move forward or call it a day.'

'Mmm.' Maggie knew better than to commit one way or the other. Whatever Eloise decided, Maggie would be ready to pat her on the back or pick her up off the floor.

'So…' Eloise hugged herself. 'Are you going to rent out your place?'

'When I find the right person maybe…'

'A single, obsessive-compulsive female with a dust allergy?'

'That's not fair.'

'Really?' Eloise paused. Then smiled. She suddenly had a plan. 'How about a single male website—'

'No…no way.'

'He's potentially very house-proud and I think if he lived on his own rather with two other man-boys we might stand more of a chance….'

'That's emotional blackmail.' Maggie shook her head slowly. 'I don't think he's the right guy for my flat. Hello? He peed in your underwear drawer. Remember, you've told me everything.'

'He was very drunk at the time.'

'I think he's lucky to be alive.'

'I remember someone vomiting in a wicker waste-paper basket in a country house hotel a few years ago.'

Maggie blushed as she recalled the indignity of it all. 'That was food poisoning.'

'The Hunter-gatherer selective recall strikes again.'

'Irregular urinary habits aside, I don't get the impression from you that he's particularly domesticated.'

'That's because he doesn't own his place.'

'And because he's male. And then there's the dog.'

'It's his sister's.'

'No pets at my place. Not even for the afternoon. Not on that carpet.'

'Not a problem.'

'Why don't you just ask him to move in with you?'

'It's too soon. It's too big a deal. Plus he's never lived on his own. I think he should try it.'

Maggie sat back. 'Finally. My points exactly.'

'For us, not for you two. I'd just like Jake's life to have a little less built-in entertainment if that makes sense. Plus, my flat will be full of your stuff.' Eloise knew she'd just scored a valuable point.

Maggie paused.

'And with a bit of luck I'll be there to keep an eye on things. Don't forget I still have a spare key.'

'I'll think about it.'

'Fantastic.'

'Hang on, I didn't say—'

'And I'm just thinking about whether you can leave any belongings at mine.' Sensing victory, Eloise beamed at her best friend.

'Hey, that's not fair.'

'All's fair in love and cohabitation.'

'That's what I'm afraid of.'

Maggie dialled Max's mobile as she walked to the bus stop. He answered almost immediately.

'Hello?'

'Hi, Relationships Anonymous here, apparently you have an addiction to cohabiting.'

Max laughed. 'How was Eloise?'

'Very excited about us.'

'That makes two of us. And hopefully three?'

'I just thought it was fair to warn you, you're about to face your toughest test yet.'

'I'm ready.'

'Do you know how much stuff I own?'

She could hear him smiling. 'So is that a definite yes?'

Maggie nodded.

'Maggie?'

'Sorry, nodding, forgot you can't see that on a mobile.'

'Fantastic news. You won't regret it. I love you. Now hurry home and let me cook you lunch to celebrate. I'll put a bottle of your favourite Chablis on ice.' Max grinned and, in the safety of his living room, indulged himself in a little air punch.

'Are you always this smooth?'

'You'll just have to wait and see.'

Chapter Ten

Maggie stared at the tired magnolia wall complete with Blu-tack craters c.1981. The chips in the gloss paint on the skirting board were exactly the same as they had been when she'd woken up stiff with fear on exam mornings. So much had changed since then and yet her room was the same. A shabby port in a storm. And yet a security blanket she had outgrown. For all its familiarity it was cold.

Maggie stretched. Back in this room, she realised that despite her adult accessories—expensive watch, cellulite, almost cohabiting partner, BMW parked outside—she still didn't feel very different. Adulthood was a myth sustained, no doubt, to ensure children could have faith in their parents until they reached an age when they were old enough to know better.

It had been her decision to leave London for Oxfordshire on Christmas Eve instead of spending the night in London with Max and, to her almost relief, she did now miss him but with the rumour of snow on its way, there was only one place she'd wanted to be.

From the lack of luminous light filtering through her rarely drawn curtains she could tell that, disappointingly, the weather fraternity had screwed up again. They were more guessers than forecasters despite the millions of pounds' worth of probes, satellites and computer programmes at their disposal. You were still better off looking out of the window first thing when you were deciding what to wear.

A lumpy stocking had appeared at the foot of her bed during the night. Mother Christmas never retired. Swinging her legs into the upright position, she rummaged around under her bed for some vintage slippers. Better still, a pair of slipper socks emerged from yesteryear, having dodged a place in Room 101 or the charity shop by hiding themselves in the dusty shadows.

Reaching for a fleece from her leather weekend bag, Maggie wondered whether her parents had decided that they would live longer if they cryogenically froze themselves in their own home. Grabbing her stocking and hugging it close to her for added insulation, she wandered onto the landing in search of her family.

Floorboards creaking as she made her way to the bathroom, her mother's voice carried up the stairs, backed by the strains of Christmas carols on the radio.

'Happy Christmas, my darling. There's fresh tea in the pot.'

'Morning.' Maggie shouted back with as much festive cheer as she could muster. 'I'll be down in a minute.'

For the thirty-second year running, Maggie remained the only child in the house on Christmas morning. She knew her mother had been hoping that there would be grandchildren by now even if, to her credit, she had never said a word. Or at least not a direct word.

Eloise couldn't be sure that she wasn't drunk and yet she was still in her pyjamas.

She struggled to hold her champagne at the best of times, but it was as if her body had no idea what to do with alcohol before noon, let alone 10.30 a.m.

Only her father would have insisted on a glass first thing and he was fitter than the rest of them put together. His incredible self-discipline and drive—which sadly for her seemed to have skipped a generation—had recently lent itself to his exercise regime and he was in training for his second London marathon in two years. Unfortunately the more energy he demonstrated the more lethargic she seemed to become. A law of physics meandered in to her thoughts from the recesses of her memory.

Every action had an equal and opposite reaction.

Newton's third law? Or just sod's? Could she really have been born without a competitive streak or had her brothers simply beaten it out of her by the time she'd reached her tenth birthday?

She wondered if anyone would notice if she popped back to bed. The house had been bustling with activity for the last four hours. The enormous turkey had almost gone in on time. Potatoes had been peeled, carrots sliced, brussel sprouts trimmed, satsumas and Quality Street devoured alongside toast and cereal until someone put the crisps out.

More out of habit than expectation she found her mobile

on the dresser and checked for text messages as she watched her three older brothers and their wives totally consumed with each other and their offspring. Alone in a crowd, she took a step away and decided to escape upstairs either to drown her slight sorrows and pending headache while there was still hot water or maybe to steal half an hour's more sleep. She'd see how she felt at the top of the stairs.

'Ellie.'

Damn her father. A couple more paces and she would have officially left the room.

She waved vaguely. 'Just off to shower, Dad.'

'What about my Christmas hug?'

'I'm not six years old.'

'I'm afraid there's no age limit. You should have read the small print. Plus you look like you need one.'

'I do?' Now in his arms, she battled to remain strong.

'My special girl.' He kissed the top of her head.

'Your only girl.'

'Exactly. Are you happy, my darling?'

Eloise nodded hard, afraid to speak in case her voice betrayed her. As her father stroked her hair tenderly she wondered if any man would ever love her half as much as he did.

'So, what's going on with this chap?'

'Chap?'

He released her in order to get a proper look.

'Your mother and I might have been married for a hundred years but we still talk to each other. Besides, I've been keeping my eye on you for half my life and you can't fool me.'

Eloise smiled at the thought of her father tracking her every move from a surveillance centre; wall-to-wall monitors and a GPS transmitter in the locket he'd given her for her twenty-first birthday. 'Jake's fine.'

'Ah yes, Jake, the invisible man. You should have invited him home for today.'

'It's not that serious.'

'You've been seeing him for a while. Besides, I'm nosy and I know the boys were keen to test his credentials.'

She knew she was lucky with her family. They didn't all manage to get together that often these days, but as she got older their combined presence was more precious to her than any gift under the tree—even the year she got her first iPod.

'He's not really a Christmas person.'

'Jewish?'

Eloise shook her head, amused at her father's logic.

He hadn't given up yet. 'Jesus was a Jew you know....'

'It hasn't got anything to do with religion. He just thinks it's all overcommercialised and a waste of money.'

'Which it is and which is why we love it.'

Her father was a self-made capitalist and it showed.

'Is he a humbug the rest of the time?'

Eloise smiled. *Humbug* was a word that always made her giggle. It was so silly and so perfect all at the same time. 'Of course not. He's not the grumpy sort.'

'Good. And do you think it's going anywhere? You know, like a church?'

'Dad.'

'What? I need to know if I should be saving.'

Eloise shook her head. 'Not yet. But he's a good guy.'

'I'm sure I could get some Arsenal tickets. Maybe I should take him to the football with the boys?'

Eloise knew better than to protest.

'He does like football, I take it?'

'Of course.'

'Well then, that's settled.'

Never going to happen without her being there keeping an eye on them both, but she appreciated the gesture.

'And I promise not to mention your bossy streak or the fact you're going to make an excellent mother, for at least an hour or two.'

Eloise smiled, enjoying the banter and the attention. 'I'm just not sure he's interested in a proper relationship.'

'No need to get too serious.'

'That's not what you just inferred. I'm getting old, Dad.'

'Nonsense.'

'I am, on paper, way past my peak fertility.'

'Do you have any idea how expensive weddings are these days?'

'Daddy.' Eloise's tone was not to be messed with.

He winked at her. 'Just joking. As long as he's good for you he gets my vote.'

Eloise nodded. Muesli was good for her. Was Jake?

'So, do you trust him?'

Eloise nodded.

'Well, that's a good start.'

It was the finish she was more worried about. She wasn't sure he was capable of taking anything in life seriously.

As Maggie descended to the farmhouse kitchen, her stocking bumping down the stairs behind her, she smiled as she recognised her mother's favourite Christmas CD getting its annual airtime. When she entered their winter wonderland, to her bemusement both her parents were wearing garlands of tired red tinsel that Maggie recognised from yesteryear.

'Merry Christmas.' Maggie hugged and kissed them both and wondered if she would ever feel adult in their company. Even when Adam died she had felt them doing their best to absorb the shock for her. Parenting was clearly a job for life.

Automatically checking the date on the milk carton before helping herself to a bowl of cereal and a coffee, Maggie took her unofficial place at the end of the table in the bay window.

A pan of water puttered on top of the Aga as the potatoes parboiled for roasting. As her father's pencil scratched at his sudoku puzzle and her mother reread the recipe for the red cabbage she only made once a year, Maggie wondered how long it would be before there was a new support group in town: Spouses Against Sudoku. The puzzles may have been great for keeping your brain in shape, but she wasn't sure their effect on relationships could be as beneficial. As she crunched through her Crunchy Nut Cornflakes she hoped her breakfast was sounding louder on the inside of her head than it did on the outside.

Her dad completed the grid with a satisfied grunt. Within seconds her mother had taken it to check; once a teacher, always a teacher.

David returned the pencil to its pot on the dresser with a victorious flourish. Now free to join them, he set his agenda for the morning.

'Are there any objections/injuries that might prevent any of the assembled company from taking part in our traditional walk before lunch? Now is the moment to submit your excuses or for ever shut up.'

Maggie smiled. 'I'm in.'

'Shame there isn't any bloody snow out there to crunch underfoot but, all the same, thought it would be good to get the heart pumping a bit before I coat my arteries in Stilton and brandy butter.'

'Remember what the cardiologist said,' her mother interjected without looking up while, using the pencil as a pointer, her hand flew across and down the rows of numbers checking for errors.

'Since when do you have a cardiologist, Dad?' Maggie gave him her undivided attention.

David Hunter glared at his wife before turning to his daughter. 'Believe me, Maggie, getting a cardiologist in your late sixties is as routine as getting a cleaner in your thirties.'

'Mum?'

'Hang on a second.' Carol rested the pencil on the square she was checking so as not to lose her place and looked up.

'Is Dad okay?'

'While it pains me to admit it, this sudoku seems perfect.'

David beamed. 'Fiendish, eh? I'll show them.'

Maggie ignored her father. 'I mean health-wise."

'Why don't you ask him?'

The man with a cardiologist interjected. 'I'm fine. Blood pressure's a bit on the steep side and cholesterol needs some attention but, other than that, I promise I'm not going anywhere, except for a walk if you'll both join me. I'm hoping we can have a family moment. Carol?'

'I'm not sure if I've got time before lunch.'

'For goodness' sake, woman, when did this family last have Christmas lunch before two o'clock? It has only just gone ten-thirty now and without wanting to draw attention to our lack of popularity this year, there are only the three of us. We could just dial for a pizza. It would be much less stressful.'

'Honestly, David. You love turkey.'

Maggie and her father exchanged a knowing look.

'Of course I do, darling. I love it most on Christmas Day and least by December the twenty-ninth.'

Carol sighed. 'I've told you, you can't get very small ones. And we're not having chicken.'

'Perish the thought. I mean they weren't serving chicken in the manger, were they?'

'David. Turkey is the traditional lunch.'

'Only since the sixteenth century when that bloke first brought a turkey over from America.'

Maggie chipped in. 'Bernard Matthews?'

Her father laughed.

Her mother didn't. 'Look, it's traditional.'

'Just like our little stroll on Christmas morning.'

Maggie remembered riding her first real bicycle on one of their walks. She'd rocked from stabiliser to stabiliser along the gravel drive, her fingers pink with cold, determined to keep up and make her father proud as he'd walked backwards in front of her wielding his cine camera.

'I'm just not sure we've got time for one of your rambles today. We all need to get ready for Max.'

'Ah yes, HRH Max of Maggieland.' David turned to his daughter. 'How is your future husband, darling?'

Mouth full of satsuma from her stocking, Maggie nearly choked and, reaching for her now-cool coffee, saved herself from certain death, although the fusion of milky drink and citrus fruit was making her insides curdle.

'My boyfriend is fine, thanks.' She hadn't even moved in yet.

'I saw something in the paper about him being part of a consortium bidding for a chain of boutique hotels.'

Maggie was embarrassed she didn't know the details. She rarely read the business section and she clearly hadn't been asking enough questions. 'He's always working on something.' She was sure it would be easier to keep across everything when they were living together.

It was time to divert attention from her inadequacies as a girl-friend. 'Mum, you do know he's not coming until five or six.'

If Maggie had her way, he wouldn't have been coming at all. He'd already met her parents twice in London.

'Have you seen the state of the sitting room?'

'He'll take us as he finds us, Carol.'

'Dad's right.'

'I was just going to do a little bit of tidying.'

Maggie and David groaned. 'That's settled.' Her dad folded his paper. 'I'm going to get some warm clothes on and make the most of the fields while we've still got some on our doorstep.'

Maggie looked from one of them to the other as her mother went over to stir something vigorously on the stove. Her father slowly got to his feet.

Maggie focused on her mother. 'You're not selling off the paddock, are you? Granny only let you have this house on the condition that you kept it just the same.'

'While she was still alive.'

'I've no doubt the developers have been waving cheques at you again, but before you know it there'll be five houses backing on to the garden and a block of flats where the compost heap is. If you're feeling short of cash, maybe I can help a little in the short term.'

Her dad perched on the kitchen table next to where she was sitting. 'That's very kind of you.'

'You could always remortgage. Or get a couple of lodgers.'

He nodded. 'We could.'

Maggie looked from one parent to the other. 'But no?'

'Actually we've been meaning to talk to you about this for a while.'

Self-protectively, Maggie tucked her hands under her armpits.

Her mum joined her dad, both now invading her personal space. 'I'm afraid it's not just the paddock. Daddy and I have decided to put the house on the market.'

'You can't…'

Pure spoilt brat behaviour. Can't, shan't, won't.

'…it's my home, too.'

'Darling, look around you, the house needs work. Proper work we can't afford. A new roof, repointing, new window frames. That's not even considering bathrooms or any of the more cosmetic stuff. And we really don't need all this space.'

Maggie shook her head. 'How can you say that? The house is full of stuff.'

'Lots of our friends have downsized. We don't want to spend our hard-earned retirement sitting at this table talking about what we'd like to do if only we could afford it. We want to live our lives while we still can.'

Maggie had to admire their joie de vivre. She couldn't help thinking that by the time she got to her sixties she'd be only too happy to sit around reading trashy novels and doing very little.

'Plus you're in no danger of needing a family home soon.'

Maggie was sure her mother hadn't meant to be quite so harsh.

'Your life is in London. You only make it down here a few weekends a year and now you're more settled, I think it's time. We've already spoken to Nigel Whittaker and he says—'

Maggie shook her head in disbelief. 'You told the estate agent before you told your own daughter?'

'You're always so busy at work.'

'Doing what exactly?'

'Sometimes I do wonder.'

'Seriously, Mum. This is ridiculous. This is what I do. And I do it well.'

'I told you, Carol.'

Maggie watched her father.

'Don't be like that, David.'

'And where are you thinking of moving to?' Briefly Maggie wondered if Max might want to invest in another property.

'Back to London and as soon as possible really.'

Maggie swallowed hard. 'I thought you loved it here.' She reminded herself it was just a house.

'We've loved every minute. But we're not country people. Not in our hearts. Plus if we're back in town, we'll all be closer.'

'You're only forty-five minutes away now. Less if you come on the fast train.'

'But if we're in London we can be a lot more spontaneous.' Her mother smiled. 'And we can make sure you're being nice to Max.'

'Mum!'

'Seriously, it'll be much easier if we're round the corner.'

For whom? Maggie groaned. 'Please tell me you're not saving up for grandchildren. Take up golf. Bowls. Bingo. Anything.'

Carol stood firm. 'You're depriving us of our second youth.'

'I'm still a child myself.'

'Actually, that's where you're wrong.'

Jake tossed Frankie the Frisbee for around the twentieth time in a row, determined to tire her out before lunch and happy to be outside while the kitchen and the turkey were dangerously overstuffed. Panting heavily, Frankie didn't look any less enthusiastic when she brought it back and dropped it at his feet. As Jake put his hands in his pockets to warm them up, she barked her dissatisfaction at his decision.

'Okay, one more and then we're going in.' He shook his head. As if she could understand a word he was saying.

His mobile rang and Eloise's number flashed up. Frankie barked again and this time he threw the Frisbee as far as he could. She bounded off in pursuit.

'Eloise.' He'd meant to call her earlier. 'Merry Christmas.'

'And to you, Scrooge.'

He smiled. 'I'm really not that bad. So, how's your day going?'

'Surrounded by family and friends. Or you could say nosy parents and brothers, noisy nieces and nephews and an embarrassing number of gifts. How about you?'

'I'm hiding in the garden.'

'What?'

'Frankie and I are building up an appetite. Susan has cooked an enormous lunch. Or rather has nearly finished cooking an enormous—'

'It's nearly four.'

'From the stress levels in there, I'd say we're running a little behind schedule. The kids have already had a handful of cheese triangles to keep them going. Not that at five years old they even like roast turkey. They'd rather have sausages or fish fingers.'

'I think it's great she cooks you all lunch.'

'Since Mum died, she's been determined to feed me and subject me to the whole ho-ho-ho thing. Now she's had children, it's even compulsory to be full of good yuletide cheer and between you and me, I'm starving.'

Christmas was all about family. And these days for him, it had become about pretending to be happy. It was the one day of the year he missed his parents unashamedly.

Eloise laughed. 'Well, I just thought I'd say hello. Maybe next year you'll come and experience the madhouse.'

'Maybe.' He wasn't sure he was ready for immersion in someone else's happy family.

Eloise immediately regretted pushing him.

Jake berated his reticence. His mood wasn't her fault. 'Or we could go away somewhere next year.'

Eloise beamed into the phone. 'Cool. I've never had a

Christmas outside the UK.' He was suggesting forward planning *and* foreign travel. Possibly the best present he could have given her.

Jake scuffed his shoe in the grass as he kicked an imaginary football. His canine spectator, having already returned, and this time waiting patiently at his feet, hurtled off only to return seconds later, confused.

'I spent the first two Christmases abroad after Mum died. I didn't want to be responsible for my nephews' formative memories of Christmas Day when I was feeling so negative.'

Eloise had learnt more about him in the last twenty seconds than she had in the last seven months. 'And of course you're so much more positive about it now.' Her tone was teasing.

'It's bloody hard.'

'I was only joking around. I'm sure it must be incredibly difficult.'

'Plenty of people have real problems. I just miss my mum and dad. I'm sure I'll grow out of it.'

'I don't know.' Eloise couldn't imagine a world without her parents in it. 'Did you unwrap your present?'

'I'm saving it for under the tree.'

Eloise wondered why she'd bothered.

'We were never allowed to do presents until after lunch as children. I guess it just stuck. And I thought we agreed we weren't doing gifts.'

'It's a really small thing.'

'You shouldn't have, but thank you in advance.'

'My pleasure. Look, I'd better go. I've promised to help Ollie build his new solar system. You can guarantee he'll have got bored in twenty minutes and I'll be doing it for hours and loving it. You can test me on the order of the planets later. Fun and games as ever.'

Jake admired her energy. 'You really mean that, don't you?'

'Absolutely. We always have a laugh even when later on, the board games get ultracompetitive. Sadly this year there haven't been any family conferences. Normally someone is having problems with their marriage/conceiving/broadband supplier. Nothing is too trivial and nothing is a secret if you're a Forrest.'

'Scary stuff.' Jake wondered what they'd said about him.

'It's quite reassuring really. And no one ever listens to any of the advice. It's just cathartic.'

Jake shrugged. 'I only have a bossy sister left and I definitely don't listen to her.'

Eloise dared herself to try and spread a little good cheer. 'What are you doing later?'

'Later?' Jake sounded surprised.

'Are you going to stay over at Susan's?'

'Might do. Or I might just head home and watch black-and-white films all night. The others are away so it'll be nice and quiet at the flat.'

'Fancy a game of Trivial Pursuit?'

'I'm not sure I'm up for a big family thing.'

Eloise changed tack. 'Then why don't we meet back at mine at, say, around ten-thirty?'

Jake laughed. 'You're crazy, you know that.'

'Yup, but looking around me today, I could have been so much worse. So what do you say?'

Jake paused. 'Why not? I'll see you at yours.'

Eloise put the phone down. She didn't know what she was doing but she was doing something. And she liked that.

Jake folded his phone closed and, helpless to resist Eloise's effervescent good cheer, bent down to give Frankie an ear rub. 'You know what, doglet, I think I owe you a drink.'

Frankie carried on panting, her expression the same. Jake wondered if dogs had become man's best friend because they always listened and never criticised.

The back door opened and from inside Jake heard Susan bellow.

'LUNCH.'

The twins used the moment to escape and, shrieking, raced to their uncle, grabbing a leg each.

'Coming.'

Tucking a wriggling, giggling, dribbling twin under each arm so he could actually walk, Jake swaggered towards the kitchen. As he reached the house and unloaded his cargo, he refilled Frankie's water bowl with tasty rainwater from the watering can. 'House special. Never let it be said I am not a man of my word.'

Max couldn't remember the last time he'd enjoyed a bog standard pint of lager so much and had seen Ed drink one so fast. Now his brother-in-law was checking the time on a day when the rest of the world was wound down. Then again they had left Emmy at home with Toby and Rosie on the one day of the year she was supposed to be able to count on extra pairs of hands.

'Two more please.' Max enjoyed catching the barmaid's attention. She wasn't bad looking, if a little young. In fact if he'd been a policeman he'd have been asking her for ID, let alone allowing her to serve a drink to him.

The pub in Primrose Hill was hot. A log fire was blazing in the hearth even though it was mild enough to have several windows open. But the landlord wasn't changing his festive scene for anyone.

Shaking his head, Ed returned his empty glass to the bar. 'Hey Max, hold up. We have to get back.'

'One for the road, come on, it's not as if your wife is an unreasonable dragon.'

'Believe me, this will not go—'

'Careful what you say, that's my sister you got knocked up. Twice.' Max raised his glass to Ed's. 'Cheers, mate. Happy Christmas.'

'Are you deliberately trying to get me into trouble?'

'Au contraire, we're celebrating.'

'Celebrating?'

'I asked Maggie to move in with me.'

Ed shook his head. 'That didn't take long. Max French, serial monogamist rides again.'

'Ah, but this one's different.'

Ed nodded. 'I'm glad you've noticed.'

Max nodded proudly. 'She is, isn't she?'

'Even Emmy approves.'

'Really?' High praise indeed. Max knew how hard it was to impress his sister. 'Maggie did take some persuading.'

'The first one who hasn't fallen at your feet.' Ed winked.

'For a moment I thought I'd scared her off.'

'Well, you can't blame her, after the whole Adam thing.'

'That was three and a half years ago.'

'Trust can take a lot longer to rebuild than that.'

Max paused. 'Do you think I should ask her to marry me?'

Ed put his glass down. 'How strong is that beer?'

'I think maybe it's time I settled down.'

Ed shook his head at his brother-in-law. 'Wait until "maybe" doesn't appear in that sentence. And it's early days yet. What's the hurry?'

'Can I tell you something else?'

'Oh God, you're not pregnant, are you?'

'No, of course not.' Max hesitated. 'I'm just having a good moment. Things are going well. I can afford to relax a little.'

'True love or timing?' Ed watched him carefully.

Max shrugged. 'I just want to take care of her.'

'I'd let her unpack first.'

'Shut up.' Max punched Ed's arm.

His phone rang. Maggie. Right on cue.

Max smiled into his handset. 'Happy Christmas to you.'

Previously alone, to Maggie's amusement her mother suddenly appeared in the sitting room. 'Merry Christmas, indeed.'

'How's Oxfordshire?'

'Cold. How's London?'

Max looked around him. 'Cosy. Or at least it is in this pub.'

'You've gone to the pub?' Maggie tried not to sound surprised.

'Ed and I snuck out for a pint.'

'Some sort of male bonding ritual?'

Max nodded. 'Exactly.'

'Because the beer at home tastes different?'

'Spot on.'

Maggie was bemused by the maleness of the logic. 'Your sister must be delighted.'

'Something like that.'

'Are you still okay to come over later?'

'That's the plan.'

'And you're not too drunk to drive?'

'Trying to fob me off?' Max quickly mentally checked hours remaining before travel against units of alcohol consumed. He'd be fine.

Ed frowned into his glass before focusing on finishing his second pint.

'No, not at all.' Her mother would never forgive her if she uninvited him now. For the first time in nearly a year she could see the surface of the coffee table.

'Is everything okay?'

'Yup. Fine.'

'Is everyone listening in?'

'Absolutely. Yes.'

Max laughed. 'So nothing weird is going on?'

'Nothing to do with you.'

'The plot thickens. I'll be there about, let's say six actually—that way I may only be a few minutes late.'

'See you then.' Maggie prepared to hang up. Carol glared at her. Maggie turned away. 'Really looking forward to it.' Without looking, Maggie could feel her mother's glare soften into a beam.

'Me too.' Max hung up. A grin appeared.

Ed smiled 'Ah, love's young dream.'

'Fuck off.'

'Long may it last.' Ed raised his glass. 'May you be as happy as Emmy and I were before you persuaded me to stay for a second pint.'

Chapter Eleven

New Year. New her. These were moving times and, finding a bottle of vodka, she decided to toast herself. Maggie stood in Max's, or rather their, sitting room. What had previously seemed spacious, felt claustrophobic thanks to the two storeys of her cardboard boxes running down the middle of the room. A great wall of china, books, magazines, DVDs and other urban essentials, they may only have been material items, the majority totally unnecessary for personal happiness or world peace, but they were hers.

In search of a glass, she picked her way through the new furniture arrangement, which wouldn't have looked out of place in an auction house. Finding a path to the kitchen, she stood, marooned on an island of clear floor space. Noisily tearing the brown tape from the top seam of a promising-looking box she'd only labelled forty-eight hours earlier, she rummaged through the bubble wrap and scrunched up newspaper until she reached her blue glass wine goblets.

As always seemed to be the case when she was willing a day to reach its end, it had only just gone six and, having filled her glass with ice cubes from the dispenser on the fridge door, Maggie poured herself a vodka, watching the clear life force crackling a path through the rocks before taking a sip. The second sip caught her throat less. The third was positively delicious. Selecting the top CD from a recently unpacked pile, Whitney Houston's greatest hits soon filled the kitchen. Ooh, she wanted to dance with somebody who loved her.

She didn't hear Max come in. At least a huge bunch of flowers had walked in with legs that looked like his and she couldn't mask her delight. Tulips were her favourite.

If he was surprised at the state of his kitchen, or the state of her singing, it didn't show. Putting his arm round her waist, he pulled her in for a very welcome kiss. At which point Maggie realised that she hadn't brushed her teeth since she'd had a furtive McDonald's for lunch, nor had she remembered to apply any make-up. Embarrassingly her standards seemed to have slipped already. Damn. She'd make it up to him later.

He handed her the enormous bouquet of red and pink. 'Welcome home, sweetie.'

Maggie ached from head to foot, the skin on her hands sore and dry from overexposure to cardboard and sticky tape, but this was her kitchen, her boyfriend, her bouquet and her life; all in all, a pretty bearable state of affairs.

'I don't suppose you've seen my slippers?' Max was grinning. 'What's for dinner?'

'Very funny.'

'Too tired for jokes?'

'Not all jokes.' She perched on the edge of the table.

'Knock knock.'

'Okay, maybe I am. And by the way, it's official—'

'I know.' Max interrupted her. 'You live here.'

Maggie completed her original sentence. 'There's no room for me. Every cupboard is already full.'

Wearily she rested her head on his shoulder as she felt him look around the room. The vodka seemed to be relaxing her muscles, and her muscles were the only things that were keeping her upright enough for unpacking.

'So we need to change some things. No big deal.'

'But you promised me nothing was going to change.' Maggie raised her eyebrow as she drained her glass. It had been mainly ice.

'You being here is already a major home improvement.'

She couldn't blame him for being so chipper. From where he was sitting, everything was just as it was before except she was there, too. She, on the other hand, wanted to go home and crash out except, as of three hours ago, this was it.

As he kissed her again—the perfect distraction—the doorbell rang. Maggie wondered if she could suggest they ignore it.

'Coming,' Max shouted as he hung his jacket on the back of a chair laden with surplus cookery books and rolled his sleeves up, preparing for work. He bounded towards the door. Maggie just waited, a slightly inebriated picture of exhaustion and inertia.

'Well hello, Mrs Home Maker.' Eloise's excitement wafted into the kitchen a couple of seconds before she did. 'Saw these tulips and thought of you.' Entering the room, Eloise's spotted the heap of similar flowers on the table and shrugged her shoulders.

'Blimey. I guess I was lucky there were any left.' She turned three hundred and sixty degrees as she took in the scene. 'This is so exciting.'

'Don't you mean so messy.' Maggie wished she could stop sounding like she was complaining. Everything she said seemed to have become distorted by the time it reached the open air.

'These things always get worse before they get better.' Eloise picked her way through the maze of packing boxes and reached several cardboard cul-de-sacs before finding her way through to Maggie, who she suspected was in grave need of a hug.

Max was opening and closing cupboards at random in a clueless search for vases.

'You know, I always thought this place was a bit bare.' He grinned as, giving up, he produced a bucket and a pint glass. 'Take your pick.'

'At last, something I can add to your life. El, find the vase box.'

'You have a whole box of v—?'

'Don't be daft. They're in with the champagne flutes.'

Eloise started reading the labels on the boxes. 'When we get rid of all this packaging, it won't look so bad.'

Max cleared a chair and made Maggie sit down before rubbing her shoulders. Eloise was already up to her elbows in a box that looked promising.

Max kissed the top of her head, reading her thoughts. 'I had meetings all day or I would have been here to help.'

Eloise looked up from her vase detail. 'How did they go? Is the hotel project a goer?'

Of course, Eloise had remembered the details. She was going to make someone an excellent wife.

'I think we could be on to something.'

Maggie never ceased to be amazed by the number of things Max crammed into one week. She used to think she made the most of every day until she met Max. Maggie felt the remains of her energy leave her body. 'You shouldn't have let me sit down. I may never be able to walk again.'

'You'll be fine.'

'I'm hungry.'

'Aha.' Eloise sounded like she had found the meaning of life in her cardboard box. 'Just so you know, Max, when Maggie actually mentions that she is hungry, you have less than half an hour before she turns into the Incredible Sulk.'

Maggie glared at Eloise. 'I'm not grump…'

Eloise winked at Max and Maggie would have got quite cross if she'd had the energy. 'She gets like this when she hasn't eaten for a while. Anything will do. Pitta bread. A chocolate biscuit.'

Since when had it been her versus the rest of the world, or at least the rest of her world? Maybe she should have read the fixtures list.

'Why don't I pop out and get a takeaway.' Max saw an escape route and picked up his jacket.

'Perfect.'

Apparently Eloise was answering for her now, too.

'Fish and Chips? Chinese?' He looked across. Maggie's expression was neutral. Either she'd spent the morning having Botox or she wasn't bothered.

Eloise chipped in. 'How about an Indian?'

Maggie grinned. 'Yum.'

Max was only too happy to oblige. 'Any special requests?'

'Chicken Balti, Peshwari Naan and Sag Aloo.' Maggie hadn't even had to move her lips. Eloise had her ultimate order spot on. She hoped Max was going to develop into as good a flatmate as Eloise had been.

'Jake is pretty excited about moving in to yours.'

Having found and fed Maggie a packet of peanuts, Eloise was making headway in the kitchen. Or at least she had successfully squirrelled a great number of Maggie's possessions away into cupboards that had previously appeared to be full.

'Mmm.' Maggie put her salt and pepper mills alongside Max's on the worktop and wondered why she hadn't just left them for Jake to use.

'I promise I'll keep an eye on him. You don't need to worry about a thing.'

'I just hope it helps you find a bit more quality time together.'

'It'll almost be like moving in together.'

'You are going to give him enough time and space?'

'Don't worry, I'll ring the bell first.'

'I'd call. He isn't renting a drop-in centre.'

Eloise gave her a withering look.

'What? For once you can't say it's none of my business. It's my flat.'

Eloise shrugged the implicit criticism off. 'Did I tell you Jake uses Ariel and Lenor, too?'

Maggie looked up from the box she was unpacking. 'Tell me you weren't comparing cleaning products.'

'Of course not. I've just been keeping an eye out. And he buys Andrex.'

'Oh well.' Maggie's tone was sarcastic. 'Then you must be made for each other.'

Eloise stood up to her best friend. 'I thought it was a good sign.'

'It's good that he washes his clothes and uses toilet paper, but that's as far as I'd push that coincidence. My only advice to you in all of this.'

'Your *only* advice?' Eloise looked incredulous. 'This hour? This minute?'

'The worst thing you can do is mirror him and create an illusion of compatibility. We've all done it and it doesn't work long term however much you think you like him.'

'I know that.'

'Good.'

Eloise was keen to change the subject. 'So how's work going?'

'Very good actually. Not to go any further, but Red called me earlier. He's back for more.'

'I thought he bought half of Somerset last time.'

'That was six months ago, he's made another film since then. Besides, this time he wants to buy somewhere for his parents.'

'What a nice guy.'

'It's just pocket money to him. Plus if he can find them a place, you know close, but not that close, then he can control how much he sees of them.'

Eloise laughed. 'Charming.'

'I don't know. I think it's quite sensible.'

'Still hoping your parents will change their minds then?'

Maggie nodded. 'I don't think it'll happen. London here they come. Yippee.'

Eloise was silent for a moment as she continued to stash items away. 'So is Red still seeing that model, actress, walking eating-disorder?'

Maggie smiled. 'I do believe he and Petra are still together.'

'Shame.'

'Believe me, El, he's not the sort of man you'd want to date.'

'That's where you're wrong.'

'Hang on, what about Jake and his matching cleaning products?'

'Fuck off. I'm talking fantasy league here.'

'Believe me, his eye doesn't just wander, it goes away for the night. He's always rumoured to be womanising.'

Eloise sighed.

'Anyway, it sounds like Jake is shaping up.'

Eloise nodded. 'Slightly, plus he'd rather be watching an obscure film at one a.m. or sleeping in than sleeping around, so that's one less thing to worry about.'

Maggie smiled. 'A man after my own heart.'

Eloise paused to check her approach. 'Which reminds me, can I ask you a favour?'

'Provided it doesn't involve a dog in my flat.'

'Relax.'

'What then?'

Eloise changed her mind. 'It doesn't matter.'

'Out with it.'

'Well, do you think, maybe, if a convenient moment arises, you could ask Red if he might want to do an interview?'

'With you?'

'For the hospital radio station.'

'Ah yes, Parky one night, Radio Night Nurse the next. What planet are you on?'

Eloise shrugged. 'Planet Possible. Surely, in the most selfish century yet, people still have time for the occasional good turn? Come on, Mags, the patients would love it.'

'You of course would hate every second.'

Eloise raised her hands in surrender. 'It would be a huge coup for me, but it would also be great PR for him. The gossip in hospitals is far more effective and faster moving than a viral Internet campaign. And it would be unbeatable for raising my profile.'

This was a man who had increased global cinema takings by twenty percent this year alone, but Maggie didn't want to be negative. 'I'd have thought it was unlikely.'

'The worst he can say is no. Isn't it?'

'I guess.'

'I know you're probably worrying about being unprofessional and him taking his business somewhere else.'

Eloise knew her far too well.

'But I'm your best friend and it's for charity. Well sort of.'

'Charidee. Save the Eloise.'

Eloise laughed. 'Exactly.'

'Do you know how many begging letters people like Red get?'

'I'm not asking you to beg. He likes you.'

'Flattery will get you everywhere.'

Eloise shrugged. 'He calls you himself when he could get his PA to do it.'

'It's personal, that's why.'

'Personal assistants know more about their bosses than their wives, their mothers or their mistresses. Believe me. I've been there.'

'Well, maybe he likes my witty repartee. Seriously, El, it's just business and he's impatient. I know it won't have escaped your notice that I have not had a long history of men falling at my feet. Let alone world-famous actors.'

'I know, life sucks when all you get are the world's most eligible entrepreneurs.'

Maggie laughed at Eloise's deadpan delivery.

'Amusingly, Max seems to think he snuck in and snatched an opportune vacancy and I don't have the heart to tell him there was quite a big window of opportunity. In fact, more of a conservatory…I mean look, I'm here, with Max…'

'I know.' Eloise giggled as Maggie finally seemed to take recent developments on board. 'So?'

'Look, I'll see what I can do. But I'm not promising anything.'

Eloise bounced over to Maggie and hugged her best friend tightly. 'This could be just what I need to finish my show reel.' Eloise blushed as she realised her mistake.

It didn't take Maggie a second to pick up on it. 'Since when did you have one of those?'

'Just something I'm playing around with. A bit of a demo. It's not really up to much yet.'

'Eloise Forrest.'

'You're the one that's been nagging me to get focused.'

'Don't think I've given up, either. Can I have a listen?'

'Get me the interview first.'

'That's blackmail.'

'Actually, that's negotiation. Max told me you have to decide what you want out of a meeting and not compromise. And if you pull this off, I swear I will do anything you like.'

The women embraced. The breast of friends.

'Now this is a sight any man would love to find in his kitchen when he gets home.' In the absence of even a few inches of uncluttered work surface, Max balanced the aromatic brown paper bag, already sporting a few telltale translucent grease spots, on top of the Aga as he dropped his keys into what used to be a sparsely populated drawer. 'Dinner is served.'

Chapter Twelve

'So if the boiler goes out you need to—' Maggie had her house file open.

Jake interrupted. 'It's just a standard combi, I'll be fine. Spare bulbs and stuff in the third drawer down, right?'

'Exactly.' Maggie was still wondering whether letting Jake rent her pride and joy was a good idea. She glanced around her kitchen, which she had to admit looked better now her cohort of condiments had been relocated to Ladbroke Grove. 'Oh, and make sure you wipe any grease out from under the controls of the hob occasionally, otherwise it does all tend to stiffen up.'

Jake looked Maggie directly in the eye. 'Grease, nobs, regularly or they get stiff. Got it.'

Maggie reddened, immediately surfacing from her self-absorbed seriousness and wondering how she'd found herself in the script of a *Carry On* film.

His expression was impish. 'I'm fully house-trained.'

Sheepish, she closed the lever arch file and handed it to him. 'It's all in there. Just call me if you can't work anything out. I'm not trying to be a nightmare landlord.'

'I'm not sure I've had worse.' He put the file down on the draining board before thinking better of it, moving it to the work surface and following her out of the kitchen.

Pausing in the sitting room, Maggie frowned and then forced a smile, as much for her benefit as for his. She wondered if Jake was a candle man. And a red wine man? Eloise had dismissed both counts, but then Eloise had an ulterior motive.

He leant against the door jamb and ran his hand over his head from back to front and back again. 'I take it my girl-friend is allowed to stay over occasionally?'

'Look, I know I probably seem a little fussy, it's just I've never had a tenant before.'

'I've never had a landlady before. All the landlords were pretty chilled out provided they got paid and we didn't set fire to anything.'

She couldn't believe she'd let Eloise talk her out of seeking character references. Lucan had been adamant it was essential, right before telling her a horror story about squatters.

Maggie glanced around her open-plan sitting room as Jake wondered whether he had just made the worst mistake of his life. Eloise said she wasn't as bad as she seemed. But going on this afternoon's performance he wasn't at all sure.

'So where's this infamous inventory?'

Maggie wheeled. Plenty of time to kill Eloise later. She was sure Jake would be able to find a new girlfriend.

'Don't worry about it.' Carefully typed out and in

Maggie's bag, she had just decided that if she lost a teaspoon or a plate she'd buy new ones. She'd taken her favourite stuff with her anyway.

'Hey. I was only joking. Plus I've got to protect myself from you too, you know.'

A sensible point. Maggie found the A4 envelope and handed her novella over. 'No rush. Go through it in your own time.'

'Cheers.'

Maggie watched Jake fold the envelope in half lengthways and stuff it in his back pocket.

'Feel free to stop by any time and check up on me. I make a mean cup of tea.'

Maggie beamed her appreciation. 'Thank you.'

'Although it might be an idea to give me a call first, you know, so I've got time to hide all the takeaway cartons, pets and sweaty sports socks.' His eyes shone. With mischief? Maggie didn't know him nearly well enough. She reminded herself that he came with the Forrest seal of approval.

Maggie's stomach growled. 'Oh, almost forgot. Great Chinese takeaway place on speed dial two and an Indian delivery on three.'

'Now that is important information. What's speed dial one?'

'Eloise.' Maggie's mobile rang and she extracted it from her bag. The office. 'I've got to take this.'

'Cool. Well, thanks for coming over and talking me through everything.'

Already distracted, Maggie walked towards her front door. 'A pleasure.'

'And I promise I'll look after the place.'

Maggie nodded and waved. Stepping out on to the landing, she pulled the door closed behind her.

'Maggie Hunter.'

'Simon Senior.' The sing-song delivery of his name mimicked hers. 'Just to let you know the Hampstead guy called back.'

'Good.' Maggie was expectant.

'And he says four-point-five mill is fine for Holland Park.'

She felt her chest swell. 'Superb. And that was faster than I was expecting.'

'You're better at your job than you think.'

'Thanks, Simon, and for letting me know.'

This was definitely shaping up to be her year.

'I'll make a start on the paperwork if you like.'

Working late, too. Maggie wondered if he was up to something. 'That would be great, but don't stay too long. We can deal with the fine print tomorrow. I won't be in until the afternoon though.' Her phone beeped in her ear. 'Got to go, another call coming in.'

'You're a popular girl.'

'You know me.' Maggie was now in far too good a mood to care about formality. 'Have a good evening.' She hung up and answered the next call. 'Maggie Hunter.'

'At last.'

'Hi Mum.'

'What's the point of having a mobile if you don't answer it? It's more frustrating than not having any hope of reaching you at all.'

Maggie was warm. 'I promise I was going to call you back later.'

'That's what you said yesterday.'

'Sorry, it was a mad day and I didn't want to get home to Max's and spend all evening on the phone.' Instead she'd popped in to Harrods Food Hall to buy Chilean sea bass and cooked him dinner. Her competitive streak had started to surface and she was finding herself determined to be the best live-in lover he'd ever had.

'Of course not. Break him in gently. Anyway…' Her mother's tone was suggestive. 'Ain't love grand.'

'And tiring…' The women shared a giggle. Maggie was suddenly aware that she could hear two sets of breathing in her handset. Either she had a crossed line with a sordid chatline or… 'Dad? Are you there, too?' She grimaced at the thought of him listening to the last exchange.

'Bat-like hearing as ever. So much for me worrying about you deafening yourself with that Walkman.'

Maggie's approach changed to one of concern. Stereo parenting was far from a regular occurrence. 'Are you two okay?' Maggie put a hand on the banister to steady herself as she continued her descent. She'd been wearing heels all day and now, next stop home, her calves were smarting with every step.

'We're fine. How about you? Learning to share?'

'Very funny, Dad.'

Her mum intervened. 'Is this a good time for a chat?'

'Good as any. I'm just leaving Little Venice. I've been inducting my new tenant.'

'Sounds painful.' David laughed. 'Is she nice?'

'He's fine.' Maggie wished they'd just get to the point.

'You're letting to a man? You know when I was a bachelor I didn't clean the bathroom in my flat once. You're very brave.'

'Hardly, David. The chap in question is Eloise's boyfriend.'

Maggie smiled. The way her mother used the term made Jake sound about fifteen. And she was sure she'd seen cleaning products next to the loo.

'Riskier still, I'd say. That girl has made some strange choices over the years.'

At the age of twenty-two Eloise had brought a boyfriend with a ponytail over for Sunday lunch and her father had never forgotten him.

Silence. Maggie shivered as the main door of the mansion block slammed behind her and she walked across to her car. She glanced at her handset. They were still connected. 'Hello?'

'Go on then, Carol.'

'Come on, you two, I don't have hours.'

'Okay. Don't shout, but Daddy and I just wanted to let you know that as of today the house is on the market.'

Maggie stopped walking. 'WHAT?'

'I said don't shout.'

'You two are RIDICULOUSY impatient.'

'Calm down. It's just, well, you haven't done anything yet and Nigel has been round three times so far.'

'He lives round the corner. What difference is a few weeks going to make anyway?'

'I don't think that's the issue. Honestly, I don't think you really want us to sell.'

'That's got nothing to do with it.'

'Really? He seemed to think—'

'Okay, I admit I was upset at first, but this is my thing. Leave that slimeball out of it. Nigel will rip you off.' Maggie sidestepped an aggressive moped driver and walked to her car. 'What percentage is he asking for? You haven't signed anything yet, have you?'

'No.' Her mother was unusually quiet.

'I told you, Carol.'

'Shush, David.'

'You two might be very academic, but you can't be experts in every field.' Maggie could feel herself getting upset despite the fact she knew that as an adult child her opinion counted for less than that of their neighbours. 'Just give me a chance to see if I can find someone who will keep the house the way it was intended to stay and not knock it down and build a row of new town houses.'

'We don't want to miss our moment.'

'You mean your cheque. Just leave it with me for a few weeks.'

Her dad had gone quiet. The boss however hadn't given up yet. 'The developers are offering really good money, darling, and we're seriously underpensioned.'

'So you have had an offer.'

'Nothing in writing or confirmed.'

'I need to know exactly what's on the table if I'm going to help you.'

Finally her dad spoke up. 'Of course. And I'm sure we can wait a week or two.'

'Great. And hesitation on your part will only result in a bigger offer if it comes to that. Let me get my head together and let's talk figures at the weekend. Got to go now.'

Maggie snapped her phone shut and, immediately feeling guilty that she hadn't said goodbye nicely, leant against her car door looking beyond the orange glow of the street lights into the night sky.

'Counting your lucky stars or praying I'm not going to trash the place?'

Maggie jumped as a dismembered voice approached from the shadows.

The size of Jake's Puffa jacket and the shortness of his hair meant that his head resembled a tennis ball resting on a duvet.

'You okay?'

Maggie pulled herself together. 'Fine. Just thinking.'

'Always dangerous.' He cocked his head. 'Bad news?'

'Not really.' It was just a house. Maggie was wrestling with herself to keep it in perspective. 'You off somewhere nice?' And then she saw it, under his arm, a skateboard. More of a snowboard on hi-tech translucent suspension wheels than the slim emery boards on roller skates that Maggie remembered from her childhood, but either way her best friend was dating a Skater Boy. She couldn't wait to speak to Eloise.

'I was just off in search of some food. Want to join me?'

Maggie paused. She had no idea how to ride pillion on eight wheels and no desire to find out. 'I think I'd better be heading home.' Maybe he had a ten-year-old brother, or a son?

'Back to "your" place—plural.'

Maggie smiled. 'I guess.'

'How about a quick drink in your favourite local pub? Consider it a thank-you.'

'I've got an early start tomorrow.'

'Go on. You may find your first tenant is less of a walking disaster than you originally thought.'

'Okay. Just a half. And some crisps.'

'Excellent.'

Jake hadn't moved.

Maggie was confused. 'Changed your mind already?'

He shook his head. 'Just waiting for you to show me the way. You forget, I'm new to these parts.'

She looked at his mode of transport. She was wearing serious heels.

He followed her gaze. 'I'm happy to walk. Or you can drive?'

The ball of her foot ached to the bone, but Maggie knew they'd never find anywhere closer to park.

'Luckily for us both I bought a flat less than five hundred metres from a great pub on the canal.'

'You can tell you're a professional. You know what they say.'

'Do one thing every day that scares you?' Maggie was hopeful.

'Location. Location. Location.'

It was an ordinary, non-big-footie-match Tuesday night at The Waterway and yet the pub was packed. It was no wonder that the British had a reputation for being a nation of drinkers. There were definitely more people here than Maggie had ever seen at the gym round the corner.

Jake elbowed his way to the bar as Maggie spotted movement at the far end of the room and deftly secured the last table, still slightly tacky with drying drinks from its last occupants, but now theirs. Using a green paper napkin, she did her best to clear up, ignoring the ring of green now on the table where she had effectively started a papier mâché collage. Napkin with lager. It could have been a modern work of art if Damien Hirst had been the man mopping. She wondered what she and Jake were going to talk about. Without Eloise and his new home, she suspected they had close to nothing in common.

Jake arrived back with their drinks and a menu tucked under his arm and indicated the large blackboard behind her with his head. 'Apparently it's quiz night.'

Maggie took a long sip of her half pint of Guinness. The dark red walls of the pub created a warm atmosphere and, no doubt, acted as camouflage for a plethora of stains.

Jake took several consecutive gulps of lager and, to Maggie's amusement, licked his lips as he came up for air. 'So what do you say? I'm game if you are.'

'For dinner?' Maggie wondered if she should check with Max first. She had definitely said she wouldn't be late. Then again she was starving now.

'For the quiz.'

Maggie was less keen. 'Just the two of us?'

'Why not? We can eat, too.'

Maggie scanned the crowd, most already seated in groups of four to six around their tables, pencils sharpened, biros chewed, brows furrowed in anticipation of their mental workouts. Bowls of chips and nachos—presumably just for energy—seemed to be a central feature and Maggie found herself gazing at the culinary equivalent of porn with some longing.

Jake was also scoping out the opposition. 'Okay, so these guys do seem quite professional, there's at least four per team. Maybe we need to go recruiting.'

'I think this might be a good time to tell you I'm not a very good loser.'

'Hey, I definitely won't be the weakest link. Although I may not have what it takes to be a millionaire…'

Maggie smiled as she stifled a yawn. She was tired. She was hungry. But she wasn't in a hurry to go home. Recently she felt like she was always installed on the sofa when Max got back, however late she meandered home from work. It would be good for him to miss her for a change.

Jake was still making his case. 'I can assure you we're not going to win, but we'll probably have fun trying. Alternatively we can drink up and head to our respective homes to sit in front of separate televisions and watch other people apparently having a good time.'

Maggie didn't have a chance to answer.

'Laydees and gents. Time to sharpen your wits and your pencils. Welcome to tonight's quiz.'

'I'll be back in a mo.' Jake got up.

'This is no time to leave me at the mercy of the question master.'

'I'll be right back. Just going to order some power nachos, as soon as I've been to powder my nose.'

Maggie hoped he didn't mean literally. She'd told him about not smoking in the flat but had forgotten to mention the no-drugs-on-the-glass-coffee-table rule. Then again she was sure Eloise would have mentioned that sort of habit.

Suddenly nervous, she called after him. 'Maybe I'll give Max a shout and see if he's around to come and swell our combined IQ.'

'Cool.'

'Want me to call Eloise and see if she can join us later, too, or maybe you want to phone her?'

Jake smiled and shook his head. 'Promise me you're just going to be my landlord. I've already got one bossy older sister.'

Maggie was taken aback. Jake was an easy guy to be around and then in came a curve ball.

'You can call her if you like.'

As Jake walked off, Maggie busied herself with composing text messages to Max and Eloise and watched her handset until they had been sent. She still couldn't get over how clever the whole SMS thing was.

Two and a half pints of Guinness later, both Max and Eloise had failed to respond to their calls to arms and she and Jake had settled in as a double act. Maggie was enjoying herself more than she'd thought possible although, despite her choice of tipple, she was definitely not as much of a pure genius as she'd hoped. Jake on the other hand had surprised her. She was sure it was all a bit lucky.

The four black-taxi drivers on the next table had generally been putting them to shame until Jake had led them from oblivion to a respectable ninth on the scoreboard. They'd played their joker on the film round. Their pop trivia, thanks to the decade being the eighties tonight, had been pretty solid, edging them up to sixth. With three rounds remaining, they had everything to play for.

'Rrrrright…' The question master stopped rolling his *r*'s to clear this throat. He sounded like there'd been a time when he'd smoked round the clock. 'On to round eight if you please. "Where in the world? Any jokers this round?"

Jake leant over to her and whispered, 'Where in the world did they find this guy?'

It wasn't that funny but Maggie giggled anyway, determined that he was going to report to Eloise that he had enjoyed their evening.

Jake took it as encouragement. 'I mean really. I haven't seen a suit as nasty as that since the eighties.'

Maggie sniggered as Jake revealed a bitchy side she hadn't previously seen—and most definitely in his favour. 'And he's wearing a wedding ring so somebody loves him.'

'He probably bought it on eBay.' As they buried their giggles in their drinks, the rest of the room fell silent and they were chided with a stare from the man with the microphone as he prepared to read the first question in this round. His dyed-brown comb-over was strand perfect.

Jake whispered to Maggie, 'Over to you. Geography has never really been my thing.'

'I thought you'd travelled loads?'

'I was stoned for most of my year off...'

Hopefully it was a habit he'd grown out of. She didn't want little burn holes in her cushions or rugs.

'...and I'm crap at remembering names.'

'Right. First question. What is the second highest mountain in Africa?'

Jake nudged Maggie. 'Fancy another drink? One for the road?'

'One for my driving licence?' She shook her head. 'Better not.'

'Go on.'

'I've got the car.'

'You can't drive after two and a half pints and another half isn't going to make your cab journey home any more expensive.'

Somehow he had made having another drink sound sensible.

'I have to drive a client in the morning.'

'So just get a cab back first thing. Or you can crash in the spare room at mine/yours/whatever we're calling the flat.'

He was asking her to stay? 'That'd be too weird.'

'So call Scooter Man a bit later, but you can't leave me drinking all by myself mid-quiz.'

Thanks to her blood-alcohol levels, Maggie forgot she could negotiate instead of doing what she was told.

'Okay, last one then. Better make mine a gin and tonic. And a glass of water. And a packet of crisps.'

'Flavour?'

'I don't care as long as they absorb alcohol.'

Momentarily a team of one, Maggie was wrestling with her concentration.

'Right, question two—Where in the world was pavlova invented?'

Maggie chewed the end of the biro, having long forgotten that she'd found it at the bar and had no idea where else it had been. She felt a little bit sick.

Someone kissed the back of her neck. She froze. From where she was sitting she could still see all four cab drivers and Jake at the bar.

'Hello, gorgeous,' Max whispered in her ear and she warmed to his touch. Her knight had arrived to save her, and hopefully in a car. 'The answer is New Zealand. Or it could be Australia. They both like to claim it was theirs. I'd put Australasia to be safe.'

Excited, she turned to kiss him. 'Timing, my love, is everything. Second highest mountain in Africa?'

One of the cabbies on the next table gave her a filthy look and tutted.

Max kissed her temple and whispered in her ear. 'Mount Kenya.'

Maggie grinned. She'd bagged a good one.

'Hello, mate.' Jake put the drinks and crisps down and wiped his hands on the back of his jeans before the men shook hands. Maggie observed the formality of the ritual. It was so much easier to be a girl with the air kiss in your armoury.

Jake glanced at their answer sheet. 'Looks like you're doing fine without me. Max, can I get you a drink?'

'A pint of London Pride would be super, thank you.'

'No problem. Back in a mo.'

Maggie looked at Max. 'What are you doing?'

'Having a beer.' Max look confused. 'Are you nagging me?'

'Of course not.' Was she?

'I find myself in a pub and I'm assuming you're not going to leave until the final round now, are you?' Max squinted at the running totals on the blackboard. 'Not that you're in any danger of winning.'

'It's not about winning.'

'Since when?' Max kissed her again.

Maggie kissed him back and then refocused. 'We could yet make it to the top four, and as there are only two of us that would be a heroic effort.'

'Trouble is these quizzes are always packed with semi-professionals. It's like jumble sales.'

Maggie looked at the man she had elected to share a bed and a life with. 'What the hell do you know about jumble sales?'

'I have a long and chequered past.'

Maggie leant across suggestively. 'I like the sound of that. Maybe we should go soon?'

The question master wasn't leaving her any time to go anywhere. 'Pens ready. Next question. Where in the world would you drink JulBrew?'

Maggie yawned as she scribbled down 'The Gambia (Banjul), Africa,' without thinking.

Max was wide-eyed. 'If that's right, you're a genius.'

'From now on I suggest you address me as Professor Margaret Einstein-Hawking. I've ordered beer all over the world and it just so happens that I have actually been to The Gambia.' Maggie was dimly aware of the fact that she was slurring a little.

Max put his arm around her proudly and protectively. 'I'm assuming you'd like me to drive you home?'

'Perfect. And it just so happens that I won't take you out of your way.'

Max grinned.

Maggie rested her head on his shoulder and batted her eyelashes. 'And maybe I could have a lift back to my car again first thing tomorrow?'

Max looked at her with affection. 'Maybe…'

Maggie beamed. There were some excellent advantages to having a cohabiting partner.

Chapter Thirteen

Maggie could still taste the bacon sandwich she'd forced down first thing to try and clear her fuzzy head. Happily, Red was currently amusing himself by flicking through a summary of London areas in the Home brochure he'd found in the passenger door of Maggie's car and wasn't requiring her to come up with any small talk.

'Green Park sounds as if it was taken from a Mr Men storybook. It'd be like having a resort called Blue Sea, or Golden Sands or a viewpoint named Grey Skies.' Red paused. 'Thanks for fitting in with me and collecting me so early this morning.'

'No problem.' Thank goodness he hadn't witnessed the reality. After a mere six hours in bed, only four of which she'd been asleep for, Maggie had clung to her duvet as if her life depended on it. When her alarm rang Super Max had started the shower for her, made her coffee and breakfast and driven her back to her car. The sense of achievement she'd felt as they'd clambered to fourth place in the quiz before Max had poured her into his Porsche and taken her home for a victory romp was a distant memory.

'You're by far the most attractive driver I've had in the last few weeks.'

Pre make-up and blusher it had been a very different story. She shuddered at the recollection of their drunken high fives as they'd left. Jake had been as delighted at their achievement as she had. Beneath his laid-back exterior was a competitive man trying to get out.

Maggie smiled. 'Any time.' She yawned as covertly as she could. Unfortunately for her, Red was wide awake.

As they sped down the M4, Red lay back in Maggie's passenger seat, having reclined it to the almost horizontal dental-chair position. To Maggie's bemusement he was wearing sunglasses. Supposed to provide anonymity but actually drawing more attention in that celebrity look/don't-look/please-look fashion.

Maggie concentrated on the road and not on the fact that arguably one of the world's most desirable men of the moment was within arm's reach. She decreased the temperature on her side of the car and wondered why, amongst all the luxury extras, BMW hadn't thought to invent one that misted cool water on to your face, slapped you on the forehead or poked you in the back to keep you focused on the road. She was sure comfortable seats and cruise control were not safety features, despite the fact they had allegedly provided ten air bags to soften any blow.

Red looked out of the window as Maggie overtook an enormous removal van.

'I can't believe you've shacked up with a guy since the last time we met.'

'Just because you've been busy saving the world from nuclear attack.' Maggie alluded to the plot of the film he'd just completed. 'Not all of our lives can be so exciting.'

'Well, as long as he knows he's a lucky guy.'

Maggie hadn't meant to tell Red. It had just come out in the midst of conversation about something completely different. She'd sort of been showing off and, unfortunately for her, having lost interest in his own personal life after weeks of self-promotion and tabloid speculation, he had singled Maggie's out as today's specialist subject.

'Of course, at your age I was still playing the field.'

Maggie glanced across. The paternal thing wasn't working for her. He was only five or six years older, plus she didn't appreciate it when her clients got too personal. She didn't go round to their places and criticise their extortionately over-interior-designed taste in bathrooms, chandeliers or soft furnishings.

'Forgive me, but after you'd been married and divorced twice…'

Red shrugged. 'Hey, I was young, foolish and desirable.'

Maggie wondered whether he took himself seriously. 'Well, I'm in no hurry to try marriage or divorce.'

She turned off the motorway and joined a line of stationary traffic just outside Bath. She always forgot that rush hours happened outside London, too. The fields on either side of the road were still largely white with frost. A patchwork that glittered as the sun gained strength.

Red turned to face her. 'You might as well get hitched.

At least that way you'll get presents. And, if it all goes pear shaped, a cheque.'

'That's romantic.'

'That's life. Diamonds are for ever. Marriage is only for life if you're lucky, or don't live very long.' He laughed at his own joke.

'We're just taking things slowly for now.'

'You modern women are all the same, pretending that you don't want or need us around.'

Maggie shook her head. 'It's not that. We need to adjust. I'd been living on my own for a long time.'

'Well, don't think moving out of the cohabiting house is any easier without a wedding ring. If anything it's far more acrimonious. On one occasion I ended up in casualty. It's amazing how much a Dunlop Green Flash hurts when being hurled from two storeys up.' Pain long forgotten, Red smiled at the recollection.

'Fortunately, I can only imagine.'

'I'd been a very naughty boy…'

Red's expression was not one of repentance as Maggie wondered why all men affectionately referred to themselves as boys and were strangely proud of infidelity. It was an arrogance of desire. For some reason it didn't occur to them that women could just as easily be unfaithful and indeed had the advantage of being able to be discreet. A man's desire to share his conquest, the same instinct that leads them to purchase two-seater sports cars when they have three children.

True to his genetic make-up, Red couldn't resist furnishing Maggie with the details. '…with the girl in question's sister.'

'Red Connelly, that is nothing to be proud of. There's close to home and there's…'

'Crapping on your own doorstep. Don't worry, I learned my lesson.'

'Good.'

'No more sleeping with women who have sisters.'

Red laughed. Apparently he thought he was hilarious this morning.

'The journalists had their longed-for hook, headline and sinker. And the fans love any insight into your personal life. Ticket sales for my second film only benefitted from that messy break-up.'

Maggie was just reminding herself that she didn't have to like him to sell him a house when her phone rang. She'd meant to turn it off. Doing her best to ignore it, each ring cycle, louder than the last, ricocheted around the inside of the car, threatening to bring her hint of a headache to the foreground and her forehead.

Red interrupted after its second ear-splitting surround-sound polyphonic cry for attention. 'Hey, please don't leave it on my account.'

'I won't be a moment.' Maggie hit a button on the dash and suddenly the car was filled with her caller.

'Hello, darling.'

'Morning, Mum.' Maggie addressed the microphone. 'You're on hands-free.'

'Is that more expensive?'

'No, but it means other people are listening.'

'Where are you?'

'In the car.' Maggie didn't see why it mattered. She was at the end of the line. 'And I have a client with me.'

'Everything okay?'

'Fine.'

'There you go again.'

'Pardon?'

'You seemed quite off with us last night. You didn't even say goodbye. In fact, you've been quite terse since Christmas.'

A mere two and a half weeks ago. Maggie sighed. 'I've just been busy. Moving, working…'

'But everything is okay?'

'All great.'

'And Max?'

'Mum, now isn't the time.'

'Well, just to let you know, Daddy and I have talked and we do want you to help us with the house but not if you're going to delay us for months.' Maggie could always count on her mother to be direct.

'I'll try and call in over the weekend.'

'Great. You can both come for Sunday lunch.'

Maggie was sure that was supposed to be an invitation not an order.

'I'll have to check with—'

'Maybe you could start going through your stuff, too. I'm sure most of it can go the charity shop.'

'I didn't realise you were in such a hurry.'

'You know what that man's like once he's made a decision. He was so much more relaxing to have around before he retired. Or at least by the time he got home in those days he was too tired to boss me about.'

Maggie laughed. 'I'll call you later when I've had a chance to look at my diary.'

'We've got Nigel coming round later to give us his verdict on the valuation.'

Maggie felt her mood swing.

'It's just one valuation.'

Maggie felt the colour rise in her cheeks. 'I'll call you later. I've got to go.'

As she cut off the call, Maggie exhaled apologetically. 'Mothers. What can I say? For life. Not just for Christmas.'

'Now you know why I'm buying my folks a place just far enough away to avoid spontaneous drop-ins. I do want to look after them, but from a slight distance.' He grinned. 'Daddy and I…' he mimicked her mother perfectly as Maggie smiled through gritted teeth.

As Maggie turned on to a small country road, they left the trucks behind and together, in almost reverential silence, watched the great British countryside speed past. It wasn't so much a green and pleasant land in January, more of a grey and chilly one but still breathtakingly beautiful. As they caught momentary glimpses of winter vistas through breaks in stone walls and between hedgerows Maggie wondered why people moved abroad. There was more to life than sun and cheap beer.

Red drank in his surroundings. 'This certainly beats California.'

'Never thought about leaving your heart in San Francisco?'

'It'd get lost in the fog. I love being home.' He paused. 'It's crazy really, all this pressure to find the one. So much money changing hands when we really only borrow one for a few years at a time. I mean they're never really ours, are they?'

If he hadn't been such a good client, Maggie could have punched him for being such a misogynist.

'Humphrey Bogart and I have shared the same view over the Hollywood hills and we will both always remember it as ours.'

Maggie smiled. 'You're talking about houses?'

Red frowned. 'What else?'

Relieved, Maggie lightened up. 'P.S. I don't think Humphrey remembers much these days.'

'Sometimes I long for a return to the days when houses remained in families for generations, when a man's identity was intrinsically linked to his plot of land.'

'It was only a good system if you had a family pile in the country.'

'Just think though, no stamp duty, no real estate agents— not that there are pretend estate agents, you know what I mean. And the more peripatetic I am, the more I long for a base.'

Maggie nodded. 'We all need somewhere we belong. Somewhere we're supposed to be, or would rather be. We crave roots, permanence.'

'Which is why I guess, for so many species, homing is an instinct.'

Maggie was impressed. She wondered how she could build that line into their literature.

'What do you think is one of the first things that every child draws at school?' She knew the answer. Home had commissioned the report.

Red thought back as far as he could and Maggie wondered how, in light of their conversation, he hadn't seen the answer a mile off. 'A dog? A boat? A dinosaur?'

Maggie laughed. 'Okay, so while most four-year-old boys

would give the majority of palaeontologists a run for their money, I could barely draw any of those now.'

Red held his hand out in self-defence. 'Hang on, you didn't say the drawings had to be recognisable to a third party. I have several scribbled abstracts pinned to my kitchen notice board. Works which my niece and nephews claim are everything from bonfires to dragons but to everyone except their parents, they are just a mess.'

Red had a flash of inspiration as he recalled the easels of his childhood.

'I've got it. A yellow ball of sun, blue sky suspended over a white paper midriff with a stripe of green grass below and a smattering of V-shaped birds.'

Maggie laughed. 'Much better.'

'But wrong?'

'I'm afraid so.'

Red thought back to his colouring books, to licking his lips raw as he tried as hard to keep his creativity within the thick black lines and his coloured pencils in spectrum order.

Maggie stole the pause. 'A house. A generic square-ish box with two or four windows, a door at its centre and a triangular roof, sometimes even a chimney. It's amazing, even the children imprisoned in concentration camps during the Second World War drew houses that way. It's something we've seen in a hundred storybooks. People don't live happily ever after in a forest or a cupboard. We all like to have a place we call home.'

'Or in my case three or four.' Red smiled. 'Good news for people like you.'

'And yet people claim to hate estate agents. I just don't get it.'

'I don't get lots of things….'

'Like what?'

'The *Matrix* movies, the attraction of Kate Moss, peanut butter, Little Britain…'

Maggie's mobile started ringing and this time she reached to silence it. 'Sorry.'

Red dismissed her apology. 'Go ahead. Although in terms of entertainment value I have to warn you that I'm not sure you're going to be able to beat your mother.'

Mentally Maggie crossed her fingers.

'Hello?'

'Hi, is that Maggie Hunter?'

'Speaking.'

'This is Dominic Drake and you're live on City FM.'

Maggie wished the Sat Nav had a time-travel option. If she could just rewind two minutes and switch her phone off or at least hold it up against her ear. But now negotiating high-walled roads just wide enough for two cars, she had no hands free.

'Jesus, Simon, this is no time to muck about. I'm with a client.'

'Huh-huh-huh. No this is really Dominic and you're live on *Date or Dare* this morning. Someone who wants to ask you out has got in touch with me.'

A shiver ran the length of her as Maggie concentrated on not clipping a stone wall. So far her morning had been stranger than fiction. And if she was going to roll the car, who better to have in the passenger seat than a man who had saved the world several times on the big screen.

'This really isn't a good time.' Maggie did her best to

sound friendly as opposed to hacked off. And if this guy was who he said he was, she assumed there were a few other people listening in.

Red moved his seat into the more upright position and leant forward to the nearest speaker. He clearly had no complaints at the latest in-car client entertainment system.

'So, Maggie.' Dominic was taking his time. 'Did you know you had a secret admirer?'

'No.' Maybe she could just hang up and pretend she had entered an area with no signal. 'Can we do this another time?'

'Let me tell you that you can either accept dinner, on us, or we can tell him no thanks and he has to take a dare.'

'I dare you to hang up now. If you don't, I will.'

'If I was to let you know the man in question is a work colleague, what would you say?'

'I'd say he should know I'm seeing someone.' Seeing someone. Living with someone. Maggie didn't know why she being so cagey. 'I've really got to get going.'

The DJ squealed. 'Now I can see why you're hesitating. So any idea who might have had an enormous crush on you for the last couple of years?'

Every way you looked at this, it was awkward. It was impossible to lose yourself in an office of twenty people. She wondered who she knew that listened to City FM.

'Any idea at all?'

Surely Lucan wouldn't have been bold enough to call a radio station? 'I'm not going to embarrass him on national radio.'

'Hey, he called us. I think he's embarrassed himself already. You'd be talking about…?'

Red nodded for her to continue. Maggie sighed. Better over and done with. 'Lucan.'

'Well now—' there was a pause of surprise '—it's not him. Any idea who else it could be?'

Maggie paused, wondering how she had let his conversation even get started. 'I'm sorry, but…'

'Does the name Simon Senior ring any bells?'

Maggie realised she was speeding up and concentrated on driving slowly enough not to lose control.

'This is some sort of joke, isn't it?'

'Um, hello Maggie.'

It was him, Simon, on the air, in the air in her car. Red was wide-eyed, almost rubbing his hands with glee. Maggie wondered if she had an ejector seat.

'You idiot, Simon.'

'I think that might be a no.' Dominic was relishing every second.

'I wanted to ask you before, but it's never the right time.'

'Let me assure you that this is not the perfect moment either.'

'Well, before it all gets too serious with that Max geezer, I thought—'

'You know where I am right now, don't you?'

'With a client.' From his mocking tone, it was clear Simon didn't believe her. 'I know you're in later, but I figured this might be easier if we were in separate buildings.'

'I think it would be optimal if we were in separate hemispheres. Sadly, I'm only in Somerset. And—' Maggie shook her head '—on the hands-free.'

'In Somerset?' There was a moment of silence as the

penny dropped and then rolled into a dark corner. 'Oh shit. You really are…' His voice quietened. 'Is he…'

'Right here. '

'So how about that date?' Dominic was back.

'No thanks.'

Simon was back on the line. 'Well, now I'm here and probably unemployed, can I just say give me a chance. You might be surprised.'

'You've got to hand it to Simon, Maggie, he's not giving in.'

'Look, Donald.'

'Dominic.' His irritation was perceptible.

'I have recently moved in with my boyfriend. It's a no.'

'No hope of a date at all?' This time, Dominic's question was met by the dial tone.

Maggie switched her phone off, resisting the overwhelming urge to throw it into a hedge and herself at the mercy of the airbags.

Two viewed properties later and lunch in a Gastro Pub that was so remote that Red didn't get any hassle except from a septuagenarian who was in search of change for the cigarette machine, Maggie was feeling much more herself. Red was having a final wander round the outbuildings at the last property they were due to see while Maggie waited by the car and finally dared to turn her phone back on.

'OHHH MYYYYY GODDDDDD.'

Maggie held the phone as far away from her ear as her arm permitted.

'That was HILLLLLARIOUS. Call me NOW.'

Damn. Eloise clearly had been listening.

Beep.

'Hi, it's me. Do you fancy the theatre this evening? I have two great seats for *Hay Fever*.' A police siren drowned Max out for a second. As usual he was using a moment in transit to make contact. 'Sorry about the noise. And the late notice. You won't believe what my morning has been like…'

His morning? But what Maggie really fancied was a night on the sofa not talking, not eating, not drinking, not applauding, not thinking, just being.

She dialled his number and he answered right away.

'Hey Mags. How's it going down there?'

'Good thanks. Listen, I've got to be quick. I've only just picked up your message and I'm not sure I'll be back in London in time for the theatre.'

'But it's only just gone three o'clock now.'

Maggie felt herself bristle.

'I'm not done yet. And by the time I do get back I'm really not going to feel like going out.'

'I've been given great seats. We can have a night in any night.'

Maggie paused for a split second, then stood firm. 'Seriously, I'm exhausted. It's been quite a week.'

'So…' Was he supposed to offer to cook her dinner or something? Max wasn't sure.

'Look, why don't you go anyway? Sounds like you're quite keen and I'll just see you when you get home.'

'You're suggesting I go on our date alone?'

'Of course not. Why not take Emmy or Ed? You're always complaining that you don't get to see enough of them.'

'They're away.'

Maggie tensed as she felt her quiet evening slipping from

her grasp. 'Hey, I know, give Eloise a call. She loves Noël Coward. Tell her she'd be doing me a favour.'

'Why don't you call her?'

Maggie saw Red out of the corner of her eye. 'I can't right now. I won't be free for a few hours yet, but I'm sure she'd love to go with you if she's free.'

'Well, it would be a shame to waste the tickets.'

Maggie loved the fact that despite his financial success and generous as he was, Max hated wasting money.

'How can I be sure you won't change your mind as soon as you hang up?'

'No chance. No offence.'

'Only a small amount taken.' Max tried to mask his nascent irritation.

'Honestly, I wouldn't be good company. Better I sleep on the sofa than in the stalls.'

Red was crunching his way across the gravel towards her humming the theme tune to *Mission Impossible*. Maggie hoped it wasn't a message about the property. 'Got to go. Lots of love.'

'See you later.' And he was gone.

Red was inspecting a pond in the centre of the circular drive, which he'd insisted on referring to as a roundabout, as Maggie wandered back over.

'So what are you thinking?'

Red frowned. 'Yes. And no. I think my folks will think they've died and gone to a stately home. And they really don't need a cinema on site. I bought them a DVD player a couple of years ago and, to be honest, they hardly use that.'

'So, too big?'

'Well, *I* don't think so.'

'But they will?'

Red nodded. 'I suspect so. They've spent most of their life in a terraced house.'

Maggie didn't like to mention that he'd asked her to find them a six-bedroom property.

'Plus they like a little more community. Neighbours to bore to death, you know the stuff. I think they could get seriously agoraphobic out here.'

Maggie reminded herself the customer was always right.

'I know that wasn't the brief I gave you but, thinking about it, I may have to change my mind a bit.'

'Fine.' Maggie did her best not to feel as if she had wasted her whole day.

'We need to find more of a family home. Lived in. Less manicured. If you know what I mean.'

Maggie nodded politely and then less politely and more enthusiastically. It could be perfect. 'If you don't mind a mini-detour on the way home and you're not in a tearing hurry, there is one other place I could show you. It's not on the market yet, needs a bit of love, a new kitchen and bathrooms, but it comes with nearly ten acres, most of it a paddock, the rest of it a sprawling mature garden and it's a great home.'

Red looked impressed. 'Sounds good.'

'The only setback is that it's a bit nearer town. The London side of Oxford and probably a good hour and a half by car from your place. Would that be a problem?'

'Shouldn't be.' Red smiled. 'And I can't wait to meet your mother.'

Maggie gave him a look.

'Hey, she sounds like a blast.'

★ ★ ★

'Is everything okay?' Eloise's tone was edged with concern. Max had never called her directly on her mobile before.

'Everything's good.'

'Did you catch Maggie on the radio this morning?'

'On the radio? She didn't say anything about—'

'She wouldn't have. It was all pretty spontaneous.' Eloise giggled. 'I just happened to be listening.'

'I've been in meetings all day. Anyway I was just wondering if you might be free to join me at the theatre this evening?'

'Tonight?' It sounded like he meant just the two of them.

'I know you probably already have plans and it's a bit of shot in the dark but...'

Eloise felt a little awkward. She really didn't know Max that well.

'It was Maggie's idea. She's going to be back late and I have two tickets to the new production of *Hay Fever* at the Savoy Theatre.'

Eloise brightened. 'I love Noël Coward.'

Max smiled. 'So?'

'Are you sure you wouldn't rather take someone else?'

Max was confused. 'Is that a yes?'

'I guess you have yourself a date. I mean not a date but a partner...or at least a theatre buddy.' Eloise gave up.

'Splendid. See you at the theatre at seven then.'

And he was gone.

Maggie pulled into her parents' drive which, to her relief, was totally empty.

As Red admired the wisteria around the porch and the

herringbone brickwork on the path, proudly Maggie sensed they were off to a good start.

'When was this place built?'

'Late eighteen hundreds.'

'How many bedrooms?'

'Four. Actually five if you include the nursery/study-sized room, two bathrooms plus a downstairs cloakroom and a cellar. All set in around ten acres.'

Red nodded to the roofs he could see to his left, 'The all-important neighbours. What are they like?'

Maggie tried to remember. 'One's a family with three children, I think, and the other was an old lady. I'd have to check with mu….the owners. Let's go in.'

Maggie was fiddling with her key in the lock when the door opened. Startled, she jumped.

'Well, well, this is a lovely surprise.' Carol looked from Maggie to Red and back again.

'I didn't think you were in.'

'You'd know if you'd phoned.'

'I did.' Maggie wished her mother would treat her like a professional rather than a teenager.

'Oh, I must have been in the garden.'

'Where are the cars?'

'Mine's being serviced. Daddy is out playing golf.'

As Red smirked at the 'D' word, he gained Carol's full attention.

'So, who's this?'

'Mum, this is Red Connelly. Red, this is Carol Hunter.' Maggie eyeballed her mother, silently imploring her to behave. 'Red is a client of mine.'

'Right.'

To Maggie's delight, from Carol's reaction it was clear she had no idea who Red was. She proffered a hand. 'Pleased to meet you.'

'And you, Mrs Hunter.'

'We've been round several properties today, but none have been quite right, and it suddenly occurred to me that this place might be of interest.'

'Shall I give him the tour?' Carol smiled and, opening the door fully, ushered them in. Maggie scanned the hall. To her amazement, it didn't look too messy.

Maggie was making tea in the kitchen and desperately trying to find a packet of biscuits that hadn't passed their sell-by date. She could hear her mother doing a fantastic sales job. Moments later she arrived in the kitchen without Red. Maggie raised an eyebrow.

'Gone to the loo and then going to walk around the paddock. He said he'd rather go alone. I think he likes it here.' Carol crossed her fingers. 'However, I do have a few concerns.'

'Go on.'

'Most pressingly, how on earth can he afford to buy this place? We've been led to believe, well, Nigel said that...'

Maggie reduced her voice to an almost whisper. 'No need for concern, he's a regular client of ours.'

'Do you think his money comes from a legitimate source? I'd hate to sell this place to anyone untoward. I mean we have the rest of the village to think about. Next door have young children. And he keeps mentioning his parents. I think he's buying the place for them. Do you think maybe it could be a gangland thing? I mean he's a bit old to be a mummy's boy.'

Maggie rolled her eyes. 'Do you know what, it's good you're moving back to London before you lose your grip on popular culture altogether.'

A car door slammed in the drive. Maggie shook her head imperceptibly. Fantastic. A full house. She heard the front door open.

'Is my little girl here?'

Maggie could only hope Red was at the far end of the paddock. 'In the kitchen, Dad.'

Ruddy cheeked, he kissed her hello. He'd clearly had a whisky at the nineteenth hole.

'Good round?'

'Not bad at all.'

'Have you been taking fashion tips from Rupert the Bear?'

David looked down. 'Do you mind, these are my best golf trousers. So to what do we owe the pleasure? I trust you haven't just popped in for a cuppa.'

Maggie shook her head. 'Prospective purchaser. Currently inspecting the paddock.'

'Well darling, that was quick work.'

'Never underestimate a Hunter.' Maggie repeated one of her father's stock phrases back at him and watched him bristle with delight.

'Keen?'

'Mum took him round.'

'Carol?'

'He just seems awfully young to be considering a property of this size.'

'Mum, I've told you not to worry.'

Carol wasn't listening. 'And what sort of a name is Red anyway?'

David's recently pilfered biscuit was held up en route to his mouth. 'Did you say Red? As in Red Connelly?'

David looked to Maggie, who nodded, impressed at her father's knowledge. 'Carol, he's huge.'

'I'd say he was five feet ten inches, nothing special.'

'No, you silly woman, he's an actor. You know, like Tom Cruise. They're talking about him being the next James Bond.'

Carol looked at her daughter 'Why on earth didn't you say something?'

'I haven't had a chance. Why does it matter anyway?'

'Well.' Carol stirred her tea vigorously. 'I might have told him a higher price.'

Maggie felt steam rising to her ears. 'You talked figures?'

'Very vaguely. I did say you were in charge though, that you always were.'

'That's terrific.'

'I wouldn't be so touchy. Clearly money's no object. And we all know the market is all over the place and that there aren't enough big houses to go round.'

'Please Mum, not another word on specifics from you until after we've gone. Dad, you have to help me on this.'

David shrugged. 'What makes you think she's going to start listening to me now?'

Chapter Fourteen

Max looked up from the hob where he was doing something clever with gravy, redcurrant jelly and a bottle of French red to go with the Sunday roast. From Maggie's demeanour, it appeared she had finally forgiven him for bringing Jamie and a couple of the boys over to watch the football yesterday afternoon. They'd ended up staying all evening and they'd ordered a pizza, but how was he supposed to know she'd been planning to cook him a romantic supper?

'So Maggie, received any calls this morning from radio stations harbouring secret admirers?' Eloise started giggling from the midst of *The Sunday Times*.

Maggie waved her mixing spoon. 'Hey Little Miss Schadenfreude, that's enough.'

'Sorry.' Eloise wiped a tear from her eye. 'Honestly Mags, it could only happen to you.'

Maggie frowned in to her sticky toffee pudding mix. 'What's so strange about wanting to go out with me?'

'Nothing darling. It's perfectly natural.' As Max winked at her, Maggie wondered when she'd been elevated to darling and whether it was less personal or more personal than using her name, or merely a tactic to soften her up. She was still smarting from getting back to a house full of takeaway boxes and beer-swilling men after work yesterday. It was his house too. In fact, it was his house, period. But she didn't like surprises, especially when they included brothers of ex-boyfriends. But today was a new day. Next time she'd call *before* she bought lobster. And then she'd been supposed to get excited about going to pub with them? She'd failed miserably. And Max said he didn't mind. *He* didn't mind.

Eloise shook her head. 'You were hilarious.'

'I wasn't trying to be funny.'

Eloise nodded. 'I think that's why. Jake said you're a natural.'

'He heard it too?'

She held her hands up. 'Okay, I confess I called him and told him to find it online.'

Eloise was slightly apologetic. 'I just needed someone to corroborate the facts. I couldn't quite believe what I was hearing. Apparently Jake was a bit hungover following a spontaneous night out at the pub with his landlady?'

Maggie felt herself blush. 'We were only going for one quick drink.'

'One of the lines used most often after eleven p.m. in the UK, I would imagine.'

'I did text you to come and help us.'

'So, how was the evening?' Eloise was fishing for Maggie's boyfriend report.

Apparently just catching up with the conversation, Max shook his head. 'I didn't realise I could get City FM on the Internet.'

Maggie feigned nonchalance. 'It's no big deal. You're much more of a Radio 4 listener.'

Max smiled. 'So has Simon handed in his notice yet?'

'Hey, give the guy a break.'

Max raised an eyebrow quizzically. 'I thought you'd been trying to get rid of him for years.' He whisked the gravy harder. 'Did he really think you'd say yes?'

'First of all he didn't think. Second of all, he had convinced himself I'd been harbouring feelings for him for years. Then you came along and, well, I guess he thought it was a case of now or never.'

'Never.' Max felt the need to emphasise his view.

'The strangest thing of all is that now I actually feel quite protective of him.'

Eloise grinned. 'Oh my God, it's worked.'

Maggie shook her head. 'I mean almost maternally, or maybe that should be sisterly?' She shrugged as she spooned the pudding mixture into a baking dish she'd greased earlier.

'It's official, Max, she's lost it.' Eloise made big 'whatever next' eyes at him.

Max shook his head. 'Men get such a bad press for chasing skirt and yet it's amazing how women behave when they know someone likes them.'

'Can I remind you that we're not talking about Simon Le Bon but Simon "I've shagged women in many of the properties I've sold" Senior.'

'No.' Eloise was shocked. 'That's gross.'

'And undoubtedly a lie. One of many claims he made at one of the Christmas parties after several tequilas. And anyway he hasn't sold many.' Maggie paused. 'I'm still not sure what is more embarrassing, that he called and asked, that he got a DJ to do his dirty work or the fact I had Red Connelly sitting next to me.'

'Hey, it's one hell of a dinner party story for the future. And what's happening with your mum and dad's place?'

Max interrupted. 'Red's going to take it for his folks.'

Maggie glared at him. 'Why not take an ad in *The Sunday Times.*'

Eloise squealed. 'You're joking?'

Maggie shook her head. 'And no thanks to them.'

'What do you mean?'

'You know, Mum being worried he'd made his fortune from trafficking drugs, that sort of thing.'

'Oh God, she didn't say…'

'It was close. Anyway despite them, he's still interested. And he's prepared to pay over the odds because of all the land.'

'Your parents must be over the moon.'

'Put it this way, I don't think I'll be getting so much stick for not returning all their calls instantly for a while.'

'Congratulations. Maggie Hunter, you're officially on a roll.'

'You know this is two hundred percent confidential.'

'Of course.'

'You mustn't mention it to anyone outside this room, that's a-n-y-o-n-e, not until everything has gone through and the Connellys are all settled in.'

'Aren't you just gutted that you won't have a room there any more? Imagine brushing your teeth next to that chest every morning and evening.'

Max looked up from the stove. 'Thanks Eloise.'

'Hey, every woman has to have her fantasies.'

Max paused as he pretended to be recalling an official document. *'Rule 55b)i) All members of fantasy league have to be unknown to the compiler and therefore fulfil fantasy criteria.* You should have read the small print.'

Maggie pouted.

'Did I mention I'm having lunch with Elle McPherson next week?'

'Just for the record I've never fancied Red.'

'I have.' Eloise licked her lips.

'When you know Red is short for Redmond, it's easier. Anyway he's in a hurry to complete, so now I need to find my parents somewhere, and fast, before he changes his mind.'

'They can always stay here in the interim.' Max's offer was instant and Maggie loved him for it. 'We have loads of room.'

Maggie noticed his easy use of 'we.' She was still perfecting hers. 'You don't want to go around making offers like that.'

'I like your parents.'

'I love them, but I don't want them living with us. We rarely have time together alone plus, they may never leave.'

Maggie cupped his bottom affectionately as she walked past him on her way to the sink. When he was arrogant he was very annoying, but when he was good he was gorgeous. 'Anyway in a worst-case scenario they can always have my flat.'

Eloise paled. 'But Jake's only just settled in.'

'You've got a spare room. Or, you could even share a bed.'

'Oh God, I meant to tell you.' Eloise sounded like she was about to be the bearer of some very bad news.

'What?' All culinary processes ceased as Max and Maggie gave her their complete attention.

'Did I mention that Rob and Helena are pregnant?'

Maggie rolled her eyes. 'Good luck to her. He was never right for you. Imagine how unhappy you'd have been.'

'But he said he never wanted to live with anyone and that he never wanted children.'

'Maybe he still doesn't. Maybe it was her idea. Maybe he meant that he didn't with you, or maybe he does now.'

'I didn't think men ever changed.' Eloise returned to the paper. Silence reigned.

Trying not to think of Max as a life sentence, on the back of that last comment, Maggie busied herself with tasting Max's gravy. When Maggie next looked over, Eloise was frowning.

'Bad news?'

Eloise closed the supplement and folded it firmly. She got up. 'Can I do anything to help?'

Maggie handed her a fistful of cutlery. 'Will it ever be a good news day? What is it this week? War, famine, global warming?'

'Just another one of those stupid surveys.' Eloise paused. The article had been buried deep in the business supplement. Maggie would never have found it. Then again Max might have, or someone would have mentioned it at work and, Cub Scout or not, surely it was always best to be prepared.

At Eloise's attempt to fob her off, Maggie's interest was piqued. 'What is it this time? Cohabiting reduces your life expectancy?'

Eloise laughed. 'Not if you're a man, I've definitely seen statistics on that. No, it's just one of those silly career things. You know.'

Maggie helped herself to the supplement, eyes skimming the pages until she found a germane headline. She started to read aloud.

'*"According to the latest survey, estate agents are reviled only a fraction less than traffic wardens. Indeed they are the third most hated profession in Britain."*' She looked up. 'Good job I'm a property finder then.'

Eloise and Max looked at each other as Maggie found herself in a no-eye zone.

Maggie balled the page and slam-dunked it ceremoniously into the recycling bin to a smattering of applause from Max.

'Where are debt collectors, telesales reps, call centre workers and politicians? Where are fake celebrities with workout videos? Where's Ken Livingstone? Where are Blair & Brown? How can I be the third most hated person in the UK?'

Eloise said, 'Um, sorry to rain on your dramatic parade but you are merely one member of the third most hated profession.'

Distracted, Maggie washed her hands for the second time in five minutes before carrying plates laden with roast beef and all the trimmings over to the table. She and Max had created a feast.

'You only have to look at the number of property sections, at the sheer number of column inches devoted to homes in papers and magazines, at the money people spend on interior design. It's the most expensive purchase they'll ever make. People need us.'

'And yet the general perception remains that estate agents play people off against each other, take ages doing everything and get paid a percentage of the value of the property whether they are any good or not.' Eloise stopped herself way too late. 'Not you. Of course.'

Maggie was silent. Her appetite had just exited, stage left.

'And they probably only interviewed ten people. Guys, this looks delicious.'

Max shouted over from the hob. 'Please start.'

Eloise was only too happy to follow instructions.

Maggie's cutlery remained on the table. 'How can we live in a conspicuously consumer society and yet people purport to hate brokers and salesmen?'

Max answered her rhetorical question with another while Eloise made sure she had her mouth full.

'How can it be that you have actually got upset about this? If I took everything to heart that I know people are saying about me…' He joined them at the table and tucked straight in.

'Er, not sure I have any sympathy for the person who was voted the one to watch by *City Magazine* last year.'

'Not to mention the thirty-fifth most eligible man by *Miss Mag*.' Eloise seized an opportunity to lighten the tone.

'Exactly. Thirty-fifth.' Max pretended to look upset. 'I mean you don't know what that does to a man's ego. Delicious carrots, Mags.'

Maggie's smile was tight. Her food remained untouched. 'Maybe you've moved up a few notches this year?'

'Hey, I'm off the market now.'

'How do they know that? Do you have to call someone?'

Max shrugged. 'Well, Jodie knows so I guess it...'

'Jodie?' It was a name that Maggie hadn't heard before.

'We had a few drinks a while back when she was research-ing the list. I think she was angling to get me off the list and into her bed.'

Maggie wondered if she was still hoping.

'Changing the subject...'

'Coward.' Maggie's jibe was playful.

'Surely you mean love of your life?'

Maggie blushed, rendered speechless by his audacity but happy not to contradict him provided she didn't have to say the L word out loud, especially in front of Eloise. 'Ah yes,' she stuttered. 'Yes, that must be it.'

'I still think you should set up a property search business on your own. Don't you think, Eloise?'

Maggie rotated her fork in her hand as if it were a deadly weapon. 'After that survey I'm seriously considering becoming a vet or a nursery nurse.'

Eloise butted in. 'Imagine though, your own business.'

Max nodded. 'And I could help in the short term—fi-nancially I mean, just until you're all set. I'm sure it won't take long before you'll be able to keep me in the style to which I have become accustomed.' He smiled.

Maggie shook her head emphatically, terrified by the prospect of surrendering her salary.

'Just hear me out. You're so stubborn sometimes.'

'Am not.'

'Are.' Eloise buttoned her lip too late. Maggie glared at her.

She loaded her fork. 'I like the way things are. I'm just a simple girl...'

'No such thing. Well, not in my experience.'

Maggie ignored him. '…I have a pension, medical insurance, paid holidays, a car, plus, I get good bonuses. They look after me pretty well.'

'Damn right they do. Your client list is starting to read like the contents page of *Vanity Fair*. People want *you* to find them a new home, a country retreat, a place in the sun. I think you'd be awesome on your own.'

'I was awesome on my own and then you came along.' Maggie felt much more comfortable keeping things light. She put a forkful of beef in her mouth and started chewing, slowly.

Frustrated at her intransigence, Max shrugged. 'Just imagine the commission you make being all yours.'

Maggie knew it was daft, but she'd never quite got her head around the idea of being a truly top earner. It's not like she was saving lives or anything and she had more than enough to live on. Plus she liked having an office to go to between clients. It got her up and out of the flat early, and Knightsbridge was a good base.

She swallowed. 'Don't forget, I get free stationery, coffees, international phone calls…plus I can just go for a run in Hyde Park at lunchtime.'

Max sat back in his chair. 'You could if you ever took your trainers to work. You're not even in the office that much these days.'

Maggie smiled in good-natured defeat as she savoured the taste of a roast potato. She couldn't imagine a world without potatoes, butter or meat. If she had a farm—unlikely as she hated getting mud under her fingernails or getting up in the dark—she would just have cows, a vegetable patch filled with spuds and a field of wheat. That way she'd always have all the raw materials she needed for a cheeseburger and fries.

The seeds of change hopefully sown, Max decided to move the conversation on. 'So, what's happening with you, Eloise?'

'Steady on, Dad.' Eloise faked indignation.

'I'm serious. Worked out how to make your first million yet?'

'Is self-worth based on salary, I don't think so.'

Max raised his glass in mock toast before taking a large sip. 'Well, that's telling me.'

'I do have a few ideas.'

Max was all ears. As was Maggie. 'Like?'

Eloise shrugged, not ready for the spotlight.

'Go on.'

'Well, there's the years-old radio plan and there's one idea I'd like to get off the ground, but it's not a business, more of a charity initiative. I know how lucky I am that I'm never going to be on the breadline, so I've been thinking that I should make the most of that and define my success in other ways.' Eloise picked up her glass.

'You can't leave me hanging now.' Max's eyes flashed with concentration at the whiff of an opportunity.

Eloise shrugged. 'It's still at the raw idea stage.'

'All you need is a good concept.' Max had the gift to bestow confidence and encouragement on the smallest plans.

'It's basically about everyone giving something back, not financially but putting aside a day a year or even a week a year or maybe even an afternoon a month to do some good, whether it's helping in a school, building a park, setting up a library for patients in a hospital or even visiting elderly neighbours and taking them for an afternoon out. That's probably sounding really trite, isn't it?'

Max had started scribbling on the edge of one of the papers. 'Go on.'

'Well, obviously companies will need to lead the initiative and need to give employees time off. But it's really just to encourage people to look outward into their communities instead of just inward into their homes and their bank accounts, to give something back to our locality, however small, a little of ourselves, to take pride and take care.'

'Sort of *Give A Little, Live A Little*.' Max wanted to check he was on the right lines. He underlined the words on the paper.

Eloise nodded. 'Perfect choice of words.'

'You are talking to the man who conceived of Feeling Fruity.' Maggie couldn't have been prouder. Her two favourite people on the same wavelength. Eloise had barely tolerated Adam. And Maggie was impressed. She'd had a conscience once. She'd run for charity, fasted for charity, cycled for charity, given clothes that didn't fit her to charity—but if she was honest, none of it had been selfless. Maybe Eloise was a nicer human being than she was. Then again maybe she could afford to be.

Max was nodding. 'I think it's a great idea.'

'You do?' A part of Eloise was delighted.

'It could almost be an umbrella initiative to link up with other charities and schemes that need help.'

'As long as they're diverse enough.' Eloise was emphatic. 'I think it is imperative that people become involved in something they care about and, wherever possible, in their neighbourhood.'

'And what about tax breaks?'

Eloise grimaced. 'For who? You see, that's the bit I have no clue about.'

'Do you see it raising money?'

'I don't know, only if the money reaches the right people. I see it more about raising communities from the dead but at a grass roots, practical level, not a load of politicians going to a golf course in Scotland to talk endlessly about where to have their next meeting and whether the smoked salmon is organic or not.'

Max nodded. 'I love it. I think it could be huge.' He beamed at her.

'Really?'

'There definitely seems to be a nascent backlash to the "me me me" mentality. We're starting to realise that if we just take and give nothing back we are only short-changing ourselves and the environment but individually no one really knows where to start. This could really capture the zeitgeist.'

Maggie was now tiring of the mutual adoration society and had almost finished her lunch. 'Arise St Eloise of Fulham.'

No one laughed. Instead Max was on his feet and pacing the length of the table, wine glass in hand. 'Seriously, if you get some hard hitters on board…charity initiatives are great for corporate image and if it captures the public imagination…'

'Would anyone like any more?' Maggie waved a serving spoon.

'Sorry, Mags, give us a second. Eloise, are you free for lunch one day next week?'

Eloise pretended to think. 'Let's see—Monday, Tuesday, Wednesday, any day really.'

'Maybe we could meet up and go through the concept properly.'

Maggie gave Max a sidelong glance. 'Who do you think you are Donald Trump, Alan Sugar with your fawning apprentice?'

Eloise interrupted, 'It'd be great to have your input. I love your title. I can see the T-shirts now, the bracelets, the posters…Give A Little, Live A Little.'

Maggie nodded. 'The title is good.'

As he started to really enjoy his lunch, Max brought his mental focus back to Sunday afternoon.

'So, before he arrives, let's get down to the nitty-gritty. How are things with Jake?'

Maggie was starting to wonder who the bigger gossip was in their relationship but saluted Max for having the balls to ask a direct question.

'Good…'

Maggie looked at her best friend, reminding her of their last phone conversation on the subject.

'Okay to good with occasional flashes of excellence and definite patches of mundanity. But it has been much better since he moved in on his own.'

Maggie tried not to think of Eloise having more sex in that flat than she'd ever managed.

Faced with a captive audience, Eloise's relationship floodgates opened. 'But I still find it all frustratingly part-time. I understand that he needs headspace for his creative stuff, but what if his big break never happens and he's kept his life on hold in case it does? It's not that I don't think he's talented. But he should be putting stuff on MySpace, using the Internet, you know.'

Max shrugged. 'Sounds like you'd be better off focusing on your career and not his.'

Maggie held her breath. Eloise wasn't going to like that at all.

Eloise sighed. 'I know you're right, but it's easier said than done. Anyway you can continue to assess him for yourselves later. He'll be here for coffee any minute.' She piled up her last forkful and chewed faster.

'Hey, all the best chefs overrun. It's part of our creativity.'

Max winked at Maggie. Only they needed to know that the delay was due to some Naked Chef activity.

'I wouldn't risk Jake's fate in my hands. I'm hardly a professional judge of character.' Max addressed Eloise.

'You seem to have picked yourself a top lady.'

Maggie beamed. That's what friends were for.

'I have indeed. As to Jake, well, just as long as you're happy—'

Eloise interrupted. 'Don't get me wrong—I'm loving having him around.'

'You love the guy or you love having a guy?'

Maggie waited for the explosion. Once again Eloise took his criticism on the chin. Max had apparently charmed his way through Eloise's defences.

'I'm just sorry he couldn't join us for lunch.' Max smiled. 'I could have done with another man around the house.'

Eloise brought her feet up and rested them on the edge of the next chair, hugging her knees to her chest. 'So, do you both think I'm mad?'

'Of course not.' Maggie's knee-jerk response was based on one hundred percent loyalty.

'In what respect?' Max was definitely a details man or just a man, apparently yet to learn that when a woman asked if she was mad, the answer was always no.

'You know, to be pissing around with Jake.'

The immediate silence was filled with sipping of wine as answers were carefully formulated.

'I mean I'd say we're pretty happy bumbling along, but I do want children.'

Maggie busied herself with clearing the table. She and Max had avoided the 'babies' conversation thus far and, still feeling like a child herself, this definitely wasn't the moment.

Max was unphased. 'Have you talked to Jake about kids?'

'Aside from discussing why snot is green and how parents manage to drive with serious sleep deprivation?' Eloise shook her head. 'Not really.'

'Afraid you know what he'll say?'

Eloise shrugged.

Max made sure he had her attention. 'You can't know what he thinks. We don't all regard having children as the end of life as we know it.'

'But it is.' Maggie laughed. She was the only one. She faded her laugh into a cough.

Max folded his hands. Eloise suddenly felt like she was at an appraisal. And she was confident that a review of her love life was not something she was ready for.

Eloise almost sighed. 'Trouble is, forward planning isn't his forte. I can barely talk to him about next month. What, if pushed, he decides I'm not worth the effort?'

'Surely it'd be better to find out sooner rather than later?'

'Hang on.' Maggie couldn't help but intervene. 'Life

doesn't come all mapped out. You have to trust your instincts. Sometimes they come through, sometimes they don't, but no one wants to know exactly what happens next, do they?'

'True.' Eloise was grateful to be rescued. She appealed to her best friend. 'Why can't I just be more chilled out about this stuff like you, Mags?'

'Beats me.'

Max raise an eyebrow. 'You're chilled out?'

'Oh yes I am.'

'Whatever you say, dear.'

'Start with the "dears" and I'm going upstairs to pack right away.'

Max blew her a kiss and Maggie pretended to duck to avoid it.

'The thing is, I look at you two.' A large glass of red wine coursing her veins, Eloise was in danger of getting emotional. 'And you just seem so together. You communicate.'

'Yeah, Max is a great communicator.' Maggie's smile was sardonic. 'His Blackberry is practically an extension of his hand.'

'Seriously…' Eloise was determined to make her point.

'I know, we're nauseating.' Maggie was doing her best to lighten the tone.

Max took her hand and gave it a squeeze. 'We're just lucky. We're going to have hilarious children one day.'

'Can't we just get a cat or something?' Maggie ignored Eloise's glare. 'Oh well, I'm sure I'll feel ready eventually.'

'I don't think you ever feel ready.' Eloise was firm. 'We've all been misled. Do you honestly think our parents were more mature than we are? Women these days are never ready. It doesn't matter if it's leaving the house, leaving the office or having a baby, they just need a few more minutes/hours/years.'

As usual Eloise was making sense, but Maggie was feeling nervous. If she managed to distance herself from the whole birth thing she could get used to the idea of children in the abstract. Provided they were healthy, cute and slept at least six, make that seven, hours a night. Ideally she'd produce a three-year-old. It was babies she didn't get maternal about.

Maggie decided to return Eloise to the spotlight.

'But El, if Jake got down on bended knee tomorrow, would you say yes?'

'There's no chance…'

'Hypothetically?'

Eloise sighed. 'Probably not tomorrow, no.'

Max interjected, 'Maybe that's your answer.'

'But who splits up with a guy because they're too easy-going? I think I get more confused as I get older.'

Maggie intervened. 'That's because the stakes are much higher.'

Max shook his head. 'You're both making this far too complicated. Just remember Jake's a bloke. When I met him he seemed like a decent guy.'

Maggie raised her eyebrows. 'You mean he bought you a pint?'

'Anyway, my point is that—'

'He had you at "What are you drinking?"'

Under the table, out of sight, Max flexed a fist in frustration. 'If I could just finish my sentence. Women never listen.'

'And men always do?'

Max ignored her and turned to Eloise. 'He won't have any

idea you are agonising over him. Men stop worrying at the point they meet someone they like.'

Maggie intervened. 'But that's just when we start. We take the baton of doubt and we run with it. I'm not even sure there is such a thing as a relationship of equals. Not really. Everyone's playing field has a slope and it's not constant.'

Eloise nodded. 'Wise words from the cohabiting commitment-phobe who has loved and lost and loved again.'

'Yup I'm a traitor, a wolf in sheep's clothing, actually this is cashmere, better make that a goat's clothing. And just for the record, it should be called creditmere not cashmere.'

Max put his hand up, as if to ask a question.

Eloise nodded. 'Go ahead.'

'Maybe you need a new focus. Stop tinkering with Jake and instead invest your energy in a career move.'

'Don't I need to have a career to move?'

Max wasn't giving up. 'I just think if you shift your attention, spend your time thinking about somebody else.'

'Who?'

'You. You're putting way too much pressure on your relationship because it's the biggest thing you've got going on at the moment.'

Maggie couldn't have briefed Max better herself. She'd been telling Eloise the same for months.

'Think about what you really want to be doing. If it's the radio thing, work on a demo and take yourself from station to station selling yourself—no one's going to call you. If it's teaching, start training, research schools and apply for positions. If you want to move on Give A Little, Live A Little, let's start putting a concept together and take it from there, but once you're moving forward on your own terms, the rest of your life will fall into place. Inertia, on the other hand, will eventually suffocate your spirit.'

Maggie was euphoric. Her boyfriend was the best if, slightly irritatingly, Eloise had ignored her advice for years only to lap Max's up. Not wanting to distract Max from his impromptu life coaching session, Maggie set about stacking the dishwasher. As she loaded the matching white Wedgwood plates in to the brushed steel hand, time and life saver, it still felt like she was playing house.

For all her nervous protestations, she'd had no trouble making the transition from her compact flat. Then again who would complain about moving from the Holiday Inn to the Hilton?

Jake's face appeared at the back door and if they hadn't just been discussing him she might have screamed. Instead she sauntered over and coolly let him in.

'Ciao Tutti.' He gave the sort of wave you expect to see Bono giving a filled stadium at the start of gig. 'Greetings from Little Venezia.'

His larger-than-life entrance was as fresh as the blast of cold air that had followed him in as he leant to kiss Maggie's cheek and propped his skateboard up against the back door.

'How is my home village?'

'Fantastico.'

'You're in a good mood.'

'Damn right. I've just done some of the best writing in ages. That flat is amazing. Great karma.'

He left Maggie beaming as he strode over to the table and gave Eloise a kiss.

Now he was there Maggie felt bad about being anything less than positive about him. He was a good guy.

'Well, it certainly smells like you've had a delicious lunch.' Jake shrugged his Puffa jacket off, revealing a black V-neck over a white T-shirt. His forearms looked tanned. Maggie wondered if she was ovulating or something.

'There's loads left. Mags, how about getting Jake some food? And maybe a glass of wine?'

She knew she was standing by the dishwasher and therefore nearest the leftovers, but Maggie could feel herself resenting Max's tone.

Maggie bobbed a curtsey and adopted a West Country accent. 'Can I get you something, surrrr?'

'I'm fine. I ate last week. Seriously, I had a sandwich this morning. And when I say sandwich, it was a monster.' He slapped his gym-finished stomach. 'I'd kill for a cup of tea though.'

Affirmative noises all round as Tea Lady Hunter sighed, a little too loudly apparently.

Jake jumped up. 'Why don't I help?'

He'd filled the kettle from the tap before Maggie had a chance to mention the Brita filter. 'Where would I find tea bags?' As he started opening cupboards, Maggie pointed him in the direction of the tea collection.

'Right, who wants what?' Jake examined the selection, opening tins and storage jars and sniffing hard as he double-checked the selection. 'Earl Grey, builders, peppermint, camomile, green, Lapsang poo pong?'

Orders established, he set about his task picking, Maggie

noted, the Superman mug for himself. Apparently every boy fancied himself as a superhero.

'Who wants milk? Sugar? Eloise?'

Maggie eyed her best friend with interest.

'Milk, no sugar. Clearly you need to be making me more cups of tea.' Maggie could detect Eloise reaching boiling point faster than the kettle.

Watching Jake make tea to an unheard rhythm, she was only too happy to give him a hand. The other two were muttering about business plans and investors.

Jake looked around him on his way to the bin with the tea bags. 'This is a sweet kitchen.'

'Sweet?'

'As in cool, the light you get from the lean-to conservatory just makes it. I reckon I could live in this room.'

'You do already. I think my flat is about this size.'

He laughed. 'I love being on the top floor there. You get to see so much sky. I didn't know sunsets in London could be so red. The sun almost bleeds in to the brake lights on the M40 flyover.'

Maggie smiled. 'Not the sort of description they put in the estate agent's details.'

'I bet you don't miss it much though. I mean look at this place.'

Through new eyes, Maggie appreciated her surroundings even more. But as she watched him stirring sugar into his tea, she wondered if she needed to exchange her mug for a bucket of iced water. In the months, make that years, she'd been between men she hadn't missed sex at all. Now that she was having it regularly, she was finding more and more men attractive and the effect seemed to be mutual. Nature was a little skewed sometimes.

As they arrived at the table, Max and Eloise fell silent.

Jake winked at Eloise as Maggie willed her to give him a chance. Jake moved his chair closer to Max's. Pack mentality.

Jake strolled into an easy conversation. 'So, when are you two going sailing?'

Max kissed Maggie's cheek as she delivered his tea. 'As soon as Maggie will let me take her. She's *so* busy.'

Maggie didn't appreciate his mocking tone. 'Hey, that's not fair. I just need to work out the best time to take a week or so off.'

'Exactly.' He turned to Jake. 'I'm starting to think she might be stalling.'

'They must owe you loads of holiday.'

Maggie reminded herself that Eloise was trying to be helpful.

'It's a very busy time of year. And I have to be back for bonus time at the end of February.'

'So go soon.' Eloise made it sound so simple.

'Are you going to bareboat?' Jake took a slurp of his tea.

Maggie waited for the answer as eagerly as Jake. She had no idea and it was her holiday.

'We're still deciding whether we should go it alone or have a captain and a crew.'

It was the first Maggie had heard on the subject.

'What sort of size yacht?'

'Ben 50.'

'Big.'

Maggie had no idea who Ben was, but big sounded good.

Jake nodded approvingly. 'They really are the best holidays. Truly independent travel, on a boat you can really access all areas.'

'I didn't know you were a sailor.'

Maggie could tell that Eloise was not only surprised but delighted.

'I crewed on a couple of yachts in Antigua and a few of us chartered one in New Zealand in the Bay of Islands when we were travelling.'

Eloise chipped in. 'I did Antigua race week a couple of years ago.'

'I've been a few times.' Jake took a noisy sip of his tea. 'Hey, we were probably getting drunk in the same bars.'

So maybe their paths had crossed before they were thirty? Maggie could see Eloise thinking it.

Max was attentive. 'New Zealand must have been really cool.'

'Freezing actually.' Jake laughed. 'But huge fun. I haven't been out on the water for a while though. Life keeps getting in the way.'

Maggie was feeling inadequate. 'I've never been sailing.' However many times Max reassured her, she was more than a little nervous. She wanted lots of crew. She didn't want blisters, raw lips or thread veins.

Jake turned to her. 'You'll love it. There's quite a lot to get your head around at first, but once you're in your groove you'll just relax into it. It's a great way of getting back to nature.'

Maggie wasn't sure that's what she wanted from a holiday, even if it was free. She'd always regarded nature fondly but

from a distance. David Attenborough had taught her everything she needed to know.

Max was thoughtful. 'Hey, I've got a great idea.'

Maggie noted his smile was almost bigger than his body.

'Why don't you and Eloise join us for the trip?'

Maggie looked at Eloise. Eloise was looking at Jake. She
was too late. Was there any way to reclaim her holiday for
two without sounding spectacularly spoilt and selfish? She
didn't think so.

Chapter Fifteen

Max joined Maggie at the bathroom sink where she was brushing her teeth vigorously, her bathrobe so tightly knotted closed it might as well as have been a nun's habit. She was pretending to be staring into the middle distance but as he moved round behind her he could see Maggie tracking him in the mirror. He put his hand on her shoulder and dared to make eye contact.

'I thought you'd like to have a holiday with your best friend. You always say you don't see each other enough. And you loved travelling with her.'

Maggie shrugged him off before spitting hard into the basin. She rinsed her toothbrush more thoroughly than normal, enjoying the focus, before dramatically pulling a yard of floss from the dispenser and relocating to the main mirror above the towel rail.

'I did when it was just the two of us. But you, me, Eloise

and the guy she's not sure is good enough for her? I can hardly wait.'

'I thought you got on well with Jake. You've entrusted your flat to him. You enjoyed the pub quiz.'

'That's hardly the same as a whole week on holiday. Look, more than anything I want Eloise to be happy and how does anyone know who's right for anybody? But then I'm not the one who'll be sharing a room—'

Max interrupted her. 'A cabin.'

He could be very pedantic. She continued using her vernacular. 'A bed with him.'

Max sighed. 'Look, he's her boyfriend. I guess we have to respect her choice.'

'But we don't have to take her choice on what had previously been billed as my holiday of a lifetime.'

'It's just a sailing trip. There'll be plenty more holidays. And they leapt at the chance.'

'Of a subsidised vacation in the Caribbean. Funny that.' Maggie couldn't believe she had moved in with a man who could be so emotionally thick-skinned.

'I'm only covering the cost of the boat. They're still paying for their flights and it sounds like Jake knows his port from his starboard. It'll be useful to have another guy there. It'll mean you'll get more of a rest.'

Maggie flushed her floss down the loo, defiantly breaking one of Max's rules and left him in the bathroom. Letting her robe fall to the floor, she climbed into bed and reached for her half-read magazine. She was too annoyed to actually read, but she didn't want to look like she was sulking either.

Max climbed in to his side before combat-crawling over

to Maggie and resting his chin on her shoulder. 'I'm sorry, okay? I thought it would be fun. I possibly should have discussed it with you first.'

'Possibly?'

'Probably.'

'Definitely. It was supposed to be my Christmas present.' She should have known. If there was no such thing as a free lunch, there definitely wasn't going to be such a thing as a free holiday.

'Maybe I'm just too spontaneous for my own good sometimes.'

'And so modest.' Maggie paused herself, unhappy with the fact she was behaving like a spoilt brat but more concerned that Max didn't think he had to consult her on decisions. 'Sorry. Just ignore me.'

Max wasn't sure whether that was a definite instruction or one of the ones that, as a man, he was supposed to know he should not follow. He rolled back to his side of the bed. 'You wait. It's going to be great. We should try and book our flights tomorrow. I'll call my contact at the marina.'

Maggie propped herself up on her elbow. 'Can I be honest with you?'

He looked at her. 'I insist that you are.'

'I'd been looking forward to some quality time, just the two of us, a bit of romance and mutual appreciation.' And sex. 'We're always doing stuff with other people. I can't even remember when we last had a quiet evening at home together with the remote control.'

'Is this still about yesterday?'

'It's not "still about" anything. It's an observation. Sometimes I don't want to have to be the entertainer. Sometimes it's nice to do nothing, to just be together. Unless, of course, that's not enough for you.'

'I probably should have called you to let you know Jamie was here yesterday. Not that I'd expect you to have to get permission to invite Eloise over.'

'I'd always tell you if I was having someone over for dinner, or for the afternoon. And it wasn't just Jamie, there were loads of you.'

'Look, we're on our own now.' As Max stroked her arm Maggie felt herself stiffen, and not in a good way.

Max pulled back. 'Do you want me to phone Jake and Eloise and withdraw my offer. I'm sure they'll understand.'

'Stop doing that.'

'Now what have I done?'

'You're trying to make me seem unreasonable.'

'I'm not trying to do anything. And maybe you are being a little unreasonable. She is your best friend.'

'This isn't about her, it's about us. And if you did call her—' Maggie visualised the moment '—what would you say?'

'I'm sure I can think of something. Or you could call her and explain how you're feeling.'

Maggie hesitated. 'Oh I don't know. Just leave it. Maybe she'll change her mind all by herself. I'm not ready to be one of Britain's most hated people as well as a member of one of Britain's most hated professions.'

Max stroked her arm. 'I'll make sure I book a night ashore in a luxury hotel. I'm sure Jake and Eloise will want some time alone too.'

He snuggled up to her and she felt herself weaken. 'Make

it two nights. And I'm sorry. I don't like listening to myself nag at you.'

Max stroked her hair. 'It's okay. I just didn't think. You know I love you.'

'You can't say that at tactical moments just to make everything feel better.'

Max paused. 'I wasn't.'

Maggie buried her head in her pillow. 'Sorry, honestly ignore me. Nice Maggie will be back in the morning.'

Max forced himself to laugh, if only to keep his spirits high. 'I hope so.'

Maggie rolled over to the edge of the bed, her back to Max. 'So do you think they're well suited?'

Max shrugged as he switched off his bedside light. 'Who knows? They've been together as long as we have, so something must be right.'

'And yet he doesn't even know how she likes her tea.'

'I don't think that can be the litmus test of happiness.'

'It's quite a basic thing.'

'Just because they have a different attitude and approach to togetherness than we do. Personally, I think Eloise needs to sort herself out and the rest will follow.'

'Definitely. I think he's a nice guy.'

'Then maybe this holiday will be good for them. You can't hide anything on a yacht…'

You couldn't? Not even a little cellulite? Maggie kept that thought to herself.

'… and if they can't cope with being together for a week morning, noon and night, it's best they find out sooner than later, don't you think?'

'When did you become Dr Ruth?'

'When I persuaded you to move in with me.'

'Persuaded?' Maggie's tone was shrill. 'I decided.'

'And now?'

'And now what?'

'Regrets?'

'No. Not really.' It wasn't the best evening to ask her. And she knew she couldn't blame moving in for everything she was feeling.

'That's what I love about you, such a gusher.'

'Hey, this is about to be the only home I've got. I'm getting there. I love being with you.' Maggie knew it sounded like she'd delivered that sentence with a gun to her head but at least she'd said it.

'What does a man have to do to get you really excited?'

'Put his clothes in the laundry basket?' Maggie smiled. 'Oh, you know.'

'Tell me.'

She wasn't a prude, but she didn't like talking about sex. Not details. Maggie pulled one of the hairs on his arm.

'Ouch. Maggie, I'm asking you seriously. You've got to let me in. How can I be your perfect man without your help?'

He wanted to be her perfect man. And in the abstract, it was a perfect approach. In reality it was somewhat nauseating and in her current mood she couldn't help feeling her perfect man wouldn't need to ask. She closed her eyes. The sooner she went to sleep, the better.

'Come on, what's the secret. What do I need to do?'

'Take me on a surprise sailing holiday…with two other people?'

If she wanted to be his perfect woman she knew she was going to have to let go of this argument. Maggie sighed. 'Just as long as you didn't invite them because you couldn't face the thought of too much time one on one.'

Max sat up. 'Oh sweetie, is that honestly what you thought?'

'Maybe, just for a moment.'

'You are a silly one.'

'Don't forget. I could leave at any time.'

'You could, your prerogative.'

Making an effort, Maggie leaned over and kissed Max. 'So you'd better make staying worth my while.'

He put his arms around her and gave her a hug. 'I'm sorry.'

'Me too.'

As he held her close, Maggie appreciated his soapy smell. She kissed him again. 'And you know they say you should never go to bed on an argument.'

'In that case…' Max pushed her backwards, suddenly on top of her. 'Let me see what I can do.'

Chapter Sixteen

Maggie stretched out on Eloise's sofa, supine and alone. She breathed deeply as she felt her face pack penetrate her pores and flexed her toes, snug in her old red Totes, as she found peace. An ancient episode of *Kate & Allie* burbled away in the background. Forget people wafting around in white with harps and lyres, this was her very own vision of heaven. Life was good. No, it was beautiful. And at the end of this evening Max was going to love her even more.

For the first time in weeks she was off the radar. Her phone was off and nobody except Eloise knew where she was. Anonymity was the only thing she really missed since moving in with Max. Those lost hours in shops, alone, at her pace, with no purpose. Reading the paper in a café wherever she happened to be. Days taking shape as they went along. Being uncommunicative and unaccountable, being able to hide out in her flat, painting her toenails, shaping her eyebrows, eating steamed broccoli followed by a bowl of muesli for dinner and relishing talking to no one when everyone else thought she was out drinking shots and having a wild social life. Tonight, courtesy of Eloise and Jake she was having a much needed retro moment.

While love's young dream snuggled up in front of her old television in her flat, Maggie was chez Forrest. She hoped that Max was home alone watching reruns of *Top Gear,* missing her sparkling wit and company.

Never previously conscious of when she was in or out, recently Maggie had started to feel she was always at home, usually getting back before Max despite stockpiling errands and meeting friends and colleagues for a drink when all she really wanted to do was watch soap operas in her pyjama bottoms. It was official, she was old.

Tonight she was looking forward to getting home feeling less battered by life and London than normal, knowing she had plucked her eyebrows and waxed her bikini line. Maybe she'd even get to surprise Max on the sofa. Their sex life was good, occasionally mind-blowing, but more often routine. Given the choice, Max was a late-night and an early-morning lover whereas Maggie preferred the evening workout unless it was the weekend. Romance, like everything else these days, had become something that almost needed to be scheduled. It might not have been dead, but it was very busy.

Maggie enjoyed the tingling feeling as her face pack got to work, hopefully drilling out blackheads and coaxing clean pores to close. Her aromatherapy bath had certainly soothed her spirit and her legs were as silky smooth as they got these days now that having continuous male company had ruled out any form of hair removal bar shaving. Just a few more minutes and she'd blow-dry her hair and prepare to make an entrance. She stretched her arms above her head and rested them on the arm of the sofa behind her. She felt almost weightless, as opposed to sixty-five kilograms. Moving in with a guy who enjoyed cooking and a glass of wine was not good for the waistline.

Max checked his watch as he waited for the taxi driver to give him his change. His meetings had overrun before relocating to a bar and somehow it had got to nearly nine o'clock. Time was definitely soluble in alcohol.

Now there seemed little point in going home and eating alone when he could be out on the town with his girlfriend. He only hoped she wouldn't mind him turning up on the spur of the moment and whisking her off for some late supper.

'I just hope she knows what she's doing.' Eloise took another sip of cold white wine, loving the at-home domesticity of her evening. She'd spent many evenings in this kitchen with Maggie and, yet, it already felt different.

'Hey, it's not like she's seeing another guy or anything.' Jake chopped the onion carefully. He always got nervous in the presence of kitchen knives. He only ever seemed to be a millimetre away from lopping off a finger and the disadvantage of an overactive imagination was that he could visualise it happening. He could even see the trajectory of the blood. 'We all need time to ourselves.'

'I suppose so.' In light of their impending maritime adventure, Eloise was giving Jake the full benefit of any doubts and so far he had risen to the occasion. Maybe they should have booked a holiday months ago.

'We're just lucky enough to be able to get our downtime during the day.'

Eloise beamed. They were a We.

'Don't forget, Maggie spends most of her life dealing with colleagues, sweet-talking clients, just having to be nice.'

She couldn't believe Jake was trying to educate her about her best friend.

'I know all that, but deception is never a good thing in a relationship.'

'Sometimes secrets can be healthy.'

'You think?' Eloise disagreed strongly, but then again she didn't want to seem overbearing or paranoid for that matter.

'Sure. I've never understood why when you start seeing someone, they suddenly think they have a divine right to know every move you make, every place you've been. I'm not condoning anything sinister. But you have to have trust. And it's not like she's at your flat with anyone.'

'True. But he thinks she's out.'

'Have you never lied about where you were?'

'Of course not.'

'Never?' Jake's tone was challenging. 'Not even a small white lie? You know, just to get out of going for some drinks, or to a wedding or a party miles away when you barely know any of the people going?'

'That's different.'

'Is it? You're not where you said you'd be. But you're not up to no good either.'

'I suppose. But Max isn't some guy having a party she

doesn't feel like seeing. I just don't think this is a good precedent. She should be able to be herself with him.'

Jake smiled. 'I think the thing you're most worried about is that this is all taking place in your flat.'

Eloise nodded. 'Tonight I feel like an accomplice.'

'Hey, Maggie's no villain. I think she's cool.'

Eloise smiled. 'Very. Possibly been allowed to have her own way for too long, but you've got to love her for it.'

Jake paused. 'Come on, we're all a little bit selfish.'

'It's just sometimes she thinks she doesn't need anyone else. I know it was the *Sex and the City* generation's goal to be independent, but the ideal seems to have got corrupted along the way. Women were supposed to be self-sufficient, not intolerant.'

'So how come you're so tolerant?'

'Brothers.'

Jake wondered whether he'd missed something.

'When it came to not getting my own way I didn't have a choice. Compromise was forced on me from the days of having to share an ice cream.'

Jake nodded empathetically. 'Although I'd say having siblings encourages you to jostle for attention. My sister and I used to wrestle each other until we had carpet burns in our bid to sort out the pecking order.'

Eloise laughed. 'I took up judo for a while.'

Jake smiled. 'I knew I was a lucky guy.'

Eloise resisted the urge to tell him just how lucky he was as she watched him busy at wok. The infusions of garlic and ginger were making her mouth water as he meticulously shredded cabbage and pak choi and added them to the

Chinese cauldron. It was shaping up to be a lovely evening. She'd arrived to find Jake in a towel. No wonder they were hungry.

Max made his way through the bar area, sashaying between groups of increasingly lairy office workers in search of a familiar face. He was sure Maggie had mentioned Kali Bar earlier but she wasn't answering her phone.

He'd almost completed his circuit when he felt a hand on his shoulder.

'Hello, mate.'

Max had no idea who he was talking to, although the owner of the hand clearly felt otherwise.

'It's Simon. Simon Senior.'

'Pleased to meet you.' Max proffered a hand for shaking. Not that pleased but pleasantly surprised at the lack of threat his self-appointed rival posed.

Simon waved his hand away and slapped Max a little too heartily on the back. 'No need to be polite, mate. If you'd asked my girl out on a date, I wouldn't be in the handshaking market, if you know what I mean. Not that I'm saying punch me or anything. So how's it all going? You're a lucky bastard. But I'm sure you know that already.'

Max wondered how many pints Simon had drunk. 'I guess I do. Is Maggie not here?'

Simon shook his head. 'Nah. She only stayed about an hour. Said she was knackered. She's probably at home, baking or something.' Simon winked. 'You have a good weekend.'

'You too. Have a good one.' Doing his best to sound as colloquial as he could, Max headed back out. He dialled

Maggie's mobile and then the land line as he got into another cab. No answer on either. Maybe she was freshening up in the shower. He undid the top button of his shirt.

Maggie yawned and pawed at her neck. It felt like she had spots everywhere—a rash? She ran her fingers over her face tentatively. Could she have leprosy? Her pulse raced and she sat up with a start. She was still on Eloise's sofa.

The flat was cold, almost icy. Stumbling into the bathroom, she washed the mask off her face and remarkably, despite a few blotches, her face no longer resembled a lunar landscape.

Her watch was on the side of the bath and she stared at its hands several times taking sample readings before coming to the conclusion that it was definitely just after one in the morning.

The serenity of her evening in tatters, she pulled on her clothes before trying and failing to do anything with her hair. If only the backwards through a haystack look was in. Finally pulling it back and knotting it with a scrunchie she found amongst Eloise's toiletries, she gave up on her model behaviour. Switching on her phone, she was assaulted by a queue of bleeps and guiltily checked the screen. Seven missed calls. All bar one from Max. Taking the executive decision not to call him back, she phoned for a minicab.

It was nearly two by the time she arrived home and, to her relief, she hadn't been locked out. Bolting the door behind her, she called out tentatively.

Thanking the powers that be for a blessed escape and considering sending a donation to Max's boarding school for training him to sleep deeply, she slipped her shoes off at the foot of the stairs and tiptoed up to bed hoping to slip in unannounced.

As she neared the top of the staircase, she could see that Max was sitting up, his chrome Anglepoise bedside light casting a spotlight on a man for whom bedtime had clearly been and went. His hair was tousled, his contact lenses had been replaced by his glasses and he had clearly been attempting to read what looked like a thrilling business textbook. Tomes like that were passion killing all over Britain and Maggie was determined to banish all work-related reading material to his study. It would be her finest hour. Just as long as she got through the next one.

Max turned his head slowly, as if forced to greet her, his gaze almost distant. Maggie smiled warmly, hoping he was noticing her nails, tamer eyebrows and radiant skin. As she leant over to kiss him, he stared at the pages of his book and the skin on his cheek didn't welcome her lips. His voice was barely audible. 'Where have you been?'

Maggie perched on the edge of the bed for a second before deciding it would be easier to deal with this cold front from a few metres away.

Rerouting to her side of the room, Maggie started undressing, lingering over the new lingerie that, only hours earlier, she had envisaged Max removing in the throes of passion.

He blinked as patiently, if wearily, he waited for a response.

'Just out for a few drinks, then I grabbed dinner with some of the team. We don't do it enough to be honest.'

'Interesting choice of word.'

Maggie looked up from folding her clothes. All was not well. Max closed the book gently. 'So, where did you go?'

'We went for…'

Max shook his head. Very definitely and just the once. 'Please don't lie to me, Maggie.'

'Why would I—'

Max spat his interruption, still not raising his voice. 'You've clearly just woken up.'

'I dozed off in the cab.'

'For fuck's sake. You haven't even had a drink.'

Maggie's stomach knotted as Max pulled back the duvet and got to his feet. He was wearing a pair of boxer shorts she'd bought him. 'I'll be in the spare room.'

Maggie's indignation was genuine. 'What are you talking about?'

'I saw Simon at Kali Bar. He said you'd left around seven-thirty.'

'You were at Kali Bar?'

'I was looking for you.'

Maggie blushed. 'I…I…I can explain.'

'I'd rather you packed your things.'

'Listen. I didn't think…'

'Clearly. Well maybe you will next time. I thought I was giving you your precious space. Now I'm thinking maybe I was just being naïve.'

Max pushed his glasses back on the crown of his head and rubbed his eyes. 'There's been someone else the whole time, hasn't there?'

'Don't be ridiculous.' Maggie was indignant. 'Do I strike you as the unfaithful type?'

'I didn't have you down as the dishonest type, so who knows.'

'After what Adam did to me, believe…'

'Please, Maggie. Don't bring him into it. You can't live in the past. I thought this was supposed to be the future.'

Maggie knew she had to keep calm, but part of her was already defensive. 'It is.'

'It was.' Max stood facing her, challenging an explanation.

'What were you doing checking up on me anyway? I don't go running around after you when you're out. Why can't you just leave me be?'

'That's probably a good idea.' He yawned. 'I'm too old for this.'

'So what, that's it?'

'You tell me you're out with the office for the evening. I had a few drinks after work, thought I'd drop in and whisk you off to dinner somewhere special. Only guess what, you weren't there. You'd gone home early. Well, at least that was the story.'

Embarrassed, Maggie studied her ankles.

Max sighed. 'You of all people should know how shitty being taken for a ride feels. You haven't been in a smoky bar, you're not drunk. You're not even wearing any make-up.'

Feeling about two centimetres tall, Maggie mumbled. 'I was at Eloise's.'

'Save it. You told me you weren't ready for all this. I shouldn't have pushed you. Go to sleep and in the morning you should probably start packing your things and go.'

'Go where?'

'We'll sort something out. Stay in a hotel. I'll pay.'

'I haven't done anything wrong. I was at Eloise's.'

'You lied to me.'

'It was a white lie.'

'I don't care if it was a fluorescent fucking pink lie.'

'Eloise is at Jake's. She's still there. You can call her if you like.'

'She knew?'

Maggie nodded. 'But, in her defence, didn't approve.'

'I spoke to her earlier. She didn't say anything to me.'

'I'm afraid friends come before significant others in the pecking order.'

'Well, that's just made me feel a lot more special. I don't like being the last to know.'

'There's nothing to know. And stop talking to me like a wayward teenager. I'm not fifteen years old.' Maggie could hear defiance in her tone. To her surprise she was angrier than she was apologetic.

'Then stop behaving like you are. What were you doing there?'

'Having a girlie evening.'

'You just said Eloise was with Jake.'

'I was by myself. I wanted some downtime. I was making myself look beautiful for you.'

'You are already beautiful and you live here. You'll have to try harder than that.'

Taking his pillow with him, Max walked into the spare room and closed the door behind him. Part of Maggie wished he'd slammed it, wished he'd shout. The strong silent approach was unnerving.

Lying in the middle of the bed, her head nestled between the two banks of pillows, she wondered if she should follow Max.

Heart beating in double time, rolling herself over to the edge of the bed and on to her feet, she walked over to the door to the spare room. She stood outside the closed door for minutes, wondering whether to knock. Finally daring herself to open the door a fraction, she was amazed to hear Max's somnolent Darth Vader breathing. Asleep at last, but Maggie was wide awake. It was hardly surprising—she had been unconscious almost all evening.

Chapter Seventeen

Bleary eyed, Maggie stood at the kettle. Only just five in the morning, it was still pitch dark outside, but she'd given up staring into space and was hoping a hot drink might tip her back from the precipice of insomnia into a deep cleansing sleep. Allegedly it was Saturday morning and, according to the calendar, February seventh. One week to go until the first Valentine's Day Maggie had been hoping to have with a man in tow since Adam, although now she suspected it might be daggers aiming for her heart rather than cupid's arrow this year.

As she squeezed the tea bag against the side of the mug, she realised she was being watched.

Max was leaning against the fridge. She smiled hopefully at him.

'Thought you'd start your double life early this morning?' Max was clearly ready to start where he'd left off.

Instantly Maggie felt her hackles rise. 'If you'd just listen.'

'I think I've heard enough.'

'Of course you have. A man, wrong, it would be a first, don't you think?'

'Don't try and make it sound like I'm the one being un-reasonable.'

Maggie sighed. 'You could at least give me a chance to explain.'

'Been working on your story, have you?' Max's tone was malignant.

Maggie felt tears forming and rationalised with herself that after less than three hours' sleep, it was merely a physiologi-cal reaction.

He saw her eyes glisten. 'I don't waste my time where I'm not wanted.'

'I can barely cope with the emotional energy of having one relationship, so I'm hardly going to volunteer for a second one.' It was a heartfelt plea.

'Eloise said she didn't know where you were.'

'Because that's what we'd decided in the unlikely event your paths crossed. Meanwhile I was eating cereal in front of repeats of trashy TV without having to speak to a soul. Until I fell asleep, that is.'

Max was staring at her in disbelief. Why did women always find an explanation when you least expected it.

'I'm very sorry. I should have told you the truth.'

Max sighed, now more irritated than angry. It looked like he too might have to apologise. Not his greatest skill. 'I still don't understand why you can't relax here.'

'It's different. I just wanted a night off.'

'From me?'

Out loud, she knew it didn't sound good. Maybe they weren't as compatible as they thought they were.

'From everyone. I'm not used to having people around me all the time.'

Max shook his head.

'Most of the time it's fine.'

'Fine? Wow.'

'Fine. Fabulous.' Although this temper was a side of him she hadn't known existed.

'I don't understand why you didn't just say something straight away?'

Maggie blushed and mumbled into her tea. 'I didn't see why you had to know where I'd been. Then you flounced out of the room.'

'I don't flounce.'

'You do now.' Maggie smiled. 'And because I knew I hadn't done anything wrong—'

'Apart from lying to me.' Max interrupted her.

'Apart from that, yes, I didn't see why I had to grovel. And yes I know I can be stubborn.'

Max shook his head. 'Come here.' As Maggie rested her head against his chest, he stroked her still-knotted hair. He sighed. 'I imagined the worst and then I imagined even worse. And when you walked in all smiles and bed hair, what was I supposed to think?'

Maggie yawned.

'Tired?'

'Exhausted.'

'Shall we try bedtime again?'

Maggie shrugged. She wasn't sure if she had the energy.

As they climbed the stairs, mugs of hot tea in hand, Max got back into his side of the bed. Maggie walked round to her bedside table and took a sip of her tea before sliding in next to him and entwining her legs with his. Under the covers he held her hand, tenderly tracing her fingers.

'I'm really here to make your life easier, if you'll let me.'

Maggie nodded. She didn't trust herself to speak.

'So now we've had our first major row.'

She sniffed. 'I don't want to be part of a couple who shout at each other.'

'Well, maybe if you start behaving like you're part of this couple…'

'I'm always going to want to be independent.'

'There's independent and there's separate and if you're in the latter category, I need to know.'

Maggie nodded.

Max kissed her forehead. 'We're okay, aren't we?'

She raised her eyes to meet his. 'I guess.'

'Can't we do better than that?'

'We're fine.'

'Fine. Fabulous?'

Maggie smiled weakly. 'Absolutely.'

'I love you.'

Maggie stared at the ceiling.

'I really do.'

'Why?' She looked at him challengingly.

'Right now, I have no idea.' As they shared a laugh Maggie rolled over and backed into her position as First Spoon. Safely staring across the room, she decided to get everything out in the open. Her mind slipped in to first gear, then second.

'Max?'

'Mmm.'

'You still awake?'

'Mmm–hmm.'

'Do you worry that we're starting to take each other for granted? I mean just a bit.'

'Mmm.' Max woke himself back up. It was important. 'What do you mean?'

Maggie blushed, grateful it was still dark. 'Well, for a start we're having a lot less sex and yet I'm supposed to see this as progress?'

'How long has this little grenade been waiting to explode?'

'A day or two.' Maggie remembered her new honesty policy. 'Maybe a week, or two.'

'Why didn't you say something?'

'I had this brilliant plan. I thought I'd make myself all beautiful and irresistible and seduce you. And then I feel asleep.'

He stroked her hair. 'You know this doesn't have to be such hard work.'

'I'm not looking for problems. Well, maybe I am a little.'

'I would agree that things have changed.'

'See.'

'Except in my world, they've changed for the better.'

'Because I just moved my life into yours.'

'Into ours.' Max paused, trying to read the signs. 'Do you think you need more commitment?'

Oh no. Maggie shook her head emphatically 'God, no. Just some appreciation of…'

'Of…' Max struggled to find the right word to finish her sentence.

'Of me, I guess. And it doesn't have to be grand gestures, in fact it absolutely shouldn't be.'

'I can only do my best.' Max hesitated and Maggie wondered if she should have kept her mouth shut. 'So we're still together?'

'You tell me.'

'You have to promise me one thing.'

'I'll try.'

'No more funny business. You can have as much space as you like here. You can have your own room if that makes it easier.'

'Don't be daft.'

'And by the way, just so you know, I'm starting to feel like the girl in this relationship.'

Maggie smiled.

'Seriously, I've never been accused of being too clingy. I have however been accused of being uncommunicative, self-centred, selfish, self-absorbed and…'

'Lucky me.' Maggie curled up in his arms. 'Max?'

'Yup.' He could feel her thinking.

'You awake?'

'I don't dare go to sleep.'

'You know they say the best thing about having an argument is making up afterwards.' She kissed him and as he kissed her back she felt relief cocoon her. 'And I have painted my nails and plucked my eyebrows for you.'

He reached down and stroked her recently exfoliated thigh.

'Max!'

He kissed her neck, slowly working down her body.

Maggie watched him for a few moments and then reached for the duvet. 'I have to get up and go to work in four hours.'

'On a Saturday?' Max kept moving south.

'Just a couple of clients and a spot of bikini shopping with Eloise. I won't be late.'

He looked up at her. 'Now where have I heard that before?'

'I'll be home before you know it.' Maggie kissed the top of his head and made a definite move towards her pillow.

Max took the hint and tried to concentrate on thinking sleepy thoughts. 'Home here?'

'Where else.'

They lay side by side, holding hands.

'And you're sure you don't need any help with choosing a bikini?'

'Positive.'

'Oh well. A guy has to try.'

'How about I model any purchases on my return?'

'Sounds like a perfect plan. Any objections to me cooking you some supper?'

'That would be lovely.' Maggie sighed dramatically. 'At last I have the wife I need.'

'Watch it.' Max rolled on to his side and kissed her again. 'At least let me pretend I wear the trousers some of the time.'

Finally Maggie felt her eyes start to close. 'Who said there are only one pair?'

Chapter Eighteen

Eloise sat in the small radio studio tucked away on the ground floor of the hospital as the last few bars of Madonna's 'Holiday' played out. Checking her microphone was faded down, she sang along enthusiastically, dancing in her seat. In seven days she was meeting Red Connelly, in twelve days they were off sailing. Take some time out of life. It would be so nice.

It always amazed her that the most popular requests from the patients were upbeat. No one ever asked for 'The Long and Winding Road' or 'We Gotta Get Out of this Place' despite the fact that most of the people she visited were weeks if not months away from being allowed to go anywhere near a dance floor.

She faded Madonna down and her in.

'Well, that's it from me and my Saturday Surgery for today. Enjoy the rest of your afternoon and have a good night. Ian will be with you tomorrow lunchtime, but now it's time to unplug yourself from the radio loop and plug yourselves back into the TV. Just make sure you don't pull on any cables you can't identify.

'I'll be with you again for three hours next week and next Saturday I will also have an exclusive interview with a very special guest. Red Connelly, yes *the* Red Connelly will be here talking about his latest film and choosing some of his favourite tracks. Plus Valentines galore. Now that's what I call first class first aid.'

Eloise brought the faders down and, singing MRSA to the tune of 'YMCA,' she tidied up the studio and filled in the log before locking up, dropping off the keys and squeezing past the gaggle of patients who had wheeled their IV drips out of the main door of the hospital so they could stand outside in their slippers having a cigarette. Eloise shook her head. Now that's what she called addiction.

It had only just gone five o'clock but, thanks to good old British wintertime, it was already dark outside. As she emerged from the overheated hospital corridors into the cold, fresh evening, she buttoned her coat and breathed in deeply hoping to displace the hospital air from her lungs. Either her vision was distorted or Jake was waving at her from across the road and he was clutching, flowers? There must have been some mistake.

He jogged across the pedestrian crossing and kissed her hello as if this was something he did every day or, indeed, ever. They definitely needed more nights in.

'Hey, Dr DJ.'

It was his little joke. One that Eloise hadn't found particularly funny the first time but she had made the mistake of smiling and now, months later, it would have been awkward to say anything.

He proffered the flowers.

Prearranged, they were garage-stocked rather than hand-tied, but they were definitely for her, and thankfully there was not a carnation amongst them.

'Thank you.'

'Hey, I saw them and thought of you.'

'Fresh. Colourful. Radiant?' Eloise went fishing for compliments.

'They were a tired-looking bunch.' Jake winked at her.

Served her right. Eloise wondered if she'd reached the time in her life when anti-ageing eye cream might be a non-negotiable necessity. How could she be heading downhill when she hadn't peaked yet?

'Anyway, just wondered if you might like to join me for a couple of beers and then maybe some supper?'

'Boys given you the night off?' Eloise chastised herself. Innocent until proven guilty, not the other way round and she certainly didn't want to discourage spontaneity.

Jake shrugged. 'Just thought it might be nice to do something together. Of course if you already have plans…'

She took his arm. 'Let's go. Do you know this reminds me of being collected from school by my boyfriend when I was about fourteen, except we'd have been snogging like mad by now.'

Jake wheeled round and kissed her urgently as Eloise giggled. He stopped. 'You already had a boyfriend at fourteen?'

'If you can call it that. Those were the days when I thought boys were for hand holding, standing you up at the bus stop, getting you into bands you'd never heard of before and then ruining them for you for ever when they then stopped calling.'

'Good to know we improve with age.' Jake took her arm in his. 'So how about we start at the pub and then head out for a pizza or a curry? Your choice.'

Not quite Gordon Ramsay, but it was a start.

'And Max called about sailing earlier. All confirmed. He's chartered a huge yacht. Re-sult.'

'Maggie and I'll be providing a focus for the sun's rays somewhere on deck if you need us.' Eloise grinned. She couldn't wait to feel the sun on her skin.

'You're all flying off on the Wednesday morning and I'm going to see you there the next day.'

'If there's no room for all of us on the same flight, why don't I fly out with you?'

'No need.'

'Oh.' Did everything have to be about need these days? When had *want* been elbowed out of consideration?

'I just don't see why you should sacrifice a day of your holiday when I'm the problem. I'm not back from the stag weekend in Prague until the afternoon.'

Eloise exhaled as hard as she could without speaking. This same stag "more-of-a-week-than-a-weekend" took him away for Valentine's Day. At least now she knew what the flowers were for. 'And are Maggie and Max okay with everything…'

'They're cool.' Jake suspected that Eloise was less so. 'I'll be with you by the time you've unpacked, done some provisioning and chilled the beers. There's always lots of stuff to do before you leave the marina.'

'Sounds like it's all sorted then.'

Eloise did her utmost not to be disappointed. It was only a flight. And now at least she didn't have to worry about looking ridiculous in flight socks or waking up with halitosis halfway across the Atlantic. 'So how was your day today?'

'Really good. I've been getting so much more done recently. I don't know where the time has come from.'

Eloise could tell him. No late-night spliffs. No deep-pan pizzas or buckets of fried chicken. No PlayStation nights.

'A few more songs and I'll be ready to book some studio time. And some of them have real potential.'

Eloise didn't think she had ever seen him so positive. Part of her was delighted and part of her wanted to have something she could be equally passionate about. 'When do I get to hear something?'

Jake shrugged. 'When I'm number one? So, good show this afternoon?'

'Terrific. I know this is going to sound silly, but there is definitely a weekend feeling, even in hospital.'

'The telly is better.'

'I think it's more than that, a lifetime of conditioning. Which reminds me, what are we going to do about paying our way on this yacht?'

'Max seems pretty insistent that the yacht is on him.'

Eloise frowned. 'We can't let him pay for everything.'

'He was going to charter the boat anyway.'

'That's not the point.'

'Why don't we just shout them a few meals, buy some booze, that sort of stuff. Plus we're paying for our own flights and they're not cheap.'

'We don't have to go.'

Jake was confused. 'Of course we do.'

Eloise beamed. Right answer. 'I can't wait.'

Eloise sat in the pub sipping her large glass of wine enthusiastically. Soon she would be on a yacht in the Caribbean with her cute boyfriend who was currently ordering her a bowl of chips at the bar.

Her mobile phone started to vibrate its way across the table and Eloise picked up just before it reached a pool of lager.

'Yo.' Her good mood was having strange side effects on her vocabulary. Or maybe that had been the R & B she'd been playing earlier—back in the day.

'Hello. May I speak to Eloise Forrest.'

'Speaking.' Eloise put a finger in her ear. She couldn't quite make out the voice because of the background noise.

'I have Red Connelly holding for you.' The voice was male and artificially pinched.

'Good one, Dad.'

'Eloise Forrest?'

'You should know.'

'Eloise?' The voice was deeply distinctive, and usually coming at her from surround sound speakers in the cinema. She froze.

'Mr Connelly, Red Connelly.' Eloise wished she could start again. 'Thanks so much for calling.'

'You may not be quite so effusive in a moment. I'm afraid I'm going to have to cancel next Saturday. I know you're a friend of Maggie's and so I wanted to let you know personally.'

'You can't make it?' Eloise put her hand over her ear to dull the noise. Much better.

'I'll get my PA to send you a couple of copies of my DVD box set to give away instead.'

'That's very kind…' Eloise felt her adrenaline surge, daring her not to give up on the highlight of her week/month/year/adult life. 'I don't suppose there is any way we could do a pre-record? I'd only need half an hour, you just say when and where. If you could get your assistant to email me your top ten tracks in advance we can just record some intros.'

'My schedule's pretty tight.'

'I'm sure.' Eloise could feel her heart sinking. 'There'll be a lot of disappointed people.' He was talking to the main one.

'Hold on for just one minute.'

There was a pause and Eloise wondered if he was calling an assistant to get rid of her. She took a big gulp of wine as her euphoria upped and left.

'Miss Forrest?'

'Speaking.' It was the nasal man from before.

'Mr Connelly can schedule half hour maximum on Monday for a pre-record.'

Eloise's mood performed a U-turn. 'Just tell me where and I'll be there. Thanks so much.'

'It'll be at Clockwork.'

'Right.' A bar? A restaurant? A watch repair stall?

'Do you know the place?'

'Yeah,' Eloise lied. 'Just remind me where…' She could search Google when she got home.

'Dean Street. Can we say three o'clock?'

'Sure.' Right now he could say whatever he liked.

'You'll have thirty minutes. Red should be done with his voice-overs by then. See you on Monday.'

Eloise promised herself she would have at least thirty-one minutes, if only to annoy the charmless assistant.

Jake arrived back from the bar to find his girlfriend on Planet Connelly. He hadn't expected Eloise to be so star-struck.

'Such a kind man to find me a spare half hour of his time.'

'He just blew you out for the live show.'

'I have no doubt his diary is a nightmare.'

'He's an actor, not a world leader.'

'He's a household name.'

'So's Cif.' Jake wasn't interested in talking about Red. 'Come on, drink up and let's go and get some dinner. Lunch didn't really happen for me today.'

'Can't you at least be excited for me?'

'I am. But remember he's just going to be a guy. A good-looking, well-toned, articulate, occasionally funny guy with a huge ego.' Jake hated him already.

Eloise raised her glass. 'Either way, it's a coup. To me.'

Jake raised his empty glass. 'To you.'

Eloise's concentration couldn't sit still, and neither could the rest of her. She turned to Jake, 'I don't suppose you feel like heading home and watching a few of his films?'

'Actually I was looking forward to getting out. I've been at home all day.' Realising his evening was on the verge of being rearranged for him, Jake felt his good mood slipping. 'Good of Maggie to organise this all for you.'

'Oh shit.' Eloise looked at her watch. 'I was supposed to be bikini shopping with her an hour ago.'

'And she hasn't called?'

Eloise stared at her phone. 'I hope she's okay.'

'Hello?' Maggie wedged her phone between her cheek and her shoulder as she loosened the halter neck on a bikini which was, despite its alleged Lycra content, threatening to strangle her. She was starting to wonder if skiing outfits would have been more flattering.

'Mags, it's me. I'm so sorry. I've only just remembered I forgot about our shopping date.'

'Don't worry about it. I've had a look round and now I'm going home to try my own liposuction.'

Eloise laughed. 'That bad?'

'Buying a bikini in winter in London is a nightmare. I swear I'd be able to get a bigger choice of boa constrictors if I put my mind to it and unless I'm in a hall of mirrors I'm not going to be able to eat or drink anything on this holiday.'

'That's what sarongs were invented for. Where are you now?'

'Harrods. I've decided to throw money at the problem. They're open for another hour if you fancy joining me?'

'I don't think I'll make it…but I do need to thank you.'

'For having bigger thighs than you? My pleasure. Maybe I should get a pedal car. It's so hard to fit in enough exercise these days.'

'Red just called me.'

'He did?' Maggie had suspected he'd pull out. She'd been amazed he'd agreed to it to start with.

'First he cancelled.'

'I'm sorry. Just bear in mind how many people he has competing for his time and no disrespect but you're not Michael Parkinson or Jonathan Ross.'

'Actually it's okay. I persuaded him to do a pre-record with me on Monday.'

'He must have liked the sound of you.'

'Or you. I'm really sorry I forgot about our swimwear mission.'

'Don't worry about it.' Having dressed and undressed several times in the last hour, Maggie was losing the will to live.

'You sound tired. Too many late nights methinks?' Eloise's voice was laden with innuendo.

'Too many tight bikinis. Plus your prediction was spot on. Max and I had our first all-out row last night. Well, actually this morning. I fell asleep at yours.'

'I know. He called me this morning after you'd left for work.'

Maggie felt herself stand to attention. 'Was he checking up on me?'

'No. I think he was just trying to understand you a bit better.'

'Then he should be talking to me and listening to my answers. I was totally honest.'

'I did tell him I've had a thirteen-year head start and still struggle from time to time.'

Back from the Gents, Jake grabbed her from behind. He hadn't given up on his evening just yet. 'So what do you fancy next…?'

Eloise waved him away. She didn't want Maggie to hear that she was trading their bikini moment for boyfriend time. 'Just be open with him.'

'I'm trying.' Maggie sighed. 'I can't wait until we're all lying in the sun.'

'A holiday for four, we're so grown-up. Go shop. I'll speak to you tomorrow.'

As Eloise hung up she turned to Jake. 'Sorry.'

'Is Maggie annoyed with you?'

'I'm in the clear. But she and Max have had their first row.'

'See, they're not perfect after all. So what's next? A curry? A comedy night? The night is young, and so are we, well I am.'

Eloise smiled. 'Don't be annoyed, but I'm going to head home. Max once told me that you can never be too prepared for a meeting and now I'm seeing Red in less than forty-eight hours.'

Jake hung his head despondently. 'Seriously?'

'I've got loads of stuff to read plus I think I'd better watch his last couple of films again.'

'Now that sounds like the sort of revision I can handle.'

Eloise drained her glass. 'Why don't you hook up with the boys? Maybe I'll catch up with you later? Okay?'

Not at all okay, but Jake wasn't about to beg. As he sat at the table alone with his pint and watched her leave, Saturday nights were warming up all around him. Reaching for his leather jacket, he found Eloise's flowers underneath. Thanks a bunch. Right now he was the one seeing Red.

Chapter Nineteen

Max sat in his car and waited for Maggie to answer her mobile phone.

A bottle of Harrod's finest pink champagne chilling in a cool bag by way of an apology for her duplicitous behaviour, Maggie extracted her phone from her bag as she got off the bus at Notting Hill Gate. 'Ten minutes away. You can start cooking.'

'Actually I'm just popping out.'

Maggie looked at her watch. It was nearly seven.

'I shouldn't be more than a couple of hours.'

'I thought you were cooking us supper?'

'There's a great new Thai place I've been meaning to try for ages and they deliver.'

'But I have surprise supplies.'

'I look forward to seeing them later. And don't think I've forgotten about your other promise.'

And to think she'd imagined candles and flowers. 'Is this some sort of exercise in tit for tat?'

Max laughed. 'Of course not. I just need to swing by the office to do a couple of things.'

'On a Saturday night?'

'I need to run some figures. I'll be as quick as I can. Love you.'

Instantly grumpy, Maggie flung her phone into her handbag. This weekend was not going according to plan.

Jake poured the last of the red wine into his glass, a few drops falling on to the rug. Bits of paper were strewn all over the sofa and the coffee table. He was barely aware of what he was doing and yet something was working perfectly and he didn't want to interrupt the muse. He picked up his guitar and instinctively strummed a few chords as he tried out the latest version of the lyrics.

You were there and now you're not
Seems to be that you forgot
I was the one who couldn't give enough to you

So now you've left me far away
I no longer rate on Saturday
Your knight has come and I'm not he

And I am seeing red, seeing red, seeing red
And you are seeing red, seeing red, seeing red
That makes me blue

I never wanted to commit
You made me see that we could fit
Together we began to knit
A home for two

But you were using me, I see
You were not making sense to me
I think I know you'd rather be
Alone again

And I am seeing red, seeing red, seeing red
And you are seeing red, seeing red, seeing red
That makes me blue

As silence returned to the flat, Jake raised his glass to absent girlfriends. He hadn't written a love-lost ballad for years and this one was going to be a beauty. Maybe Red Connelly wasn't such a bad guy after all.

Maggie squinted at the level in the bottle. She'd drunk over half of the champagne and instead of making her giggle it was only making her more and more angry. Alcohol was a definite mood enhancer.

She tried Max's mobile and as once again it transferred to voicemail she flung her head back on to the sofa cushion. She was convinced Max was making a point. The figures he was running had better be numerical.

Padding downstairs to the kitchen, she opened the door to the fridge and stared at the miserable lack of contents. Despite his earlier promise to cook, Max hadn't even been out to buy more milk and she hadn't yet had enough to drink for her appetite to have become a distant memory.

Opening the freezer, she spied a packet of fish fingers and laid two on the grill pan. They looked forlorn, a portion for a peckish six-year-old. She laid two more down and two more until ten were lined up in front of her—a handful of fingers. As a child she had fleetingly believed that a cod had bread-crumbed digits. Around the same time as she'd longed for a bed with brass bed knobs that might be able to fly.

On all fours, Jake stared at the expanding new dark birth-mark on the cream rug. The glass of Pinot Noir had been on the coffee table for hours and then suddenly it had flung itself, lemming-like, over the edge. He rolled on to his back and laughed. And then, full of alcohol, empty of food, he thought he might cry. His life wasn't as much of a mess as Maggie's rug but, instead, a black hole of underachievement. And while for the last few months he'd had a great girl in tow, he hadn't been looking after her at all. He dialled Eloise's flat, determined to make amends.

'Hello?' Eloise paused Red mid-air before he'd guided his parachute to safety. Meanwhile his enemies were still at the airfield. She couldn't believe she was going to be in the same room as him. She knew she'd been going to the gym all these years for a reason.

'Is that my lovely girlfriend?'

Bemused, Eloise shook her head. 'Jake Chambers, you are stoned.'

'I'm not actually.' He stumbled over the last word. His *t*'s needed sharpening.

'Drunk?'

'I may have consumed a small amount of creative juice.'

'It's only creative if you write the stuff down.'

'Which I have. Tonight you inspired me to write a song, a song that could be great.'

'I have?' Eloise softened. 'Will you play it to me?'

'If you come over.'

'Now? I can't. I'm right in the middle of—'

'Seeing Red…' Jake giggled.

Eloise was distracted. 'What's so funny?'

'Nothing.' Jake paused. 'I could come over and help?'

'Why don't I come to yours for brunch tomorrow and you can play it to me then?'

'I'm not sure it's a brunch anthem. It'll be better after dark.'

'How about dinner then? Or you can come here. But I'm going to try and get a vaguely early night.'

'Whatever suits you.' Jake felt more sober already.

'Great. I'll see you here then, tomorrow evening.'

'Maybe.' Jake didn't want to be hanging up yet. 'So how's it going?'

'Good. He's more interesting than you think.'

'Not difficult.' Jake lay on the carpet and stared at the ceiling rose.

'Seriously, there's more to him than meets the eye.'

'That's a relief.'

'Do you think I should mention Give A Little, Live A Little and see if he's interested in being involved?'

'Do you have anything on paper to show him?'

'Max is working on a proposal at this very moment.'

'Sounds like you've got everything under control. Let me know if there's anything I can do to help.'

There was a moment of silence. Jake could sense Eloise wanted to get on.

'Well, don't stay up all night. I bet you know more about him than he does. I'll see you tomorrow.'

Jake put the phone down and, in need of uplift and distraction, waved his magic wand cum remote control and instantly transported himself to the repeat of the day's big football match. After a few minutes he surfed off to the movie channels in search of more permanent company, hoping to invite Angelina Jolie or Steven Seagal into his evening. Carrying on past them all, he paused at MTV for a look at the competition and then decided to spend the next hour with Coldplay on VH1. It was that or Red Connelly picking his favourite hits on one of the lesser known music channels. That man really got everywhere. He picked up the phone.

Eloise's phone rang and rang before the answerphone kicked in. He hung up and pressed record on his Sky Plus to capture Red's music picks. Maybe now she'd be more interested in coming over to see him tomorrow.

Maggie was glued to VH1. Watching Chris Martin and co. in various guises as their best known anthems flooded the sitting room, she wondered what was she going to be remembered for?

She had just finished her eighth ketchup-soaked fish finger when she heard the front door. Fortunately for Max, her champagne journey had almost reached the too-tired-and-inebriated-to-be-cross leg.

She heard him pause in the hall, wondering where she was. 'Have you started without me?'

'Started and finished.' Maggie's delivery was perfunctory.

He appeared at the sitting room door. 'I thought we were having dinner together?'

'I thought you were cooking for me and we were spending the evening together, just the two of us?'

'We are.'

'It's after ten. Your phone's been off. I was starting to think you might have dozed off on a sofa somewhere…'

Max smiled.

'It's not funny. You could have called. Texted. Something. You could have been dead. I apologised for yesterday and yet you're behaving like a child.'

As Maggie waggled a ketchup-covered finger at him, Max shook his head. He'd never been so frustrated by a woman before. Maggie Hunter was nothing if not an original. And he was enjoying the challenge. She really was very cute when she was annoyed.

'I was at the office.'

'Exactly. Bloody phones everywhere. And you said you'd only be a couple of hours.'

'Oh well, we'll just have to try the new Thai next time, unless…can you eat any more?'

'Not if you want me to wear a bikini.' Maggie sighed.

'I thought you wanted more time at home alone.'

'That's not even funny.'

Max came over and put his arm around her. Maggie shrugged it off.

'I'm sorry. I lost track of time. I promise I'll make it up to you.'

No doubt he'd just take her somewhere hideously expensive and difficult to get a table at. Maggie bit her lip. 'Next time don't leave me in limbo. I had no idea what to do about food.'

'Looks like you found something.' Max stared at the remaining limp fish fingers with disdain and cleared her plate.

'All you bloody well had to do was call me.' Maggie's voice cracked. 'All I've wanted to do for the last hour is go home. Only, guess what, this is supposed to be it. I've only been here five weeks and yet you seem to assume I'm going to be here for ever. Well, not if it's like this.'

'I'm really sorry.' As Max approached the sofa to make amends, Maggie didn't move a muscle, staring tight-lipped at the television. As Max spotted the champagne bottle next to the sofa, he felt worse. 'It was just one of those things. Now, what can I get you? I'd offer you a drink, but at a guess I'd say I was a little late on that front.'

Chapter Twenty

After thirty-nine hours of intensive preparation, Eloise was having the best Monday ever.

As she emerged from Soho into the rather tired end of Oxford Street, she felt like the most beautiful girl in the world. There was nothing like flirting with a screen god to make your day.

In the flesh, Red was better looking than he was on screen and a much more useful size. It was a relief to Eloise to find he was a normal five foot ten, his skin less perfect than make-up artists, directors and airbrush technicians had thus far allowed the world to see, and he'd been charming.

Clutching the bag containing her precious minidisc player tightly under her arm, Eloise wove her way along the pavement like a pro. Oxford Street was the M25 of the pedestrian world. At least six lanes of constant stop/start traffic

with no highway code and enough retail distraction to ne-
cessitate many an emergency stop.

Right now she was dying to get home so she could review
and relive the interview and edit the package together. Then
a sneak preview to a tame journalist and, bam, she was going
to be the best known hospital radio DJ in West London, at
least for a few days. The potential was almost causing her to
hyperventilate. Finally she understood what Max and
Maggie had been nagging her about.

Her mobile rang and she reached for it greedily. On her
current high, even a double glazing salesman would have
received a warm welcome.

'Eloise? Red Connelly.'

Surely her day couldn't improve.

Eloise stood still. 'Hi.'

'You left your disc behind.'

Eloise hesitated. She'd taken it out of the player to label
it and check the levels in the audio suite, but she was sure
she'd put it back.

'I did?'

'The good news for you is that I could drop it off later.
Am I right in thinking you mentioned you lived in Fulham?'

Eloise stared at the pavement. 'Yes. That's right.'

'So why don't I drop it off on my way back from the studio?'

'I could just pop back now. I'm not far—'

'We're just about to restart. Text your address to this
number or call my assistant. I know a great place in Chelsea
for dinner and you can fill me in a bit more about this time-
raising idea of yours. I'll pick you up at eight.'

Whatever was in her diary, it was about to be rescheduled.

As he hung up, Eloise realised she had become an island of inertia in the middle of the river of fast-moving pedestrians who were wordlessly parting and reforming around her. In a world of her own, she slipped her bag off her shoulder and in the pickpocket hot spot of London, emptied everything out on to the pavement. Just as she'd thought, and as clearly as she remembered mentioning Fulham, she knew she hadn't mentioned Jake.

Maggie stared at the clock in her office and wondered whether a second hand could actually be deemed to be an instrument of torture. With no appointments in her diary for the remainder of the day, she had no choice but to get on with the backlog of expenses and all the paperwork she'd been avoiding for weeks. When her phone rang she pounced on it gratefully. 'Maggie Hunter.'

'Mags, it's me. Thank goodness you're in the office.'

Maggie looked at the piles of paper needing her attention, rising like stalagmites from the floor.

'I'll be here for at least a year. Where are you? You sound like you're panting. You're not jogging or anything healthy like that, I hope?' Maggie eyeballed the empty Twix wrapper in her bin. She wished she had more willpower. 'Oh my God, I almost forgot. How was Red?'

'Charming. Amazing. So normal all things considered. But you know that already. What you didn't tell me is that he's even better looking in the flesh.' Eloise was babbling.

'He's a decent looking man but, believe me, he knows it. I prefer them a bit rougher and readier.'

Eloise laughed. 'Yeah, that sounds like Max.'

'He occasionally has stubble by the end of the weekend.'

'The cleaner irons his T-shirts for goodness' sake. Anyway, back to me.'

Maggie was relieved.

'Not only did Red give me so much more time than his assistant had promised.'

'He'll no doubt get it in the neck from one of his women later.'

Eloise paused. 'What do you mean?'

'He has a bevy of personal assistants. They all seem to be called Rachel, Raquel or Rebecca apart from Joel, the token gay man. Basically they overorganise his life for him to the minute and then he does pretty much what he likes. I'm sure he's a nightmare boss.'

Eloise dared herself to come clean. 'I think I may have a bit of a situation.'

'Go on.'

'He's invited himself over.'

'Joel? I honestly would have put money on him being gay.'

'Red.'

'Red?'

'I know it sounds crazy, but he's just engineered a reason to come round to my flat and take me out for dinner.'

'Where?'

'Does it matter? Somewhere in Chelsea. Apparently he wants to talk about my charity idea.'

'Of course he does.'

'You don't believe him?'

'With his reputation?'

Eloise shook her head. 'Me neither. So what do I do now?'

'What do you think you should do?'

Eloise squirmed. 'I don't really want to cancel him.'

'Have you asked Jake what he thinks?'

'Of course not.'

'Do you think maybe you should?'

'Do I even have to tell him? Actually, shit, now you mention it I think I was supposed to be having dinner with Jake. I cancelled him last night, too.'

Maggie smiled. 'Well then.'

'This is hardly a normal pattern of events.'

'Well, well, it's good to see even the queen of the moral high ground has double standards when it comes to telling the truth to her man.'

Eloise knew when she'd been beaten.

'And if you don't mention it, it definitely looks like you have something to hide. I've just learned that lesson.'

'It's business.'

'And I'm Princess Leia. I presume Red thinks you're single?'

'I don't think it came up.'

'El.' Maggie didn't like being taken for a fool.

'Could you believe how amazing it would be if I could get someone like Red interested in Give A Little, Live A Little.'

'Is it still a coup if you sleep with him first?'

'Maggie!'

'I think he's probably more interested in your underwear.'

Eloise bit her lip. If part of her quite wanted to find out, did that make her promiscuous?

'And is it really worth screwing up things with Jake for one night?'

Eloise's response was meek. 'We don't know that's his game plan.'

'I think we probably do.'

'What if it's not just one night he's interested in?' Eloise fiddled with her hair.

'Sleep with him by all means. He's a single-ish, eligible guy, but please don't be naïve. Red is Red.'

'What happened to Petra?'

'Who knows? Maybe she slipped down a drain grate?' Eloise giggled.

'But he's definitely on the prowl at the moment. You must have seen the papers. Perhaps he does just want to take you out for dinner and then he'll shout you a taxi home, but I think we both know that's not the case.'

'You won't say anything to Jake, will you?'

'Yeah, because I talk to him all the time...' Maggie was enjoying being facetious.

'I'm serious. I'm an adult. I can do what I want.'

'You wouldn't have called me if you didn't want the truth.'

Eloise nodded. She'd never been much of a gambler. Then she smiled. She had an idea.

'Hey, how about if I borrow Max?'

'What?'

'Max. He knows all about the charity thing. He could be my co-person.'

'You mean your contraceptive.'

'Or at least my handbrake.' Eloise blushed, relieved Maggie wasn't in the same room.

'And what if you change your mind?'

'Then I'll ask him to leave.' Eloise felt reassured. It all seemed so simple.

Maggie didn't sound convinced. 'Hang on, if Max knows, then you definitely need to tell Jake, at least that you're having some sort of *meeting*.'

'Couldn't we ask him to, you know…'

'You can ask Max whatever you like, just remember, boys, beers, boasting, boating, it's bound to come out on holiday if not before and then it'll just implicate you in some sordid romp, which isn't even guaranteed to happen. And I'd rather you and Jake weren't at war. I think it'll probably be choppy enough at sea.'

Eloise fell silent as Maggie moved a few piles of papers around on her desk.

'El? You still there?'

Eloise was desperately trying to conceive of a plan that at least sounded sensible.

'But say, just say, George Clooney came to see you professionally about finding a London pad, then changed his mind about wanting a property but asked you out for dinner. Would you tell Max?'

Maggie was silent. She knew she shouldn't have moved in with someone while George was still single. 'It's never going to happen.'

'And at least with Max there I have to think twice.'

'You could of course cancel Red altogether.'

True. She did have the disc. 'I'm not sure I'd ever forgive myself, or Jake for that matter, not that he'd know what he'd done wrong.'

Maggie sighed. 'I sense danger.'

Eloise grinned. 'I like the sound of that.'

Maggie decided to cancel her lecture. She wanted to ensure she'd at least be kept in the loop. 'Well, you'd better give your prospective chaperone a call, but remember—'

'Red's not your client tonight.'

Maggie put the phone down and sighed at her in-tray. Her business. Her client. Her best friend. What could go possibly go right?

Chapter Twenty-One

Finally Eloise's flat looked like a slightly tidier version of itself rather than a shrine to Red Connelly. She'd put the pile of printed-out articles relating to him in the recycling bin, returned the DVDs to their covers and put them in the cupboard, plumped up a few cushions and, while she didn't want to seem too eager, she had showered and re-applied her make-up since arriving home—much to Max's amusement.

'Just business, eh?' Max looked up from the safe haven of the sofa from where he'd been observing the domestic goddess at work, while half watching television and half attempting today's sudoku puzzle in the newspaper.

'I got really hot and sweaty on the tube.' Eloise checked her appearance in yet another mirror as she came in from the kitchen before disappearing to substitute her trainers for heels, immediately feeling better.

He noticed her sashay back into his field of vision. 'Oh crap. I didn't bring a change of shoes.'

'I didn't invite you along to mock me.'

Max smiled. 'I'm just teasing. You look great.'

Eloise did her best to ignore the nascent wave of excitement in her stomach. 'It's just a chance to talk to him about Give A Little, Live A—'

'Just relax.'

When the doorbell finally rang, over half an hour late, Eloise jumped from her pretending-to-be-chilling-out-on-the-sofa pose and, leaving Max helping himself to another beer in the kitchen, descended to the front door to find Red standing there in the same jeans, black polo neck and charcoal overcoat he'd been wearing earlier.

With no apology for his tardiness he leant down and kissed her hello, twice. The first kiss landed firmly on her cheek, the second not quite making it round to the other side and finishing lightly on the lips. Quite a promotion from the handshake she's received five and a half hours earlier. Eloise looked left and right in the hope that there was at least one eyewitness but that it wasn't Jake. From his silence, she assumed he'd picked up at least one of her messages.

She took a step back into her flat encouraging Red to follow. 'So I've got the disc.' Her tone was laden with expectation.

Red ran his fingers through his hair. 'I just thought we might have more to talk about. I have to be careful about what I say these days and in front of whom, not that the papers seem to need any actual facts before publishing stories.'

Eloise nodded. 'Well, I'd love to tell you more about Give

A Little, Live a Little.' She'd been practising her pitch in the shower. 'Think Comic Relief, think Live Aid, it'd only be good for your public image.'

'And my conscience.'

'That too.'

'As opposed to stealing you away for dinner.' He smiled.

'Which is probably not good for either.' Eloise teased.

'Oh, I don't know.'

As Eloise climbed the stairs in front of Red, she had never been more grateful to the inventor of the cross-trainer machine. Max was there to greet them.

'Hi.' Max proffered his hand to Red.

'Hi.' Red smiled slowly and turned to Eloise for an explanation.

'Max is helping me put the proposal together. I didn't think you'd mind if he joined us for a drink.' Eloise hoped Max wasn't offended that his tenure had already been reduced. 'Max French, this is Red Connelly.'

'The smoothie guy?' Red's tone was disbelieving.

Eloise looked from one man to the other. 'You know each other?'

Red shook his head. 'I read a profile a while back in one of the Sunday supplements.' He addressed Max. 'Berry Berry Good is my personal favourite. The originals are often the best. I even got them to stock it in my local deli.'

Max beamed as they shook hands. For a second Eloise felt superfluous and achingly underachieving.

'And actually we did meet briefly, at The Man of The Year Awards at the Grosvenor House a few years back.'

Red nodded. 'Quite possibly, good memory.'

'I'm sure it's just that I meet less people than you do.' Max's self-deprecating charm was well received.

Eloise stood between them, an awkward host. 'Can I get either of you a glass of wine? A gin and tonic?'

Max watched as Red looked at his Rolex submariner. He bet it had never been used for deep-sea diving.

'We should really get going.' He addressed Max. 'I'm afraid I only booked for two.' He paused for effect. 'But great to meet you.'

Eloise didn't want to be rushed. 'Maybe we could manage five minutes here first? I'd really like Max to talk you through the basics and then you can take the proposal with you and consider it in your own time.'

Red reluctantly took a seat and picked up the copy of *Vanity Fair* Eloise had only discarded moments earlier. As he started absently flicking through it, Eloise wondered if he was looking for himself. He looked up. 'Okay, five minutes, and I'll take you up on that offer of a glass of wine. Cold white.'

In the kitchen, Eloise deliberated between opening an expensive bottle of Chablis she'd been saving and giving him the last glass from the started supermarket best Sauvignon Blanc in her fridge door. Pouring out the latter, she downed it in one herself, before opening the new bottle.

Max sat opposite Red in the armchair. 'So where are you taking her?'

'A little place in Chelsea.' Checking Eloise was nowhere to be seen, Red winked at Max. 'Chez moi.'

Max did his best to smile just as Eloise arrived back.

'You really think I'm going to come to your place, just like that?'

Max had never been more grateful that women could do a minimum of two things at once.

Red shrugged. 'It's easier for me than going out. I get less attention.'

Eloise stared into his soft brown eyes and allowed herself to imagine she was his leading lady. 'Absolutely not.'

The Connelly tractor beam working, Red smiled. 'Any way I'm going to persuade you?'

'Nope.'

'Then how about the best steak you've ever eaten?'

'Surely you don't want me to cook?'

He laughed gently. 'Not tonight. There's a great boutique French brasserie a few streets down. It's a favourite of mine.'

'Well, I've always found it difficult to turn down a good piece of meat.' Eloise smiled, mainly to relax herself. She could feel Max staring. 'Do you think we'll get a table?'

'Not a problem.'

'Just don't get any grand designs on coffee.' Eloise let her hastily-consumed wine do the talking.

Red feigned shock. 'Who do you think I am?'

'I know exactly who you are, that's the problem.'

'You shouldn't believe everything you read.'

Max guessed it was probably time for him to make himself scarce and yet he was determined to stay a little longer.

Red walked over to the bay window and looked out on to his driver parked in his car below. 'My trouble is I can't just go to any old restaurant these days and certainly not with a beautiful woman in tow.'

Eloise elevated her current outfit of Seven jeans, green silk top and sale-purchased Jimmy Choos to her all-time favourite.

Part of Max admired Red's easy charm. Part of him despised it.

Red crossed the room dramatically, extending a hand to Eloise to help her up from the armchair. 'Steak frites it is. You can pick dessert.'

Max drifted across to the door from the sitting room to the hall on his way to the bathroom. Eloise was far too smart to fall for that sort of line.

Eloise turned to her guest. 'Is Max invited too?'

'Not quite what I had in mind, but everything is possible.'

It was the probably the most charming way anyone had ever told Max to get lost and if he'd been a gentleman he'd have taken the hint. But now he quite fancied a steak. And, if he stood up straight, he was sure he had a couple of inches on Red.

Maggie peered into her grill, Jake standing alongside her. Gingerly she extended her hand into the rising temperature, being careful not to touch the metal trays.

'Well, it seems to be working fine now.'

Jake nodded. 'It probably knows better than to mess with you.'

Maggie nodded seriously. 'Rumour has it I am feared by most electrical appliances.'

Jake smiled. 'So what can I offer you? Drink? Pub quiz?'

'Not on a Monday. In fact I'd better head off, I'm cooking tonight.'

'Very impressive.'

'I always try to start the week as I mean to go on. By Wednesday I'm usually screwed.'

Jake laughed.

'And when I say I'm cooking, actually Gordon Ramsay is, I'm just following the instructions and looking at the pictures. Thought I'd try and add another dish to my repertoire which is feeling limited now I can't be seen to be eating the same thing every night. I tell you, this live-in relationship stuff can be exhausting.'

'Can I recommend the cooking for six and eating it three days running approach?'

'I remember it well. Sadly now I'm supposed to be a domestic goddess as well as everything else.'

'Now you're making me feel bad to have dragged you here for nothing.'

Maggie shook her head. 'I'm just delighted everything's working. Let me know if you have any more problems with it and I'll send an electrician over. I guess there might be a loose connection.' She still couldn't believe he'd called tonight of all nights. Maggie looked around. 'The flat's looking great.'

'Is that surprise I detect in your voice?'

'Possibly.'

'Is now a good time to confess there are a few drops of red wine on the rug in the sitting room? I've done my best to spot clean. I've tried the salt trick and white wine, I've depleted the ozone layer with "miracle" chemicals but so far, no good.'

'Don't worry. It's just a rug. An IKEA special, purchased to protect the expensive fitted carpet underneath.'

Jake nodded. 'Cool.' Definitely not time to mention the

small spoon of tikka masala that landed on that a few days ago then. He was sure there was something in the world that would remove the stain.

'I'm glad this place is working out for you. I loved it here.'

'I do have one more confession to make.'

Maggie looked around the room again. Everything seemed to be in order. She checked the walls for pen marks, handprints…

'The grill was fine when I called. There's something else that hasn't been working very well and I really wanted your advice.' Jake poured her a glass of red wine without asking. 'It's Eloise.'

Forgetting she'd promised her liver and her new bikini an alcohol-free week, Maggie took a large sip and wished she had no idea where her best friend was at this precise moment. Until four hours ago, if apprehended and questioned, she'd have been totally innocent. 'Don't you think you should be talking to her not me?'

'Probably, but she's been so unpredictable and prickly lately that I just thought you might be able to give me some advice. I know she didn't think I was around enough at first, that I didn't take enough of an interest…'

'Oh, I don't know.' Trying not to think about Eloise and Red in some sort of Hollywood clinch, Maggie attempted to make light of the situation. 'Her expectations have always been sky-high.'

'There's nothing wrong with that. When we first started seeing each other I wasn't exactly a contender for boyfriend of the year or even the month but, and this is going to sound like an excuse, and I guess it is to some extent, but I hadn't had a proper relationship for a while. No one I really cared about at any rate.' Jake took a thoughtful sip of his wine. 'If I'm honest, for the last few years I've been more interested in me than anyone else.'

Maggie took a minuscule sip of her wine in case it was some sort of truth serum. 'It happens.'

'It was a lousy habit, but the thing is I thought we'd been doing much better recently. It was starting to feel, well if I say "comfortable" I mean that in a good way. And then thanks to you the holiday opportunity landed in our laps and that's all very exciting…but in the last week or so I've started to feel like I'm just getting in her way.'

Maggie laughed falsely. 'I'm sure that's not the case.'

'The other night she blew me out to watch Red Connelly videos.'

'There's no accounting for taste.'

'I mean it would be one thing if she had actually been meeting the guy.'

Maggie looked at her shoe.

Jake shook his head. 'But just staring at him on a small screen?'

Maggie nodded, then shook her head, no longer sure of what she was condoning and what she was condemning. 'With the right exposure that radio interview could be a very big deal indeed.'

'I know it's important and I am excited for her, but then take tonight. She was on such a high after she'd finished re-cording the interview, we arranged to go out, and then she left me a message, a message, to say she was going out with some of the radio people and she'd love to see me tomorrow.'

'It's been a huge day for her. It's good to go out with the

team, important even.' Maggie wondered if Eloise would ever be able to repay her.

'But I could have gone along, too. I'm pretty media-people friendly.'

'Don't take this the wrong way, but do you think you might be a little jealous?'

'Of the opportunity or the man?'

'You tell me.' Maggie congratulated herself for batting that one straight back.

Jake was thoughtful. 'Actually, it's more that I feel as if she's been using him, this whole thing, as an excuse for an increasing range of intricate fob offs.'

'It is important you do things separately.' Maggie hoped Red was behaving himself.

Jake shook his head. 'I taught her that. Okay, example number two. Last week we were walking Frankie for Susan in Richmond Park and she was cooing over children in mittens and woolly hats.'

Maggie shook her head. 'That's normal for her, I'm afraid.'

'Believe me I know. But yesterday I mentioned something about how life-enriching kids would probably be if you could cope with the total sleep deprivation. I mean I was only being hypothetical, and she turned on me. She got on her high horse about the importance of her career which, incidentally, hasn't happened yet.'

'Sounds like a bad case of premenstrual tension to me.'

'Damn, I thought I was over that.' As Jake assumed the voice of a camp diva, Maggie couldn't help but laugh.

'Or.' Maggie stopped herself. Thinking aloud was a dangerous thing in company.

'Or?' Max peered at Maggie.

'Or, nothing.' Maggie wondered if there was any way that Eloise could be pregnant.

'Do you know something I don't?'

Mentally Maggie crossed her fingers. 'I'm sorry. I was letting my imagination run away with me.'

Jake nodded. 'Believe me, I know how that feels. And she's been less interested in sex recently.'

Maggie shook her head as if hoping to prevent that latest detail from settling. 'Too much information.'

Jake raised his hand in apology.

'And I think it's great that she's finally found a focus. It'll certainly take the pressure off you to be her be-all and end-all.'

'But do I still feature?'

'Everyone has peaks and troughs. Maybe you two are just having a bit of a valley moment?'

'I suppose we have both been busier than normal.' Jake paused. 'And it's difficult when these days she almost spends more time with Max than with me. By the time I get to see her, she's all talked out.'

'He's only been giving her a hand because he's got some time on his hands and partly as a favour to me.'

'It's very kind of him. But last Saturday, the night she blew me out to watch movies, he spent the evening doing projections for her charity thing and then dropped them over. But how urgent could it have been? And I'm not normally a jealous guy.'

It was true, Maggie hated surprises.

Jake hesitated. 'I don't have anything concrete to go on, but I just sense something is different.'

'Have you talked to her about all this?'

Jake nodded. 'And she says we're fine.'

'Well, there you go then.'

'But I just sort of wanted to double-check.' Jake fiddled with the stem of his glass. 'Am I on relationship death row?'

'Of course not.' Maggie wondered if he believed her. She really needed to make time to see Eloise one on one.

'I know girls keep secrets for each other.'

Maggie shook her head. 'I honestly don't know what's going through Eloise's mind at the moment. I've never seen her so goal oriented. Unless you count her pursuit of the rugby captain at university.'

'Successful?'

'Only for a term. As to Max getting behind the venture, between you and me, I think he can almost see his name in lights, and of course the world being a better place thanks to him.'

Jake smiled ruefully. 'And I suppose it's easy for me to sit here and be cynical. Someone's got to try and make a difference.'

'Well, let's see if Eloise manages to. She's talking to Red about her ideas tonight.' Maggie counted to three and wished she was somewhere, anywhere else.

Jake frowned. 'I thought she was having dinner with her radio colleagues?'

'Definitely. She is. But I think she was also due a call with Red earlier.' Maggie decided to brazen it out. 'I think Max was going to pop along to the dinner, too, so I should get the low-down later.'

Jake was circumspect. 'And you don't think it's strange that she's invited him and not me.'

'Or me? I may not be dating her but I've known her a lot longer.' Maggie was doing her best. She hoped it was good enough.

Jake nodded. 'So, any idea as to how I can get her attention back?'

'Take her on holiday? Let's see, how about sea, sails and…'

'Your boyfriend's already taken care of that.'

'Well, what are you doing for Valentine's Day? Maybe you could cook the hopelessly hopeful romantic a special dinner?'

Jake grimaced. 'Bit difficult, I'm on a stag weekend. And then I'm coming straight out to meet you guys.'

'Your weekend ends on Wednesday? I want to live my life according to your calendar.'

Jake grinned. 'I didn't organise it.'

'You've still got a couple of nights before you go. Take her out for dinner and then why not leave a card or a present for her to find on Saturday—it doesn't have to be huge, just thoughtful. No teddy bears, helium balloons or greatest love CD compilations.'

Jake laughed.

'But surpass her expectations.'

Thoughtful, he stroked his eyebrows from the nose to the ear. 'That shouldn't be hard.'

Maggie resisted the urge to agree. 'Just remember, I'm hardly a relationship guru.'

'No need for a disclaimer. You and Max seem to have got the relationship thing down to a fine art.'

Maggie scoffed. 'Hardly.'

'It looks like that to me, and to Eloise, for that matter.'

'No two couples are the same.'

Jake part-filled and then raised his glass. 'Cheers to that.'

'Well, it certainly keeps it interesting.' Maggie sat at the table in her old sitting room. It was good to be home.

As Jake rocked back on her dining chair until it was resting against the wall, Maggie reminded herself he was paying rent and that she had a full month's deposit.

'Then again you deserve someone like Max.'

'Deserve?'

'Eloise told me about the guy who died. That's quite hardcore.'

'Not as difficult as losing your parents, I would imagine.' Maggie shrugged. 'It was just lousy timing. I mean we were finished way before he was. And then there I was publicly grieving, and mainly for me. Everyone else thought it was all about Adam.'

'That must have been an incredibly difficult funeral, not that any are exactly easy.'

Jake was the first person who had thought so.

She shrugged. 'Fortunately I'm not an expert.'

'At least with my parents we could see it coming, we could say goodbye. For my mum it really was a relief.' Jake blinked hard. 'I only wanted her to keep going for me and for Susan.'

Maggie felt tears in the corners of her eyes and tilted her head back slightly, hoping they might head back to where they'd come from. 'It's infuriating. He didn't deserve me and yet…'

Jake leant across the table and gave her hand a squeeze. 'Hey, we need to be needed, to be part of a bigger frame-work. Whether it's friends, family or bloody pets, it's human nature. I mean we weren't the sodding Waltons or anything, but not a week goes by when I don't miss my parents. And I don't mean a passing thought, my soul literally aches.'

Maggie was enchanted by his honesty. 'Are you finding that the time-is-a-healer cliché has its basis in fact?'

Jake smiled. 'Five years down the line and it *is* getting easier. But it's taking time. And to be honest, it doesn't make me want to rush out and get close to people who could hurt me.' He paused. 'Now listen to me. I'm behaving like a mummy's boy, with no mummy.' He shook his head. 'Repeat any of this to Max and I'll smear jam on your walls.'

Maggie was thoughtful. 'It's weird, much as I like to complain about my parents, having them around does mean I can still behave like a child when it suits me and get away with it.'

'Yeah, I miss that. And Mum's funeral was the worst. Everyone said it was nice that she and Dad were together again, but I don't believe that they're up there chatting away, bickering about the things they used to. They're dead. Gone. That's the hardest thing to get your head round. That and the fact you're next in line. That's why the idea of the after-life makes it all so much easier.'

'We don't know what happens.'

Jake frowned. 'Do you really think Adam's up there, keeping an eye on you? I'd love it if mine were peering down, although somehow I don't think this is quite what they'd hoped for me.'

'You're doing great. You're a good person. You've got a successful career—potentially two. You're self-sufficient.'

'I'm renting your flat.'

'You'll buy somewhere in time.'

'Maybe in a developing country. London house prices

depress the hell out of me. And the idea of a mortgage for hundreds of thousands of pounds scares me to death. I hate borrowing things. And what if I just want to up and leave?'

'Have you ever done that before?'

'Not since I went travelling for the six months immediately after Mum died. But I've thought about it.'

Maggie nodded, their heart-to-heart causing introspection on her part. 'Did Eloise tell you she was at Adam's funeral?'

'I'm sure she was a rock. That girl has remarkable inner strength.'

'Not Eloise. She. Her. Eve. She came over to tell me how sorry she was. She even held my hand. I couldn't see her eyes because of her sunglasses. So there I was, looking at a reflection of myself in her polarised lenses, wondering whose benefit she was there for. It certainly wasn't mine. In a soap opera I'd have had my hands round her neck. In the real world I had to just let her walk away.'

'Do you know what?' Jake paused and, grateful for a fresh perspective, Maggie waited for his philosophical words of wisdom.

And waited.

'I think I'm going to open another bottle of wine.'

'To Give A little, Live A Little.' Max raised his glass.

Red followed suit. 'I'll talk to my agent in the morning.'

'So what's your secret?' Red looked across at Eloise. 'You have a real buzz about you.'

Max watched her with pride. He'd never seen Eloise so fired up. It suited her.

On the spot, Eloise could only think of one secret and she

was sure it wasn't the one Red was looking for. 'What you see is what you get. It's all natural.'

'No narcotics at all?'

Eloise was insulted. 'No!'

'Is there a man in your life?'

Max found himself clearing his throat.

Eloise glared at him. 'Sometimes.'

Intrigued by the ambiguity of her answer, Red raised an eyebrow inquisitively.

'It's all very modern. We see each other when it suits us, but it's hardly a great romance. Max is the man with one of those.'

Jake was in the kitchen waiting for the microwave to melt the cheese to pour over the nachos he'd dug out as a much needed bar snack. Unbeknownst to him, Maggie was gingerly leafing through the piles of paper on the coffee table.

He peered through the door. 'Hands off.'

Startled, Maggie dropped the papers as Jake entered with a volcano of calories piled up precariously on a plate. Forget haute cuisine, her mouth was watering.

'Okay you can look, but just bear in mind, without music most lyrics can seem a little on the simplistic side.'

Maggie nodded.

'That said, if they're good enough and touch a nerve, people do remember them.'

'Or in some cases—' Maggie blushed at her own short-comings '—make them up to fit the music.'

Jake laughed. 'It doesn't really matter as long as you take something positive away. Very few cut it as poetry.'

'I don't know that's true. How many of us can recite a favourite poem? Yet, lots of us could probably recite the lyrics of at least one verse of our favourite songs. And if it touches to that extent who's to say that it's not poetry?'

'Anyone who loves literature?' Jake munched his way through another handful of nachos. I mean I love Kylie for a dance floor, but she's no Dylan Thomas.'

'How about Bob Dylan?'

'Well, he was a poet.'

'Okay then, Sting, Coldplay, Jill Scott—anyone who paints a word picture. The music just adds a dimension.'

Jake was surprised at Maggie's passion. He'd had her down as a compilation album sort of a girl.

'If I just think back to the tough years in my life, I'd listen to the same songs over and over, listening to the words, taking them to heart.'

'Well, hopefully, you've been looking through most of my first solo album.' Jake allowed himself a moment of pride. 'Although after this conversation, I think I may need to do some tweaking.'

'I'd trust your instincts.' Maggie was impressed. 'I wish I could be creative.'

'Everyone's creative.'

Maggie shook her head. 'It's okay. I know my limitations.'

'Honestly, it's just a question of stumbling across your talent when you've got time to do something about it.' Jake paused. 'And of course you need a bit of serendipity.'

Maggie nodded. 'Don't we all. So when am I going to hear a song of yours?'

'All in good time.' Jake put the plate down. 'They're all works in progress.'

'And what happens next?'

'I record a few demos and just go out there and find myself a record deal.'

'Simple as that, eh?' Maggie smiled.

'Or, more likely, I am turned down repeatedly, try to remember not to take it personally, give up hope, re-find hope and more cash for studio time and pray that eventually someone in the music business sees the light. It's the best stuff I've ever done. And at least I have some contacts in that world.'

Maggie thought of her job. 'That's so exciting.'

'When it's not terrifying.'

'And I think you'll find that clause 5c) of your lease reserves me the right to demand that at least one song written on the premises is performed for me a cappella.'

'I knew I should have read the small print.'

To Maggie's delight, Jake reached behind the sofa for his guitar. She didn't feel bad. It hadn't taken much persuasion.

As he played the first few chords, Maggie felt the hairs on her neck stand up. As he started to sing, his eyes fixed somewhere else altogether, she felt her nipples harden on the inside of her bra. Enthralled, her hands firmly clasped, as he finished the final chorus and looked over to her for approval, she felt sure she was either going to cry or kiss him. Definitely time to go home.

Finally Red excused himself for a moment, leaving Max and Eloise at the table.

Max leant over. 'So shall we share a cab?'

'Now?'

'Probably best to quit at the top of our game. If we call

his agent tomorrow afternoon and try to get something signed then, bam, we have a legitimate charity initiative. There'll be no stopping us. Celebs will be queuing up with endorsements.'

Eloise fiddled with her napkin, suddenly awkward. 'Why don't you get a cab?'

Max raised his eyebrows questioningly. 'You're not seriously thinking…'

She held her hand up to silence him. 'Not thinking at all but not ready to go home yet, either.'

'We can stay longer.'

'You should get back to Maggie. You've given up enough of your evening already. Thank you.'

'Hopefully we've set out on our way to doing some good tonight. Going on your current rates of persuasion we'll have signed up the Queen by the end of the week.'

She reached over and kissed him hard on the cheek. 'Thanks Max. I really appreciate your support.'

'Any time.' Max put his hand on hers and then retracted it. He raised his glass, the last sip looking less inviting than the first had. 'To Giving a Little.'

'And Living a Little.'

As they toasted themselves, Red returned. Max noticed he'd done something to his hair. He hoped he hadn't brushed his teeth.

He hesitated at his chair. 'So, can I get anyone a brandy? Or a port?'

Eloise nodded at Max.

Max shook his head at he started to get up. 'Just a cab for me, I'd better be off. Thank you.'

'Delighted to meet you. Look after Maggie now, won't you.' Red's expression was making Max feel uncomfortable.

'Of course you've met…'

'We've spent days together in the search for the ideal home. I gather you're providing hers at the moment.'

'So far, so good.'

'Bright girl. Best in the business, I'd say.'

'My best friend.' Eloise beamed proudly. 'Taught her everything she knows,' she teased.

'Tell her I'll be in touch as soon as I can afford to be.' Red smiled.

Max nodded. 'I'll pass that on.'

As the men slapped each other heartily on the shoulder in a charade of camaraderie, Eloise wondered what she was doing. If she stayed she was sure it meant only one thing. Then again if she left, she wondered if she was going to regret not sleeping with Red for the rest of her life or only for the next few months. She tried not to worry about what Max was thinking. This was none of his business.

Max kissed Eloise goodbye. He whispered gently as his lips brushed against her cheek. 'Call if you need anything.'

Max raised his hand in a farewell salute, and Eloise watched him with affection as he left the dining room. She must have drunk far more than she'd thought. Everyone was suddenly looking attractive.

Chapter Twenty-Two

'Thanks for a lovely evening, Miss Forrest.'

Eloise laughed at Red's faux formality as he put his arm around her in the back of his car. 'My pleasure. Sorry if it wasn't quite what you were expecting.'

'Hey, I like your idea and Max is an interesting guy.'

Eloise wished Red would move on from Max. He seemed to be omnipresent at the moment, her guardian conscience. 'I've known him since university.'

'Really?'

'Although he wasn't that inspiring back then. So we'll send the full proposal to your agent tomorrow along with a draft contract.'

Red admired south-west London through the tinted windows. 'You do that.'

For the first time that evening, Eloise wondered if Red was a better actor than they'd given him credit. And she'd sent her safety net home.

As the car arrived outside her flat, the driver automatically looked for a space and parallel parked. Presumptive or well practised, Eloise wasn't sure.

Red looked at her. 'So, what now?'

'Coffee?' Disappointed with herself, she went for the cliché. But then she didn't have a scriptwriter. And absolutely no guarantee of a happy ending. She'd been hoping he'd take the initiative, thus removing any responsibility from her shoulders.

Red kissed her. And for a moment she stopped worrying. Quite a few moments in fact. As he cupped the back of her head gently in his hands, she resisted the urge to check out his six-pack. They were definitely not teenagers.

A montage of images of Red in action mode flashed through her mind, almost a video compilation of his greatest hits; their current clinch—as she imagined it must look—was featured alongside several of his leading ladies. She felt herself smile in the midst of everything. And then suddenly he had his hand under her top.

She pulled back, very aware that there was a third person in the car.

'Maybe we should relocate?'

Red looked nonchalant.

'I mean, what about the driver?'

'Don't worry. Steve's seen a lot worse.'

'Oh.' Eloise pulled her coat closed.

Realising his mistake, Red swore noisily and punched the seat next to him.

Eloise paused as she gathered her poise. 'I think I'd better head upstairs.'

Red flung his head back dramatically and sighed. He wouldn't even look at her.

Eloise could feel the disappointment creeping in. 'Thanks for a great night.'

'Coffee's off?'

'For now.'

'It wasn't meant to sound…'

'It never is. Thanks for dinner. Good night.'

Eloise tucked her bag under her arm and slammed the door closed behind her. As she unlocked her front door, she was relieved to see the car pulling away and if she wasn't mistaken Steve was smiling at her.

Eloise shook her head. What had she been thinking? She was far too old to be a groupie, almost drunk enough to call Jake and demand his presence and tempted to call Max and trumpet her fidelity.

Max found his sleeping beauty on the sofa, remote control still in hand. It had clearly been another music television evening. Max wondered if she learned lyrics by osmosis. It would explain her impressive knowledge.

Leaning over the arm of the settee, he kissed her. Shocked at the assault on her dream-like state, she sat bolt upright and only thanks to his Ninja-worthy reactions did he avoid being knocked out.

Realising he wasn't the enemy, she flopped back to the horizontal position.

'Hey. Girlfriend in a coma. It's serious.' Max knelt down beside her and stroked her cheek. Full of steak and red wine, he was feeling like a real man and, surprisingly, not at all sleepy. He kissed Maggie again. 'You've been drinking, young lady.'

'So have you.'

'But I'll bet you forgot to eat dinner.'

'I had some…'

'Cereal?'

She smiled. Maggie was sure nachos were cereal. Or at least corn was a cereal crop. 'You're good.'

'I know you. And while the man's away…'

'I was supposed to be making a terrine, but I ran out of time.' Maggie didn't feel the need to mention she'd only been back about an hour.

Max ran his finger lightly down from her neck to the V of her jumper and beyond.

Maggie grinned. 'I should send you out with Eloise more often. How was it?'

'Fine.'

'A Red-letter day or even a French-letter day for her?'

Max grimaced. 'I hope not.'

'Is Red interested in the project?'

'Seems to be.'

'And Eloise?'

Max placed his finger on her lips. 'Enough talking. Not enough kissing.' As he undressed her on the sofa, Maggie relished the moment of seduction, eyes firmly closed lest she become distracted by the questions she had. Finally her evening was back on track and she tried not to think about Jake sitting crossed-legged on the floor, guitar in hand, and focused instead on the man of her university dreams.

★ ★ ★

Eloise sat on her bed, a fresh pint of water on her bedside table, two ibuprofen currently surfing their way down her oesophagus on a mission to save her from a hangover and a guilt complex worse than death. She pressed play on her answer phone whilst texting Max the not-so-good news.

Thanks again. Home alone.
Suspect Red may not be on
board after all. Give a little,
take a little, more like it. Fun
evening tho. One 2 tell the
grandchildren if not the
boyfriend!

In the background her answerphone played back a selection of messages, apparently all from Jake.

Hi, it's me. Give me a call on your triumphant return…

Dr DJ, it's Jake, um, no doubt you're still out celebrating. Do give me a shout when you get back…

Me again. Don't worry if it's late. I'm going to be working into the night—got to get a site up. Anyway sleep is for wimps and for mornings. Cool. Call me…

Relieved she was more or less still in one emotional piece, Eloise picked up the handset and dialled Jake.

'Finally she returns from her fans. Did you have a good night?'

'Yes thanks.'

'Pissed?'

'A little.'

'What a day you've had.'

'Believe me, I'm still reeling.'

'Did you remember to eat?'

'Yup. Went to a cool brasserie in Chelsea actually.' Eloise wondered whether to come clean about the real company she'd been keeping. 'My steak was delicious. We should go out to eat more.'

'We should. I'm really looking forward to our holiday.'

'Me too.' Right now Eloise had never felt in more need of a great escape.

'I'm sorry I won't be around to fly out with you.'

'I wouldn't worry about it. Maggie and I can get our traditional magazine fix on the way there and I can watch crappy girlie films without you rolling your eyes. So how was your evening?'

'It started off pretty low-key and ended with a deadline. I totally forgot I'd promised to get a site live by tomorrow morning, seem to have lost a day or two somewhere.'

'Lost in music perhaps.'

'No turning back.'

Eloise smiled at his knowledge of the lyrics. Just gay enough.

Jake sighed. 'I guess I better get on.'

'I don't know how you do it. I need my sleep.'

'Shame. I'd love to see you.'

'Now?'

'Always.'

'I'm tired and drunk.'

'Sounds perfect.'

'What's going on? You're not about to reveal you're off on a gambling trip with the boys?'

Jake laughed. 'Now there's an idea.'

Eloise closed her eyes, ashamed of her evening, which was already tarnishing. She yawned.

'I heard that. I'd better let you sleep. Today Red, tomorrow the world. I'm going to be proud of knowing you one day, I can feel it. Sleep well.'

'And you, when you get round to it.'

Eloise lay on her bed. Not proud. Just tired. And confused. And right now, very relieved to be alone.

Max prepared to turn his Blackberry off for the night. Out of habit he checked his inbox, read Eloise's text and smiled.

Touch-typing on the minikeyboard, he dashed off a reply.

Not a setback as far as I am
concerned. Plenty more fish
in the sea. Mx

As his words flew across London, Eloise slept soundly.

Taking his glasses off, Max stretched out under the duvet as he waited for Maggie to finish her ablutions. He really needed a holiday. Nine days and counting.

Chapter Twenty-Three

All at sea

Sweating, Maggie rummaged through her suitcase in search of the perfect first outfit for her new incarnation as a sailor girl. She couldn't wait to get her plane clothes off.

There was a knock on the hatch above her head. 'Right, we're off, unless you want to come along too?'

Up on deck, Max and Eloise were clearly itching to get going and strangely energetic, taking the humidity, heat and time difference into account. Maggie conversely felt she was running on borrowed time.

'You go. I'll guard the ship.' Maggie really had no desire to go to provisioning. She hadn't flown all the way to St Lucia to get excited about going to a supermarket and a cash and carry.

'Cool. Any special requests?'

'A gallon of cold water and a straw, good weather, calm seas, the usual, fresh fruit, melons, mangos, surprise me...'

Leaving London in February for sunnier climes should have been compulsory. Grey may have been the new black, but it wasn't good for the soul. Maggie hadn't stopped smiling since they'd left home.

She poked her head out of the hatch to be sociable and Max knelt down and kissed her. She was sure this was just what they needed. In nine months her life had changed completely. No patter of tiny feet, just Max's size ten Timberlands cluttering their hall.

'I've got the mobile if you think of anything you can't live without.'

Already wearing deck shoes, faded shorts that doubled as swimming trunks and a short-sleeved shirt, he was clearly on vacation. She couldn't wait to follow suit.

Waiting until she felt them both disembark, Maggie peeled off her cotton trousers and the T-shirt she'd been wearing for nearly twenty hours. She'd have had a shower if she'd been able to find it. Instead, naked, she stood up in the only three square feet of floor space in her and Max's cabin, ready to apply sun cream.

From the outside, their yacht had looked impressively large for four and yet their berth was smaller than their bathroom at home and the mattress was thinner than her suitcase, which was still half full. No one had bothered to tell her there was hardly any storage space although, judging by the size of Eloise's and Max's holdalls, it was clearly something that those in the know knew and she didn't.

Already glistening with sweat, Maggie reminded herself

that despite the cell-like conditions she was in St Lucia. Setting about her task as fast as possible so as to be able to get out into the sun, she soon learned that applying sun cream in eighty percent humidity was futile. Her hands aquaplaned along her legs as a layer of sweat formed between her skin and the expensive lotion, which was water resistant and therefore obstinately refusing to soak in.

Alone, Maggie decided to finish the job in the main cabin. Finally finding enough air circulating to stop her actively sweating, she patted herself dry with a beach towel and started to cream herself properly. She had her leg up on the sink and had yet to do anything to her top half when she felt the boat rock as someone set foot aboard.

'Hello?'

Maggie instinctively flung herself on the floor commando style and grabbed her beach towel just in time to preserve her decency as Jake's head appeared in the companionway.

'Anyone home?'

His eyes might have been hidden behind the mirror lenses on his retro sunglasses but she could feel them smiling.

'Sorry. Bad time?'

'What the hell are you doing here?' As nonchalantly as she could, from her prone position, Maggie forced herself to give him a smile. She hadn't seen him since that night at the flat. 'You're a day early, you could have knocked or something.'

'Lovely to see you, too.' He retracted his head. 'I managed to get on an earlier flight. Hooray for BA.'

Maggie checked all around her. From the volume of his voice he hadn't gone far and there seemed to be windows everywhere.

Maggie got up slowly, wrapping the towel around herself carefully. 'Yippee for me.' Her tone suggested otherwise.

Jake tactfully walked to the bow of the boat and, taking in a 360-degree view of his location, let out a low whistle. 'You've got to love February in St Lucia. And she's a beauty.' Jake murmured approvingly.

Maggie craned her neck to see who he was talking about. And then as she surfaced on deck, she realised he was referring to, and indeed stroking, the boat.

Jake walked back towards her and peered past her into the galley. 'Is the fridge on? I could do with a cold drink.'

'Good job you don't have one on you, because right now I would murder for one. They've gone shopping.'

Maggie was currently somewhere between light-headed and a migraine and had already sucked dry the bottle of Evian she'd carried from London. Water, water everywhere…

Jake slid his sunglasses down to his nose. 'You look very flushed, you feeling okay?'

'General embarrassment aside…' Maggie nodded, relieved to be outside. 'It's just bloody hot down there and the air con isn't on yet.'

Jake laughed. Maggie hadn't realised she'd cracked a joke.

'Why don't you finish getting dressed and I'll see if I can find us a cold drink. I'm sure I passed a bar on the way in. The secret to this sort of holiday is spending as much time drinking outdoors as possible.'

Jake threw a bag the size of Maggie's hand luggage into the saloon.

Maggie looked around for the rest. 'Is that it?'

'Don't know about you, but I'm planning on spending the next eight days in shorts. Plus once you set sail, everything just gets damp and salty so there's no point trying to be stylish.'

'Wish someone had bothered to tell me.' Maggie had kitten heels in her cabin and linen trousers that needed ironing.

'You what?'

'Nothing.'

Jake clapped his hands. 'Nearly thirty years old and I still get childishly excited when I arrive on a holiday. May I never grow up.'

Nearly thirty years old. It was only a three-year age gap, but for a moment Maggie felt like Mrs Robinson as she watched him disembark nimbly, her beach towel tight around her. As soon as he was out of sight, she popped down below to organise a bikini before digging out her favourite shorts to cover the as-yet-untanned cellulite at the top of her thighs. Thankfully she'd shaved her legs before leaving London. It was about the only preparation she'd had time for, but then Eloise hadn't just sold an eight-bedroom house in Hampstead or found a penthouse for Australia's newest fitness guru. She could smell the commission already.

Abandoning any attempt at style, Maggie tied her hair back into a scrunchie and immediately felt a few degrees cooler. She was really looking forward to spending some time catching up with Eloise. There'd been a time when they'd have debated each item they'd packed and yet while she'd been busy at the office, her best friend seemed to have been carving out at least two careers for herself.

★ ★ ★

Bemused, Jake watched Maggie drain the bottle of mineral water in one.

He waited until she'd swallowed the last drop. 'I wasn't thirsty anyway.'

'I assumed you'd…I didn't think…'

'Don't worry about it, I'll have a beer.'

'Let me go and buy more water.'

'Honestly, I'm good to wait until the others get back. For what they're charging at the bar, I'd hope that bottle was hand filled in the French Alps.'

Maggie was doing her best to ignore the constant bobbing of their boat in the water and the slight feeling of nausea it triggered in her.

Reminding herself that thirty-six hours earlier she'd been at work and wearing several layers of clothing plus tights, she lay down on deck and relished the sun on her skin. She was still far from comfortable.

'I don't suppose you know where the sun loungers would be?'

Jake nearly spat his mouthful of beer all over him.

Maggie sat up. 'Don't tell me this is it?'

'I can probably find you a cushion or two.'

When she next opened her eyes, strains of Bob Marley were wafting past on the breeze. As he made way for Groove Armada and then Otis Redding, Maggie eased herself on to her elbows and gradually upright before gingerly making her way back to the cockpit, as Jake had assured her the bit by the wheel was called.

'Everything okay?' He looked up from Eloise's copy of *Heat*.

'Seriously perfect music selection.'

'You can't have a holiday without a mix CD.' Jake stopped at a double-page spread. 'Honestly this Red guy gets more publicity and more girls than anyone else by miles.'

'He loves it.'

'Oh, and thanks for the Valentine's tip. It was a winner.'

'She loved the card.'

Jake frowned. 'And the perfume?'

'Aftershave.'

Jake stopped flicking. 'I bought her Chanel.'

'Pour homme.'

'Oh shit.' He laughed. 'Well, at least we'll both benefit.'

'That's exactly what she said.'

'Great minds.'

'Mind you, it wasn't the first thing she said.'

'I'm sure.' Jake stretched. 'It's the thought that counts, isn't it?'

'It's definitely a good starting point.'

Jake looked very at-home on her holiday and, suddenly guilty that Eloise and Max were running errands while she'd been snoozing, Maggie ventured back to her cabin to finish the unpacking, or rather to cram as many clothes as she could on to the three shelves and three hangers before stuffing Max's bag into a corner and wondering where she could stow a suitcase. Now she was here, she was determined to take to sailing like a duck to water, or something.

Doing her best to get the idea of how she looked full-length via the strategic use of a compact mirror and a chrome bar, she was just about shipshape when she heard footsteps directly above her and a high-pitched shriek as, no doubt,

Eloise realised Jake had arrived ahead of schedule and was only wearing a pair of shorts.

Provisions unpacked and stowed in every available area, the as-yet-untested crew sat around sipping local rum and Diet Cokes. Having now been shown the ropes, literally, Maggie was starting to feel like a salty sea dog, or at least a sweaty sea puppy, a guise she might be able to carry off provided no one discovered that she'd packed a hairdryer, hair straighteners, or red nail varnish.

Despite the Beneteau 50's high specification, she was starting to suspect it was going to be more akin to a luxury caravan than a five-star hotel and she'd never been on a camping holiday in her life. Eloise and her brothers had clearly whittled themselves a ridge pole every summer and Maggie was impressed at how at ease her best friend looked in their current surroundings. She and Max were organising things in perfect synch.

Finally out of chores, Max lay down next to Maggie, resting his head in her lap. He stared up into the light blue sky.

Stroking the hair off his forehead, Maggie followed his gaze. 'Not a cloud in sight.'

He frowned. 'No wind, either. The forecast for tomorrow is similar.'

'So we have to go to a hotel?' Maggie was hopeful.

'We'll motor out. There'll be wind out there and we'll find it.'

Of course they would.

'And I'm going to suggest we make an early start as we haven't got long.'

Maggie wondered if that was her cue to apologise. But it was her busiest time of year.

'I was thinking of setting off at seven, latest.'

Maggie smiled at Jake and Eloise just in case either of them had been under the misapprehension that they were on a holiday, before returning her attention to Max. 'Do you ever unwind?'

'Give me a couple of days.'

She couldn't wait.

'By then we'll be functioning like a real team.'

Maggie rolled her eyes and noticed Jake spotted her. She wasn't being disloyal, just herself.

Chapter Twenty-Four

02:40 in the morning. Maggie lay next to but not touching Max in their cabin as he slept. Airless, despite the open hatches, mosquitoes hummed as they circled their prey. Maggie rereached for the cotton sheet she had already discarded several times, in the hope it might provide adequate protection from proboscises. Covering herself as lightly as possible, she could feel every pore of her skin reaching out for the glancing breaths of air that were being generated by the small plastic fan in the corner of the cabin. Glistening with sweat, Maggie wondered if, based on its noise levels and apparent inefficiency, it could be generating more heat than it was removing.

02:44. Maggie turned the fan off. Blissful peace at last, she prepared to embrace sleep.

02:46. At least three mosquitoes taunted her with Red Arrows style flypasts. Maggie wondered whether she could now hear them because the cabin was quieter or because the fan wasn't blowing them off course. Or maybe it was just one with a high work rate and an attitude problem.

02:47. Open season declared after a mosquito threw down its tiny gauntlet by flying dangerously close to her ear. Max narrowly escaped assault as Maggie reduced the resident mosquito population by one, although clearly after it had dined. Maggie turned the fan back on.

02:51. Maggie placed a sheet over her entire body and head and tucked it underneath her. Due to the small size of sheets provided, the shroud system only worked if she assumed the very foetal position.

03:10. Max still asleep. Almost hallucinating with heat and exhaustion, Maggie stubbed her toe painfully en route to the deck in search of fresher air. Close to tears, Maggie wondered if now maybe the mosquitoes could just help themselves directly from her wound and leave the rest of her alone.

A figure appeared unexpectedly from the darkness. 'You okay?'

'Jake?'

Their voices were a whisper. Above their heads, the halyard intermittently clinked against the mast.

'Can't sleep down there, thought I might take my chances out here, but that's not really working either. Fancy a rum?'

'Trying to drink yourself to sleep?' Maggie couldn't believe she hadn't thought of that earlier.

'I thought it was probably worth a try.'

Maggie reached for the bottle with one hand. The other was still holding her throbbing toe.

He bent down. 'Want me to have a look at that?'

'It's nothing.'

Too tired to protest, she allowed Jake to examine her foot. 'It's bleeding quite a lot. Stay there a minute.'

Maggie sat and stared into the darkness. Where did he think she was going to go?

Jake appeared with a bucket on a rope and threw it overboard before presenting it to Maggie. 'Dunk your foot in there. That'll clean it up. I'll get you a plaster.'

Maggie was only too happy to do as she was told.

'So.' Jake dressed her toe and cleaned the deck. 'Can I assume from your presence up here that you hate mosquitoes as much as I do?'

Maggie nodded. 'And they bloody love me.' She lay down alongside the table and yawned.

'I'd get yourself back to bed.'

'Can't I sleep out here?'

'You can do whatever you like, but the bad news is that the little buggers are out here too.'

'I might sleep though.' Now dozy, Maggie forced herself back up and, stumbling towards the companionway, without thinking, stopped to give Jake a kiss on the way past.

03:40 Maggie was back in bed. Still asleep, Max rolled over and rested his arm on her for several minutes before she moved it away on grounds of overheating. Finally, her body gave up the fight and she passed out.

06:15 Maggie woke to discover she was alone and in desperate need of a holiday. Either she was hallucinating or could smell toast. Pulling on the same shorts and T-shirt she'd worn to dinner the night before, she surfaced to find a hub of activity on deck and in the saloon.

'Morning.'

Eloise was sounding unfeasibly cheerful for a woman who appeared to be up to her elbows in mayonnaise, tinned tuna and sweetcorn.

'Help yourself to some juice.'

As Maggie poured carton long-life orange juice into a thick plastic glass, she felt like she was on a picnic.

'More tea on its way. Cereal on the table and you can grill yourself some toast if you fancy it.'

'Aha, sleeping beauty.' Apparently fully rested and refreshed, Max popped his head and shoulders through the companion-way and gave her a kiss. 'You've just missed the most amazing sunrise.' He disappeared as quickly as he'd arrived.

Bleary eyed, Maggie sat on the top step and watched Eloise. 'Are you making sandwiches?'

'Just the filling, in case we have to have lunch on the move.'

'Where's Jake?'

'Still sleeping. If you want to have a shower on dry land, you better get going. Max wants to leave in forty-five minutes.'

'This is my holiday, right?' Maggie yawned.

Eloise looked up. 'You okay?'

'Exhausted, shell-shocked…'

Eloise registered surprise.

'It's just not what I was expecting. And to think Max thought we could do this, just the two of us.'

'I think he would have got a skipper and a crew.'

'What changed?'

'We signed up.'

'There's still room for a captain. He can have my half of the bed.'

Eloise laughed. 'You'll acclimatise.'

'Don't even think about patronising me.'

'I'm not, sweetie. And just look at Max, he's in his element.'

Maggie watched Max checking the charts and taking readings from a compass. He did look as though he was having a fantastic time. She was glad at least one of them was.

'And you wouldn't want strangers on board, would you?'

'I'll let you know in a few days.' Maggie stretched. She'd forgotten that, first thing in the morning, Eloise's innate optimism could be wearing.

Day one and she was already longing for a breakfast buffet, fluffy towels, an ensuite bathroom, a massage and a pool. She'd never pretended to be Ellen MacArthur.

Chapter Twenty-Five

'Ready to go about?' Max checked his crew were in position as he stood at the helm. Oakley sunglasses on, feet slightly apart, barking orders, he looked every inch a captain and, with a winch handle in her hand to give to Eloise any moment now, Maggie had bluffed her way in to feeling part of the team.

'Leigh-ho.'

As Jake freed the sheet from the winch and allowed the jib to fly, Max steered them on to their new bearing and let the wind do the rest. The boat heeled as Eloise winched the jib hard into its new position and, with her soon to become thighs of steel, Maggie managed to stay upright. So far, increased muscle tone looked to be the best unsung bonus of this trip.

Maggie sat down with her book, determined to make the most of the lack of activity required on her part until their next tack. At sea and at sail there was, finally, thankfully, a continuous breeze.

Three days in, Maggie could now understand why Max loved sailing. For a boy who didn't like reading for hours, or indeed even an hour, there was always something to do. Sails needed "trimming" (basically, adjusting), the route needed plotting and replotting with gadgets that resembled the contents of a giant maths set, the wind speed and direction needed to be monitored, beers needed to be chilled and when everything else was done, the horizon needed to be studied.

For those new to the game, who hadn't yet mastered the basics, there was endless food to be prepared, washing-up to be done, hatches to be closed, decks to be hosed down and holding tanks to be emptied. Maggie had felt more like an au pair than an international bright young thing as they'd set off but now, London life a world away, she was starting to relax into her new role.

Next Christmas she'd settle for a cashmere jumper or a double CD. And maybe she'd buy them for herself. Away from home, she'd had more doubts about her and Max than she could bear to admit although, rationally, she knew that upward of four hours' sleep a night would definitely have helped his (and her) cause.

Max pressed a can of cold lemonade against her back and Maggie gasped. 'Hey.'

'Thought you might like one of these?'

'I don't suppose there's a can of something without eight teaspoons of sugar in it?' Spending twelve hours a day in a bikini definitely made a girl more self-aware.

'There's beer. Or water?' As Max kissed her neck Maggie hoped she tasted musky rather than sweaty. Her real-life action man was looking incredibly healthy, if not quite as toned as his deputy.

'I'm fine actually.' Leaning up against him, Maggie re-immersed herself in her book as he drank her can of drink in a few noisy gulps before burping loudly.

As the yacht cut through the water, for a moment there was silence aside from a rhythm Jake was drumming on the wheel with his fingertips and the waves splashing against the bow.

Max closed his eyes and leant back, enjoying the feeling of the sun on his face and his girl at his side. 'So how about I teach you some knots later?'

Historically, she had always been very bad with ropes whether they were for tying or for skipping. Her first trainers even had Velcro fastenings although she vaguely remembered learning a few basic knots at Brownies; a reef and maybe a half-hitch or something with cloves.

'I can tie a lovely bow.'

'How about a fender knot? And maybe a bowline.'

'If you can do them, I'm fine though, aren't I?' Maggie was only half-joking.

'But what about when we're on a boat, just the two of us, no Jake and Eloise to help out?'

'Thinking about tossing them overboard already?'

Max laughed. 'There's still plenty of the world I'd like to see.'

'And flights are so cheap.'

'You are enjoying yourself though?' Max opened his eyes and looked at her.

'Of course.' Maggie paused as she wrestled with her conscience.

Apparently her poker face needed work. She couldn't

bear the look of disappointment on his face. 'Hey, I'm still learning the ways of the sea and—' Maggie looked around her '—it really is incredibly beautiful out here.'

As they left land behind them heading south to St Vincent on a bearing of something Maggie didn't understand, she wondered if anyone else had noted that they were sailing away from the sun and towards a large cloud.

'DOLPHINS,' Jake shouted as he raced up to the bow. Max was only steps behind him, as was Eloise. By the time Maggie had tied her sarong and found the camera, the dolphins had gone. Bloody wild animals.

However Jake had now noticed ominous clouds approaching as a cooler and stronger breeze started blowing in. 'Hey guys, I'd grab your waterproofs.'

Max took over from autopilot at the helm and squinted through binoculars as the sea started to roll. 'Throw all the books and towels down into the saloon. Mags, run down and check all the hatches. I'd say we're about to get pretty wet.'

Run down and check all the hatches, *please*. As Maggie did her best to scamper round to every cabin, the boat was starting to surf the waves and, to her stomach's dismay, the pictures on the wall were starting to hang at alarming angles. She made it back into the fresh air just in time to avoid disgracing herself.

Breathing deeply and concentrating on the horizon, Maggie lowered her sunglasses and zipped up her waterproof only moments before an exfoliating cloudburst drenched them all. Twenty minutes of strong wind and heavy rain later, the spin cycle was apparently finished, but she was shivering hard.

Max whooped as the sun returned. 'Everyone okay?'

Grey lipped, Maggie peeled her waterproof off, teeth chattering.

'Here you go, babe.' Jake chucked her his towel as Maggie tried to generate some warmth. Hair plastered saltily to her head, this wasn't quite her sailing fantasy. More like *Survivor*. But in a perverse, she will not be beaten, we shall overcome, stiff upper lip British fashion, the more the ocean threw at her, the more her eyes stung, the more she was determined to enjoy herself.

The clouds cleared as fast as they'd appeared, and a vision of calm seas, verdant hills and sun-filled valleys unfurled before them. And as they sailed past rows of lollipop trees on one side of the lush volcano on St Vincent, Maggie did her best to restore her core to holiday temperature. When finally they sailed into Walillabou Bay, where lush palm trees outlined a crescent of sand, Maggie couldn't stop grinning. This was how she had imagined the Caribbean and to her delight they were the only yacht there.

Max barked orders from the cockpit as Jake led Eloise forward to the windlass. Maggie hoped if she just kept quiet and hung out next to Max she wouldn't have to do a thing except read their depth out from a digital display.

Safely at anchor and with a couple of hours of sunshine left, finally this was shaping up to be more like the holiday she'd been hoping for. Eloise lay down on a towel next to her.

Maggie turned to face her. 'Isn't this bay beautiful?'

'You were a bit grumpy with Max earlier.'

'I know.' Maggie hated it when Eloise criticised her, not least because, usually, she deserved it.

'Look around you. I mean, what more could a girl want?' Eloise murmured as she felt the sun relax her.

'A sun lounger of some sort, a poolside restaurant that serves something other than sandwiches, an ensuite bathroom with a shower that isn't also the mixer tap and, um, don't take this the wrong way, but, Max and I've hardly spent a moment together.'

'Well, excuse me if we're cramping your style.'

'Oh no, I'm so glad you're here. Apart from the fact it's a treat to spend more than a few hours together, I can't honestly imagine it being just the two of us. I mean Max and I.'

'Really?' Eloise was surprised. 'But you live together.'

'Not, thankfully, twenty-four consecutive hours a day.'

Maggie rolled over on to her front, trying to find enough room between the hatches to get comfy and somewhere flat enough that, if she did have the good fortune to doze off at some point, she didn't run the risk of rolling into the sea. 'So how are things with Jake? Where is Jake?'

'Taking a nap.' Eloise checked the coast was really clear. 'He's strangely in a relationship mood at the moment. To be honest it's a little weird. Terrible isn't it—they behave well and you get suspicious.'

Maggie didn't like to point out that Eloise's behaviour hadn't exactly been exemplary of late.

'I told you about the card he left.'

Maggie smiled into her towel, delighted her pep talk had paid off.

'The thing is, I also got a dozen red roses.'

'From Jake?'

'Don't be daft. From Red.'

Maggie pushed herself up and Eloise pulled her down.

Maggie reduced her volume to a whisper. 'Why didn't you say something earlier?'

Eloise shrugged. 'There's nothing to say.'

'Of course not. Only the other day Tom Cruise sent me a box of chocolates, just because…'

Eloise laughed. 'Okay, okay.'

'Max and I sat next to you on a plane for nearly eleven hours and you didn't say a word.'

'I didn't fancy a chorus of disapproval and for all I know he sent forty bunches of roses to women all over the world. He was probably just clearing the air. Or hedging his bets. I'm assuming you saw the feature in *Heat* magazine?'

Maggie nodded. She hadn't wanted to be the one who brought it up. '"Painting The Town Red."'

'Five women in five days, Petra had a lucky escape.'

'If you're feeling cynical, her association with Red was definitely to her advantage. I mean who outside the fashion world had heard of her before they started dating, and now she has her own television career.'

'True.'

'Anyway, thank goodness one of those random women pictured in the article wasn't you.'

Eloise's eyes widened as she thought of Jake. 'Could you even imagine…'

'I'm not sure you'd be up for girlfriend of the year any more.'

She reduced her voice to a whisper. 'Between you and me, Jake's enthusiasm is only making me nervous.'

'Not excited?'

Eloise paused. 'I just keep thinking about Red. And Max.'

Maggie raised an eyebrow. 'Max?'

'Only in that I'm constantly comparing Jake to him and, well, it's not pretty.'

Maggie shook her head. 'They're just different.'

'You don't need to worry. I know what you're saying.'

'I'm a Jake fan.'

Maggie's efforts were in vain as Eloise flitted back to her other wavelength.

'You know Red hasn't got back to us about Give a Little?'

Maggie sighed. 'Then it probably wasn't meant to be.'

'Maggie Hunter, the unlikely fatalist.'

'We've all got to believe in something. And I did warn you about Red.' Maggie frowned. 'Not that he's ever made a pass at me. Typical.'

Eloise laughed. 'Probably only because he can't afford to get on the wrong side of you. Have you met his folks yet?'

Maggie nodded. 'They're very down to earth and, if anything, a bit embarrassed by his success, not at all what I was expecting. But they loved the house.'

'And are your parents okay about not being multimillion-aires?'

'They got well over a million. Plus their conscience and karma is intact.'

'They must be so proud of you.'

'Actually I think they're feeling very pleased with themselves. The neighbours even threw them a little party to thank them for not inflicting a whole cul-de-sac of new build houses on them.'

'Have they moved in to their new place?'

Maggie checked the date on her watch. 'Any day now. It's a tiny cottage in Kew. There's barely room to swing a cat.'

'Or a grandchild.'

'They don't need to be worrying themselves about that.'

'I'm sure Max will want herds of children.'

Maggie paused thoughtfully. 'Seriously, do you think that can work?'

'If you have lots of help, I don't see why not. And it's not like he can't afford nannies and all that stuff.'

'Forget the next generation, I meant Max and me.'

Eloise looked around nervously until she positively identified Max swimming a few metres away from the boat. She reduced her voice to a whisper anyway. 'Do you really think this is the time or the place for this conversation?'

'When do you and I ever get a chance to have a heart-to-heart these days? I can't wait until we're forty-something or to schedule a coffee for a week on Friday. And I've had plenty of time to do some thinking while we've been away.'

'You know I think he's very good news.'

'That's pretty obvious. But the two of us?'

'Two of my favourite people.'

'Together?' Maggie forgot she was supposed to be keeping the volume down.

'It looks great from the outside, except when you're being snappy.'

Maggie knew she had lots of faults, but being short-tempered had never been one of them.

'Maybe this is as happy as it gets.' Maggie sighed. She couldn't help suspecting otherwise.

Eloise propped herself up on her elbow and leaned in to Maggie.

'Do you think there's any chance that Red might want more than a one-night stand?'

Maggie shook her head. She couldn't believe that in her hour of need they were back on Red, then again part of her was relieved. 'Maybe a two- or three-night stand. Surely you're not thinking about giving him a second chance? You said it all felt a bit sleazy.'

'It did. But I think that's because we were in the car.'

'I'd relish your far more unique position in being the only one who said no.' Maggie lowered her voice further. 'I'm just not sure that Max and I are truly that compatible.'

'How can you say that? He's your childhood sweetheart.'

'And then I grew up.'

'I think it's unbelievably cute that you're together. It's like a happy ending.'

'Ending. Exactly. Look at us. We live in his perfect house. This is his perfect holiday.'

'He was your perfect guy.'

'Before we'd spent any time together.'

Eloise rolled her eyes. 'If you're determined to find fault and pick holes—'

'Hey, I know successful relationships are always going to involve compromise, but I don't think he even really knows who I am.'

'He'll get there. Remember Max French is a success at everything he does.'

'So is Maggie Hunter.'

'And you say you don't have anything in common.'

'It's just sometimes I feel like I'm just here to amuse him. That he wants to retrain me. Fundamentally we're very different.'

'Not as different as Jake and I.'

'Different can be good.'

'That's not what you just said.'

Maggie sighed. 'Sometimes I feel like he wants me to be more like him.'

Eloise was silent.

'What, so now I'm not allowed to even express an opinion? And I think you should steer clear of Red. Just remember, the grass is always greener on the other side of the bed. Plus it's not like Jake isn't attractive.'

'Maggie!' Eloise giggled.

'I can't help it. He sits around semi-naked all day. The man has a six-pack for goodness' sake.' Maggie wondered if a skateboard could be the answer.

Both women blushed when, as if on cue, a hatch opened a few feet away and Jake's head appeared.

'Hey, Forrest…'

Maggie cringed at the possibility she'd just been over-heard. She buried her head in her towel.

The white cable from his headphone was hanging round his neck. Eloise hoped he'd been listening to something very loud for the last twenty minutes.

'Don't suppose you could spare me a moment? I could do with your help down below.'

From the crease on his cheek, it looked like he'd been asleep and his tone was still dozy, if suggestive.

Maggie pretended not to be looking as he lowered Eloise through the hatch, no doubt directly on to their bed.

Maggie crawled a little further forward and put her iPod on, turning it up to total isolation level. She wondered if she was getting old if she thought it was far too hot to be even thinking about having sex at the moment. Or maybe that was just the sort of sex she was having.

What she'd really love now was a massage. She wondered whether Max was still swimming. As she stared up at the furled jib sheet she smiled to herself. There might have been a forestay on a yacht but there was certainly no foreplay.

A few songs later, a cloud blocked out her sun and Maggie opened her eyes to find Max causing the eclipse, a beer in one hand and a packet of nuts in the other.

'Hello, gorgeous. What do you fancy doing now?'

'Now?'

His hair had been roughly towel dried and, with the sun behind him, was beautifully highlighted.

'I reckon we've got about an hour and a half more daylight. Want to go ashore?'

Maggie peered at the deserted beach. 'Are there shops?'

Max laughed. 'There might be a bar.'

Maggie reached for his beer and took a sip. 'I think I'd rather catch the last few rays from here. Want to join me?'

Max sat himself down behind her and Maggie rested her head in his lap, closing her eyes. When a moment later she opened them again, he was staring at her.

'What are you looking at?' Maggie wondered if he could possibly have overheard her earlier.

'I was thinking. How about tomorrow night we leave the

kids to fend for themselves on board and we spend the night in a hotel.'

Maggie smiled as she reached up behind her and pulled his head down until their lips met in a salty kiss.

He grinned at her. 'I'll take that as a yes then?'

Visualising white sheets and a power shower, Maggie closed her eyes as she kissed him with heartfelt gratitude. The holiday was by no means over.

Chapter Twenty-Six

A night on Mustique; dinner for two served on china, a bed with linen sheets and mosquito net in a room with air conditioning, eight hours' sleep and a visit to a spa and Maggie was feeling like an attractive woman. And now an afternoon in the Tobago Cays, the most stunning blue and turquoise sea that Maggie had ever seen.

Eloise and Max had decided to swim to a nearby sandy beach. From her position as unofficial life-guard she could now see them walking, if not jogging, along the crescent of sand. Part of her was glad Max had found someone to teach navigation to before breakfast; it was just interesting that it wasn't her. A far from impartial observer, Maggie couldn't help but notice that Eloise and Max were more compatible than either of them realised. And here, anchored in the middle of nowhere, she was surprisingly unbothered.

Jake was currently sitting on the bow with a notebook,

staring into the blues. Maggie put down the novel she was half reading and, as the sky started to gain colour in advance of the sunset, started thinking about a sundowner.

'Hey, Chambers, want a cocktail?'

Jake looked up and flashed a smile. 'I'd rather have a beer thanks. You're a star.'

Humming to herself, Maggie rummaged around in the fridge. She was a star. Jake said so.

In three days they'd be home and now the end was in sight, she was really starting to enjoy her holiday. Max was currently enjoying a renaissance in her affections, if in more of a sentimental than a passionate way. Even if she wasn't quite ready to admit it yet, she could feel herself coming to terms with the fact they weren't likely to be together for ever. Getting over a man was always easier when he was still there to remind you what it was that wasn't working and when it was sunny and twenty-seven degrees centigrade.

'Penny for your thoughts?' Jake surprised her with a personal appearance and Maggie dropped an unopened bottle of beer on the floor. As it rolled under the table, they both scrabbled after it, laying hands on it at the same time.

'Yours.' They both surrendered and as the bottle rolled further out of reach, Maggie giggled as Jake combat-crawled into the shadows to retrieve it.

As he got up, he twisted open the bottle and drank the beer as quickly as he could to prevent a frothy explosion, before wiping his mouth on his arm. 'I realise now that lying on the floor semi-naked is a crew tradition.' He did his best to disguise a burp. 'Excuse me.'

Maggie blushed as she thought back to their first day and

looked at Jake, all tan with fluff from the floor now stuck to his sweaty torso. 'At least I didn't have a chest wig.'

Jake looked down his front. 'Guess I'll just have to dive in and wash it off. God I hate holidays. Going to join me?'

As they sprang off the back of the boat, for the first time in a long while Maggie honestly didn't have a care in the world.

'Don't you just love sunsets?'

Eloise watched the warm lava glow spread over the sea as Max inspected their yacht from his position on the beach.

'I've thought about buying a boat.'

'They're seriously expensive though, right?'

Max nodded. 'And you wouldn't want to keep it in the UK, plus the running costs would be huge.' Max was predominantly talking to himself.

'I can't believe we have to head home.' Eloise sighed as she watched the sun reach the sea. She wondered why endings were so much more dramatic than beginnings. And not just in nature.

'I'd like to sail round the world one day.'

Eloise looked at him with a mixture of admiration and concern. 'Isn't that dangerous?'

'I don't mean in a race. Ideally you'd take a year or so to do it.'

'A girl in every port.' Eloise grinned.

Thinking logistics, Max didn't rise to her goading. 'You can always pay a crew to sail the difficult passages and fly part of the way.'

'At which point you probably decide to go along on board just for the ride.'

'Exactly.' Max nodded.

'You should do it. I think it would be awesome.'

'And what do you think about Maggie?' Max burrowed his feet into the sand, searching for a cooler layer.

Eloise paused. 'I wouldn't suggest a year at sea just yet.'

'But do you think she's enjoying herself?'

Eloise could feel him eager to please. 'Look around you. Who wouldn't be?'

Max shook his head. 'After last night I think she'd rather have had a week in a hotel.'

Eloise wondered how truthful he wanted her to be.

'Well, our girlie holidays were traditionally largely sedentary with the exception of multiple runs to the lunch buffet. And I think it did take her a few days to adjust to life on the open sea, but I think she's slowly being converted.'

They both watched as Maggie dived off the side of the boat. Eloise turned to Max. 'I'd say she's settling in now.'

Max was relieved. 'So, have you heard from Red recently?' He sensed her discomfort. 'Hey, don't worry, there's no way they can hear you.'

Eloise raked her toes through the sand. 'As everyone predicted, it looks like he was probably only interested in one thing after all, and it had nothing to do with charity.'

Max's expression was grim.

Eloise watched as the sun started to fade and the water started to change colour from turquoise to purple towards inky black.

'We'd better get back while we can still see.' As she waded into the sea, she stretched her arms above her head before diving under the water and surfacing a few metres ahead, the salt stinging her eyes and today's sunburn. Max was right behind her. As he swam a few extra strokes to bring himself level he pointed out the moon rising.

'Amazing.' Eloise looked from the sun to the moon and back again. 'Is there always an overlap?'

'One goes down, the other rises. The cycle of life.' Max paused.

'I think there's one of those at my gym actually. Actually, maybe that's a Lifecycle.'

Max splashed her.

'Hey.'

Max was bored of treading water. 'So, fancy a race back to the boat?'

'Okay, Mr I've-done-a-triathalon, that's hardly going to be a fair competition.'

'There are no losers.'

'Yeah right.'

But Max wasn't listening. He'd already flipped over on to his back, kicking hard enough to create a pillow of water for himself as he splashed his way back to the boat, Eloise in hot pursuit.

Full of fresh tuna they'd caught on their way to the cays and barbequed off the back of the yacht, Maggie crept to the middle of the boat and lay down on her back to admire the canopy of stars. It was actually less of a canopy and more of a fitted sheet. Max had not undersold the stargazing. The night sky here was more luminous than any she had ever seen before. A halo of mist surrounded the moon. A moon rainbow apparently, although monochrome and a complete circle it was more of a moon polo.

Dinner plates pushed to one side, Max was studying the chart for their return passage.

'We should leave as soon as it gets light.'

'You've got to love the great outdoors,' Jake joked. 'I can't wait to get home and have a lie-in.'

Max double-checked the distances. 'We've got a long way to go tomorrow.'

Eloise nudged him. 'You can count me in for the sunrise shift.'

'Thank you.'

Jake stood up and stretched. 'Count me in for the one after that.'

Feet away in the dark, Maggie pretended she wasn't listening.

Eloise raised her glass which was, once again, almost empty. 'Thanks so much for having us along, Max. It's been fantastic fun.'

'Yeah, thanks. It's been awesome.' Jake drained his beer bottle and went to the fridge for another one.

At the table, Max turned to Eloise. 'So when we get back who are we going to approach next? I think we need at least one big name behind Give A Little, or at least one who's seriously interested, before we can take it much further.'

'What happened to Red?' Jake butted in.

Eloise looked up. 'Where have you been?'

Maggie flinched at Eloise's tone. Apparently she wasn't the only one who could be grumpy.

'Last I heard he was interested. *"Such a great guy"*— remember?'

'He was. And then he wasn't…' Eloise didn't want to get into this now.

Max had apparently drunk away his tact and sensitivity. 'Just say he didn't get exactly what he wanted from the deal.'

'He tried to negotiate conditions on a charity project?' Jake shook his head disbelievingly. 'I always knew he was a wanker.'

'Exactly.' Max concurred heartily. 'He was fine at first, charming at dinner but ultimately he didn't get what he wanted. So he went off the idea.'

Jake turned to Eloise. 'I didn't realise you had dinner with him?'

'Max and I did.' She answered breezily. 'It must have been while you were away.'

On deck Maggie almost stopped breathing. Inhaling and exhaling was making too much noise and there was a live soap opera unfolding on her yacht, or maybe that should have been boat opera? She didn't want to miss a moment.

'You both had dinner?' Jake looked from one of them to the other and then shrugged. 'How cosy.'

Eloise froze. Max was pissed. So was Jake. Now at least one of them was going to be pissed off. Her tone was impressively insouciant. 'It was just business.'

'I didn't think it was a threesome. I'm just surprised it didn't come up. I mean you practically repeated the interview for me verbatim.' Jake's attempt to appear unbothered wasn't fooling anyone.

Max sensed the need to smooth things over. 'We just talked everything through over dinner at a local brasserie.'

Eloise hoped Jake's memory wasn't photographic.

'A brasserie?' Jake's eyebrows performed a Mexican wave. 'The same one you went to with the radio team?'

A safe distance from the action, Maggie did her best to zone out. She'd never been good at confrontation.

When she next opened her eyes, Max was lying next to her. Her stealth boyfriend had made it all the way to her side. He slid his arm underneath her and pulled her close for a kiss. She surrendered to the moment.

'Thought I'd better let those two have some privacy.'

'Do you think that's a good idea?'

Max squeezed her. 'I knew you'd been listening.'

Maggie shrugged. 'I told her she should have said something at the time.'

Max kissed her forehead.

'What's that for?'

'Nothing.' He smiled. 'Everything. It's been a great holiday, hasn't it?'

'I loved Mustique.'

'I love you.' He kissed her again. 'And next time, I promise it'll just be the two of us.'

Maggie smiled. 'Thank you. But…'

She stopped herself. No need to ruin the moment.

'What?'

'Nothing.' Everything could wait until they were back on dry land.

Chapter Twenty-Seven

Maggie stood in the cold light of their tiled, dry, exquisite bathroom on terra firma and slathered herself in cream. It was a futile attempt to glue the surface, and brownest, layer of her skin to the others. She wondered why she'd even bothered getting an all-over tan. The only bits of her that had been exposed since her return would have been sufficiently bronzed in a V-neck and shorts.

She could have sworn when she was a child that March equalled spring. Looking out of the window when she'd got up in the dark nearly an hour ago, it still looked like winter. But with heating and carpet in the bedroom and hot water, mirrors and a hairdryer in the bathroom, she was a very happy bunny.

Using the remains of her suntan lotion to moisturise her face and neck, Maggie clung on to that holiday feeling. The scent would not only ensure her holiday mood lasted until at least the second week of their return, but this way she might actually finish the bottle instead of keeping the last third for the next five years—never full enough to justify packing for another holiday but too much to feel guiltless about throwing it away.

As she pulled her tights on, she marvelled at the pleasure that having dry feet and straight hair could bring. She was clearly more superficial than she'd realised. Or too spoiled and the way this week was going, it was only going to get worse. She loved it when the city bankers got their bonuses. She'd had two happy customers already since they'd got back. Bonus time for her, too.

One leg in tights, the other still naked, Maggie hopped across the room to answer her now ringing mobile. Could it be she was up for a hat-trick? She glanced at the screen. Nope.

'Ahoy there.'

Eloise wondered if Maggie knew how often she'd answered the phone to her like that recently. 'Sorry to call so early.'

'No problem.'

'You around this morning?'

'Sadly not.' Maggie checked her watch. 'I shouldn't even be here now. Why?'

'Thought you might like a coffee and to gee me up for my radio rounds.'

'I'd hire you on the spot. Just make sure you walk in there confidently.'

'I'll do my best.'

'Just be you. Call me as soon as anything happens…or before.'

'Will do. So, everything good your end?' Eloise was just

going through the motions, hoping Maggie would ask her the same question.

'Yup. Busy, but great.'

'Max?'

'He's somewhere in South Africa on business.'

'God, that man gets around.'

'You might want to think about rephrasing that.'

'Hey, do you think he's diamond shopping?'

'I think he's thinking about investing in a hotel group, but thanks for winding me up.'

Maggie's mind started racing, and not in a good way. They hadn't had a moment for a personal conversation after they'd got back before he'd left. 'He's back later today.'

'Perfect. How about lunch?'

Maggie sensed something artificial about their conversation. 'What is it, El?'

'Oh, just so you know, Jake and I called it a day last night.'

Maggie did an aural double take. 'Just so I know? Have I been demoted to the position of your aunt?'

'It's no big deal. All very amicable, in fact. He wants to focus on his stuff and I want to focus on mine. He needs his space, and to be honest, so do I—from him. We weren't good for each other any more.'

'Does this have anything to do with Red?'

'I'd say no, but Jake's written a whole song about it, so now I'm not sure.'

Maggie wanted to tell her Jake had penned it weeks ago but realised she probably wasn't supposed to know.

'I don't want you to think we didn't have a great holiday though. We both had a wicked time. I just think we've both realised that "we" were as good as we were ever going to get so it was time to move on. It was all very rational. No shouting.'

'No tears?'

'Actually no, not yet. A few stray solitary ones but no sobs, no heaving chests…'

Maggie hadn't realised there was a Beaufort scale when it came to crying.

'Oh, and did I tell you that the hospital has asked me to be chairman of the radio station?' Difficult news delivered successfully, Eloise's pace picked up at the good stuff.

'I only spoke to you two days ago and that's two major announcements I've missed.'

'It's been a hectic couple of days.'

'I can't believe you didn't call to tell me.'

'I'm telling you now, aren't I? I'm also thinking of pitching a weekly show that broadcasts simultaneously at all the London hospitals in conjunction with City FM.' Eloise's excitement was tangible.

'Sounds like a great idea. Congratulations. And I have to be honest, you sound better than okay.'

'The way I see it, I've gained a younger brother and lost an immature boyfriend. I don't know why it took me so long to face facts.'

'I thought the sex was great?'

'There's more to life than sex.'

'Thank goodness.'

Two women in life, they shared a giggle, Maggie laughing a little too hard. 'Well, good for you for tying things up.'

'Actually he was the one who initiated it. I would have in time, but I don't know, I was sort of waiting.'

'To meet someone else?'

Eloise paused. 'I read a survey that said women in relationships were far more attractive to single men than single women.'

'I do wish you'd stop reading crap like that.'

'My time will come. I'll meet the right man. You'll see.'

'I thought, according to a previous survey, you already have met him?'

'Touché.'

'And speaking of wrong men, any word from your celebrity bastard?'

'Truthfully, I thought about sending him a text only this morning, but then I thought better of it.'

'That's my girl.' Maggie paused. 'And I'm genuinely sorry things didn't work out with Jake. He's a fun guy.'

'Thanks to you both for such a great holiday.'

'I'm sorry it didn't have the desired result.'

'We needed to know where we were headed, now we do. It was exactly the holiday we needed.'

The latest news slowly percolating, Maggie had a sudden thought. 'Are you still cool with Jake living in my flat?'

'Of course. If you are?'

Maggie wondered if that was a loaded question, some sort of loyalty challenge? It was too early in the day for mind games.

'I still care about the guy. I'd hate for him to be homeless.'

'Good.'

'Anyway, I think he's looking to buy. He's decided it's time to grow up. It seems to be the case that men date me and then change for the better.' Eloise laughed. 'Anyway, got to go. I haven't finished preparing for my meeting at City FM and I've only got one of my tights on.'

Maggie looked at her reflection in the mirror and laughed at the symmetry of their mornings. 'Snap. Let's try and have a coffee soon or maybe we can manage an alcoholic beverage or three one evening.'

'Definitely. I'm around. And weekends are going to be good for me. Again.'

'Call me if you need anything, or just a rant.'

'Of course.'

'And let me know if you have any news after your meeting at City. If we could return to the same-day news service I'd really appreciate it.'

Eloise was apologetic. 'I'm so sorry. There was just a lot going on.'

'I know how that feels.'

'But—and this is going to sound weird—in some ways I couldn't be better.'

Maggie nodded to herself. It didn't sound weird at all.

Chapter Twenty-Eight

'The first round's on me.' Maggie didn't feel compelled to mention that the company credit card would be footing the bill. Grabbing Lucan for assistance, and because he was tall enough to pick out the best route through the crowd, she headed to the bar.

Struggling to recall the blue of the sea and the feeling of the sun on her back, in the spirit of team bonding, and readjusting to life with less alcohol and no sundowners, Maggie had finally succumbed to one of Simon's suggested team outings to the nearest pub.

Home was where her life was and they were having a fantastic month. Everyone was working crazy hours, but employment spirits had never been higher, hers included, and when the big boss had deigned to put in a rare appearance, it had been one compliment after another. And then a pay rise. No bartering required.

Trays full of drinks, elbows out, they made it back to their pushed-together table almost intact and distributed the glasses.

Maggie raised her large spritzer. 'To us all. May we continue to be hot property.'

Everyone laughed. Possibly because they were holding a free drink rather than because she had been funny, but Maggie didn't really care. She was enjoying being part of a happy team.

Simon stood himself next to her. 'So come on then, exactly how bling was the yacht? Are we talking white leather?'

Maggie laughed. 'Nope. Nor gold fittings. But the bluest sea you've ever seen. And believe me, Max can certainly sail.'

'Aye-aye, whatever rocks your boat, I guess.' He drank half his lager in one.

Maggie decided not to react in case it encouraged him. 'So, what's going on with your personal life?'

Simon shuffled a little. 'Not much.' To Maggie's amusement he was being defensive.

'So nothing in the rumour that you're seeing Cherie's daughter?'

He looked nervously in Cherie's direction. 'Yeah, well, she's pretty fit, if you know what I mean. Top drawer.'

Maggie smiled to herself. Simon was every future mother-in-law's worst nightmare.

'Shoulda known there'd be no secrets round this place.'

'Not if you date people's daughters, especially for a few consecutive weeks.'

Simon shrugged. 'We'll see. I'm not sure I'm her type.'

'I thought you were everyone's type?'

Simon frowned. 'It's difficult being a bloke these days.'

'Don't you of all people go all new man on me.'

'I'm serious. Girls want you to do all the running, all the calling, all that, but then they don't play ball. If you know what…'

Maggie didn't need him to finish.

'Someone's calling you.'

Maggie looked around the group. Everyone seemed to be deep in their own conversations.

'On your phone.' Simon shook his head.

'Thanks.' Maggie rummaged in her bag, only then hearing her ring tone. 'Maggie Hunter.'

'So, how about I cook you dinner tonight?'

'You're home already?'

'Home, unpacked, shopped, just waiting for my gorgeous girlfriend to join me.'

'I'm having a quick drink in the pub with the office. Really I am.'

Max laughed. 'What time will you be back?'

After being home alone for the last week, Maggie reminded herself it was a reasonable question.

'I don't know. Around eight?'

'So if I have supper ready for eight–thirty?'

'Better say nine. That should be fine.'

'Fine, fabulous?' She could hear Max smiling.

'Exactly that.'

Walking up the path, she reluctantly removed her glove to rummage in her bag for her house keys and glared at the sky, daring it to snow. Apparently March was the new December. She hadn't got as far as putting the key in Max's lock when the front door opened.

Max stood there freshly showered, dressed in jeans and the Smedley jumper she'd bought him for Christmas, his holiday tan topped up by the South African sun. He looked great. 'You're late.'

'Very busy day. All peopled out.' Suddenly she remembered she hadn't called Eloise back. Very bad friend.

Maggie gave Max a glancing kiss before taking her coat off and hanging it over the banisters. The house was lovely and warm.

'But good news for me—big pay rise, possible shares to follow.'

Max gave her a hug. 'Good for you. You deserve it.'

She was sure his praise wasn't meant to sound patronising. Maggie knew she was oversensitive about her earning power versus his. 'So, how was your trip?'

'Good. Missed you though.'

'It wasn't even a week.'

'I'd got used to having you within my sights all day.'

'You'd think you would have been dying for a change of scene then.' Maggie followed Max down to the kitchen. She'd been enjoying being back at work.

He held up a chilled bottle of white wine from the fridge. 'Want to start this now or shall we pop to the pub for a drink first?'

'I think I'd rather have a cup of tea.'

'I thought it would be nice to go out.'

Maggie filled the kettle and flicked the switch. 'It's freezing and I've just come from a pub.'

'Think roaring fire. Leather sofa for two.'

'Right now I'm thinking packet of crisps.' Maggie stared

into the cupboard. 'Lunch passed me by. I did buy a sandwich, but I must have left it on my desk.'

'Just hang in there, supper's all taken care of. I've made your favourite.'

Maggie grinned. Eloise was right, Max could be too good to be true. 'Lasagne?'

Max frowned. 'Thai Green Curry?'

Maggie laughed. 'You mean *your* favourite?'

'Our favourite?'

'Nice attempt at a recovery.'

'Let's go and get a pint and then eat.'

'I'm quite happy here.'

'Go on, just one. I've had a ridiculous week and I want to unwind with my girlfriend.'

Maggie reminded herself that he had cooked dinner. And it wasn't fish pie.

'I don't suppose I could sit on the sofa for ten minutes first?'

'Later. If you sit down now, that'll be it.'

Returning her empty mug to the cupboard, Maggie wondered when her life had become an endurance event.

Silently she followed him up the stairs to the hall.

'So, I spoke to Emmy and Ed today and guess what, Tabitha had kittens.'

'No.'

'Why not?'

'It'll shred the sofa, swing from the blinds and the house will smell faintly of cat pee. Everything we own will have cat hair on it.'

Max wondered if maybe he should wait until after dinner. Then again, he always had been impetuous.

Maggie had never been able to decide whether she thought domestic animals or babies were more destructive. 'We do not want to be getting a pet.'

'Let's at least think about it. You did mention once that you wouldn't mind having a cat.'

'Okay.' Maggie had done all the thinking about kittens that she needed to. Now she was thinking about Eloise and Jake and the fact she really hadn't talked to Eloise properly about it. She was sure Max wouldn't mind if she called her.

Max had already put his jacket and shoes on and reluctantly Maggie trailed in his wake. At the front door he turned. 'Hey, have you got keys?'

Maggie felt her coat pocket. 'Nope.'

'Can you grab mine? They're just on the stairs.'

Maggie sighed wearily as she picked up the bunch and, just about to chuck them to Max, she stopped. And stared.

There was another ring on the key ring. And this one had a huge diamond in it. Kitten forgotten, this was a sodding great cat among the pigeons.

She looked up. Max was no longer at the door. Much worse, he was on one knee.

'Does Mrs French sound good to you?'

Maggie's head was spinning. Sometimes she wondered if they were in the same relationship. Then again she hadn't exactly been keeping Max in her mental loop. She'd been waiting for the right moment. And this hadn't been it.

'I had a wonderful holiday. And I think you'd make me a wonderful wife.'

Maggie knelt down to join him and, putting the keys

down, rested her hands on his shoulders. 'Thank you so much…' Max certainly had balls. No one had ever dared to propose to her before.

He leant to kiss her. She held her hand up to pause him in his tracks.

'I can't say yes.'

Max just stared. 'What do you mean, *can't?*' His face darkened.

Maggie looked to the heavens, or at least to the ceiling, and asked for advance forgiveness for ruining his day/ week/month/year. 'It's not what I want. Not now.'

'There's no rush. We can wait a few months.'

Maggie shook her head slowly but certainly as weeks of doubts crystallised into an unstoppable force.

'It's not so much the wrong time. I think I'm the wrong person or at least not the person you think I am. I'm sorry.' Irrational tears sprang to her eyes. Maggie sat back on her heels and then sat on the floor, her back against the bottom stair. Max was still kneeling.

He shuffled towards her, forgetting he had the full use of both legs. 'I don't understand. We're so happy.'

'You're so happy.'

'What are you—'

'Long term, I don't think I'd be enough for you.'

'Surely that's my call?'

'I'm sorry.'

'You can't do this to me.' Max could feel his disappointment and shock turning to anger.

'To us. And I'm afraid I have to. Surely it's best I say something now.'

Max shook his head grimly. This was not going according to plan.

Maggie watched him nervously, wondering what happened next. 'I'm really sorry. It's not you, it's me.'

'Right.' In shock, Max got to his feet and dusted his knees down. 'I definitely need to go to the pub now.'

There was bouncing back and there was denial. Maggie wasn't sure where he was emotionally. 'I think we should talk about this.'

'What is there to say? You don't love me. I'm a bright guy. I get it. No point in hammering it home.'

Maggie sighed. 'I do love you or at least I used to. I'm just not sure I'm in love with you.' She stopped herself. Everything she said at the moment made her sound cruel and unreasonable.

Max shook his head disbelievingly. 'A line I've used successfully in the past myself and it feels pretty shitty at this end of it, let me tell you.'

'I've felt better myself.'

'I guess I'm supposed to be grateful that you're being honest.' He paused. 'Were you ever in…?'

'Of course, and we probably could have tootled along for a few more months, even a year or two. You're the one who called a summit meeting.'

'I didn't think this was going to be the outcome.'

'I didn't think I'd ever be able to trust another man enough to give love a go.'

'Delighted to have been of service.' Max doffed an imaginary cap.

'Don't be like that. We have been a revelation for me.'

'Be like what? Fucking hell, Maggie, I just asked you to be my wife and you said no.'

Maggie felt her eyes fill with tears again. 'I could have said yes now and no later, would that have been better?' Being the bad guy didn't suit her.

Max shrugged.

Maggie couldn't bear the pressure. 'Have you spoken to Eloise today?'

Fists clenched, he crossed his hands in front of his chest. 'Brilliant tactic, Mags. Textbook. Always easiest to change the subject.'

'She and Jake have called it a day.'

'So what? Are you going to tell me it's catching? You two don't have to do *everything* at the same time. Well, I hope you have a great time out on the pull together. How sweet.' Max disguised his hurt with aggression.

'Don't be like that. She wants to find the right man, not just a man, before committing. You can't fault her for that.'

Something about him softened. 'Good for her. They were an unlikely couple.'

'I don't know.'

'She needed someone more, well, interested, hands on.' Talking about Eloise, Max was animated, involved. 'She really doesn't need to be tied to one place and one person. Not until she's found herself.'

Suddenly low on energy, and remembering what had just happened, Max sat down on the stairs. 'You really don't want to marry me?'

Maggie shook her head. As she looked into his eyes, she almost changed her mind out of sheer guilt. 'I'm so sorry.'

'So you keep saying.' Max shrugged. 'I guess you don't want to marry anyone.'

'I didn't say that.'

'You're not helping.'

'But really you're a great—'

Max waved his hand for her to stop. Maggie could see him battling to control his emotions.

She sat down next to him and took his hand in hers. 'Thing is, Eloise isn't the only one who deserves better.'

'I did my best.'

'Not me—you.'

'I thought I had the best.'

'Well.' Maggie managed a watery smile. 'I'm up there, but…'

Max pulled his hand back. 'This isn't fucking funny.'

'Well, you know me.'

'Can't face up to reality.' Max's expression was grim.

Maggie could feel her hackles rising. 'I've had to deal with more reality in my life than most. I'm just trying to be honest with you. You'll thank me for this in the long run.'

'What about compromise?'

'We're not discussing a choice of car—we're talking about the rest of our lives. You want a kitten, you want kids and I don't want you to change. Most people would say you're pretty perfect as you are.'

'Just not for you.'

Maggie nodded. 'Exactly.'

'So, that's it.' He exhaled slowly.

Maggie couldn't quite speak.

'What I don't understand is, if I hadn't proposed, would you still be leaving me?'

'Probably not today…' Maggie sighed.

'So you hadn't already decided?'

'No. Not exactly.'

'But you'd been thinking about it.'

She nodded.

Max looked around. 'I can't believe it. The first woman I ask to marry me says no.'

'Maybe it'll be second time lucky.'

Max looked at her. 'Now you've lost me.'

'I thought you were an intuitive businessman.'

'Meaning?'

'How about applying some of your instinct elsewhere?'

Max hadn't thought he could become more confused.

'It isn't a trick question.' Maggie made sure she had eye contact. 'What makes you happy? Who really makes you happy?'

Max raked his fingers through his hair distractedly. 'God, I don't know.' He paused. 'Eloise thought you'd say yes.'

'You spoke to Eloise about proposing to me?'

'Only briefly. I wanted her advice. She reckoned you'd probably panic at first, say yes eventually and that you'd be a fool not to.'

'Oh really.'

'Something like that. She said she'd have been over the moon if I'd asked her.'

'She did?' Maggie's eyebrows almost reached her hairline. 'And what did you say?'

'Relax. She didn't mean it like that. So any chance you're still panicking?'

Maggie shook her head.

'So Eloise doesn't always understand you, either. That makes me feel a little better.'

'Why don't you ask her what she meant?'

'I really don't want to keep raking it over.'

'You could at least ask Eloise out for dinner.'

She got to her feet and Max followed suit.

'Eloise?'

'I know you think she's fantastic.'

'I do, but not…' Max stuttered to a halt.

Maggie folded her arms, delighted that the mood had started to change. 'I could see it working.'

Max looked at her. 'Now you're being weird. I just asked you to marry me.'

As Maggie took a step towards the door, she realised she already had her coat on. 'I think I'm going to go out now.'

'To the pub?'

Maggie shook her head. 'I need a moment alone.'

'Where are you going to go?'

'No idea.'

'Won't you at least stay and have supper first?'

'I couldn't eat a thing.'

'But you can't just go out.'

Maggie felt herself bristle. 'I can't?'

'I'm not letting you.'

'It's not up to you any more.'

'It never was though, was it?'

'Don't worry, I'll be fine.' Maggie hugged Max. 'And any minute now, you'll realise you are too. That this would have been wrong, we'd have been making a mistake.'

Max still wondered how she could be so sure. 'Are you coming home later?'

Home? 'I think I might just go and crash at Mum and Dad's.'

Max sighed. 'I can't believe today is ending like this.'

'Better a day, than our marriage.'

'Say hi to Carol and David from me.'

'Of course I will.'

'Take care.' His voice cracked.

'Hey, it's not like we're not going to see each other again.' As Maggie opened the door she felt a surge of relief.

'I can't believe you turned me down.'

'Honestly, I'm surprised you asked me.'

'I wish I hadn't now.'

'We don't need to tell anyone.'

'How can you be so clinical about this? Are you going to call Eloise and tell her?'

Maggie kissed him on the cheek. 'Absolutely. But why don't you give her a call first. I don't want to talk to anyone right now, at least for an hour or two.'

Stunned, Max watched Maggie get into her car and automatically waved her off. No wonder so many men were gay. For all his success, the female brain remained an enigma to him.

Chapter Twenty-Nine

Maggie stared at the granite headstone. It was the same colour as Max's kitchen work surfaces and almost as shiny. She was sure Adam was more weathered by now.

It would be four years in July since she'd last been to the cemetery. But she'd obviously been paying more attention than she'd realised on the day of the funeral, because she had just navigated herself to a part of north-west London she barely recognised. Illuminated by street lamps on the periphery, the centre of the cemetery was darker but surprisingly not at all eerie.

She walked around the grave before squatting down in front of it. Somehow it felt more appropriate to be on a level. 'Hello Adam…'

Maggie glanced at the headstones on the adjacent plots. 'So what are the neighbours like?'

Self-conscious at the sound of her voice in the dead calm, Maggie hesitated. But she talked to her houseplants when no one else was around and her basil had certainly perked up when threatened with the bin. With the air full of invisible streams of communication from text messages to television channels, who knew who could hear what? And she wanted to be clear. For them both.

'Hey, I'm sorry I haven't been for a while. At all in fact. Which, if you are managing to keep a log of visitors—which I doubt you are—you will have noticed. But I don't like cemeteries. And, for a while, if I'm honest I didn't really like you, either. But you can't blame me for that.

'You're probably wondering what I'm doing here. Honestly? I'm not sure. I used to wonder what would have happened if you hadn't been knocked down. Whether we'd have tried again, gone for third time lucky, or if you'd have left me for her? For a while, not knowing left me in limbo. Or at least that's what I told myself. Now I suspect it was just a useful smokescreen. And I am sorry we parted on such acrimonious terms. Not that you left me much choice. Not that it was my fault. You know what I mean.'

Maggie paused to do her coat up as high as she could. Her nose was dripping.

'So I went to your dad's wedding. He seems happy and Ivy's a good sort. Jamie was on great form and Max was there too. Max French. Remember him? Turns out he is a friend of Jamie's from school. I knew him from university and we've sort of been seeing each other, well we were.'

She watched her breath curling upward from the plot like a spirit. Maggie rubbed her gloved hands together and shifted her position while she still could. Her feet were almost numb.

'Everyone thinks he's perfect. Even more perfect than

you. Hah. And Max just asked me to marry him. Before you get a swollen head, I am not here to ask for your permission. And I said no.'

Maggie noticed a couple of withered bouquets just to the right of the headstone. If she'd planned her visit at all, she'd have brought him flowers, or a magazine or a Kit Kat or something. Kit Kats were always his favourite.

'I said no. I didn't have to think twice about it. I just knew.'

As she moved a few shrivelled leaves from the first bouquet, a dirty, weathered florist's card fell from the centre.

THINKING OF YOU…on your birthday. Hope you're having a peaceful one. Miss you every day. Lots of love, Dad
x

Of course. Feb 11th. Always two reasons to have dinner out in one week. Guilty tears sprung to her eyes. She really had put him behind her.

The second bunch was damper but just as dead. Maybe that's how Adam liked them these days. The card had been thoughtfully placed in a Ziploc bag. 'On your birthday. With love now and always. Your Evie.'

Her. Again. And clearly she was a much nicer person than Maggie, or she'd loved him more, or she had a reminder in her Outlook.

'I see you still have a way with the ladies.'

It looked like he'd picked the right girl after all. She wondered if things had been different, whether Eve would have left her husband for Adam. Maggie added Jeremy's card to the bag for safekeeping and longevity before leaning them up against the headstone.

'It's funny. I was thinking on my way over tonight, do you even know how many times I'd hoped you'd spring a ring box on me?

'Anyway, it's fucking cold here on earth so I'm off. I just wanted to let you know that you didn't ruin my life after all. You didn't break me. If anything you made me stronger. So, well, I'm sorry. Just generally.'

Maggie turned to leave and then stopped again.

'Do you know it's funny, usually around Christmas time or my birthday, I half expect to get an email from you letting me know how you are.' She shook her head at her own insanity. 'I stood here nearly four years ago and watched them lower the coffin into the ground and I still think you might call.'

Maggie took a step back towards the path and the land of the living. For the first time in their relationship, Adam had been a good listener.

London was apparently as crowded after death as it was in life. As Maggie picked her route carefully back to her car she wondered if the men in white coats were gathering. She felt strangely calm. Max might have been the man of her dreams ten years ago, but he wasn't the man of her future. And neither had Adam been.

It was edifying to know that she was coming out on top. And the great cop-out about being a fatalist is that she believed everything happened for a reason. Then again, you did have to be in the right place at the right time. You had to help you help yourself.

Chapter Thirty

Recently thawed by mobile state-of-the-art German heating technology, Maggie rang the bell to her flat. She hadn't spoken to anyone other than Adam since leaving Ladbroke Grove and now she found herself at home although, it appeared, she was there alone. Luckily, she'd never taken the set of keys to her flat off her key ring. She let herself in.

Perching awkwardly on the sofa, she wondered what she was doing. Aside from trespassing, that is. But she needed to go somewhere she'd be welcome for the night and she wasn't ready to have Eloise tell her how stupid she was yet. But this wasn't her place any more. Time to revert to her original plan. Time to tell her parents. Time to face the music. Then sleep. Turning the television off, she left as anonymously as she'd arrived.

Max had finally moved from the stairs. He'd sat there for a while, replaying the evening's drama and now he was in the kitchen with a bottle of wine and a Thai Green Curry keeping warm on the Aga.

He picked up the phone again. This time he was going to actually call. He dialled Eloise's mobile.

It rang. And rang. And rang. Almost relieved, Max started composing his answerphone message. And then she answered. 'Hello?'

'Eloise. Hi. It's Max.'

'Hi. How's it going? I've been meaning to call you.' Eloise walked into an area of Selfridges that had slightly less of a nightclub vibe than Spirit. She wandered through into the cosmetics hall, slaloming between several women brandishing bottles of perfumes.

Max was in a better mood already. She sounded as effervescent as ever.

'You have?'

'Yup, I had this meeting today at City FM and I mentioned Give A Little, you know just the concept and our outline. Anyway they sounded really interested. Potentially good for increasing awareness, don't you think?'

'Could be great.' Remembering why he was calling, Max was struggling to sound enthused.

'Is everything okay?'

'I'm not sure.'

Eloise stopped in her tracks, wishing she had a less active imagination. 'Maggie?'

Max could hear the panic in Eloise's voice. 'She's fine. Well, I think she's okay. But she's not here.'

'That girl spends far too much time at the office.'

'Actually, she's left.'

'Her job? And to think she had the cheek to tell me off this morning about withholding information.'

'Me. She left me.'

Eloise froze. 'When?'

'About an hour ago. Have you heard from her?'

'No.' Eloise wondered why she hadn't called, especially after this morning's promise. Maybe she was at her flat? Eloise started walking towards the main doors. 'Why?'

'I just wondered if she'd spoken to you.'

'Why did she leave?'

'Lots of reasons.'

'Had you mentioned the proposal?'

Max sighed. 'That was definitely the catalyst.'

'Oh shit, I'm so sorry. I feel like such a fool.'

'I think I win in that category at the moment. I can't quite believe it.'

'Of course you can't.'

'I think I'm in shock.'

'Of course you are. Maybe you should have a whisky? Or tea? Sweet tea.'

'Maggie told me to give you a call.'

'She told you to call me?'

'I promise those were her explicit instructions.'

'I take it you've heard about Jake and I?'

'Yes. And I was going to call.'

'And now you have. Clearly this is the week for starting afresh.' Eloise paused. 'Between you and me, I feel better already.'

'Good. That's good.' Max hoped that, in time, he'd be

able to claim the same. 'I don't suppose you want to meet for a drink?'

'Tonight?'

'I definitely need one and a friendly face would be a real boost. Any chance you can come over?'

'Why don't you come to me?'

'I have food here.'

'Actually I think I better call Maggie first.'

'Of course.'

'Where did she go?'

'No idea. She said she wanted to be alone.'

'If she's not careful, she's going to spend her life like that.' Eloise was talking to herself.

'Sorry, I didn't catch that.'

'Not important. Look, I'll call her and if you don't hear from me in the next half hour assume you're fine to come over. Make it an hour. It'll probably do you good to get out of the house.'

'I've only just got back from Johannesburg.'

'Max French. Don't be facetious.'

Max nodded. She was right as usual. 'Okay, if I don't hear from you I'll jump in a cab in a bit. Have you eaten?'

'Not yet.'

'Fancy a Thai curry?'

'Yum. My favourite.'

'Excellent. Hopefully we'll see you later then.'

'We?'

'Me and Le Creuset.' Max put the phone down. It was certainly the strangest evening of his life so far, but surprisingly not the worst.

Eloise jogged along Oxford Street looking for a taxi with its light on. If Maggie was at her flat, she needed to get there before Max did. First checking for missed calls and text messages, now on a rescue mission, she dialled Maggie's phone.

Maggie's parents' new place might have been small, but it did have two bedrooms. Three if you counted her dad's 'study'—basically a shed substitute. Finding herself face to face with the third front door that evening, she rang the bell, ignoring her phone as it rang out in her bag.

'Darling. What a lovely surprise.' As her mum embraced her, Maggie held on for dear life. At least this sounding board had a heartbeat.

'I was passing and saw the lights were on.'

'You've been working late again.'

Maggie didn't contradict her.

'Can I make you a cup of tea?'

Maggie followed her mother into the kitchen. 'A cup of tea would be great. And maybe some toast? And a bed for the night?' She leant in the general direction of her father, who art on sofa. 'Hi Dad.'

Now they had Sky, her father could always be engrossed in one of the news channels. David raised an arm in silent greeting.

Her mother stirred vigorously. 'Did you say a bed?'

'Yup.'

'Is Max still away?'

'Well, the good news is, I got a pay rise today and the bad news is…' Maggie sighed, anticipating her mother's reaction. 'I'm sorry to report we've split up.'

'Oh no.' Maggie saw her mother steady herself.

'It's for the best.'

'What went wrong? You've just been on holiday and I thought that for once, well, you know…' Her mum was already looking more upset than Maggie was.

'There's nothing like ten days at close quarters to bring everything to a head.'

'So now you're single again?'

Her mother made it sound as grave as being HIV positive.

'It's hardly the end of the world.'

Carol shook her head. 'When will you appreciate that things are changing. You're getting older.'

'I know how old I am.'

'Your generation may not look your age, but you can't cheat nature. What about children?'

'Luckily we don't have any to fight over.'

'Maggie.' Her mother's tone was one not to be messed with.

Maggie wrapped her fingers round the mug, seeing how much heat she could absorb.

'Am I to take it, from your cocksure and sunny disposition, that this was your decision?'

Maggie nodded as her mother shook her head. She found a stale croissant in a white paper bag on the breadboard and started nibbling.

'He asked me to marry him.'

'Oh darling.' Carol's eyes filled with tears.

'I couldn't say yes.'

Her mother winced.

'I honestly think some of it was about timing for him. And surely it's an even bigger deal if you say yes and don't mean it?'

'You'd never have had to worry about anything again.'

'I'm assuming you mean financially?'

'Well.' Her mother paused. 'Yes.'

'So it doesn't matter if I'm not in love with him as long as he can pay all the bills?'

'That's not what I said.'

'Trust me. I did the right thing.' Maggie stared into her tea contemplatively. She could feel her mother staring at her. 'The more I think about it, the more I'm certain he should have been asking Eloise.'

The more times she said it, the more reasonable it seemed.

'Your Eloise?'

'They're perfect for each other.'

'Don't be absurd. Max was going out with you.'

'And now he's not.'

'He chose you.'

'Actually, I chose him years ago. Turns out I was wrong.'

'Good Lord, Maggie. I didn't bring you up to be so cold. It can't be good for you.'

'I wasn't in love with him. That doesn't make me emotionally retarded.'

'And what does Eloise have to say about all this?'

'Actually I haven't called her yet.'

'What?' Carol's tone was one of shock. 'You must.'

Maggie shook her head. 'I thought it'd be better if Max spoke to her first.'

'And what's he supposed to say? Poor chap. You should call her and let her know you're okay.'

'I've had quite enough confrontation for today. I'll call her tomorrow.'

'She's your best friend.'

'I want her and Max to be her idea.'

Carol shook her head. 'Even if she is head over heels in love with him, and I suspect it is an "if", she wouldn't do a thing.'

Maggie thought back to Eloise's recent behaviour. Maybe. Maybe not.

'She'll be too busy worrying about you and your feelings. You mean more to her than any bloke.'

Maggie shrugged. It was a valid point. 'I don't know.'

'I do. This isn't some sort of twisted friendship test, is it?'

'Of course not. I genuinely want her to be happy, and Max too for that matter. Maybe I can be the best man and the bridesmaid at their wedding?'

'I don't know how you can be so glib.'

'I can't tell you how relieved I feel.'

'Is there someone else?'

'No. Now you sound like Max. He sends his love, by the way.'

'But you haven't given up men for all eternity?'

'Of course not.'

Maggie noticed relief in her mother's expression.

'Well, that's progress, I suppose.'

'This isn't like after Adam.'

'This isn't about you taking control because you can?'

'This is about me doing the right thing. I've just had a walk to collect my thoughts and it all feels good.'

'On your own? At this time? Don't you read the papers?'

'It's only nine o'clock. I popped in to see Adam.'

'David. DAVID.' Carol rummaged in the kitchen drawer and produced a vial of Rescue Remedy. She handed it to Maggie.

'Forget counting drops, just take a swig.'

'Mum, I'm fine. It was about time I went to the cemetery.' She proffered the little brown bottle. 'Maybe you should have some?'

Carol didn't need any encouragement.

Her dad came over and hugged her. 'Sorry darlings, fascinating footage of the space shuttle. What did you want, Carol?'

'She's gone and left Max.'

Maggie wondered why her mother was talking about her as if she wasn't actually there.

David smiled. 'Oh well. Nice chap.'

Maggie watched her father carefully. 'You didn't like him?'

'Nothing wrong per se but quite serious, I thought, and rather pleased with himself.'

'David.' Carol's tone was reprimanding.

'If you're allowed your opinion, then surely I get to air mine, too? I mean Max obviously has great credentials on paper and he's a good-looking young man but—'

Maggie wondered whether she'd just witnessed the end of her parents' marriage.

Carol interrupted. 'Well, I thought he was lovely.'

'Really darling, you've never said.'

'Maggie, I wouldn't be doing my job as a mother if I wasn't honest with you right now. Call him. Apologise. I think you'll live to regret this.'

'He's not my future.' Maggie shook her head, relieved that she hadn't had a single second thought.

'How can you say that?'

'It's an instinct. A gut feeling.'

Maggie's phone started to ring in her bag and she ignored

it. Her mother however picked up the handbag and rummaged for the handset.

'Maggie…?'

'Actually it's her mother. Hold on one second.'

Carol handed Maggie her phone.

'Maggie Hunter.'

'I'm reporting a break-in.'

'Jake?' Her blood sugar might have been low and her mind slightly scrambled, but Maggie was sure she'd locked the door behind her.

'I've just got back from the pub and someone's been in the flat.'

She smiled sheepishly. 'Are you sure?'

'The cushions on the sofa have been plumped up, the calendar in the kitchen has moved from February to March and someone's been watching E4. Why didn't you leave a note?'

Maggie blushed. 'I was just passing. I shouldn't have gone in. I just wanted to say how sorry I was to hear about you and Eloise.'

'So you weren't coming over to give me my notice?'

'Of course not.'

'It's just I thought I might be out on my ear.'

'No, you're fine where you are. She seems quite calm all things considered.'

'It was the right thing to do. It wasn't easy but, well, that's the whole point of relationships, isn't it?'

'What is?'

'Some work, some don't. You just have to know when to walk away before anyone gets really hurt.'

'I don't suppose you want to repeat that to my mother, do you?'

'Pardon?'

'Nothing.'

'And besides I was getting a bit tired of fighting for her attention.'

'Red's just a phase she's going through.'

'It's not him I was worried about.' Jake had been wondering whether to say anything to Maggie for a while. 'So, how are things with you?'

'Don't you know?' Her whole world had changed and no one suspected a thing.

'You just sat on the couch—you didn't leave a message…'

Maggie wondered if Max was hoping this was all going to blow over.

'If I'd known you were popping over I would have stayed in *and* opened a packet of crisps.'

'I was literally just passing. I wanted to let you know I'm moving.'

'Are you two buying somewhere together?'

'Not exactly.' Maggie walked away from her parents. There wasn't far to go and she was still within earshot, but by turning her back on them she at least created an illusion of privacy for herself.

Jake's focus was inward. 'I've been meaning to call and apologise. If Eloise and I had been honest with ourselves and not gagging for a holiday, we probably shouldn't have come sailing at all. Or at least not together.'

'What are you talking about? It was great to have you guys

there. It's not like you were arguing or anything, and if you two hadn't been there, Max and I would have split up long before we got home. I prefer my holidays to be a little less salty and, thanks to you, at least I didn't come back with larger biceps.'

Jake laughed. 'Could you do me a favour and find out how much I owe Max for my share of the yacht charter?'

'I think he's got it covered.'

'I'd feel better if I'd paid my way. Especially now. So how's Eloise doing?'

'I haven't actually seen her yet, which I'm taking to be a good sign. We had a chat this morning and she seemed fine. That said, we were both rushing. How about you?'

'I miss the fact she's not going to call. I can be quite perverse when I put my mind to it.'

'How's the album coming along?'

'Not bad. I'm going to call some people next week.'

'Call them tomorrow.'

'I've got a load of sites to update.'

'There'll always be something more mundane to do.'

Jake nodded. 'Domesticity versus creativity, the house wins every time.'

'And it's always going to be easier to do the ironing than put your neck on the line. Book yourself some studio time or I will.'

'Pep talk received loud and clear.'

'Good. Catch up soon, I hope.' Maggie hung up. She didn't know when. And Jake clearly hadn't been listening or, at least, not astutely enough.

Maggie's parents were now deep in conversation, sitting

side by side on their sofa. Maggie squeezed between them, kissing them in turn. 'Mind if I stay here tonight?'

Her mother stroked her hair. 'Of course not.'

A bed secured, Maggie got up again walked over to the dresser and helped herself to a banana and an apple. 'I might just head up now. I'm bushed.'

'Where are you going to go next?'

'Sorry?'

Carol wondered whether all daughters could be this exasperating. 'You said something on the phone about moving?'

Maggie shrugged. 'I'll try and explain everything tomorrow.' Just as soon as she'd worked it out herself.

'Yes, you will.'

'Night all.' Maggie picked up her handbag and headed up the stairs. She didn't even have a toothbrush with her.

'I'm worried about her.' Carol turned to face David, who was glued to the television again. She picked up the remote control and pressed the mute button. The breaking news story of their hour had just gone upstairs.

'I'm not.' Now deprived of volume, David didn't take his eyes off the screen. 'She's got that look in her eye. The one she always gets when she's excited about something.'

'What if she doesn't know what she wants any more?'

'Maggie? No chance. Leave her be. Perhaps it just wasn't meant to be.'

'Now you even sound like her.'

'We've done our bit. Now we have to trust in her. I wasn't in a hurry to settle down at her age. I wanted to live life to the full before I threw myself into marriage, and I've no regrets.'

'But you were a man. She can't wait for ever.'

'As long as she's doing what she wants and it's not illegal, I'm happy. I taught that girl everything I know about life.'

Carol sighed. 'Maybe that's the problem.'

Chapter Thirty-One

Back at her flat, Eloise opened a bottle of wine and raised a glass to herself and her future. A pilot for City FM was no guarantee of a regular slot, but an hour in a studio bigger than a broom cupboard had to be a good start to her dreams of a commercial career. She'd left the interview on a high, and as a result had received three smiles and a wink before she'd even left their offices. Then, in Self-ridges, she'd found the mac she wanted—in her size—and a great handbag. Things were looking up. This new chapter of her life was only a day old, but it was already feeling very promising.

She did her best to relax despite the fact that there was no sign of Maggie, no message, no nothing, and not a trace of Max even though he'd called her over an hour ago. She could have sworn he said he was going to jump in a cab if he didn't hear from her. Maybe they'd got back together already.

Walking over to her front window, Eloise peered out into the street. There was a man in a baseball cap, pacing the length of her front wall. A baseball cap she recognised. She put her wine glass down and, raising the wooden venetian blinds, opened the sash window.

Favourite grey wool scarf tied firmly round his neck, casserole dish on the pavement and no longer tepid, Max paced up and down. He hadn't rung the bell and he'd been there over ten minutes.

Above his head, he heard the window open. Damn.

'Max?'

He looked up.

'It's customary in these parts to ring the bell.'

He shrugged. 'Sorry. Just having a think, it's been a confusing day.'

Eloise sighed, glad she'd already had a moment to celebrate herself. 'I'm on my way down.'

Wearing, or rather swimming in, a pair of her father's flannel pyjamas, Maggie lay in an unfamiliar bed. As she replayed the last few hours in her mind, she realised her mother, as usual, was right. She should have called Eloise first. If there was one person she wanted to keep on her side for the rest of life, she was the one.

Propping herself up on the pillows she dialled Eloise at home and then on her mobile and was rewarded with two answerphones. Leaving messages on both, she dialled Max at home and dictated message three. She hoped he was okay and not still sitting on the stairs staring at the door and ignoring the phone. Determined to at least exhaust all avenues of possibility in tracking down Eloise, and hoping to confirm that Max was still breathing, she dialled his mobile.

'Maggie? Where are you?' Max had wondered when she was going to call. They'd had dinner and finally he'd been rewarded with a trip to the pub, three hours later than scheduled.

'At my parents' place.'

'I was getting a little worried.'

Maggie hoped he realised that she'd really left.

Instinctively Max got to his feet. 'Look, you know you can stay at home until you sort yourself out. You can have a spare room.'

Maggie was impressed. He definitely understood and, so far, no attempt to persuade her that she'd made a dreadful mistake.

'Maybe tomorrow. We'll see how the dust settles. Are you doing okay?'

'Better. And hard as it is to take, I do appreciate your honesty.'

'Thank you.' Maggie had almost been hoping he'd be upset for at least a day or two. Just for ego purposes, of course.

'It's not been easy.'

'No.'

'And you should have told me you weren't happy.'

'It wasn't that I was desperately unhappy. I just couldn't imagine us in a few years' time.'

Max instructed himself not to get angry.

Maggie remembered why she'd called. 'I don't suppose you know where Eloise is, do you? I've just tried to call her flat and her mobile.'

'We're at The Horse's Mouth.'

Max was in Fulham already? Interesting.

'We popped out for a drink after dinner to celebrate.'

'Celebrate?' A stray second thought disappeared instantly.

'She's about twenty feet to my left, playing on the jukebox.'

'So she knows?'

Max paused. Surely he couldn't have done the wrong thing again.

'It's okay, I told you to tell her.'

'And I did. But she'll be really relieved to hear from you. She tried to call you a few times earlier. And she's got some good news.'

Maggie was relieved. At least that would explain the celebrating. There was a muffled exchange and finally Eloise came on to the line.

'Why didn't you phone me? I felt like a right idiot when he called.' Eloise was taking no prisoners. She walked away from Max in search of at least semi-privacy and a quieter area.

'I'm really sorry. I needed some time away from people.'

'I'm not "people".'

Maggie was sheepish. 'I know.'

'So where did you go?'

'To see Adam.'

'Always easiest to go and see the one who can't answer back.'

Maggie regrouped. 'Are you cross with me?'

'Still think you did the right thing tonight?'

'I know I did.'

'You're a stubborn fool, but I love you anyway.'

'So I gather you have some news.' Maggie took a breath.

'It's just a pilot—there's no guarantee that they'll commission a programme.'

'What?'

'The City FM offer.'

'They made you an offer? That's fantastic. They have one new listener already.'

'Thank you.' Eloise laughed at the thought of Maggie sitting by her radio. She paused. 'So what were you talking about?'

'Sorry?'

'Maggie. You thought I was going to say something else.'

'A pilot for your own show. Go Eloise.'

'Margaret Hunter, I'm warning you.'

'You really should have been a teacher. You'd be terrifying.'

'Don't even think about changing the subject.'

'All the signs were there, but I guess I wasn't looking. It only actually dawned on me this evening.'

Eloise wished Maggie would stop being so cryptic. 'Any chance of a normal conversation?'

'I know Max isn't the right man for me—' Maggie psyched herself up to finish the sentence she'd started '—because he's the right man for you.'

'Max?' Eloise felt herself blush, grateful that this exchange was taking place over the phone. 'You can—'

Maggie interrupted. 'Listen, I know what you're going to say and if I've learned anything over the last few years it's that love doesn't necessarily occur at first sight. Indeed I would almost say you should be wary if it does. It's a bit like light travelling faster than sound. Appearances can turn out to be deceptive.'

'At least when I quote my surveys they have their basis in fact. So that's it? We all live happily ever after. Me with your cast-off.' She shook her head. 'You do crack me up.'

'Why not? You've always said you liked him.'

'While he's been going out with you.'

'You should think about it. You two would be perfect together.'

'What about the bit where you change your mind, get insanely jealous and never talk to me again?'

'It's never going to happen.'

'Finally you say something sensible.'

'If you're honest with yourself and you two were on the other side of the world, not worrying about hurting my feelings, I think you might already be a little bit in love with him.'

Eloise paused. It might be more than a little bit true, but if she admitted that to herself then she would never be able to ignore it.

Maggie continued. 'By the way, I'm not expecting you to answer that.'

Eloise walked further away from Max, out of eye and earshot. 'How could it possibly work. It's all a mess.'

'Define *mess*. It's just life. Honestly, he's your one.'

'How can he be? He was your one.'

'No, he wasn't. My mistake. He was my unrequited crush from over ten years ago, but when the nostalgia evaporated Max wasn't my soul mate. Not even nearly.'

'So now you're trying to recycle him?'

'Look, it's not like he'll have trouble finding a girlfriend. I just wanted to make sure you two were both looking in the same places.'

Eloise shook her head. 'Mags, is this some sort of ruse to make you feel less guilty about saying no.'

'Not at all.'

'He is devastated.'

'You say all the right things, but this time you're wrong. He's shocked. He's angry even and I can't blame him for that. Max French is a man used to getting exactly what he wants when he wants it. But it's so obvious. You both talk about each other all the time. Even Jake noticed.'

'Max talks about me?'

Safe at her parents' house, Maggie rolled her eyes. 'He thinks you're incredible. Which you are. And you met him before you were thirty, so it's perfect.'

'Very funny.'

'I know it probably seems a little weird.'

'Weird? It makes wife-swapping look like badminton.'

Maggie laughed. 'I can't help that. Look, at least consider going on a date together.'

'Are you going for some sort of sainthood and life of celibacy?'

'You two make perfect sense.'

'And you're sure these aren't the late-night machinations of someone feeling bad about leaving a guy in the lurch?'

'It's true, if he hadn't got down on one knee this evening, I wouldn't have left today.'

'Exactly my point.'

'And it was his earlier. But I would have left eventually. Probably not soon enough, and it's much better like this.'

'You don't get to play cupid. Who says you get to make all the decisions round here?'

'I know you're thinking I'm crazy, but why is he there now? He could be with any of his mates, with his sister, with his brother-in-law, but no, he's with you.'

'He said you sent him.'

'Since when men do anything they're told unless they want to?'

Eloise paused. She wasn't sure what she thought. 'So where are you now?'

'I'm at my parents' for the night.'

'If only they'd bought a larger place.'

'Small is good. This way I definitely can't stay more than a couple of nights.'

'And then what? You know you can always come and stay with me.'

'That's a very kind offer.'

'You see, it's awkward already. And nothing has happened yet.'

'Yet?' Maggie couldn't disguise the glee in her voice.

'Just a figure of speech, you know.'

'Look, I promise it's not awkward. You and me are fine. I hope we always will be. That said, you need some time on your own, or at least without me around. I can always go home.'

'To the flat? But Jake's there.'

'Don't worry, I won't boot him out unceremoniously. So maybe I'll have a flatmate for a few weeks while he looks for somewhere else?'

'You hate sharing.'

'I loved being your flatmate, and it'll only be for a bit. We can eat pizza and watch crap DVDs. I'm at work during the day. Jake's out a lot in the evening.'

'He used to be.'

'Look, in the short term it might be fun.'

'Is Jake okay with it?'

Maggie paused. 'Of course, he doesn't know yet.'

'Be warned, he likes having that place to himself.'

'He used to have flatmates.'

'Not über-tidy ones.'

'So I'll chill out. I'm just looking forward to being back there.' Maggie paused. 'But most importantly, are we going to be okay?'

Eloise swallowed hard. 'We'd better be.'

Maggie sighed with relief. 'Good, because after everything that's gone on today, that's honestly my biggest worry.'

'You're not worrying about Max?'

'Not now I know where he is. He may not be one hundred percent convinced yet, but when he wakes up tomorrow and his pride reboots, he'll realise I've just done him a huge favour. In fact, he owes me.'

Eloise no longer knew what she thought. 'So how about lunch very soon? Just the two of us.'

'Most definitely.' Maggie hung up and closed her eyes in an impromptu and informal prayer of thanks. Everything was going to be okay eventually. She could just feel it.

Eloise handed the phone back to Max.

He slipped it into his coat pocket. 'You see, I told you she was in a funny mood.'

Eloise shrugged as she looked him up and down.

Self-conscious, Max watched her. 'What?'

'She sounded pretty normal to me.'

'And do you understand what she's going on about?'

Eloise turned to Max and smiled. As he smiled back, she wondered if she should allow herself to get her hopes up. 'Do you know what, I think I do.'

Chapter Thirty-Two

Twenty-two hours later and not one of them spent at the office, Maggie was standing in her kitchen while Jake poured her a glass of wine from a bottle in her fridge. Little did he know she had an overnight case in the boot of her car just in case he liked the proposition she was about to make.

It had taken her three hours to get past Gestapo Mother earlier, not least because Carol had taken Maggie's car keys hostage until she'd had answers to all the questions she'd dreamed up overnight and, free at last, Maggie wasn't planning on going back there to stay any time soon.

Jake handed her a glass. 'You see, if you call first, you even get wine.'

Maggie smiled. 'Thank you, and I'm so sorry about yesterday, I know I'm not supposed to just let myself in.'

'Don't worry about it.'

'It was a homing instinct. I just didn't know where else to go.'

He looked up. 'I'm sorry. I don't understand.'

Maggie took a breath. 'Yesterday evening Max asked me to marry him.'

Jake paused, clearly puzzled. 'And you're having a glass of wine with me in your old flat.'

Maggie smiled. 'Absolutely no congratulations required.'

'You turned down multimillionaire Max French? Now that could be toast-worthy.' Jake raised his glass. 'To life post Max.'

'I know I probably need my head examined.'

'It's your life.' As Jake supportively and fleetingly put his arm around her shoulder, Maggie felt herself relax. He didn't appear to have judged her at all.

'Not least because then I went to see Adam.'

'Adam?' Jake frowned. 'I thought he was…'

'He is.'

'I think you should come and sit down. You've clearly been working far too hard since we got back.'

As Maggie followed Jake into her sitting room, she felt herself relax. She was home.

Jake watched her doing an inventory of the room. 'May I say, you seem very calm.'

'Nothing like ten days in each other's pockets to help you determine how you really feel about someone.'

Jake nodded. 'Don't I know that scenario…'

'Sorry, how self-absorbed of me. How are you coping with your return to single status?'

'Honestly?'

'Eloise won't hear a thing. Tenant-landlord confidentiality is in place.'

Jake paused 'Well.' He almost looked apologetic. 'I'm loving the sense of freedom, not that she ever really stopped me from doing anything but…'

'You don't need to explain.'

'So.' Jake sucked his cheeks in. 'Do I presume you're here because you want to move home, not because you fancied a free glass of wine?'

Maggie nodded. 'And sooner rather than later.'

Jake looked around the room. 'I guess I could be out of here in…'

Maggie couldn't miss the disappointment on his face.

'…a couple of weeks, couple of months tops.'

'I'm not throwing you out.'

'There's always my sister, but young children are not very compatible with an insomniac website designer who works from home and needs his own space for making a noise after seven p.m. I was actually thinking about maybe even trying to buy somewhere.'

'Really, there's no hurry.'

'Where will you go?'

'I could move in with my parents. Max, ever the gent, has offered me one of his spare rooms but, if you can handle it, I thought I might move into the spare room here. I mean if that's okay. I just want to be home.'

'Okay with me? It's your place.'

'You didn't rent it with a sitting tenant. Of course I'll reduce the charge.'

Jake paused. 'Are you sure I won't drive you mad?'

'I could ask you the same question.'

'I guess there's only one way to find out.' Jake grinned. 'When were you thinking of moving back?

'Tonight?'

'Tonight?' Jake hadn't been into the spare room for days. He hadn't seen the surface of the duvet cover for weeks and he wasn't sure if he'd even washed it once since he'd moved in.

'We could leave it until next week if it's easier?' Maggie wondered if the sofa at the office was comfy. She could always shower at the gym.

'Just give me a few hours.' Jake paused. 'Don't take this the wrong way, but does Eloise know about us sharing?'

'I think she's worried I'm going to make your life a misery.'

'She said that?'

'Almost.'

Jake shook his head. 'She can be a little bit scary at times.'

'What about me?'

'Direct, yes but scary, no. Anyway, I guess if Eloise doesn't like our arrangement, she and Max can gang up on us together.'

'If they haven't already.'

Jake's eyes darkened. 'Do you think they've been…'

'…sleeping together? Absolutely not. But with a bit of luck they'll get it together eventually.'

'I can't believe you just said that.'

'I can't believe you're pretending to be surprised. Those two have been an accident waiting to happen for some time and now there are no potential casualties at the scene, it's more of an inevitability. There's clearly an attraction there.'

Jake nodded in defeat. 'So what now?'

Maggie stood up and walked over to the door. 'I'm just going to get my overnight bag.'

'Now this minute?'

'Would you rather leave it for a few days? In which case, can I be really cheeky and have a quick shower before I go…'

'Of course. I mean sure. Stay. Now. If you like. It doesn't bother me when you arrive, or if you never leave. This is your place. I was just keeping it warm for you.'

Overcome with relief, Maggie nodded. 'Thank you. I really appreciate it.'

'I'll go and clear the bed.'

Maggie giggled.

Jake blushed. 'Okay, I know how that sounded.'

'In that case—' she waggled her eyebrows in fake flirtation '—I'll just nip down to the car and get my things.'

Maggie climbed the last flight of stairs with her carry-on suitcase, pausing to rest on the top landing before wheeling herself home.

She stood at the entrance to the spare room. Either it had become haunted since she'd moved out or Jake was somewhere in the duvet cover he was changing.

She watched him for a few moments. Little to no progress was being made. 'Here, let me do that.'

'No, no, I insist.' Jake hoped she wasn't looking too closely. The newsprint from some of the supplements he'd been saving seemed to have rubbed off on the cotton cover that was now a whiter shade of grey.

Finally shaking the freshly covered duvet out, he laid it on the bed, making sure the pinprick of red ink from the pen he'd just rescued from one of the crosswords was face down, out of sight. 'There you go.'

Maggie watched him plump the pillows and add the bed-spread before folding it down.

'I could get used to having housekeeping.'

'So it's all quite straightforward, shower and loo in there. Make sure you hold the flush down properly or the cistern won't empty fully.' Jake aped her rather well. 'Kitchen is all as it seems. Watch out for greasy nobs. Grill works perfectly. If you could not touch the piles of paper in the sitting room I'd be eternally grateful. I'll sort them out tomorrow or the next day. Have you eaten?'

'Nope.'

'Follow me.' He opened the fridge and peered in. 'I can do you chicken fajitas—shop bought, lots of additives—home-made spag bol or—' he checked another cupboard '—lasagne?'

'You cook?' For some reason Maggie had imagined Jake being a slave to the microwave.

'Only the basics. And when I do put pan to stove, I tend to make enough for the rest of the week. I mean who'd want to cook every night? So, what do you fancy?'

'Is lasagne the most complicated to prepare?'

'The bolognaise is already cooked, so it'll be about forty minutes, an hour max.'

'That would be perfect.' Maggie walked over to Jake, who was now squatting by the fridge. 'Thank you.' Without thinking, she bent down and kissed him.

His face was a picture of surprise. 'Whoa. Is this what swinging is like?'

'No. I don't think so. In swinging, you go back. Not something I do.'

Jake stared at her.

'What?' Did she have something on her face? She wiped her hand across her mouth and cheeks as subtly as she could.

'Sure you don't want to kiss me again?'

'Sure. Not sure.' Maggie went for second time lucky. And for the second time Jake stopped her in her tracks.

He pulled back. 'Actually I think we should probably just quit while we're ahead, don't you?'

Maggie pouted. 'It was your idea.'

'No offence, but I think I need a bit of me time. And do you know what, I think you do too. My head's all over the place. You're probably on the rebound...'

Maggie wondered if only the dumped rebounded.

'And if we're going to be living together for a bit, this is a very bad idea.'

Maggie wasn't used to someone else being the sensible one.

Pretending the last few minutes hadn't happened, Maggie wondered if she should move out, the shortest lived flatmate ever. 'Is there anything I can do to help with dinner?'

'No, go and settle in. Seriously, take it easy. Sounds like you've had quite a day or two.'

'If you insist. I'll be on the sofa.'

'I'll just stick this in the oven and I'll be right in.'

Maggie watched him. 'Are you sure you're okay for me to stay here?'

Jake looked up from the baking dish. 'I was about to ask you the same question.'

'I'd love you to.'

'Well, that's settled then. Just no more funny business while you're under my roof.'

Maggie grinned. 'Whose roof?'

'And tomorrow, I'll start looking for somewhere to buy.'

'I can help if you like.'

'I'm not sure I'm in your property league. I mean the commission probably won't even cover one of your pairs of shoes.'

'I wouldn't charge you.'

'It's a very kind offer, but I think it's time for me to stand on my own two feet. You've done more than enough. And probably best to keep business and friendship separate, don't you think?'

Maggie reclined on the door frame, hoping she looked like a good-time girl.

'It just might mean you have me here for a couple more months.'

'I'm sure I'll cope.' Maggie's heart sank at the thought of having to repatriate all her possessions. 'Moving sure beats having a real hobby.'

'With a bit of luck, it'll keep us both out of trouble.'

'Until the next time.' Maggie refilled her wine glass and lay down on the sofa. Until the next time.

Epilogue

Jake waved his new house keys at Maggie who was spring-cleaning the kitchen. Okay, more like autumn cleaning, but since Jake had packed his stuff up, the dust in the drawers and cupboards had become far too visible to ignore.

'I've got them. I am finally complete.'

'You've completed.' Maggie corrected him without thinking.

'Whatever. But I am no longer on the road to nowhere. I am a man of property. As of an hour ago, I finally got my big toe on London's property ladder.'

'Congratulations.' A couple of months had become six months, but who was counting.

'Hey, I couldn't have done it without you.'

'What a load of old codswallop. You haven't let me do a thing.'

'I know.' Jake rubbed his hands together with glee. 'How annoying am I?'

Judging by the arrival of a little black cloud that had been following Maggie round her flat since first thing this morning, not that annoying at all.

'And thank you for patience.'

'The time has flown. Speaking of which…' Grateful for the diversion, Maggie turned the radio up as Eloise's lunch-time show was about to begin. Only in its third week, it was turning out to be the best way to really keep up to date with what she was up to. And it was a bit like having her around. Same excitable chit-chat, same dodgy taste in music.

Jake poured himself a pint of water. It was a drink fit for a new homeowner and frankly all he could afford for now.

'This is Eloise Forrest and you're listening to City FM. Coming up on today's show…'

Jake smiled. 'She sounds so professional.'

'She sounds so newly engaged.' Thankfully, Max had traded in the ring he'd bought for her and Eloise had designed herself a very different one. And Eloise wasn't planning on moving in until after they'd got married. Maggie was still hoping they might buy somewhere new.

'And so happy. I must invite her and Max round for dinner when I've settled in to my place.'

'Ditto.' Maggie sighed as she thought about the cardboard boxes stacked in the sitting room that had arrived from the storage people yesterday. Not that she'd be admitting it to anyone, least of all Max, who had kindly funded her return, but she hadn't actually missed any of her possessions. Plus Jake didn't seem to be taking much with him. Maybe she'd use the opportunity to have a serious clear-out. From now on, her life was going to be less cluttered.

'Later on I'll be previewing next week's hot single releases, revealing my download of the week and giving away tickets to next year's big gig in Hyde Park. Remember this is the only station that can get you in to the party that everyone is going to be talking about. As the world gets ready to give something back, you can come and Live A Little with us.'

Jake turned to Maggie. 'Can you believe she's actually doing all this?'

Maggie nodded. 'Of course I can. I'm so proud of her.'

For the last fifteen years they had always managed to be there for each other one hundred percent in spirit, even if in recent months they had only managed to catch up for an hour or so a week.

'Anyway, before I play today's golden oldie, as chosen by you, I'm going to treat you to a repeat play of something I previewed a couple of weeks ago. I've had so many emails and calls since I played it. It isn't out yet, but it will be and when it is, just remember that you heard it here first. The name to remember is Jake Chambers. The track, of course, is "Seeing Red."'

Maggie looked at Jake as he stared out of her kitchen window listening to his demo, a smile playing at his lips. 'She's been good to me.'

'It's not all selfless—Eloise is going to get the kudos for breaking a hot new artist. And it sounds great. Some things do happen for a reason.'

'Shall we phone in?'

'Can you imagine?' Maggie giggled at the idea.

Jake clapped his hands. 'Right. Time for me to be making a move and only four months later than scheduled. You know I can't thank you enough for putting up with me.'

'Not a problem.' She could feel herself welling up and yet she'd promised herself she was going to be cool about this. She blinked hard. She'd loved living on her own before. 'It'll be weird now not to have you here.'

'You mean you'll have to do your own washing-up?'

Maggie laughed. 'Yeah, that mainly. So can I give you a hand with anything?'

'Nope, I'm all sorted.'

'Where are the removal men?'

'You're looking at him.'

'You can't do it all yourself.'

'I told you, I'm not going far.'

Maggie shrugged. 'I give up and I can't believe you haven't let me check out the new place yet.'

Jake grinned. 'Never give up. All in good time, I just want to get a few things straight first.'

'At least let me help you to the van with the light stuff.'

Jake shook his head.

Maggie picked up his guitar. 'I'm taking this hostage until you let me do something. I'm stronger than I look.'

Casting her eyes over the cardboard boxes filled with CDs and DVDs, it was a brave claim.

'There is no van.'

'No van?' Maggie was confused.

Jake smiled. 'I figured you're probably a woman who likes to be on top,' Jake continued. 'Or should I say on top of everyone and everything.'

Maggie tried and failed not to blush. 'What are you talking about?'

'I'm only moving downstairs.'

'Seriously?' Again Maggie could feel tears in her eyes. Only this time they were accompanied by an unexpected wave of sheer excitement. Christmas had come early to Little Venice.

Jake nodded. 'As of an hour's time, I'll be on the ground floor if you need me.'

'If?'

'When.'

Maggie gave herself an extra squirt of perfume for luck and rechecked her appearance in the mirror. She'd swapped her jeans for a skirt. She was sure girl upstairs was a slightly smarter look than girl next door. Plus Jake had seen her looking pretty ropey over the last few months, so anything was going to be an improvement. She grabbed the mug of sugar she'd prepared earlier and removed the bottle of ice-cold Veuve Clicquot from the fridge before heading downstairs.

As she rang his bell, her smile was on full beam.

'Not today thanks.' Jake had only opened the door a fraction.

'I just wanted to welcome you to the building.' Maggie proffered the champagne. 'Quick, let me in, before it gets warm.'

Jake opened the door. 'Now that's what I call loving thy neighbour.' He looked at the mug in her other hand. 'Sugar?'

Maggie was sheepish. It had seemed funny upstairs. 'Come on, it's what neighbours used to borrow from each other before champagne came along.'

Bemused, he watched Maggie attempting to peer round him, desperate to get a look at the flat. 'Would you like to come in?'

Maggie punched him playfully as she pushed past. 'I thought you'd never ask.'

'I know you're more interested in my square footage than me.'

'Rubbish.' But as Maggie inspected each room, she was already taking mental notes.

The curtains needed replacing, the walls needed a bit of love, but the floorboards had been sanded and varnished and the layout was one she was very familiar with.

The sitting room walls were a welcoming deep red and as she walked in to the room at the end of her tour, Maggie did a double take. The boxes were piled high but, at the far end, a dining room table had been laid for two, complete with candles and a wine cooler. Only now did she notice that the smells wafting from the kitchen were very promising. And he was wearing a shirt with his jeans.

Flustered, she took a step back towards the door. 'I'm so sorry, I just assumed you'd be here unpacking…of course you're going to make the most of your first night of freedom.' Maggie turned to go. 'Enjoy the champagne. You must have been desperate to get your own place.' He'd certainly played that one close to his chest.

'The woman in question isn't usually at all patient.'

'But circumstances being what they were…'

Jake smiled. 'Exactly.'

'Well, forgive me for barging in. Give me a shout tomorrow if you're free or you need a hand with anything.' Maggie continued to back towards the door.

Jake watched her. 'Where are you going?' Striding over, he put his hands on her shoulders and walked her to one end of the table. 'I've been waiting for you to show up for hours. This is already the second set of candles. I guessed you'd be down here by six at the latest.'

'This is for me?' Maggie was overwhelmed and under-dressed. Mind you, Jake wasn't even wearing shoes.

'I just wanted to say thank you.'

Maggie held on to the back of chair. 'You didn't need to go to all this trouble. It's been a real pleasure.'

Jake stood next to her, 'And, if you still want to kiss me…'

For once Maggie didn't have to think twice, and this time Jake didn't pull away.

Jake opened the champagne a few minutes later. 'So it would appear the neighbours here are pretty friendly.'

'Not all of them, I hope.' Maggie grinned as she looked around the sitting room. 'This place is great.'

Jake watched her. 'What are you thinking?'

'Venetian blinds would be good. Maybe an uplighter in the corner and definitely paint that mantelpiece.'

'I meant about us.'

She held his gaze. 'Everything.'

He kissed her again.

This time it was Maggie who was the first to pull away.

Jake's face was etched with concern. 'Something wrong?'

Maggie's smile spread as she studied his face. 'Something right. I think I just might be falling for the boy downstairs.'

What do you do when the other woman is you?

Lizzie Ford is London's most popular agony aunt who's been sitting on the bench for three years waiting to get back in the game. So Lizzie can't believe her good luck when she meets Matt Baker, only there's one problem – Matt's wife may not be happy with this new arrangement.

The strange thing is that even while she's hoping that Matt will get a divorce, she's actively helping a writer · to her column save her crumbling marriage – a marriage that bears more than a passing resemblance to Matt's…